I0669332

SONG OF THE COMING FIRE

TYLER JAMES

SONG
OF THE
COMING FIRE

TYPEWRITER PRESS

Copyright © 2023 by Tyler James

All rights reserved.

No part of this publication may be reproduced, distributed, or transmitted in any form or by any means, including photocopying, recording, or other electronic or mechanical methods, without the prior written permission of the publisher, except in the case of brief quotations embodied in critical reviews and certain other noncommercial uses permitted by copyright law .

This is a work of fiction. Names, characters, places, and incidents either are the product of the author's imagination or are used fictitiously. Any resemblance to actual persons, living or dead, events, or locales is entirely coincidental.

ISBN: 978-1-951996-04-8 (e-book)

ISBN: 978-1-951996-05-5 (paperback)

Book Cover designed by MiblArt

First edition 2023

Typewriter Press

Visit the author's website at: www.tylerjamesbooks.com

CONTENTS

Song of the Coming Fire

1

THE PRICE OF A LIFE

I t fascinates me how quick they are to destroy themselves. All they needed was a simple whisper, a gentle push, a single nightmarish dream. Their ships sail now, not for distant shores, but for their own. Voices scream into an empty air, tears fall to a thankless soil, a song fills this great void. And I am free.

-The Last Bridgemaker

There is nothing simple about a mask. Especially one that is made from lies and half-truths, misconceptions and direct falsities. It is a thing worn, but it is also something enacted. Not just clothing, but action and movement and speech.

A mask is an identity. It is all that makes up a person except for the fact that it is unreal, fake, a facsimile of truth. Yet there are those that prefer them, to hide and skulk behind them. The merchants wear a mask of confidence and honesty when their hearts are cruel and full of dishonesty. The sailors have masks of determined strength, but within they are filled with self-doubt, resentments, and the knowledge of their inferiority amongst their brethren.

Gulamira's mask was by far the most well constructed. It calmed and it seduced, cheered and relaxed. Those who looked upon it knew what it was to desire a woman. They knew what it was to hate a woman.

A smile. A simple smile took the centerpiece of the mask. A perpetual smile, one that hadn't left her face in nearly eight years. In that time, no one had seen he true face, not even her.

She had no mirror to examine the smile, yet she knew it well since she had slowly crafted it piece by piece over the years. Some people had masks made of the thinnest materials, ready to shatter at the faintest insult or aggression. Not hers. She made hers with the hardiest of deceits, the kind that layered atop one another with such density that nothing from outside could penetrate through and nothing from within could escape. It was made of jovial tears and false sincerities, hearty despairs and cruel mercies.

Gulamira put on her mask this morning, feeling its coyness drape across her mouth like a sheer veil while playful teasing filled her somber eyes. Without a mirror, she could not see it, but she felt her beauty, her allure, emerge for the world to take advantage of. Before perfumes coated her silvery-gray skin, before she massaged lavender oils into her curled, black hair, just before she adorned her cheeks and lips with rouge, she strapped on her invisible mask.

The oils and perfumes flowed into her nostrils, driving out the musk that still permeated the room from last night. She sat upright as she let the pleasant smells surround her and take her mind past the throbbing pain in her thighs, breasts, and everywhere in-between. Gulamira paused and glanced over her shoulder at her bed, where the three human men snored soundly, all as naked as ever.

Gulamira's smile was pleasant and typical, yet there was only a sick twist in her stomach. She hated doing groups. Groups rarely came to her because of the need for release or because of some profound loneliness they couldn't handle. No. Groups only saw her when they really, really wanted to hurt a tatzon like her. When they wanted to feel powerful, violently powerful. Groups urged each other on, encouraging each other to keep going, to be even harsher and rougher than the last.

She had needed the extra coin. Because of last night, she finally would have enough. And that had to be worth it. She told this to herself as she struggled to walk to the bedroom door and leave them behind. Normally, she had to wait for them to leave or for them to be kicked out, but she did not want to see them awake again, to hear what derisions those humans had to say to her.

Gulamira moved slowly through the River's Delight, keeping a hand on the thin wood slats that made up the walls. She stopped when she came to a window that had swung open in the night. Outside, she saw the dilapidated constructions of Archoz, a once thriving port town in Rajalend. The constructions stood three stories tall, though their bases sloped and sunk into the increasingly swampy ground. Some homes leaned onto their neighbor, as though needing coerced help, while others bent outward, over the street. Most people had running bets on how long it would be before these leaning structures fell.

Beyond the frayed roofs and collapsing human residences, the wall surrounding Archoz loomed high and impassable. No matter where in Archoz you were, the wall was there within sight, forever a reminder that the *Cleansing* was coming.

Gulamira shivered at the thought, but she nodded firmly to herself. This last month had been hard, but it would all be worth it if she escaped the *Cleansing*.

She shut the window as other doors in the hall opened, with other patrons heading out, some with aching hangovers, others with romantic farewells to the women who accompanied them all night. But when the patrons caught sight of Gulamira, they seemed to forget everyone else in the room momentarily.

She ignored them. In the past, she'd count how many looked at her with throbbing passion and how many glared with heated disdain, but she didn't care to count today. No, her mind was centered on a single goal. She entered the central room of the River's Delight, where the other women were already cleaning or getting ready to entertain other guests. She marched past and into a side room that none of the women went in: the master's office.

The lecherous old man sat at his desk, gleefully gathering coins into a leather pouch. While the rest of Archoz slowly wasted away, he was among the few that still profited from the misery. The Rajals had given him a special pass that, as long as they shared in his coin, they would keep him from harm. And he'd brought them much coin.

He spun at her entrance, his lanky and bony hands reaching for a dirk on the table, but he relaxed when he saw it was her, though he furrowed his brows so deeply she wondered if they'd fall off.

"What are you doing in here?" he asked, shifting in his chair to block her view of the pile of money.

"I'd like my earnings from last night." She stayed close to the doorway, since she hated being even this close to the man who owned her.

"Heh, bet you would! You wouldn't believe what they offered to pay. Surprised you're even standing." He leaned in with his own foul smirk. "You'll get paid when you always do, not a moment before. So, get out."

Songs tickled the back of Gulamira's throat, wanting to pour forth, but she held them back. This pitiful excuse of a man was not worth her needing to use such powers. No, she'd much rather use Medhi's dagger, which she had hidden in the small of her back.

"I shall leave promptly. As soon as you hand over my earnings, of course."

"You going deaf now? I told you to leave." He paused and that smirk of his turned into a most Prikur-like grin. "Unless, of course, you wanna do a trade? I barely could sleep thinking about what those three wanted to do to you. So, for my wellbeing, how about you tell me a story? Give me all the little details of last night and, sure, I can slide over your coin early."

Her smile stayed stalwart, and she wanted to roll her eyes so desperately, but she held back as that would give him the tiniest bit of pleasure. She had no intention of giving him any.

"You know how tatzons hang from bars when we sleep?" she asked and raised her priarm, longer and thicker than her other, with markings of twisting branches covering it. "Our priarm grabs onto the bar and we hang from it all night. It never weakens or tires. It holds us up for hours upon hours." Her gaze fell to her prihand and she delicately plucked at the air as she took slow strides toward her master. "Do you know why we hang from only our priarm and not any other arm?"

He cleared his throat. "What's your point? Step back."

"It's because," she said as she splayed her prihand's seven fingers. "Our priarms have a somewhat unnatural strength." With that, she took two quick steps and rammed her prihand against his throat, shoving him off the chair and into the wall.

The weak old man fought back, but he was nothing but bone and spite. "Let me go! I'll have you beaten for this! I'll—"

She squeezed slightly. "Did you know that we tatzons can make our prihands lock once we've gripped something? It's why no matter what, we won't fall once asleep. Once we lock our hand, nothing can pry it open. Not even a Colossal beast." She leaned into the man. "Should I lock it?"

His squirming ceased.

"Good. Now, about that coin..."

He swallowed and shakily reached for the money bag on the table, slowly counting out her earnings.

She shook her head. "Actually, I've changed my mind. I think I earned double for last night, don't you?"

His eyes widened. "Double? Are you insane? You think—" Her hand squeezed a bit more. "—I mean, of course. Double. Take it!"

She could have just killed him. Her hand itched to reach into the back of her dress and ram Medhi's dagger into his belly. In the past, the Rajals would have hunted her down if she'd laid even a finger on their illicit enterprise. But, after today, they would never find her. Even so, she held back.

Gulamira grabbed her coins and added it to the pouch on her belt. It felt heavy enough. "Thank you."

She shut the door behind her, not looking back once at him. She wanted the last image she had of him to be his terrified face.

The other women of the brothel watched her as she left the office, obviously wondering what the master would have done to her. Gulamira let her gaze fall over them. She was the only tatzon among all the women of the River's Delight and she didn't have anyone here she considered a friend. So, it wasn't difficult for her to turn from them and follow the patrons out of the brothel and into the muggy air of Archoz.

When Gulamira first arrived in Archoz, or rather when she'd been sold here, there had been no wall. There had only been the bustle. Dense with traveling merchants heading either inland or out to sea, this town was a top contender for the most successful port in all of Rajalend, with opportunities for tatzon and human alike. Once she landed in the River's Delight, she drew in crowds of customers, most human.

She remembered the disperse people that flocked to the town, from affluent tatzons to sun-baked sailors. Money flowed like a flooded river here, which could be seen in the tall constructions painted in bright greens, in the shops that displayed ostentatious finery, and even in the streets themselves which were decorated in tiled mosaics.

That felt like a whole other world now, a whole other life. As Gulamira walked toward the eastern gate, she gazed at the streets, which were muddied or shattered. The shops she passed were void of people, let alone merchandise. The homes and stores and warehouses of Archoz had rot creeping through their foundations, corrosive moss eating away their sides, and flooding had turned the solid ground into churning mud.

So much had changed. All because of that wall.

With a single edict, the Oligarchs had turned Archoz into a prison. In a single day, no one could sell or buy or leave. They were told to fester and wait for their execution. For the *Cleansing*. Yet, while no one left, more and more came. The dregs of Rajalend were sent here in droves. Criminals, discontents, humans in the wrong place, they were all sent here to Archoz, which was like pouring a disease into an open wound. Things were bad here, and then they worsened.

Gulamira saw many of these people on the streets she wandered, though none even looked at her. Most when they arrived had rebelled. Early on, there had been small uprisings, and the streets ran with blood. But it was like this place had the curse of the Abyssal itself, because even the most rebellious spirit gave up in time. Some still fought on their own, some even banded together to create criminal organizations within this prison, but as a whole, they were like the people she saw now.

A man sat on an overturned cart. He stared at his hands, unblinking. He neither moved nor did he seem to notice when a few kids threw rocks at him.

A woman leaned against a wall. A swaddled baby lay at her feet, crying and crying. She looked at the babe and only shook her head.

A young man stood with a young woman. He spoke of the recent rain and she commented on seeing a bird fly overhead. They became silent, stared at each other for some time before the woman's lip trembled and she hurried away. The young man didn't follow.

Gulamira understood. The *Cleansing* was expected any day now, and once it arrived, this nightmare would feel like paradise.

However, as she strode through the decayed town, she couldn't help but feel a growing lightness to her step. It wasn't hope though. She was not ready to let herself feel that.

Because she was getting out of here. She'd acquainted herself with a pair of guards at the east gate and these bedfellows had told her that they'd be willing to let her out of Archoz, for the right price. They even promised to get her an escort to the town proper, which laid deeper in the forest. A month of hard work would finally pay off, with her being free. One bribe and she could say goodbye to Archoz and all it meant.

Gulamira kept her coin purse hidden as best she could. Though most in Archoz had already drowned in their despair, there were those that had chosen the path of the madman instead. However, she caught sight of the gate without getting assaulted.

The gate seemed busy today. Besides the two tatzon guards she came to see, there was a crowd of people lined up against the wall with a few other tatzons stationed nearby. It almost looked like people were being arrested, but that made little sense. Who arrested someone already in a prison?

As she neared, she saw that those lined up were all women, with interconnecting ropes tied around their throats and wrists. In front of them, a fat human man looked each of them up and down, and Gulamira realized what was happening. This man owned the only other brothel in town, another man who thought himself a king in this prison town. It seemed he was purchasing new merchandise from the outside.

"Not really impressed with what you've got me this time," the fat man said to a pair of tatzons walking alongside him. "Where'd you find them? Some plagued village?"

The tatzons beside him wore the uniforms of officers in the Rajal army and neither looked amused with the brothel owner's joke.

"They match your customers," one officer said. "You're not serving a Beneficiary."

The fat man continued to grumble and deride the women before him, but the gate guards caught Gulamira's attention. They waved at her and she remembered her reason for being here.

"Wait now," the fat man said. "This one. Is this one for sale?"

"Technically. We planned on presenting her to some of the land-owners nearby."

"No, I must have her. She's exactly what I need."

Gulamira was heading up to the gate, but out of curiosity she glanced over to see who they were....

Her steps faltered and she found herself unmoving, her eyes locked on the woman—no, the girl they were speaking of. A girl who couldn't be older than eight. A little tatzon girl.

"We don't sell tatzons to humans," one officer said.

The man didn't look at them. His eyes drank in the little girl. "One exception shouldn't hurt. You paraded her in front of me, after all." He stroked the girl's cheek, but she snarled and bit him. "Ah! She's got some fight in her. Ha, good. I'll take her for double what I normally pay you."

The fat man turned to the officers, the three engaging in their barter, letting the number of their greed determine the life of this tatzon girl.

Just as it had happened to Gulamira.

"This seems reasonable to us," the officer said. "I'd say we have—"

"Stop!"

Gulamira had rushed forward before she realized what she was doing. The three spun toward her, and all the eyes of the women and nearby guards were on her. On seeing her, the fat man groaned and folded his arms.

"What're you doing here?" he asked. "Your bastard of a master send you here? Tell him this is my line."

Gulamira didn't answer. She didn't speak. She wasn't even sure if she breathed. Her eyes darted from the three men to the girl. Hearth's Fire, what was she doing? Things like this happened all the time. People were taken, sold, robbed, killed, and worse. The worst of Rajalend filled this place and she'd seen it all. Of all times, why intervene now?

She needed to turn around and simply march through those gates, forget any of this happened. Just a few steps away....

But the girl called to her. Or rather, a girl called to her. An always ignored, fully abandoned, nearly forgotten fragment of a memory the Rajals had tried to kill so many times before, but which had always fought back, fought to live. That girl, that memory of a past stolen from her, drew Gulamira to the beaten and bruised tatzon in front of her. She locked eyes with the little girl and noticed something for the first time. This child, hurt and beaten as she was, showed no fear. This child was all defiance. A will to fight.

"I want the girl." The words escaped her mouth before she could stop herself, but as they entered the air, she knew she would not stop. She could not.

"Sorry, what?" the officer said.

Gulamira knew what needed to be done. She squared her shoulders and smiled her most deceptively alluring smile. Then Gulamira stirred a song in her throat. A soft, simple song, one of the lower ones. The song danced through her, tickling her throat as a cold numbness washed over her tongue. She interlaced the song with her Rajal speech, hiding it deep within the words so that no one would hear it, so no one would notice the subtle voice that influenced their thoughts, shifted their emotions.

"I see these women are for sale. I wish to have this tatzon girl." The soundless song left her mouth and went into the world, a song to dull their senses, to encourage receptivity. Her words carried the undercurrent of this song of power, filling the air with a melody only she could hear.

The tatzon officers nodded. "I'm unsure who you are, but of course we can do business."

"Wait, what?" the fat man said. "We were about to settle our deal. This girl is spoken for."

Gulamira wanted to frown, but her smile remained. Her songs could indeed influence, but the lower songs could not control the mind, and this human desired the tatzon girl too greatly for her song to have much effect. She'd need to deal directly with the officers.

However, they broke eye contact and glanced back at the man. "Hm. That is true," one said. "I am sorry, we did already decide to—"

"Don't you think," Gulamira said, pouring more of her song into her words, though not so much that they might hear the melody, "it would be better to sell a tatzon to tatzon? It seems wrong for a human to have the primary rights to our kind."

The officers considered this, but the fat man stepped past them. "Rich for you to speak. What right do you even have to purchase?"

Oh, she was tempted to use a different song on him, one that would make his skin crawl and insides rot, but that was a higher song. Those she dared not sing anymore.

The officers conferred with each other briefly, and she did not let her song die down, though she kept her words silent. They at last turned back to her. "We like the idea of kind with kind. However, he has offered quite the sum for her. We will forgo his offer if you instead pay her original price."

Gulamira's heart pounded as her attention became all too aware of the coin pouch at her side and the gate behind. "And how much is that?"

"Five hundred ivories."

Her heart sank. Her purse carried that much, but only just.

The fat man looked ready to protest, possibly tripling his offer, to provide the officers with something not even her songs could distract them from.

She practically leapt forward and thrust the pouch of coins into their hands. "Deal."

They nodded and had the girl untied from the rest of the line and handed over to Gulamira, all while the fat brothel owner shouted and complained beside them. She ignored him and quickly took the girl from there before anyone changed their minds or came after them.

Gulamira didn't look back at the gate. She couldn't bear it.

A few minutes later, she stood frozen in the middle of a street. What had she done?

She looked at the girl, who only glared at her. Gulamira blinked. "Come on."

Gulamira took a few dazed steps forward, but the girl didn't follow. In fact, she looked ready to bolt.

"Listen," Gulamira said. "If you want to run, go ahead. Just know there's plenty of humans here that will do far worse than what that fat man earlier wanted to do. I will not hurt you and I'll get you food. Your choice."

The girl looked her over, as if trying to be doubly sure that Gulamira was a fellow tatzon. After a moment, she looked Gulamira in the eyes. "I'll follow you."

And so she led the girl through the decaying port town to the only place Gulamira knew she could go. Not a safe place, for those didn't exist in Archoz, nor even a good place, for those didn't exist anywhere.

She returned to the River's Delight and Gulamira's smile, her perfectly constructed mask, began to strain.

2

AN INSANE TASK

I know I'm not a military expert, but I've heard some rumors about the Veirs and I'm confused why no one's looking into it. The Zaruf pulled back much of his army from the Wall and even the sea. According to a friend, the Veirs are looking to develop better weapons based on scrolls the Sefaran brought with them. Yet, no one around here seems to care. What if they develop the power of the quintal? Or what if they recreate the Sefaran disease? We can't recover if they do.

-Raza, the one who rambles a solid concern.

Isra had never hated the sight of a tree so much before. Well, maybe once before, but that had been a very particular tree.

Today, she glared at a sespen oak, which was a Common sized tree. Maybe less than a hundred feet tall with a good thirty foot diameter at its thickest. There were hundreds of trees just like it here in Archoz, all massive and stretching high into the sky, just like every other tree in the entire world. And just like a good tatzon town, these trees had homes and businesses and stables and storages all Built right into them. Not constructed with extra material like a human's place. No, these were all designed by plant-possessing Builders who got paid to grow and shape these luxurious places of life for these gray, self-important creatures.

But that was all usual. Normal. A Built dwelling was safer and longer lasting than any constructed one. That's not what made her hate this tree. Nor was it even the people inside the tree waiting for her. It was what coming to this tree meant.

It meant she had to sell another fragment of her soul and grind it into dust.

She sighed and stared at the tree canopy high above her. There was no sight of the sky, not through how thick the Builders interlaced the branches, but she could still taste the oncoming rain. A quick look around the tree-connecting bridges showed others noticed the rain as well. Tatzons hurried with their Partners to their next destination, some also went with their spouses and lovers. Sometimes they had their Partner's lover or their lover's spouse or their spouse's Partner. But no matter what, they traveled in pairs. No matter what, tatzons didn't go anywhere alone.

Which Isra imagined had to get annoying. Not that it mattered. She was just trying to distract herself from what awaited her in the tree ahead.

She left her little nook above the stairwell, brushing some rotting wood out of her thick, black hair. Isra adjusted her tunic, a rough cotton as brown as her skin, and emerged onto the bridge, which drew the gaze of a dozen onlookers. Humans were a rare sight in the town proper, and none walked the bridges as she did. The bridges were thick branches that a Builder had shaped and nurtured so that they formed straight walkways from one tree to the next. A priest of the Ethereal Tree often blessed bridges like these. Isra wasn't sure if her walking on these was actual blasphemy, but most tatzons acted as if it were.

But she kept her head down and didn't look anyone in the face. Which wasn't hard, since tatzons stood a head taller than her, and she didn't consider herself short by any human standard. This act of deference was enough to mollify anyone watching, just enough for her to cross before someone called the guard. Which had happened before. Twice. So, mouth shut and eyes down, she marched across the bridge to the walkway curving around the tree.

Isra took a glance toward the rest of Archoz, to where the humans lived. She'd never visited this area before the wall went up, but she'd heard of the liveliness of the port. Even at her vantage point, she couldn't see over the wall, but it wasn't hard to imagine what these tatzon Rajals did to the people inside that prison. It brought to mind stories Isra's grandmother had told her about. Humans crammed in cages and tied to trees for beasts to eat.

But, of course, the humans in her grandmother's stories had been Sefarans. So no one, other humans included, had cared what happened to them.

As she headed to her destination, she passed by a notice board with dozens of announcements and requests nailed to it. Most had to do with new policies in the town. A couple were job offerings, and a few others appeared to be updates on the war with Veirzen. As always, these updates emphasized how amazing the Rajals were and how impenetrable the Vined Wall was. Besides that, there was a wanted poster for two fugitives from the Iron Mountains. A deserter and an ordîn had escaped the prison up there, and had quite the bounty on their head. Which was a bit of an oddity. Isra didn't know ordîns could break the law.

With nothing else interesting to stall herself with, Isra walked to the door of the tavern she was told to go to. Well, "door" wasn't quite the proper word. Humans made doors. Tatzons Built "openings", which were sealed passages only to be opened or closed by a Builder possessing it. But this wasn't that rich a town, so not every tavern was going to have some Builders on staff. Instead, this place had a larger, circular metal partition that rolled into the wall when open and rolled back out to close.

So, a door.

Two tatzons waited just beyond the opening, sitting at a table with a game of chance going. Both had four thick arms matching their thick necks. Like all tatzons, they each had markings covering their body. One had markings that looked like irregular circles, and the other had a triangle pattern, both in light brown colors. Markings were the best way to tell these creatures apart.

The two narrowed their eyes at the sight of her and one grabbed three axes, the other only two. Before they introduced those metals to her flesh, or threw her off the forty-foot drop, she showed her medallion. These guards would recognize it. Most people did. The medallion was a little smaller than her palm and made of a Common beast's ivory, and so had brown swirls throughout. The coin displayed the symbol of two crossed wings on one side and a symbol of a thorny branch wrapping around the moons on the other. A Medallion of an Appointed Servant. The fanciest title the Rajals had thought of to call a human slave.

The guards took the coin and examined it, but it wasn't like they were guarding the Oligarch's crystals or anything. They couldn't disallow her entrance. Not with that coin.

Regardless, the two stepped toward her, looming over in the way only self-important tatzons could. Both glared death at her. She returned it in full.

"Obey the rules in here," one said. "One misstep and—" he tapped his axe to his head.

Isra took back her coin and headed inside without a second glance.

It wasn't the busiest tavern she'd seen, which she thanked the Lady for. The fewer of these people she had to deal with, the better. From her count there were only eight other people here, including the two barkeeps who stiffened at her entrance. With an eye roll, she held the coin between her middle and index finger and rested it by her shoulder, the expected stance of an appointed servant when their master wasn't around. This way the tatzons would not... well, she'd still discomfort them and they'd prefer her gone, but they wouldn't throw her out unless she gave them good reason to. For now, she looked for her table.

The tavern, like most Built rooms, was rounded and smooth, with slits on the sides to allow in fresh air to combat the thick musk of the mushroom ales. Lightstone lanterns hung from the ceiling in several places, though the crystals were too small to light up everything. The owners had painted the room in bright Rajal colors, though bright for a Rajal was just a lighter shade of brown and green. Color was for those Veirs, after all. Or maybe even an ordîn.

Isra took a seat at the farthest green table from the opening and sat with her back against the wall. No one bothered her. No one asked her what she wanted. They took a glance or two and went back to their talk. A human here was unnerving, but Rajals excelled at ignoring her kind.

And it seemed the people she was here to meet were taking their time to get here.

She sighed and leaned deep into her chair. This could be a long wait. Better she used the time to prepare. No one looked her way right now, so she rolled her sleeves past her elbows, revealing her own "human markings". These tattoos were black on her skin, but they'd have confused anyone looking at them. Each arm had three circles—one on the palm and two on the inside of the forearm. A thick, curving line connected every circle to one another, making her arm resemble a series of twisting roads. One of these "roads" ran up along her index fingers to the tips. To most people, these were a strange choice of tattoo. People often ignored them. And Isra liked that.

Because then they'd never know the secret behind them.

Of the six, three were empty circles. The other three had strange symbols inside. Symbols that to this day she couldn't decipher. Sometimes she thought they resembled things, but other times she was sure it was some forgotten or lost language. Or just one she didn't know. That didn't prevent her from feeling the contents of the circles.

Isra looked at her circles and ran her finger along those on her right arm. She stopped at the circle on her palm with a symbol that she knew better than any other. She touched it and Released its contents.

Instantly, her ivory stylus materialized in her hand and the symbol in her palm circle vanished. Isra then got to work.

The table in front of her was circularish, but with many imperfections. She'd start there since it'd be the largest area she'd have access to in the space allotted.

She pressed the stylus into the wood and carved a faint circle, deep enough for it to work but not deep enough anyone would notice right away. The wood was tough, but even ivory from a Small beast was as strong as iron. Carving perfect circles into wood used to be a laborious process, given the grain often fought her, but years of practice yielded a circle of perfection. No edge or warped curve. A perfect circle.

Without removing the stylus from the wood, she carved a line from the circle down the edge of the table, and stopped just underneath so it was within reach. The barkeeps looked her way, so she stopped drawing her circles. And then two tatzons walked into the tavern, looked right at her, and she scowled. Seemed her meeting had begun.

They sat with a nod. She returned the gesture. They both sat with total composure, befitting a well-groomed servant. She sat with the total apathy of a wilting mushroom.

They were two women of middling age, which for tatzons was something close to seventy, an age few humans lived to see. Loose green wraps, the latest trend in Rajal fashion, covered them from shoulder to mid-calf, though remained open and flowing enough to showcase their bodies underneath. They had to be of thick Rajal tatzon descent, considering both had skin like iron and markings as light brown as dying leaves. One woman had markings that looked like a series of hooves stamped all over her body with no sense of order. The other had the most orderly horizontal lines for markings. No matter how many tatzons Isra had ever met, she'd never gotten over how random markings were in a person. Though, tatzons preferred the term "unique" over random.

"Nu'Isra of the Brier," the one with hoof markings said with a tone of such natural superiority that Isra wanted to punch her in the face. "I am Verta Austr Hanska Con-Sala."

"And I," the other said, "am Sala Perto Pesta Con-Verta. We are here to issue your direction from the Lady Brier."

Isra gripped her ivory stylus hard underneath the table, out of sight. Why tatzons needed to use such long names was beyond her. Why these two dared bring up her family name was another infuriating matter. Sometimes, only sometimes, she wished her father had not made the Brier family rich and influential. But he had. And that's why she was here.

When she didn't answer either of them, Sala reached into her satchel and rifled inside. "Yes, we were told you weren't one for conversation. That should make this simple."

She handed a sealed parchment to Isra, stamped with the symbol of the thorny branch wrapping around the three moons. Seeing her family's crest made her right shoulder, and the tattoo of the same crest, itch and her insides burn. She snatched the letter from them and shattered the seal open, though she noted the woman had placed their satchel on the table. Isra made quick work of the instructions inside.

And sure enough, she'd found a new way to hate her step-mom.

She looked back at the two women and raised a brow. "Is she mad?"

"The Lady Brier is of excellent health," Verta said. "We will pass on your concern for her."

"As for the letter, is there something you require assistance in understanding?" Sala asked.

Isra gave the deepest glare she could muster and shook her head once. The letter was clear enough. Step-mom wanted her to fetch something, again. But this time, the damn woman was asking for the impossible.

"An idol of Mirr," Isra said.

"The Lady Brier has learned of one's discovery," Verta said. "Doubtless you understand the importance of her acquiring it before anyone else."

Isra nodded. She knew little about the legends or religious significance of a Mirr idol, but she knew the practical value of one. The Oligarchs, the six rulers of Rajalend, long ago offered to grant a single request for one of these idols. And there were no limitations placed on the request.

"When?" Isra asked.

Verta smiled and folded her two hands, one bigger than the other. "The *Cleansing* is expected any day now. You'll need to find your way onto it before it leaves the shores. We have a few contacts that might help you in getting onto the ship. Though returning will be up to you."

"Money?"

"The Lady Brier gave us a small sum to bribe your way to the ship." Sala patted Verta's bag, which Isra now noticed bulged more than a regular messenger bag. And it still sat on the table. As if they were just begging her to Catch it.

"How long?"

"The Lady Brier requires it within the next four months."

Isra sighed, looking at the letter again.

The *Cleansing* was coming here. A prison ship sent by the Oligarchs to purge Rajalend of all the criminal lowlifes of the land. Empty every prison and jail cell and dump everyone onto islands in the Dragon's Maw to work plantations until they dropped dead. And thanks to the Temple of the Ethereal Tree burning, being a human had unofficially become a crime.

And instead of running as far from this death ship as she could, like any sane person might try, she had to get onto it and survive long enough to obey the will of this despicable woman.

Isra paused and rubbed her right shoulder and the weight of responsibility it carried. She eyed the two women.

"If I fail?"

"Then the Oligarchs shall grant Con-Breks and Con-Ure the north meadows and beyond to Tutchal." Sala, whether paid to look it or genuinely felt it, appeared downcast at saying this. "The Briers will lose a major source of trade."

And Isra's people would suffer for it.

She folded the letter and handed it to Verta. "Burn it." They nodded. Likely, they planned to do so anyway. Better no one else knew what secret the *Cleansing* held in its hold. Less competition.

"Shall we head to our associates in town?" Verta asked. "We'll want to begin the process as soon as possible."

Isra waved a hand and placed her stylus on the table. "No need."

Sala cocked a brow. "Oh? And you believe you'll be able to start these bribes on your own? Our associates don't particularly deal with your kind."

Isra, for the first time today, smiled. "No need."

She connected the tattoo line on her index finger to the line carved into the table and, with her other hand, she tapped one of her empty circles that connected to that line. She winked at the tatzons and Caught everything on the table. The satchel, the burning candle, her stylus and medallion, everything vanished, and she felt them course through the lines and into the circle on her arm where a new, complex, symbol appeared.

The two women stumbled out of their chairs. Hard to tell if Isra's step-mom had warned them about her power. No one ever could make sense of it. After all, humans weren't supposed to have magic.

"Thanks for the coin," she said and, using the frustration that had continued to build since she'd first received her step-mom's summons, she launched herself at the women, fists clenched and striking fast.

They weren't fighters nor were they possessors, so Isra gave them a fair beating before the two guards from the opening came in and tore her off of them. The two women glared at her through a bruised eye and bleeding lip.

"The Lady Brier will hear of this!" Verta said as they dragged Isra out.

Isra was laughing at this point. She couldn't help it. "Good!"

Despite the guards' earlier threat, neither could kill her. She had an official servant's seal. And she'd only done a minor infraction. Small enough to get a drunk tatzon thrown out. But for a human like her?

They handed her over to the town guard, who took her to the lowest levels of one tree and tossed her into an outdoor pit with a metal cage atop. It'd begun raining at some point, so she fell into the warm mud with a splatter. It covered her clothes and got into her hair, but those punches had felt just so good.

Besides, this was most direct route to the *Cleansing*. After all, the ship was coming for many kinds of people, but, primarily, it was coming for one specific group.

Criminals and trouble making humans.

Troublemakers like her.

3

---◆◯◆---

PURIFICATION

R *az, I love you and your wandering and curious mind, but don't
expect me to take part in your musings. I already have too many
actually important things to worry about. The Zaruf's army is behaving
weirdly, I'll grant you that, but I doubt they are looking at Sefaran
designs. They may be Veirs, but they are still tatzons. They will not listen
to a human, let alone a Sefaran.*

*Also, thanks for the red thistle leaf. I appreciate it. It always makes me
think of home.*

-Beneficiary Syeda Softbark, a proud sister of a rambling brother.

Warm rain dripped down the shutters of Gulamira's window,
which she normally shut for a rain like this, but today she had them
wide open. She stood at the window, wind blowing rain into her
face, her gaze toward the ocean. The River's Delight had no view
of the waters, only of the rotting, dead homes of humanity. But
she looked all the same, as if looking long enough would grant her
vision through the constructions sinking into the mud, past the
towers of her imprisonment, and beyond the malaise of Archoz to
the open seas of freedom.

But staring granted no such boon. She drank deep from her
mulled mushroom wine. Maybe if she drank enough, she'd see the
ocean.

She wiped rainwater from her face and turned away from the
window, though the room she was in wasn't a better sight. Fad-

ed curtains and ripped drapes decorated her small residence. A red-tinted lantern sat in the corner and heavy perfumes clung to the air in order to mask the burning whale fat. A bed sat in the center, taking up a fair amount of the space, with green-patched blankets covering the rotting straw beneath. Above the bed was a sleeping bar she'd had installed a while back. At first, it had been so she didn't sleep on the ground like a beast or human, but there were some customers who wanted to make use of it, too. There was also a single portrait of two unknown Partners which she hung on the wall to cover a hidden hole the brothel master had often used to watch from. Beside the bed was a single chest that held all three things she owned. Right now, Medhi's dagger sat atop it.

The dagger had an ivory hilt, with streaks of red marbling which meant it came from a Large beast. The blade was curved and made of iron, though if one took a closer inspection or just waited for the dark they'd see specks of glowing green and blue crystal. This made it a perfect weapon for a human, since without crystal a weapon had little chance in the Abyss to hurt a possessor. The ivory and crystal made this little weaponry worth a lot in Rajalend. It would fetch enough ivories she could have bought her freedom months ago.

Yet, whenever the thought to sell came to her mind, she never found herself able to part ways with Medhi's only gift to her.

There was little else in the room, little else in this den of pleasure and loneliness.

Except the girl.

The girl sat on the bed and stared at the discolored portrait, recovered from all that happened this morning. She had not spoken a word as Gulamira dragged her along into the brothel, though the girl likely didn't know what this place was. No one had stopped them as they came in.

And Gulamira was here, back in the River's Delight to rot away until the *Cleansing* ended her. All because of this girl.

Gulamira took another long drink. The stuff tasted as horrid as they came, but after a couple of bottles, she wouldn't even notice. It was this first bottle that was the hardest.

Gulamira stayed near the window, water trickling down her back, and looked the girl over. For one, the girl seemed fed. Most urchins, tatzon and human, were leaner and bonier, but she didn't have that look about her. A lost girl, maybe, but not a street dweller. Though, she also wasn't plump, like some tatzon children. No, she looked more... muscular than deprived. And she was clean, at least compared to Archoz standards, with solid gray coloring to her skin, which was not as dark as most Rajals, but not quite like a Veir. Mixed heritage, most likely. The girl had markings of deep black that resembled circles with broad lines striking through them. Her markings spread out evenly across her skin.

Gulamira sat on the bed across from the girl and glanced at the final oddity. This girl had an undeveloped arm. Every tatzon was born with only their priarm, and only through possession did they grow any more. But, it took tatzons months upon months, even years, to grow a new arm. And more than that, despite every tatzon being able to grow at least one arm, most didn't start until they were at least ten years old and they rarely finished in under three years. This girl didn't look over eight, and this new arm was almost full grown. Maybe the girl was older than she looked.

"Hey, do you need anything to drink or eat?" Gulamira asked, not sure what she was supposed to say. "We have little here, but we could scrounge up a half eaten loaf of bread, maybe." Of course, the bread would either be stale or have a few inhabitants inside.

The girl shook her head. "Not hungry."

Gulamira was with the girl on that. She didn't have an appetite either. "Right. Well, despite earlier, I'm not interested in owning you. You're free to do as you will."

The girl looked back at her. "So, you're just freely helping me? Why?"

Gulamira wanted to laugh. That was the very question she'd been asking herself. And she didn't have an answer. But she had to say something.

"We're tatzon," she said. "We look after our own."

The girl didn't look convinced and stared back at the portrait.

"Do you have a name?" Gulamira asked.

"Of course I have a name. What's it to you?"

This kid was a lot gruffer than most children Gulamira had met. But given she was being sold by slavers, a little distrust was understandable. "My name is Gulamira. It's alright if you don't want to tell me your name, but it will feel odd for you to know my name and me not know yours."

The girl glanced at her a moment before looking back at the portrait. Gulamira shrugged and took another drink. Children were not her expertise. With shy or more forceful customers, Gulamira would incorporate certain songs into her voice and let them permeate the air so they would not hear but would feel. These would help relax a person, encourage them to trust Gulamira, or even appease a bit of their anger. These songs had been her secret to her advancement in Archoz, as well as her survival for all these years.

Songs that could influence the minds of people and even the movements of spirits.

The effects weren't harmful, unless she meant them to be, but she would never use her songs on this girl. Only once had she used her songs on a child. She would not again.

"My mom named me Kamaria," the girl said, her voice quiet.

"It's nice to meet you, Kamaria."

The girl turned toward her, a shy and uncertain smile coming and going on her lips. "Why are you being so nice?"

Gulamira shrugged. "I know I'd want some kindness if today happened to me."

"You didn't have to help me, you know. I would've been fine."

Gulamira nodded. "Of course. But I wanted to make sure, just in case."

Kamaria sat up straight and stared Gulamira right in the eyes. And there was that same strength and defiance Gulamira had noticed there before. "I would have been just fine. Because I'm going to be the strongest Guardian to ever live and not even those men could've stopped me."

She spoke with power and determination. And it was the strangest thing, because for a moment Gulamira believed her.

The girl had dreams. Though, all children did at one point. Even Gulamira once had dreams. Once she had seen herself adorned with the garments of the High Priestess, overseeing the life of all Veirzen, with her Partner at her side.

The thought of the promised Partner she never had caused her to take another deep drink from the wine bottle. Thoughts like that did her no good, only brought irritation and a cold, sick feeling to her stomach.

Dreams were dead. Kamaria would learn that some day soon.

Gulamira leaned back on the bed. "Then you're growing a Guardian arm there?"

Kamaria puffed her chest out. "I've been training all year. Tsuran says I'll finish my first arm soon."

Gulamira coughed on some wine and sat up. "Fiery Breath. Agh." She turned to Kamaria. "Wait, you've only been training for a year?"

"Well, almost a year, I think. I'm still learning how to track time. I don't get it, but Tsuran says it's important."

Less than a year? And her first arm had grown this much? That was not impressive. That was full on impossible. You'd have to train every hour of every day to do that.

A sick feeling swept through Gulamira and she scooted closer to Kamaria, scanning every part of her she could see. The girl wore tighter clothes than most Rajals, but enough skin showed for Gulamira to look her over.

Kamaria leaned away. "What are you doing?"

"Sorry, I'm... Kamaria, during your training has any part of you..." Exkel above, how was she supposed to ask this? "... become different?"

"You mean Remnancy?"

Gulamira nodded.

"No, I don't have any of that. Tsuran never lets me train long enough for my skin to turn into anything."

"Is Tsuran your teacher, then?"

"Yeah, he's teaching me how to become a Guardian. I want to get as good as him. He'll stop worrying about me, then." She leaned toward Gulamira and whispered in a conspiratorial manner. "Sometimes, I train when he's not looking. Even deep into the night."

Plenty of questions rolled into Gulamira's head, but she stopped them and pushed them aside. Why was she bothering with this girl? She was an oddity, for sure, but why talk with her as if today was just another normal day.

The *Cleansing* was coming for Archoz soon. And the Oligarchs' declaration didn't care if they were tatzon or not. To them, to the *Cleansing*, Gulamira and Kamaria were the same filth Rajalend needed clearing of. The Abyss was coming in the guise of purification.

Gulamira went for another drink but found her bottle empty. She dropped it and pulled herself to the corner of the room to grab another. But why was she even bothering with numbing herself? This weak stuff couldn't protect her from the misery before her. And there would be misery. Everyone knew there would be. There'd been stories of life on the three Oligarch ships. Stories that drove people to desperate means. People tried to escape Archoz, preferring to face beasts and spirits and guards than the *Cleansing*. Others abandoned any kind of purity and engaged in every licentious and depraved pleasure. Gulamira even knew of parents who drowned their own kids in order to protect them from the nightmare that sailed for them.

And it was coming. There was no stopping it. Soon her life would end. Again.

She bit into the wine cork to pull it out, but the rotting thing broke apart, leaving a chunk of it still plugging the wine. Gulamira groaned and leaned back against the wall. And she wondered.

She wondered if she were as strong as those parents had been. They knew what awaited them and their kids, and they did something about it. They knew the world had nothing but agony for them, and so they deprived the world of its sick pleasure. Gulamira sat on the splintered floor, staring at the horrid wine, and wondered.

But she knew the answer: no. She wasn't strong enough to end her life, to end her misery. And she wasn't strong enough to endure it either. All she could do was close and lock the doors of her soul, huddle in the darkest corner, and refuse to let anything in.

Something stirred deep inside her, deeper than anything else could. A song. A song that spoke of release. It stirred down below her heart, underneath her spirit, just behind her soul. The song moved with power and purpose, with the intensity of the Dragon's Breath. It grew, inviting itself up through the layers of her being, wanting to grow in her throat and burst free through her mouth.

Gulamira recognized the song. Her parents ingrained it in her before she could even walk. It was one part of the Heritage they'd passed to her and no one else.

The Song of the Coming Fire.

It was of the higher songs, those that held the greatest power of the Heritage. The lower songs could influence and suggest. But the higher songs were commands. This song promised so much to her. It promised to release her from this life of pain. It promised to make the world burn. No more hiding. No more fearing. Only release. She was not strong enough. This song was.

Last month marked ten years since she'd dared sing a higher song. It seemed appropriate that as a higher song began her misery, so too should one end it.

The song rose from the depths, like a growing heat ready to engulf her. The Coming Fire rose. It would be easy, almost too easy, to unleash it.

"Were they Guardians?"

Kamaria's question drew Gulamira from her reverie like a waft of stinkweed. "What?"

The girl pointed at the portrait. The two Rajals in the portrait had four arms each, meaning they were active possessors. "Were they Guardians?"

"I do not know who they were. Given that there's a painting of them, I'd guess they were Builders or something. Might even be a pair of ditherers."

"Dither... wer?"

"Someone who has arms in multiple possessions."

Kamaria frowned. "But they're not Guardians?"

"People don't paint Guardians."

"Why not? Guardians are the best!"

Gulamira shrugged. "Possessing statues just isn't as useful as possessing plants or beasts."

Kamaria looked back at the portrait, but with more disdain now. "Well, I don't think that's right. When I'm a famous Guardian, I'll have everyone make paintings of me."

The window shutters batted against the wall as the winds picked up. Gulamira groaned and forced herself to the window to latch the shutters closed. "I know it's raining, but now that you're safe, maybe we can try to find your parents."

Kamaria quieted, and for the first time, the fire in her eyes dimmed. And Gulamira did not need her to say anything. She recognized those eyes, that haunted look.

Kamaria didn't have parents.

"I'm sorry," Gulamira said, as if that meant anything to the girl. "Do you have anyone to go to? This Tsuran fellow?"

Kamaria nodded. "I travel with him. He's kept me safe since…" She swallowed and dropped her gaze. Her parents must have died recently. The pain in her voice was all too fresh.

Gulamira knelt next to the bed and touched Kamaria's knee. "Is he here in Archoz? Is it safe to bring you to him?"

"I don't know where he is. I… ran away a few nights ago. Someone caught me and brought to this place." Kamaria grabbed Gulamira's hand. "But he'll find me. He always finds me when I'm lost."

She said it as if trying to reassure herself. As if repeating what she'd been told many times over. Gulamira didn't know what to say. Because if this man had not found Kamaria yet, then there wasn't any more hope for it. The *Cleansing* was coming.

And her song waited. It was ready. The Coming Fire was ready. The song rose in her throat and she knew that her release would come swiftly.

But Kamaria squeezed her hand. And the song… Gulamira wasn't sure how to describe it, but it was as if the song retreated from her.

"Can I ask you something?" Kamaria asked and the song, which had been so near before, ebbed away.

"I guess so."

Kamaria tried to smile, but it was half-hearted and pain leaked through. Though maybe it was pain only Gulamira could see. "You've smiled since I met you. How do you do it? Why do you smile?"

Gulamira paused and resisted touching her face. Was she still smiling? She hadn't even noticed. But she felt it now. Yes, the smile was there, small and subtle, but there. A mask she'd carried with her through all these years.

And the girl's question echoed in her mind, Why do you smile?

But as it sounded in her ears, she did not hear the voice of a girl, but of an older man. Her teacher and mentor.

Why do we smile, High Priestess? Priest Salma had asked. Why do we live? Come, you know your lessons. You know why we priests must smile. So never forget.

Those were his last words to her as the guards whisked her away to safety. That had been the last priest of Exkel she'd ever seen, on the day her life had ended. When she had become an orphan.

An orphan like Kamaria here.

Salma's words were loud in her mind. Why do we smile?

Gulamira shook her head. She knew the answer. Even after a decade, that lesson was still firm in her mind. Priests of Exkel smiled in order to bear the burdens of the world, in order to ensure everyone else that life would be alright. But that answer was for a life she no longer had. She still smiled, but not as a priestess of Exkel. She smiled as Gulamira alone.

Gulamira gripped Kamaria's hand tight. "Sometimes, when you're in the most pain, when you feel the most defeated, all you can do is smile. Even if you've lost, you don't have to let anyone else know it."

Kamaria met her gaze. "Are you defeated, then?"

Gulamira's chest tightened and in the recesses of her soul, the song of the Coming Fire stirred once again. But, as she looked at this girl, this fellow orphan, something else stirred. Something even more frightening and more intense than anything brought about from the Coming Fire.

The whisper of hope rose in her.

And against her better judgment, against her soul's cry for relief, against the fact this girl would change nothing, Gulamira pushed the song of the Coming Fire down and away, locking it back up inside of its chest. And a rare, but genuine, smile graced her lips. "I am not. And neither are you."

Kamaria smiled.

From outside, trumpets and drums resounded through the port. Kamaria looked to the window. "What's that?"

Gulamira hung her head. "Archoz is announcing it."

"Announcing what?"

Gulamira opened the shutters, the wind and rain pelting her again. Other houses in the Deviant Quarter did the same. Everyone knew what this meant. "The *Cleansing* is near."

And that whisper of hope that had built became even quieter than it began.

4

THE CLEANSING

*W*hile looking over some old records, I found something... odd. *Did you know the Oligarchs had at one point agreed to develop weapons and ships based on Sefaran designs? They claimed to "harness the thunderous power of the Quintal". Tatzon scholars presented these designs, so no one outright dismissed them and in fact everyone agreed to look into it. But nothing came of it. I've looked and I can't find any of these designs anywhere, nor any other record of them. Further, those scholars have been missing for over five years. Right after the Oligarchs agreed to develop the weapons, these scholars vanished.*

-Raza, a puzzled man. Also, you can drop the "Beneficiary" when writing to me. It makes me roll my eyes every time.

The *Cleansing* arrived in the heat of the day, amidst a warm downpour. It came like a Colossal specter of death, emerging from the gray waters without fanfare or dirge. And like the mighty beast it was, it laid in wait, ready for its prey.

Soldiers emptied each of the port quarters. The entire morning, Gulamira and Kamaria listened to the screams and shouts and fights breaking out all over. When soldiers came for them, the most belligerent of the humans were already lying dead in the streets, the rain washing away their blood in little red streams. Everyone else had iron around their ankles, wrists, and necks. They didn't chain every human right away, but every tatzon was. After all, tatzons couldn't possess through iron.

The soldiers clasped iron around Gulamira and Kamaria and put them in with a group of humans. She avoided using any of her lower songs. Nothing subtle would help her, only something more forceful. However, doing that risked her being discovered given how many soldiers were here. At that point, they would see her as more special than they needed to.

There were so many being taken today. Hordes of humans and many tatzons stood crammed together in the streets, trudging to the docks. Several smaller boats ferried groups from the docks through the opened gates to the *Cleansing*, which was too large to fit through the wall's opening. Gulamira wasn't sure how many people were in the port itself, but she'd heard estimates of a thousand or more humans.

They had emptied the Deviant Quarter first and Gulamira's group came close to the front within two hours. The rest of the port would take a couple of days to empty. But that did not stop the soldiers from forcing everyone to stand outside in the pouring rain.

Gulamira watched group after group walk onto the boats and ship off. Her group would board soon so she pulled Kamaria close to her. She had already fought through a throng and endured a whipping to keep the child next to her and she wasn't about to lose sight of her. Kamaria's small hand squeezed hers and Gulamira tried offering her a reassuring smile. The girl held her undeveloped arm tight to her chest, gaze jumping from one person to the next as though everyone were about to snatch her up.

Gulamira tugged her close. "Don't worry. I won't let anyone touch you."

"Where are they taking us?"

Gulamira looked up toward the *Cleansing*. Exkel's Breath, how was she supposed to explain this? Straightforward truth, she supposed. "They're shipping us off to the Dragon's Maw. Far away from here."

Kamaria held her hand firm. "That's bad, right?"

"Yes. It's bad." Though, Gulamira dared not think of how bad it'd be. For now, she'd stay safe behind her smile.

"I don't want to go," Kamaria said.

Gulamira stared forward, unable to look at the girl.

"I don't want to leave."

"I know."

Kamaria sniffed and Gulamira saw tears inside those young eyes. A crying child. What was she supposed to do with this?

"Hey, hey. No need for that. It's going to be fine. I hear... I hear the Maw is pretty and—"

"I want Tsuran." Kamaria hugged onto Gulamira's leg tight, almost tripping her over. A few people next to them glanced over, some with pity, others with pleasure to see tatzons in pain.

Unsure what to do, Gulamira patted the girl's head. "Well, maybe he's coming. Why don't you look for him?"

"Everyone's too tall," she said.

"What's he look like? I'll look for you." It was pointless to look, but maybe giving the child hope would distract her from what was happening.

"Well, he wears tight gray clothes. He's got hair like mine,"—Kamaria pointed to her braided hair, which Gulamira recognized as a Rajal warrior braid—"and he's got four arms, but no priarm."

Four arms, but no priarm? That would stand out. "And what about his markings?"

Kamaria looked at her hands, her own markings covering them. "Black crescents on his right side."

"And his left?"

"There's nothing on his left."

Gulamira raised a brow. Markings on only the right side? That didn't seem likely. Such a thing didn't exist. Markings by nature covered the entire body. Of course, sometimes they didn't cover the face entirely, like her own, but they always went around the rest of the tatzon.

"And his Partner?" Gulamira asked. "What do they look like?"

Kamaria shut her mouth and looked away as soldiers with clubs and whips ushered them forward. Only two more groups ahead of theirs.

"Kamaria?"

"You'll never see the monster."

"What?"

Kamaria only shook her head and mumbled something.

"I didn't hear that." Gulamira knelt closer. "What'd you say?"

Even this close, the girl's voice barely rose above the rain. "Just find Tsuran. Please."

Another boat took off, and the next took its place. One more group.

Gulamira straightened but didn't look away. She kept her eyes on the girl. Kamaria had faced four drunk humans this morning without a shred of fear. But she closed herself off now, eyes downcast, body still. All at the mention of Tsuran's Partner. This "monster". A single person held power over Kamaria, power to rob her of all her bravery and gumption at the mere mention of them.

Gulamira understood that. She'd known too many people like that. Every day, she felt their whispers trying to pry through her walls, trying to break her smile. But she kept her mask steadfast.

"Right, next up," a voice called from behind. It was her group's turn to board.

Gulamira bent down to Kamaria's ear. "There are many monsters in this world, Kamaria. They will all try to break you." She turned the girl so their eyes met. "Never show them they have."

"Go on, all of you." Soldiers pushed them forward onto the boat. Gulamira kept Kamaria close to her, never letting go of her hand.

Row after row of seats filled the deck and strong looking humans manned the oars, though they neither looked pleased nor rested. The soldiers kept pushing person after person onto the boat and once Gulamira was drowning in human hair and limbs, they set off.

Kamaria clung to Gulamira's legs, though her head bobbed up and down, trying to get a last look at the docks. Maybe she thought her friends would burst from the crowd. Despite herself, Gulamira also looked.

But no one came for either of them. And the *Cleansing* awaited.

As they approached the prison ship, Gulamira realized that not a single rumor or imagining had prepared her for just how massive the ship was. It sat deep in the water, yet even then still had so much ship left. There were no less than six masts and more than a dozen decks. She couldn't even see the top deck from the water. The entire ship loomed above her like a waiting beast, with her boat its next meal.

That was the *Cleansing*. The prison ship designed for the specific prupose of carrying off all the undesirables of Rajalend and carting them to the Dragon's Maw for the glory of the Ethereal Tree.

Well, "designed" wasn't the best word. Because there was an even greater difference between every other ship she'd ever seen or sailed on and the *Cleansing*. All those other ships had been constructed. Human in design, constructed using human labor, and sailed by human sailors.

But the *Cleansing*, oh, she was different. She was Built. Not the product of cut wood mixed with tar and iron. The entire ship had once been the trunk of a living tree. A living tree that dozens of Builders had possessed and shaped and morphed into what Gulamira saw before her now. A ship made from a single tree, where every deck, every window, every stair, every hull was all one piece.

Their tiny boat reached the side of the mighty ship where a walkway, which might have once been a branch, lowered for the prisoners to walk up. With some curses and a few stinging whips, the prisoners loaded onto the walkway and marched up. It had a railing on either side and ridges for the feet to grip, otherwise no one would have made it up in the constant rain. Going up the walkway felt like trying to climb into the sky. The water fell further away and the clouds drew closer. She thought even close enough to touch.

At the top of the deck, she met an unexpected sight. Midship the crew had put up two makeshift canopies, creating a slight barrier to the rain. Underneath each, a group of tatzons waited, all wearing clothes distinct from the sailors around. The deck itself was as wide as a Small oak, a hundred, maybe a hundred-fifty feet across. The colors of Rajalend flew overhead and Rajal soldiers stood by to keep order. A contingent of soldiers stood in front of the aftcastle, where two prominent tatzons, the captains, stood. Gulamira's attention, though, went to four tatzons behind the captains. People seemed to avoid their space. Each had four arms and two had large metal boxes on their hips.

Four possessors, two of which had to be Soulborn, spirit possessors.

She for sure could use none of the lower songs now. They worked because people didn't notice them. But Soulborn knew to listen for them.

Besides them, the deck had quite a few sailors, all watching from the sides. The sailors, all human, wore tight green trousers and open-faced shirts, perfect clothes for warm weather and working in the rigging. However, those under the canopies wore loose, flowing black wraps, though their arms were sleeveless. They brought the prisoners under the tents one by one and Gulamira realized who stood under the canopy. The ship surgeons.

"Next!"

She squeezed Kamaria's hand, let it go, and entered the tent.

"Mm, a tatzon. Early twenties. Female," one surgeon said. He brushed his long hair out of his eyes, showcasing light brown square markings all over his gray skin. His Partner, another man, took notes on parchment, with markings that resembled warped and wriggling lines. "Alright, remove."

The two guards on either side grabbed her dress. And she let them. Iron clasped her throat, chained her legs, locked her heart. She'd had her chance at a fantasy of freedom and that was dead now. She was back to this familiar old truth. The faces and mode were different, but the master was the same. There was no Gulamira. Only someone else's property.

And so, she made sure her smile was as wide and pleasant as ever. She smiled big, and behind that smile she hid and shrunk into nothingness.

The dress ripped off and was discarded onto the rest of the growing pile. The surgeons raised their brows at her wrapping, but the guards grabbed her and removed Medhi's dagger.

"Add to the confiscated pile," one surgeon said, and glanced at her legs. "This one is muddied. Water."

Cold water dumped over her, sending spine-tingling shivers down through her toes. The contrast with the warm rain brought her a blaring acute awareness of everything she tried to ignore. The way the surgeons looked at her as if judging breeding stock, the way the irons dug and chafed, the way the sailors had stopped to leer and laugh. They she tried to ignore the most. She was not shy, but they leered without someone berating them and so it was all too easy to wonder what else they could do to prisoners and get away with.

A hand gripped Gulamira's chin, and she nearly yelped, only just hanging onto her smile. The surgeon was ready for her.

He turned her head side to side, examining the size, or maybe checking to see whether she had fleas. "Head seems clear," he said and his Partner scribbled away as he turned her around twice. "No signs of Remnancy." He grabbed her second arm, the one she grew as a little girl. "Type of possession?"

It took her a moment to realize it was a question directed at her. "Beast."

He pointed back at the crowd behind her. "Which is your Partner?"

The warmth of the air and rain vanished from her and she struggled to speak her practiced lie. "Dead."

The surgeon showed no sign of pity, he simply continued with his examination as his Partner jotted down notes. He ran his fingers along her ribs underneath her priarm. "No sign of further growth. Non-active possessor. Light gray skin tone denotes Veir ancestry. Note on the markings: resembles twisting branches. Symmetrical and black. Runs down chest and back, wrapping around hip and thighs. Half-marker on the face. Marking curves under both cheeks."

His hands, rough but precise, moved throughout her body, describing a half-dozen things that meant nothing to her. However, with everything the surgeon said, his Partner seemed more and more disappointed. She started to tune it out, to descend behind her smile and become numb, but the man was thorough and her secret dread came to fruition.

He lifted her left breast, and she swallowed the urge to punch him.

"Hm," he said, staring. "There's an incision here. Under the left breast. It's thin and no longer than a finger. Nearly unnoticeable."

"Intentional?" the other asked.

"Childhood accident," Gulamira said. "Ran after a friend and into a thorn bush. Got scratched up, but that one was the worst of them."

The surgeon stared at her and back to the scar. Whether he believer her or not was irrelevant, because he would not know the truth. The truth would only worsen her situation here. Telling people that the quintal stole her ability to possess had the tendency to do that.

The surgeon left her and spoke in hushed tones with his Partner a moment. After reaching a consensus on something, the surgeon nodded to the guards. "Forward hatch."

The guards tossed Gulamira a loincloth and breast wrap. It seemed she'd join the majority.

She wrapped herself, hiding the scar away from view. The guards then moved her to the group heading down the hatch to wherever they'd hole up for the journey to the Maw. Gulamira glanced back for Kamaria. She did not know what to do about the girl. She'd have to figure out some... wait. Something was wrong.

Kamaria's surgeons finished with her but they did not remove their gaze from the girl's undeveloped arm and they looked more than pleased. Both nodded to the nearby soldiers and Gulamira went cold.

The guards grabbed Kamaria. They did not give her any clothes.

"Hey," Gulamira said before she could stop herself. "What are you doing?"

A guard prodded her in the chest. "Back in line."

They were taking Kamaria to the other hatch. They were taking her away.

"Hey, wait," Gulamira said. "Stop!"

A sharp whip slashed Gulamira's back, and she yelped. "Mouth shut and in line."

"That girl. Please, she's with me! Where are you taking her?"

The whip cracked. Gulamira winced. Everything in her told her to shut up. Let it be. Don't cause anymore trouble.

Kamaria caught her gaze. Her eyes were wide and Gulamira could tell she was struggling to not scream, struggling to not let them break her. And something deep in Gulamira, more visceral and real than anything else in the world, boomed through her entire body. *SAVE HER!*

She lunged forward, arms reaching for the girl.

Her chained legs tripped underneath her and she crashed onto the deck as they pulled Kamaria aftward. The guards next to Gulamira flexed their muscles, gripped their flogs, and began their delightful work. Through a gritted smile and a single tear she hadn't restrained, Gulamira watched them pull Kamaria down the other hatch and out of sight. The rain poured, the whips cracked, she bled.

The guard gripped her shoulders and pulled her back to her feet, shoving her along with the rest of the group. She didn't resist. She fell behind her smile and choked down every bitter tear. Worst of it was she could not be sure for whom or what those tears were for. Not all for Kamaria.

Not all.

They marched her down through the ship, descending deck after deck until she was sure they had left the ship and dove into the depths of the Abyss itself. The ship had no lightstone, only oil lanterns that created a thick, musky smell of a rotting beach. With every level, the smell, the heat, the cramped quarters all worsened beyond what could be survivable. In fact, everything worsened the deeper they went. Decks became disorderly. Lanterns became more and more rare. People they encountered were dirtier and dirtier, and not just the prisoners. And they did encounter prisoners. Haunted, emaciated, dirt-encrusted humans who scrubbed floors, rolled barrels, hoisted ropes. All chained.

They went down so many decks, she lost count. And then they stopped. She wasn't sure why, not in the dim light of this deck. There was talk ahead, but inaudible. Whatever was said, the prisoners in front started shuffling and moving, but in two different directions. It looked like the men were being separated from the women and children.

She wondered if they'd have her go somewhere else since she was a tatzon, but they pushed her into the group of other women. The men headed down another deck, but the guards filed the women one after the other into a dark room. Gulamira shuffled in, not wanting to run into the woman in front and trip. But stepping into the room was one of the hardest things she'd done so far, because of the absolute horrid smell that crashed from the room into her. It pummeled her nose with such intense ferocity she wanted to vomit. Somehow she kept it down, but many other women were not so lucky. Gulamira had spent over two years in the most putrid swamp of a place filled with the absolute worst filth humanity and tatzonkind could muster, and yet that had been a field of flowers compared to this.

And when the guards brought in a lantern, she'd wished they'd left them to the darkness.

Hungry, desperate, fearful eyes appeared in the darkness, reflecting the lantern light. And not a few. The room was fit to bursting with women and children. There looked to be nothing in the room but these people and they lined every inch of the place. If she had to guess, they Built the room to handle a hundred people. No less than four times that many women were here, crammed up against each other, not having room to move or stand or live. As the guards forced her in, she noticed some bodies slumped over and—Abyss, were they decomposing?

This time, Gulamira couldn't hold it in. She heaved up whatever forsaken food she'd consumed that morning, only then realizing she'd vomited all over some people. No one noticed, themselves covered in their own dirt and filth.

Salma's words, his last lesson, tried to entreat her mind. Tried to encourage and strengthen her.

But he was dead. Everyone was dead. Gulamira could no longer fight. She could no longer live.

The guards slammed the door shut, locking it behind them. The darkness became absolute.

And, in that darkness, Gulamira broke.

5

---◆○◆---

FROM THE DARKNESS

I will ask Lamia about it, if you'd like. She wasn't a Beneficiary back then, but she was around so maybe she heard something. But I doubt it's that great a mystery. It was Sefaran design, so they dismissed it. Nothing more to it.

However, as to your actual job, have you learned anything more about Ma'Jra? Oligarchs Hyder and Zaid are interested in knowing how the Veirs leveled such a well defended town. We need to know if we're to protect our people.

-Beneficiary Syeda Softbark, the one proud of her station and who will flaunt it in your face as often as she can.

Isra took in her surroundings. Low light, awful smell, cramped space, moaning thieves, all enclosed in a wooden cage. So, not the worst scenario she'd imagined.

After last night's jaunt in the town's mud-jail, tatzons had whisked her away and onto this insane ship. One strip search later, they shoved her into a wooden jail in a long line of cells. Seemed they kept actual criminals separate from the rest of their "cargo". Isra glanced behind at the other occupants in her cell. There were five other humans, all women, a small blessing. She doubted the men locked up here would have too many qualms about forcing themselves on her.

The only light in the place came from the lantern a few guards had as they checked each of the cages. Or at least, that's what they were supposed to do. Instead, they kept harassing some women down the way. Regardless of race, men were the same. Isra moved away from the door and took a place in the shadows, though the other women had already taken the best shadows for themselves. They eyed her, but none attempted to talk. Hard to say what brand of criminals they were, though it was possible they'd just been in the wrong place at the wrong time.

Not Isra. She was here on purpose.

That didn't make the itchy modesty wraps any better, though.

Unlike other jails Isra had visited, the people here were quiet like the dead. There were no rebellious spirits here, for they all knew where they were heading and what was to become of them. The guards left. And the people sat in the darkness. And... well, it was strange how the darkness affected a person. Kids feared the night and then grew out of it. Children grew up to think that a little lack of light was nothing compared to all the things in the world to fear. Not compared to all the things tatzons did to them. And then these brave adults met with Night and she instilled the fear back into their bones. Because it was in darkness that monsters were born.

And these folks here would know all about that. They were accustomed to the night, they were children of the night. But there was a long line of difference between the night and true darkness. True darkness was rare, since at least two moons always beamed on the world in their fullest glory. You had to go deep, deep inside a Colossal or even Behemoth tree to find darkness. You had to dig deep into the earth or hide away in the caves of mountains. It was only there, in those kinds of places, that true terror laid.

The *Cleansing* was such a place. It was blacker than the Abyss, thicker than whale blubber. In this emptiness, you saw no one else and only imagined you saw yourself. You floated in a nothingness that spoke to you and told you that there was no safety, there was no warmth. No one was meant to be in darkness like this, a darkness so true it seemed to consume a person's very body. They were nothing but drifting souls now. And no one spoke. The toughest, strongest, bravest of these thugs quieted. Darkness gripped them by the throat and strangled them. The only sound was the clicking and distant moans of the ocean that waited just through these wooden walls.

The unease even entered Isra, but it only motivated her to move instead of freeze and shrink. She shuffled to what she hoped was the door and reached through. She found hinges and a lock on the outside. A padlock, it seemed. At least one thing was going for her.

She ran a finger along her arm to her palm. Every time she ran over one of the tattooed circles, a sensation like a half-dream pressed into her as she felt the contents of the circle. She could only feel the size and mass of the contents, nothing more specific than that, but these were her circles, and she knew what she had.

Isra touched the circle on her palm and Released her ivory stylus. While in the mud jail, she'd already moved Sala and Verta's satchel and her medallion to different circles. With her stylus in hand, she crouched and pressed it into the wooden floor. Circles were the foundation of her magic. Without them she couldn't do anything. Problem was, it needed to be a perfect circle. Perfectly round and proportioned. None of those pathetic ovals. Thing was, it was darker here than the hole in her step-mom's heart. Well, at least nearly as dark.

She had to let go of sight and trust that her hand knew the motion. Isra closed her eyes, though it didn't make a difference, and scratched the floor with her stylus.

"What's that?" one woman in the cell asked, voice hushed.

"What?" another said.

"That scratching. Is... is something trying to get in?"

"Hope it ain't a Small crab or nothing. Had a cousin killed by those monsters."

The first woman cursed, and it sounded like she shuffled away from the wall and in Isra's direction. No matter. She'd finished the circle.

But she was ready. She tapped a circle on her left forearm and Released her pouch, which materialized on her arm. Isra felt around inside, feeling the dozens of different sized wooden discs until she found one the size of a good fist. The padlock had been the size of her fist, so this would work just fine.

She reached through the door bars with the disc and found the padlock. With delicate care, she lifted it and placed the disc under it, being very careful that only the padlock touched the perfect circle.

Careful to not have her fingers go inside the circle, she moved her index finger to a small indent she'd made underneath the disc, where the line from her finger would connect with a line carved into the wood, connecting her to the disc circle.

She tapped an empty tattoo on her forearm, and she Caught the padlock. However, she Caught it into the wooden disc instead of the circles on her arms, since she liked to keep those free for the most important things. The padlock vanished, and she put the disc, now with the lock inside it, back into her pouch, which she now placed onto the larger circle and Caught it back into one of her arm circles.

Her magic had been simple to learn. In fact, she was pretty sure she learned the basics of it in a single day, back when she was a young girl. All that was needed were two circles and a line connecting them.

One circle did the actual Catching and needed to be large enough to encompass the entirety of whatever she wanted to Catch, which wasn't always simple. Every circle had an invisible dome—at least, in how she imagined it—that was as tall as the circle's radius. Even though her circles were flat, the power and affected area was hemispherical and whatever she wanted to Catch had to fit within the hemisphere. It usually wasn't a problem unless she had to Catch something taller than it was wide. It ended up with a lot of guesswork.

The second circle did not need to be the same size. She used it for initiating the Catch and it could be whatever size she wanted. Isra preferred using her circle tattoos to make the Catch, them being the most convenient. All she had to do was tap the starting circle and she Caught whatever was in the first, transferred it into the circle itself. It'd taken practice, but she now knew how to channel the Catching so she could choose which circle stored what she Caught. It made it easier to transport large things by putting them into circles she could carry.

Her grandmother had taught her as much as she knew, but that knowledge was secondhand. This power popped up in the family from time to time, but not consistently. Isra was the first since her grandmother's grandfather, something that was cause for both celebration and concentrated secrecy. No one could know about her magic. Tatzons weren't kind to their inferiors who tried to grow in power.

With the door now "unlocked", she eased it open. It creaked a bit, but only as much as the rest of the ship. She slid out and shut it again. Ideally, she'd put the padlock back on, but it was still locked and there was no way she could Release it just right so that it materialized back onto the door.

She placed a hand on the cells and turned to her right, toward where the stairs were. There were no lights here, so she stepped carefully, not disturbing anyone or anything. She left the people in their darkness.

The cell area turned into something like a hallway that ended with a stairway. Without a plan, but with the knowledge she had to keep moving, Isra began exploring the ship.

The ship looked huge on the outside, yet, somehow, felt even bigger inside. She couldn't keep track of what deck she was on or the purpose of it. The lowest decks made sense, the tatzons kept all the humans down there, but a few decks in the middle seemed empty. These middle decks had more rooms and cages, space for the next batch of slaves, but there were also large rooms filled with dismantled machines and headless statues of some tatzon or another. Storage rooms, but ones that didn't match her initial idea of what the *Cleansing* was supposed to be.

Each deck she snuck through was like a maze of corridors, empty rooms, random dead ends, and stairs. This made it easy to hide from guards, but easier to get lost.

After those few empty decks, the ship became something else. No longer a human collecting ship of death, these decks looked more like some luxury estate near the nectar tree of Al'Rajak. The ceilings were higher, the halls wider, and the air breathable. Some halls had windows to the ocean, bringing in natural light to reduce the need for lanterns burning, as well as to help air out the area.

Coming to these decks was like entering a different world, with all of its painted floors, decorated archways, and many, many stuck up tatzons lolling around the place as if they were the single most important person in all of existence.

This was perhaps the strangest part of these decks. Along with the ostentatious displays of plastered wealth, there were many here who were neither slaves nor part of the crew. They were passengers. Most looked like merchants, with long flowing green robes that trailed behind, and Isra guessed they had something to do with all of those machines and equipment on the middle decks. Though, why they were on the *Cleansing* of all ships was beyond her. It was as if this ship couldn't decide its purpose.

The more important thing she noticed was the humans. A group of them hurried and moved throughout these upper decks, with no one stopping them or even noticing them. Isra could use the confusing layout of the ship to hide and sneak her way through, but her progress was slow compared these humans. It didn't take many observations to realize they were slaves from the bottom of the ship, but had been... "recruited" to become servants to these upper deck tatzons. Seemed, even out here on the ocean, these bastards could not go a day without ordering a human around.

Each "servant" wore fitted black clothes, showing their status around here, and hurried about with little order. They didn't appear assigned to any tatzon pair and so went to whoever called for something.

It was a strange experience to watch those on these decks act as if there weren't hundreds of lives in the holds.

Isra pushed down the rising fury and went about getting a pair of black clothes for herself.

Procuring them wasn't as difficult as she'd imagined. The servants lodged together in a single room and nearby they kept crates of black clothes in a separate storage room. There weren't that many servants, so they'd notice her, but hopefully they wouldn't see a difference between her and any other human. But she wasn't planning on joining the serving staff, only to impersonate them. Besides, doubtful a human would rat her out. Humans stuck together in situations like these.

She found a pair of clothes that fit and without hesitation rid herself of those itchy wraps. Isra couldn't imagine going another day wearing those. Once clothed, she checked the hall, took a breath, and left the shadows. A pair of guards entered the hall near to her. She held her breath.

The two barely glanced at her and moved on.

Isra nodded. As long as she wasn't an idiot, this could work.

A bell rung and Isra froze, glancing around. Within moments, she caught sight of other black-clothed servants filing into the hall she stood in, all heading to the servants' quarters. She turned, hoping to duck into a side room, but the two guards who'd passed her stood at the end of the hall, next to the quarters, watching the servants head toward them. Isra calmed her breathing, though she couldn't do much about the frustration building in her. If she tried ducking away, the servants and guards would see her, and while she wasn't sure what the bell meant, it'd be stupid to walk around when all the other servants weren't.

Not wanting to draw anymore attention to herself, she turned to the quarters and went inside.

The rest of the servants arrived, but instead of relaxing and lying on their beds, they lined against the walls. Isra joined them as they circled the room, though she tried to ignore how imperfect the shape was, and tried to gauge the others here. The first thing she noticed was that all the servants were women. Second, they looked agitated.

One woman noticed her, looked over her shoulders, and headed over to Isra, who braced herself. The woman sidled next to her, and other women gave her a curious look.

"New here?" the woman said.

Isra looked the woman over and nodded.

"Looked it, seemed confused."

Isra nodded again, though she kept her eyes on the other women. Many of them looked at her with subtle grins, while others looked sad. The rest ignored her.

"New assignments. Happens time to time. Don't worry too much about it, but you are standing all wrong."

She was standing wrong? There was nothing wrong with how she stood. "Meaning?" Isra said.

The woman leaned toward her. "You're slouching and scuffing along like a breathing shroom. Might've worked for you back on the mainland, but not here. They don't like seeing weakness. Weakness gets you thrown in the waters. Just stand up straight and always look em in the eyes all respectful-like."

Lady above, she had to act respectful? Well, best she try until she understood the place better. Isra nodded to the woman. "Thanks."

"We're human. Gotta look after our own." The woman smiled and skirted away at the same time others started shuffling to the sides. Seemed some tatzons headed this way. She had not meant to join this staff. But she only had to keep this charade up long enough to escape notice. The guards entered and Isra held back a sigh and stood upright, looking them right in the eyes. If she had to go through this, she might as well—

"What's with this one?" a guard said, scowling at her. The other guards saw her too, and only too late did Isra notice that everyone else, including the woman who'd spoken to her, kept their heads bowed and backs bent. Isra saw the edges of a smirk on that woman.

Damn it all.

One guard slapped Isra across the face and she let it drop her, trying to look as nonthreatening as possible.

"Looks like we've one with some backbone," the guard said. "Well, if you're not tired, then why don't we put you to work?"

Isra shook, trying to act as afraid as she could. "I'm sorry," she said. "I don't mean—"

Slap.

The guard tossed her toward the door. "Looks like we've a volunteer for hauling duty!"

The others grinned and two pushed her out of the room and toward a set of stairs leading up. Isra took a glance back, glaring at that damnation of a woman, who glanced up and winked at her.

Isra's blood burned hot and her fingers itched to reach for the third circle on her right arm. She resisted and hurried along the path these guards shoved her on.

They took her to the top deck, where a light rain drizzled down her face. They shoved her toward a growing group of humans, though none wore black clothes like her, meaning servants didn't typically do whatever this work was.

The crew—the enslaved, human crew—worked hard hoisting crates, barrels, and other goods on board. Boats ferried the goods from land to the ship and the crew here used these massive cranes to pull the new cargo up. Though they did so by attaching the cranes to the boats and hoisting them to the top of the deck.

The sailors and crew were mostly human men, though she saw a few women sprinkled throughout. They looked surprised—and amused—with Isra joining them.

"Haven't seen a black shirt volunteer for this work before," one man said. Like the other sailors, he wore tight trousers and a fitted shirt, though he also wore a long brown scarf which he had wrapped tightly around his neck. He sat atop a barrel and grinned at her. "What got you?"

Isra turned from him. "Stood wrong."

"Ah, yeah, they're touchy on that here. Been in trouble a few times myself for that. Though I thought you shirts were smarter than that."

"It was suggested."

The man and other crew nearby laughed and nodded. "You got done in by a bootlicker. You must be new here if you fell for that."

Isra cocked a brow. "Bootlicker?"

"Some on board turn others in for their own benefit. Extra food, fewer lashings." He spat and frowned. "Not everyone looks out for their kind."

Before Isra cared to ask more, a pair of important looking tatzons arrived surrounded by guards and two Isra guessed to be Soulborn, since they both wore metal boxes on their hips. Judging by the fine silk, these important tatzons were the captains of the ship. The human crew quieted and bowed their heads, all except the man with the scarf. The captains glared at him and then addressed everyone else.

"We want everything secured by sundown," one captain said. "Everything we've hauled on board goes to the iron holds below."

A few sailors started to groan but cut themselves off. Doubtful these overlords appreciated outward expressions of... well, anything. But Isra at least now knew what task they had assigned her to. She looked at the mountain of crates and chests they brought and then glanced to the sky. They had six hours of sunlight left, but she didn't see how this crew could haul all of this down the entire *Cleansing* in six hours.

The captains didn't seem like they were looking for suggestions, though, and the hauling began.

The captains put every human here to work, grabbing the cargo and bringing it down to the hold, deck after deck after deck. Everything was heavy, and she needed a partner to help carry the chest she picked up. As they descended into the *Cleansing* again, she kept looking for a way to escape, but there were too many people to notice her disappearing.

The stairs they descended through did not go through the lavish areas of the merchants. These stairs were sectioned off to ensure the merchants never encountered filthy humans.

Isra hated every moment of this. This was not why she was here. She was supposed to be smarter than this. By the Lady, not even her father would have fallen for such an easy manipulation. People often took advantage of him, but he'd always allowed it. They'd always been part of his calculations, part of his grand vision and plan. No one manipulated him without his say so. No one until Isra's step-mom.

Thinking of her father and that Abyssal of a woman put a fire in Isra's bones, and this helped her descend the steps. She would find a way out of this mess. Just like she'd some day find a way out of her father's mess.

She followed the crew to the bottom of the ship, where they entered the hold, which was larger and taller than she'd imagined. It was easily four times her height and ran the entire length of the ship. Towards the bow, cargo filled the hold all the way to the top, but another sight met her when she looked aft.

A massive metal wall cut the hold in half, top to bottom, side to side.

They all stood before this wall and Isra noted it had a single door—an actual door, not an opening. The door sat inside a rather large alcove which the captains approached with their lantern while everyone else stood back, though the Soulborn took a single step forward. Some sailors looked worried, like they were ready to run away. The captains took out a key and put it into a hole in the wall, no padlock for this place. There was an audible clicking and grinding, but the captains did not touch the door until the sound stopped. Even then, they waited as the Soulborn approached and opened the door themselves. Isra wasn't sure what was going on, but when the Soulborn nodded, she heard a collective sigh of relief escape many of those around her, including a few guards.

The door opened to a second hold, lit with a bright, unwavering light. Which could only mean one thing: they had lightstone in here. Sure enough, as she carried the chest in, Isra spotted several chunks of the white-cyrstal embedded in the ceiling throughout the room, which was expansive. It looked even bigger than the hold behind them. And metal covered the entire place. Floors, walls, and even the ceiling. And filling the room were dozens of metal cages, some as short as ten feet, most as tall as twenty. Lock boxes and chest filled every one of them, all with unknown, but well secured, riches. But there was only one she cared about. Only one she needed. And she hardly believed it when she saw it.

She'd set down the cargo, her eyes scanning every cage they passed, when her attention found a cage emptier than others, yet more secure. Inside the cage sat a second cage, and inside that a third. The iron was thick and green-crystal embedded all the metal, strengthening it beyond anything else here. And in the center of that third cage stood a secured pedestal decorated with gold, fine gems, and a glass dome that encased a small metallic idol, no bigger than a hand.

The idol of Mirr. The very idol she came to retrieve.

Her heart picked up its pace, but she knew she couldn't get it now, not with so many eyes watching her. Besides, she first needed to get past the locks on those three cages which, unlike her cell, didn't use padlocks. She didn't have any skill in lock picking so she'd need to find the keys first, though it was also possible she could make a circle large enough—

Clang.

Isra jumped at the sudden noise. She turned toward the wall as another clang sounded alongside a loud banging. The other humans smirked and puffed their chests, which was for show—Isra saw how their timid eyes darted to the same wall.

"First time here?" one said. "Yeah, I remember when I first came here. But what can they do to us now?"

Isra looked from the woman to the wall. "What is it?"

A bit of the woman's posturing leaked out as she spoke the word. "Remnants."

Isra shot them all a look. She could not have heard right.

Another spoke up. "It's how they guard all these valuables. The door to the place doesn't lock, but if you come in without the key, these walls open and the Remnants come out."

"When I came to the ship," another woman said, eyes closing as if to forget the horror. "Had a few friends stupid enough to listen to one of them bootlickers. Damn idiots came in here for some treasure and..."

The women moved on, heading back outside the hold. There was still work to be done, but Isra stayed put just a moment. Because her work just got a lot more complicated.

Traitorous humans she could deal with. Tatzons wanting to hurt her were simple obstacles. But Remnants? No, she was not equipped to deal with that.

So, with a last look to the idol, she rejoined the rest to lug cargo to various holds, all the while her mind worked, and it worked hard. She didn't have words like her father, nor did she have his way of envisioning things. But she had his flexibility for when plans needed changing. Her initial ideas would not work, but her next goal was obvious. Before she could grab the idol, before she could even attempt to break through those cages, she needed to get her hands on the captains' key.

6

THE STRENGTH OF A MASK

I can't thank you and Lamia enough for access to the ordîn level and their library. Helps to have family in high places, I guess. This place is amazing. It's been tricky moving around since they suspend everything in the air and I don't have wings. However, everything is so vibrant here, so full of color. It's like a massive rainbow, which makes sense for ordîns, but it's still so different from the browns and greens of the rest of Rajalend. And this library is immense! I'm so glad they obsess over knowledge. It's going to make my job far easier. Syeda, I feel like I've died and gone to the Lady's side.

-Raza, a speckle of umber in a chromatic sky.

Back aching, arms numb, hands raw, Gulamira continued to scrub the deck under the watchful eye of the guards. Lanterns lit the hall with a yellow glow and a musky smoke. They were on the deck above the women's "lodging" and hundreds of prisoners filled the halls and massive rooms, all on their hands and knees, scrubbing away.

She wiped away sweat from her eyes and dunked her bristle brush into the bucket of... honestly, she still wasn't sure what it was. It smelled like spoiled mushroom and had this strange, thick, sticky texture to it. People here called it "swib". Whatever it was, it soaked deep into the wood. She'd heard one of the other scrubs, the guards' pet name for them, say it kept the wood strong, limber, and from rotting away in the ocean. Another said it helped people not slide around during enormous waves, helped with footing. After several days of scrubbing deck after deck, Gulamira had her own theory: it was to keep prisoners tired and busy and weak.

The guards, all tatzon, never allowed breaks. Prisoners scrubbed the decks from dawn until dusk, eating gruel with one hand or not eating at all. Stopping received lashings. Requesting a break received beatings. Complaining resulted in going topside and never being seen again.

Gulamira spoke to no one and stayed to herself, though never far enough that Solitude came. She never spoke up, complained, resisted, or reacted for a single moment. It would have been futile to even try. She was a slave, a prisoner, a corpse waiting for her unmarked grave. Gulamira stopped tracking who was around her, how much time passed, what people said, or even what she ate. She'd lost count of how long she'd been in the underbelly of this beast. It felt like months. It could've been a week. Everything bled into itself and she retreated deep inside herself. There was no escaping this Abyss. Her life had already ended ten years ago, anyway, so she fled from the *Cleansing* to the recesses of her mind where reality could not touch her. Where there was no one and nothing.

Where she was no one and nothing.

Gulamira sat up, arching her stiff back and ignoring her stinging knees. One good thing about these decks, though, was the lack of splinters. A small blessing. Today, she was a part of a group scrubbing an off-shoot room that stored extra tools and supplies. She chose a corner to do her work, easier to escape the focus of the guards that way, and set down her bucket.

Something moved in her direction, and she looked over. Two women and a girl made their way toward her. They didn't say a thing as they set their buckets near her and crouched down to start the drudgery of the day. Gulamira had half a mind to move again, but a couple of guards glared at her, so she dropped and grabbed her brush. The girl, perhaps twelve in age, glanced at her and then back at her swib bucket.

"Get scrubbing, girl," one woman said under her breath. The girl obeyed. Gulamira eyed them for a moment and then returned to the floor and scrubbed. They were in somewhat of a spacious place, so they didn't have to work near her, but it also wasn't wrong for them to either. She glanced around but didn't see another spot for her to work in. However, she noticed one woman giving the guards sidelong looks, as if watching them.

"You've a name?" the woman whispered.

Gulamira paused and looked up, but the other woman spoke first. "No, don't look up. Just keep working. Don't bring attention to yourself."

She dropped her head and gripped her brush firm.

"So," the woman whispered again, "name?"

"Why do you care?" Gulamira asked. No one had spoken to her yet on this ship. Most of the humans avoided her as best they could. Except some men, but a few lashes from the guards ended any of their lustful hopes.

"I'm Sari," the first woman said. "This here is Natil. The little one is Ruer."

Out of the corner of her eye, Gulamira saw the girl peek at her before dropping back to the brushing.

"We've been on this ship nigh on two months now," Sari said. "We've not seen the sun in all that time. Seen many die around us. Barely surviving as it is."

"We came with twenty-three others." Natil paused just a moment. "Now there's only eight from our village here."

Gulamira slowed. Hoping the guards didn't notice, she looked at the women in front of her. She had tried hard to ignore the state of the others here, tried to focus on herself or nothing at all. But now she saw what months on this ship did to them. All this work and lack of actual food had left them more bone than human. Their heads looked disproportionate to their bodies, which were nothing more than brown skin stretched around small sticks. Hair was falling out of their heads and much of whatever beauty they once possessed had now starved away.

"Hardest of all has been with Ruer," Sari said, nodding to the child. She looked somehow worse than everyone else. She moved slower and weaker than the others. If a small breeze came in, the girl would topple over. "She's outlived her cousins and other siblings. Not sure how long she'll go now."

"You're pretty open about that," Gulamira said, eyes still on the girl, who didn't look up.

"Ruer knows it better than us. Fact is, we'd all given up on her living another day. Given up on any of us living much longer." Sari glanced at the guards, but they were harassing someone else, and she turned her head — no, her smile toward Gulamira. "Then you started scrubbing with us."

Gulamira cocked her head to the side. "What do I have anything to do with you?"

"I like your smile." This small voice came from Ruer.

"My... smile?"

"Girl wouldn't shut up about it first day you were with us," Natil said. "Wasn't long before we noticed it too."

"You're always smiling," Sari said. "No matter what, we've only ever seen you smiling. At first, we wanted to dismiss you, thinking maybe you were one of them bootlickers sent to catch slow workers." Gulamira quirked her head at this. She hadn't considered whether people would think that. Despite herself, the idea of slaves turning on slaves twisted something bitter inside. Sari kept on, "After a time, we didn't think bootlicker more than just a fool. A fool idiot who'd learn better soon enough. One who'd break like the rest of us and face reality." The woman paused, lifted her head, and smiled. "And then you kept smiling."

Gulamira stopped scrubbing and resisted reaching for her face. She... she was still smiling. She hadn't even noticed.

"No matter who yelled at you or if you got a lashing or nothing." Natil sounded awed by her. "Always smiling that stupid smile. And you know what? It got Ruer smiling, too. Damn kid actually smiled for the first time in months."

"By the Tree," Sari said. "I even caught myself smirking something a couple times."

Natil nodded. "Same. And we doubt it'll do much. Doubt we'll live longer cause of it, but..."

All three looked up at her. All three smiled.

"But we wanted to thank you for helping us remember," Sari said.

"Remember what?" Gulamira asked.

"What the sun feels like."

Gulamira tried to find words, but none came. She couldn't help but stare back. Back at a few grateful faces.

"So," Sari said, "your name?"

"Gulamira Con-None."

Ruer smiled. "Thank you Gulamira. Thank you."

"Hey!" a guard called out. "Back to work, the four of you!"

And they did. They bowed their heads and scrubbed away. But Gulamira wasn't there anymore, but neither did she retreat into herself. She was in the moment of three humans smiling at her. Of a girl thanking her. All for smiling. And for this one moment, Gulamira's smile shifted from her masked version to a most genuine, eye wrinkling, heart twisting smile. It'd been the first happiness she'd felt in a while.

Ruer died the following day.

Sari died the day after and some guard threw Natil overboard the day after that.

Gulamira watched from a corner as the guard raged at Natil. No prisoner stood up to him, no prisoner uttered a sound as he pulled her screaming up the stairs and away forever.

Gulamira stopped scrubbing. Only a few days ago, she'd met them. Only days ago, they'd thanked her. And now they were gone. But they haunted her thoughts. Especially the image of Ruer. That girl would not leave her mind. That small emaciated child trying to hold on to life with all her strength. And when Gulamira thought she could not bear the image any longer, it morphed and changed into Kamaria.

From behind Gulamira's smile and behind her masks, behind her walls and beyond her present, from depths she ignored and hated and missed and needed, a call rang in her ears. The same call she'd heard when she'd first seen Kamaria. The same call that made her body move despite her protests. A call from a little tatzon girl. A girl lost, alone, and needing a friend. A girl hated and orphaned. A girl she desperately needed to save.

A girl just like Kamaria.

A girl named Gulamira.

That Gulamira, that child, was dead. Any fragment of her that still existed laid buried under years of struggle and pain, unable to stand underneath it all. But Kamaria lived. Her heart lived, and the world had not yet torn her down into nothing.

Save her.

She shook her head. She had to be a fool. A complete and total idiot.

But no one had been there for her when her world ended. Maybe it wasn't much, maybe it wouldn't do anything, but she could be there for this girl. Kamaria didn't need to become—no, she could not become like Gulamira. At the very least, she could get the kid off of this damned ship.

Gulamira didn't know how she'd do that, but for a start it meant she could no longer hide in the depths of her mind. She had to face reality, which meant she needed to get back to scrubbing before she was in trouble. She spotted a place down the hall and away from the others, so she started her way there, but then stopped. Four guards blocked her way.

"Pardon me," she said, smile as bright as ever.

One of them stepped further in front of her. "Oh, are we in your way?"

She shook her head. "I just need to scrub over there."

"Oh, do you now? How you doing that without swib?"

She blinked at him, confused. The man knocked the bucket from her arms and the foul smelling swib poured all over her and the floor. The guards exclaimed and jumped back.

Another pulled out his whip. "What you thinking there? Clumsy bitch. Got swib all over my trousers."

"I—"

One of the four came behind and pushed her to the ground. Swib splattered across her face and the stench burned her nostrils. "Go on," he said. "Clean up your mess."

Lips pressed into a tight smile, she grabbed her bucket and brush and started sweeping up the swib. They'd get bored with her and move on to someone else, so she kept her head down and focused on the mess they made. The swib was thick enough that a good amount of it could go back into the bucket. The rest she'd have to scrub into the deck.

"Hold on a moment," one of them said and dangled his leg in front of her. "You got some of it on me. Get it off."

She smiled with a nod, giving a furtive glance at the whips in their hands. Gulamira brought up her brush to get the swib.

"No, not with that," he said. Then he grinned along with his friends. "Brush gets it in deeper. I want it off me. Only way I hear it works is if someone sucks it off."

The others chuckled and nudged each other. Gulamira hesitated. These looks weren't good. If she entertained them, who knew how far they'd go? She needed them to ignore her, so she summoned a song and interlaced it with her words. She hadn't cared enough to use her songs so far, but, damn it all, she cared now.

Looking the man in the eyes, she flashed a smirk. "I'm sure it will wipe right off. I wouldn't want to take much of your time."

He struck her across the face. Her lower song had been too subtle to take immediate effect and before she could recover, he bent down and grabbed her by the face and squeezed. "Did I ask for your back talk? No, I didn't. Did I fellas?"

"No," another said, still grinning. "You asked a simple request."

"That's what I thought." He paused and considered her a moment, eyes focusing on her lips, which were still, somehow, a smile. "I've heard of you. Some others been talking about you. A fetching tatzon who's always smiling." His grip tightened. "I don't find that too attractive in a slave. Makes me think you're having... ideas."

He let go, and she pulled away. "Please, I don't want to make trouble," she said.

"Oh, you don't?" The guard looked back at his friends. "She doesn't want to make trouble. Ain't that sweet?"

One twisted his whip, letting the leather creak with tension. "The sweetest."

The man crouching turned back to her. "If you didn't want trouble, then you shouldn't have started it."

He grabbed her by the hair and yanked her up. She yelped and grabbed at his hand, but he slapped her again, hard. The other guards stood on all sides of her, and the other prisoners stopped to watch.

"I did nothing, please," she said. She ran her mind through the songs she could use, songs that would turn their gaze away, to make them ignore her.

"Oh, but you have," one said and cracked his whip across her back. She yelped, but maintained her smile. "Guards ain't the only ones who notice you. Smiling and smiling no matter what's given to you."

Another whip lash, from a different guard. "The other slaves like having you around. They like seeing that smile. Been hearing others are smiling, too."

Another lash. Gulamira cried out, but couldn't focus on a song. The one grabbing her hair slapped her again. "No, no. Won't have you screaming like that. You asked us to do this. You wanted us to do this."

One with the club smashed it against her side. Another lash. And another.

Tears bombarded the back of her eyes, wanting release. But she smiled and kept them back. She poured a song into her mouth.

"I'm just smiling. I'm just—"

Another slap, interrupting the melody. "Smiling gives ideas," he said. "Smiling makes them think they've a chance. It tells them they might escape. You get none of that here!"

The room filled with cracking whips and stifled screams. They did not let her get another word in and her songs, which had never failed her, were kept from her now.

Her legs gave out, but the guard held her up by the hair and they beat her like hanging fruit. She tried to cover her face, but this motivated them to hit harder. She tried to push away, and this had her thrown face first into the wall. Blood splattered against the wood, more dripped down her back and sides. She slid against the wall and to the floor, breathing hard.

But still smiling.

She grabbed onto the barrel beside her and slowly, painfully, pulled herself to her feet. She wobbled some, but stood upright. And faced her assailants.

Their grins had gone. There was only rage and malice now. At once, they'd become Prikur. Instead of four guards she saw the man who'd tormented her most. He that had stolen her, sold her, ruined her. And there were so many others she saw in their faces. So many other Prikur-like lowlifes that danced and laughed in her head, all at her expense. She saw them all, their abuses wanting to fracture her again, and so she did what none of them had broken, what she had vowed none would take from her.

Gulamira, bloodied and bruised all over, smiled.

Not for the slaves, not for these captors. She smiled for herself. To hold herself up. To keep herself strong. They would not break her mask of iron. They would not see all the pain and weakness it hid. This mask would remain intact and solid, and there was nothing they could do to take it from her.

She smiled.

And they growled.

One yanked her to the side and threw her into a beam in the center of the room. "Get me rope. Now!"

The prisoners scattered, tripping over their swib buckets and into each other. Someone brought him a rope and he and another guard tied Gulamira's hands to the post above her head. The rope chafed and dug into her wrists.

"You think you're brave or something?" the guard asked. "You think you're better than us? Well, guess what, there are plenty of ways to make a tatzon lose their smile." He turned to the others gathered. "Alright, everyone, out! Out of the room. We're leaving."

The prisoners looked at each other, and even the other guards paused.

"Chiuk, you're not thinking of—"

"I am." He glared at Gulamira. "Let's see what a bit of Solitude does to that face of hers."

It was only by pure stubborn habit she didn't lose her smile now. The rest of her stilled. They wouldn't do that to her, would they? Another tatzon? Even if they hated her, no one would... they couldn't... no. By Exkel's Mountain, no.

"We'll only be gone a bit," the one called Chiuk said as he glared at Gulamira. "Just enough for it to mess her up, but won't kill her."

"Don't do this," Gulamira said, her throat hoarse from her earlier screams. "You don't have to do this."

Chiuk walked up to her. "Oh? You got something to say now? Got a little frown for us? That's all we want. Just want that smile to leave. Do that and no Solitude."

She stared into his twisted face, only seeing Prikur's sadistic snarl. Gulamira grinned and said, "See you after Solitude."

Chiuk's nostrils flared, and for a moment she thought he'd slap her again. Instead, he turned and whipped the rest of the prisoners out of the area, cursing and swearing with all his energy. Seemed she struck a nerve with him. Good. Good...

Everyone left. And it came. A looming feeling at first, like the anticipation before a fall, but then sharp and stinging. Then twisting and ripping. Breaking and shattering. Forming and dying.

Solitude came.

It felt like a gut punch. Air sucked out of her as she tried to breathe. But her throat felt more constricted than before, more so than the collar. Her leg spasmed out from beneath her, a stabbing pain shot through her lower back, pressure built in her ears and only continued. Her spine arched, eyes bulged, and fingers creaked and cracked.

And it only worsened with every moment of being alone. Solitude built upon itself, gaining strength from her pain and misery, twisting it into a burning reality. Because Solitude would not break her. It would kill her. Twist and bend her body while boiling her insides until there was nothing left of her. Not even a smile.

7

━━━━━◆○◆━━━━━

THE SMILE OF A BROKEN PRIESTESS

I might be on the ordîns' nerves up here. No one was thrilled to have me to begin with, but they've been even less happy when I try talking with them. For instance, one woman came by and I thought to ask her thoughts on a few of my musings. She was a fellow scholar, so I thought she'd be interested in talking. I was wrong. But she looked at me long enough I had a good look at those gray eyes of theirs. She had this azure blue skin that mixed so well with her white hair... these people are so fascinating. But I'm getting distracted. I still have an entire table of papers to sort through.

-Raza, a man with too many musings.

Solitude consumed. Solitude destroyed. Solitude was all, and all was Solitude.

No breath. No sight. No feeling. No self.

A dark forest, beasts all around, an endless thorned path. Winding, winding, winding through the darkness. It was the pain of every ignored memory, every lost opportunity, every disconnection. Pleasant pasts were erased and potential futures burned. There was nothing but darkness. And it would consume and destroy until it was all. Until the self was utterly and totally gone and forgotten.

Never ending.

Never ending.

Never... ending.

Never... never...

Gulamira opened her eyes and tried breathing again. The all-consuming presence of Solitude... it no longer increased. In fact, it was lessening, weakening. And there was something else. Something warm. A presence? It was hard to tell... but yes. A presence. Someone was here.

Gulamira's eyes trailed across the room, which was hazy. Black spots stuck in her vision, distorting what she saw, but after a moment something moved just ahead of her. Blurry, but it had the shape of a person.

A person. Someone was here.

"... help..."

Gulamira barely heard herself. It would be no surprise if this person hadn't either. The image of the person, blurred and shadowed, stopped a few feet from her. And it stared. She tried to lift her head, to stare back, but her neck had no strength and she realized it twisted to the side as though her chin tried to meld into her shoulder. How pathetic she must've looked. But she called again.

"... help... please..."

"Hm, you're alive."

Those words, that voice, broke through all the silence of the ship and all the raging fury of the Solitude like the very voice of Exkel. It was enough that Gulamira felt tears streaming down her face.

"Touch..." she said, trying and failing to turn her head. Her throat ached and her lips were sore, so words were beyond difficult to form. How was she supposed to recover, to grow strong, if she couldn't even—

A firm warmth touched her side, and it was like a jolt of life. Gulamira gasped in the thick, dank air as her neck snapped back into place and her tongue loosened, though this meant she tasted the vile mucus in her mouth. With every heartbeat, another jolt pulsed through her from the touch.

The darkness ebbed away.

It was enough, for now, for her to see. Most of the black spots faded, so she looked at her savior.

And found a human.

A short, wide human in dark black clothes in their mid to late twenties. Someone's personal servant, or rather their personal slave. And it looked like they were alone. At least, Gulamira couldn't see anyone else. Just this... well, maybe it was her poor sight at the moment, but she couldn't determine whether this was a man or woman. Gulamira squinted, and it looked like the servant had breasts. It'd have to be "she" for now.

The probable woman removed her hand and looked Gulamira up and down. But, it looked like her gaze settled on Gulamira's lips. Right now, they were formless. The mask had dropped.

Although she didn't have the strength to do so, although it was pathetic and worthless now, Gulamira formed the smallest smile.

The woman crossed her arms with an amused look, and the ship swayed, creaking around them. The woman stared, as if waiting. And the longer she stared, the more Gulamira found the pure defiance in her blood to make her smile even more solid than before, reforming its tears and cracks. Not pretty, not desirable, not alluring. But strong. Sealed. Her one defense.

The woman watched, staring into Gulamira's eyes for some time. "You still smile."

Gulamira huffed, Solitude still biting and snapping and eating at her since it would take some time for it to leave her body entirely. But she held onto this smile, unwilling to let go. "Always."

The woman smiled at this. "A fighter."

"A survivor."

"Name?"

A pause. But what did names matter here? "Gulamira Con-None."

"Isra."

Gulamira nodded, or rather let her head drop to her chest. Her neck hurt, her arms strained, and her whole body longed to sleep and rest.

"I watched before," Isra said.

"Before?"

"You kept smiling."

Gulamira, with a decent effort, lifted her head. Isra hadn't moved. "You were here when the guards tied me up?"

A nod. Gulamira waited, but the woman said nothing else.

"How long?" Gulamira asked. "How long have I been here?"

Isra shrugged. "Ten minutes."

Gulamira coughed up a bit of greenish bile and stared at the floor, eyes wide. Solitude had done this to her in only ten minutes? She'd heard and known of the pure destruction of Solitude, but this was her first time experiencing it. How much longer until she'd have died?

"Thank you," she said. "For coming back."

Isra looked her up and down again, returning to the smile. "Why continue smiling?"

Gulamira had asked herself that question for years. "Too much goes into that answer."

"One reason."

"One reason? Why is everyone so obsessed with my smile?"

No reply.

Gulamira peered at Isra through stinging eyes. There were only ever four kinds of people in relation to her smile. Those enchanted, those amused, those confused, and those who were enraged. Right now, Gulamira couldn't decipher which Isra was. "You want a reason? Then how about because it helps me hide the pain?"

Isra shrugged. "Is it why?"

"Sure." She dropped her head. Her body ached so much and sharp stabbing pains danced through her legs. It was too much effort to even think about moving or doing anything else. Gulamira closed her eyes and breathed deeply, trying to find some part of her not trying to kill her. After a moment she glanced up and Isra was still there watching her. Didn't look like she'd moved at all.

"What?" Gulamira asked.

Isra looked at her, eyes drifting from head to foot. "Want out?"

"Do I... want out? Of this?"

A nod.

Gulamira paused. If Isra was offering to release her, she wasn't going to do it for free, otherwise she would've already. No, she was here because she wanted something. "Yes, of course I want out."

"How bad?"

Gulamira coughed, and a shiver ran through her. Solitude's effects lessened, but her mouth was still so dry and talking took a lot of effort. She took a moment to breathe before looking back at the woman. "What?"

"How badly you want out?" Isra asked. She didn't make much of any kind of expression. But she looked like she was... evaluating something.

Gulamira eyed her. " Are you offering to let me out of these ropes?"

"Off the ship."

"Ah. Great. Wonderful. How do you expect to do that?"

No reply.

"Right."

Isra fidgeted with her fingers, again looking Gulamira over. And a twisting burn seeped into Gulamira's blood.

"What do you want?" Gulamira said, holding onto her defiant smile, though it strained.

Still no reply.

And maybe it was the Solitude, maybe it was the days of hunger, thirst, and sleeplessness coming upon her, but mask cracked and she snapped, "Hey, can you hear me? Or are you just an idiot? Oh, never mind. Who'd thought Solitude could be preferable to—"

"I'll leave."

"No!"

Isra stopped mid-step. Gulamira's body had gone rigid. Both looked at each other. Solitude waited.

"I... I didn't..." Gulamira's throat constricted and warmth flooded her cheeks as the next words tried to form. "... don't..."

Isra cocked her head to the side, but didn't turn back to Gulamira.

Gulamira swallowed something impossibly large. Blood, spit, pride, whatever it was, it nearly lodged in her throat. "Please don't leave me."

Isra didn't take another step. She didn't turn around. She stared.

"Would you smile?" Isra asked.

Gulamira smiled and nodded. Of course she'd smile. She smiled every single damn day. She'd smiled for every man who'd ever owned her. Smiled for every woman who derided her.

Isra waved a hand at her. "No. Would you smile if I left?"

Gulamira paused. What kind of question... what was with this woman and her smile?

"Sure, why not," Gulamira said.

"Would you?"

"I always smile."

"Would you?"

Gulamira breathed out a heavy breath. "Yes!"

Her voice echoed off the walls, not enough to carry far, but enough she heard it. And maybe it was the defiance boiling in her, maybe it was exhaustion from lack of sleep and food and rest, maybe it was the beatings and the Solitude, but she knew, beyond any creeping doubt, that she would carry her smile to her most excruciating death.

Isra crossed her arms, a small smile on her lips. "Why?"

Gulamira wished her hands were free to strangle this woman. "Why? Because! Because... because..."

She paused as a dozen scenes sped through her mind in rapid succession. A decade's worth of hurts and pains and betrayals passed her vision. A decade's worth of memories she shoved away, chose to forget, tried to ignore. They clawed at her from behind her smile, trying to shatter that masked wall.

But she swallowed hard and the mask held. It had to. Because of this mask, she was able to think that she could bear another day in the world. That she could live. That she was safe.

She held up her head and looked into Isra's eyes through her smiling mask. "My smile tells the world it can't hurt me."

The words flowed like a stream without a dam, like a breath held in too long.

Isra stared at Gulamira. She stared back. Silence sat between them.

And a door opened down the hall. Voices followed. Voices coming this way.

Down the hall in front of her, turning around the far corner with gleeful twinkles in their eyes, her four tormentors entered view.

"Looks still alive," one said as they entered the open space.

"Who're you?" Chiuk said, glaring at Isra. "Servants don't come down here."

Two others crossed their arms, while another stepped up to prod Gulamira with his club.

"She's still smiling," the prodder said.

"What?" Chiuk pushed past him and grabbed Gulamira. "How? Solitude should've melted your smile right off."

"Seemed it just made you uglier," Gulamira said.

He smacked her across the face and spun on Isra. "This your doing? You stuck around with her?"

Isra, surrounded by the four large tatzon guards, maintained a blank expression.

"Answer, human." One with a whip tightened a grip on his handle. "Black shirts don't protect you from lashes."

Isra ignored them and began rolling up her sleeves.

"Hey!" One grabbed her shoulder and tightened his grip. "Answer!"

Chiuk turned back to Gulamira. "Ignore her. Probably an idiot. They sometimes do that for servants. 'Sides, we've got a bit of fun to have."

The prodder sidled up with Chiuk. "Sure we can't just kill her? Be simpler."

"But where's the message?" Chiuk asked. He licked his lips, as if the thought of hurting Gulamira made him hungry.

She didn't drop her gaze. She strengthened her smile.

"A hanging dead body is message enough," the guard said.

"Gots to say, I'm with him," another said. "If Solitude didn't take the smile, she's likely mad already."

"Or the idiot happened in here," Chiuk said and glared back at Isra. She'd finished rolling up her sleeves and there were strange tattoos on her arms. "Maybe we have fun with this one while we let Solitude do its thing again."

They chuckled amongst each other. And then flesh slit. A guard gurgled. The body fell.

The shock kept the three guards still for the briefest of seconds. Gulamira had already recovered, so she watched Isra, hand gripping a blood covered sword she did not have a moment ago, slice into another.

He screamed as one of his arms dropped to the floor. The other two finally moved. They jumped at Isra. They were big and bulky men, but they had whips and clubs, good only for tormenting.

She had a sword.

And she knew how to use it.

Gulamira's gaze dropped to the guard on the ground as he screamed, holding his severed arm. His gray skin seemed to lose even more color than she thought possible. Red blood flooded from his wound and he tried grabbing it, tried stopping the flow. He screamed and caught her gaze. His eyes pleaded with hers.

Her lips curled. "Why don't you smile?"

He groaned. His head dropped to the side. The eyes dulled.

Gulamira looked up to see Isra's cutlass cutting Chiuk up the center. With a pitiful sound, he slumped onto the ground on top of the other. Isra stood over the dead guards, blood dripping from the blade, a fiery expression across her face.

She bent and wiped her blade on Chiuk's trousers and surveyed the scene.

Gulamira didn't look away from the sword. "Where did that come from?"

Isra didn't look up.

"People will have heard them screaming. Soon there's going to be guards coming and they're going to kill us both." Not that she was going to live much longer, but there had been hope.

"Only if they find the bodies."

"How you going to hide four... what are you doing?"

Isra had laid her sword down and grabbed one guard and pulled him over to Chiuk and Todd. She then grabbed the other one and pulled him to the pile as well. Then, with an ivory stylus, she carved into the ground around the bodies.

"I need help," Isra said, not looking up. "A tatzon's help."

Gulamira watched her finish drawing around the bodies and start drawing along the floor to the wall. "You want my help?"

Isra nodded, bringing the line up the wall to head height. "I need something. I need a tatzon to get it." She drew what appeared to be a small circle on top of the line. She looked back at Gulamira, who now had the strength to stand and not hang.

"You can't do this with another human?"

"It'd be hard."

There was no change in her expression, but Gulamira guessed that this was an understatement. This human sure liked to keep her lips tight and information limited. It would be hard to trust her to not stab her in the back.

"And what does any of this have to do with my smile?"

"Needed to know." Isra leaned against the wall, eyes dropping to her stylus.

"Know what?"

Isra kept her eyes on her ivory piece and placed a hand on her right shoulder. "Obstinate tatzons are common. Tenacity is rare." She left the wall, expression unreadable, and stood before Gulamira.

Gulamira looked back at the bodies. The woman knew her way around a sword, which could be useful. Icy Abyss, she was right now the only one willing to free Gulamira. Yet, she had killed four tatzons without hesitation and Gulamira had had too much experience with people who held a vendetta against her kind. Problem was that staying here was not an appealing option either. But she had negotiated with unappealing options before.

"What do I get?"

Isra nodded at Gulamira's bondings. "I'll set you free."

Gulamira scoffed. "That's not an exchange. You'd need to free me no matter what to get what you're after."

"I'll help you off the ship."

"That's a given. I'm likely to help you escape this ship just as much."

"I could kill you." Isra raised her sword to Gulamira's throat, but she did not flinch. She kept her smile steady, though this woman could leave her to Solitude or kill her outright. Gulamira chose her next words with care.

"Yes, you could. But that would delay your plans, and I'm sure you don't want to stay on this ship long."

"I'll find someone else."

"Another tatzon willing to help you? Yes, I'm sure there's a line of them waiting to join. All with... tenacity."

The sword rested just under Gulamira's chin and the two watched each other with no changing expression. Gulamira waited. This woman was no fool. She had to see the logic in keeping Gulamira alive. But desperate people often did foolhardy things. And it was a fine line of desperation that separated Isra from freeing Gulamira and killing her.

Isra lowered the sword. "Have something in mind?"

"A girl," Gulamira said, letting her smile lessen. "I came here with a girl. I... I help if we save her, too."

Isra rolled her shoulders and sighed. She looked between the bodies and Gulamira and reached up to the wall, to the circle she'd drawn, and tapped it.

The bodies vanished.

Breath froze in Gulamira's throat.

"What... what just... how did..."

Isra picked up her sword. "They won't find them now."

"But... that was... that was..." What had that been? That wasn't possession. It wasn't the ordîn magic either. She knew nothing of this.

Besides, even if it had been possession, some twisted version of it, it still shouldn't have happened. Humans didn't have magic.

Gulamira watched Isra approach her, a strange coldness in the back of her head. "What are you?"

Isra paused a moment, then smiled. "You decide."

She sliced through the ropes and Gulamira dropped to the floor. Without helping her up, Isra went to where the bodies had been and placed her sword on the floor. She touched the circle with one hand and then with the other, tapped one of her tattoos.

The. Damn. Sword. Vanished.

Gulamira looked up at this impossible woman. A woman who shouldn't exist.

Well, then again, many said the same about Gulamira.

Her legs buckled beneath her, but she pulled herself to her feet. She huffed only a little before sucking it back behind her smile. She would not complete a deal from the floor. Isra smirked at her. Well, Gulamira would let her. This woman was dangerous, that went without saying. But so was Gulamira.

"I'm guessing then, we have a deal?" she asked and held out her hand.

Isra did not hesitate to grasp her hand. "Deal."

8

A NEW ALLY, A NEW BURDEN

S yeda, I don't know what I've stumbled upon, but it can't be good. It was a random thought, but I realized Ma'Jra's destruction happened not too long after the anniversary of the Florella's assassination at the Summit of Blood. I wondered if the Veirs had done some ten-year commemoration or something, since that was the event that pushed us into this renewed war. I found nothing that connected the two events. Except one. Oligarchs Argul and Ortu were supposed to be sitting right next to the murdered Zaruf, yet on that day, they excused themselves from the meal for unknown reasons. And, more recently, the Oligarchs were also supposed to go to Ma'Jra on the day it was destroyed but canceled their plans in the last moments. And Syeda, there's more. The Bramble's death, the Black Swallow's betrayal, our loss at Green Gully, the Oligarchs are connected. Small coincidences, but they are adding up.

Syeda, I think the Oligarchs may be traitors.

-Raza, a frightened man.

Isra peeked around the corner into the next room, one finger close to the circle holding her sword. The tatzon, Gulamira, leaned against the wall behind her, tired and breathing hard. They stood in a dimly lit section of the hall, but it turned into a wide open room filled with disassembled farming equipment. Lanterns illuminated the large number of slaves cleaning all the tools. Guards supervised from the corners. With still half of the day left for work, it would be hard to sneak all the way to the third deck, her eventual target, so she'd need a back-up plan.

The hall continued past the equipment room and stretched on for quite a distance, though she hadn't found a hall yet which stretched from end to end of the ship. No matter how long this hall was, it would branch off into others. Isra gestured forward, and Gulamira nodded in acknowledgment. They crept past in silence, though the tatzon struggled to keep up, until they reached a point where the hall split off in opposing directions. As before, she followed the path of least noise. The halls branched and curved so often, with the light diminishing more and more, making it easy to lose their way. However, getting lost had fewer consequences than getting caught. And right now Gulamira increased their chances of capture the more she was in the open. And this woman was not worth failure.

Besides, there was still the question of whether this tatzon was the right one for the job. Sure, she'd shown grit and determination earlier, but those weren't good enough grounds to trust her with this task. Only good enough to test. Hopefully, Isra didn't need to find another tatzon to do this with her, but... she glanced back at Gulamira. The tatzon walked as slow as before, her gray skin somehow looked pale, and Isra knew she posed no physical threat. Solitude had already sapped her of any strength she might've had. If she wasn't worth the risk, it would take no effort to dispose of her and move on.

Sometimes it amazed her how these tatzons, with all their inherent magical power, couldn't handle a little alone time. They could possess gigantic beasts and spirits and trees, reshaping the world however they saw fit, but as soon as someone even threatened to leave them alone, they crumbled like dried leaves.

There was much unknown about this woman, and that was a problem. Hard to control someone Isra knew nothing about. But Solitude made Gulamira weak, so maybe it would make her more open to suggestion. It was worth trying, at least.

Isra glanced back. "Why'd they take you?"

"What?"

Isra gestured to the surrounding ship.

"You mean why take a tatzon on a human purging mission?" Gulamira's smile remained as still and lifeless as before, but a shadow crossed her eyes. "Not all tatzons are ranked so high in this world."

Isra waited, but Gulamira said nothing more. The hall branched off again, so Isra held off questions as she determined which way to go. As always, silence was her guide, and it led them into quieter and darker places on the ship. She stopped just outside the next room, which was the darkest yet. Only a single lantern hung from the ceiling to light an expansive room. No one worked inside, though further ahead there was a pair of guards, a lantern between them, heading in her direction.

Something hit the floor behind her. She started and spun around. Gulamira lay groaning on the ground, trying to pick herself up again.

"My legs gave out," the tatzon said. "I... not sure how much further I can go."

Isra looked the way they came from. It was a long way until the next room and corridor, and those hadn't been empty. She glanced back into the darkened room. The guards were most definitely coming to their hall, but their lantern light wouldn't reveal the two for a bit yet. She scanned the rest of what she could see in the room.

The room was longer than many others, but seemed empty except for the rows and rows of shelves that lined both walls. And these were sturdy and tall shelves. Isra guessed the shelves were large enough for a person to lie on. If they hurried, they could make it to the floor shelf before the guards' light reached them.

If they hurried.

Isra knelt next to Gulamira. "Up. Move quietly."

Gulamira shook her head. "I... I think I'd rather sit here just a moment."

"Don't have a moment. Up." Isra glanced back. "Guards coming."

Gulamira sighed and groaned, but didn't complain anymore. With her strained smile still plastered on her face, she pulled herself to her feet. She turned back down the hall.

Isra grabbed her arm. "No." She pulled her to the corner. "Under those shelves."

"Are you mad? Those guards are right there."

"Then hurry."

"They'll see us."

"In the hall, yes."

"I can't move that fast."

"Pleasant knowing you." Isra crouched and hurried into the room. The ship creaked around her, masking her footsteps, as she slunk through the shadows to the edge of the room. The guards took their time, chatting as they walked, but they weren't giving her a lot of time to hide. She felt for the shelves, dropped to her belly when she found them, and pulled herself under.

The shelves were much deeper than she'd expected, as deep as a human was tall. Perfect for hiding, so she chose not to imagine this place with hundreds of people crammed side by side together, stacked like bundles of sticks or quarried stone.

With shadows covering her, she turned back toward the hallway entrance. There was just enough dim light from the room's lantern for Isra to see the rough outline of Gulamira, who left the hall and limped toward Isra's place.

Isra looked back at the guards. Their lantern light was creeping ever closer. Gulamira, a tired, beaten, Solitude-filled tatzon had moments before they discovered her.

Isra ran a finger along the circle holding her sword, just in case she needed to silence a few tatzons.

Gulamira inched her way toward the shelves.

The guards plodded closer.

The lantern's light was nearly on them.

Isra narrowed her eyes and lowered her finger to the circle, but did not Release the sword. Not yet.

Gulamira found the shelf and Isra reached out, tapping her leg, which cause the woman to tense. "Drop."

Gulamira complied and bent her way down.

"Faster," Isra whispered, eyes on the guards. They had seconds before the light revealed Gulamira.

Gulamira mumbled something, fell to the floor, and started to crawl under the shelf. But by the Lady, this woman was too slow. Isra grabbed her arm and yanked her deeper into the shelf just as the lantern's light reached them.

Both stayed still, unmoving.

The guards walked up to where they hid. And without breaking step, they passed on to the hall.

Isra breathed out as darkness covered them once again.

"That was too close," Gulamira said in a hushed tone. "Do you usually take risks like that?"

The shadows were too thick to see anything, but Isra still looked toward where Gulamira laid and held back a snort. Gulamira was a far greater risk than hiding under these shelves.

"How long should we wait before moving on?" Gulamira asked.

"A few hours."

"A few hours?"

"At least."

Gulamira shuffled next to Isra. "Why so long? This place is not comfortable. Think they're coming back?"

"Maybe. Maybe not." Isra expected further incessant questioning and so continued, "You're a problem. Weak, useless, discoverable. When the ship's asleep and you can walk, we move." And, if Isra decided Gulamira was too great a risk, then this would be a great place to hide a corpse.

The only accompanying sound in the darkness was that of the ship moving through open waters. The wooden deck groaned and griped, as if it were too precious to be subjected to carrying cargo overseas. Occasionally, there was a random clicking noise, muffled by the thick hull and the watery prison, but still very present. The ocean was a strange place. She wondered if it was a sea beast sizing up the *Cleansing*, though there was no telling if dealing with a sea monster would be more a help or hindrance to her plans right now.

After all, there was a potential hindrance lying beside her.

Isra ran her finger along the wood, making small circular motions. Time to determine whether Gulamira was worth the trouble.

"Who's the girl?" she asked.

"Her name is Kamaria," Gulamira said, voice quiet. "They took her during the initial examination."

Isra grimaced. That examination had been unexpected, and it wasn't good that they had a detailed report of her and her tattoos. They didn't recognize the emblem on her arm, but it was still a way to track her down.

"Have you heard of what happens to those taken?" Gulamira asked.

"Never asked."

That was half true. She didn't ask, but the servants up top whispered about it from time to time. Those that worked further to the stern came back with tales of closed off walls and haunting noises coming from the other side. No one knew for sure why people were taken, but most ideas were less than pleasant. Whatever happened to this girl, she was probably dead already.

"Appearance?" Isra asked.

"She's a tatzon, about eight, I think. Her markings are ovals with lines striking through them, and they are grouped together evenly throughout her body. Oh, and she already is developing an arm."

Isra rolled her eyes. That was a tatzon description, alright. Markings and a number of arms were all they cared about. To them, there were no other distinguishing markers of a person. Isra suspected that was why most tatzons had such a hard time telling one human from the next.

However, the developing arm was interesting. Isra knew the basics of how tatzons grew arms. The more they practiced their magic, the more the new arm grew. There was more to it, but she'd never cared too much to ask. However, even she knew kids didn't start their possession training until age ten. From what she understood, it either wasn't possible or was not good for them. At the very least, it was their initial steps out of childhood and into adulthood. Only villains in children's stories tried forcing a child to leave their innocence like that.

"You training her?" Isra asked.

"Gods no. I... I'm non-active." She cleared her throat. "Besides, I have only just met her."

"Not your daughter?"

"No, I met her the morning the *Cleansing* took us."

Isra paused. Only that morning? And yet she was what Gulamira made a deal over. Isra ran a finger along her tattoos, feeling the contents until she came to her sword circle.

"Just met her?" Isra asked.

"I saved her from being sold to a brothel. She's a sweet kid, doesn't deserve any of this."

"Her family on board?"

"I don't know her family."

"Didn't know her before?"

"Just ran into her."

"Protective."

"I'm just..." Gulamira hesitated, and Isra waited. "Like I said, she doesn't deserve any of this. I get it might seem strange, but I am concerned about her wellbeing. Maybe it's a tatzon thing I don't know."

Oh, but she did. She did not fool Isra for a moment. Gulamira was lying, for sure. There was something more to this girl than she was telling, something that made her worth the trouble to find and rescue. Maybe not to anyone else, but the girl meant more to Gulamira than she let on. Isra didn't need more details than that. As long as this tatzon wasn't about to vanish on her, she was fine in letting her keep her secrets.

"And what about you?" Gulamira asked. "I'm still not clear on what you need me for."

Isra smirked. Seemed the tatzon wanted to change the subject. "I want a key."

"Why can't you get it?" Gulamira asked and from how her voice came, it seemed she shifted onto her side.

"Not a tatzon."

"And?"

"Key's on top deck with the officers. Human servants are not allowed there."

"And you don't think anyone would recognize I don't belong?"

"New slaves come often."

"I'm sure. And what is this key for?"

"Metal room in the hold. Key keeps Remnants locked up."

Gulamira leaned into Isra. "Remnants? Are you serious?"

"Open the door without the key and they're let out."

"That seems... extreme for a ship of slaves."

Isra nodded. "Ship's more than they say."

"I gather. And what is it you're aiming for? Ivory? Weapons? Crystal?"

"Focus on the key."

"Ah, a secret, then. Alright. Everyone is entitled to those." Gulamira shifted and something hard hit the floor. "Fiery Hearth, I hate these collars."

Isra eyed the darkness Gulamira lay in, but then turned her attention back away.

"So, tell me," Gulamira said. "Do you have an escape plan?"

Right, escape. Isra would need to dedicate time to figure out how they'd accomplish that. The ship had a few boats, but getting them into the water would be complicated. She'd need to steal food and water in preparation, too. No telling how long they'd be stuck on the water.

Isra shrugged, knowing the woman wouldn't see. "Don't worry about it."

"I'm sorry, we're trying to rescue a girl, rob the hold, and steal from officers and you don't want me to worry about our escape? If you don't have a plan, that's fine. I can try coming up with some ideas."

Isra eyed the darkness Gulamira lay in. "I have it handled."

Gulamira paused. "Do you not want help?"

"I want to succeed."

"And yet you decide to waste a valuable resource."

Isra narrowed her eyes. This woman was already getting pushy. Already, this tatzon was forgetting who was in charge here. "Solitude is not a resource."

A hush arose between them, neither speaking nor moving or breathing. Even the ship seemed to quieten, as if wanting to listen. No strange clicking, no creaking and cracking of the wood.

Gulamira ended the silence. "I was in Archoz long before it became a proper prison. I was sold to a brothel there about two years ago. For months I was poorly fed, barely clothed, and didn't sleep.

People derided me on the streets and cursed me in the bed. There was no place where I was welcome. By the time the *Cleansing* took me, I was the most influential person in town. I stopped criminal factions from warring and I saw to the fall of those that opposed me. I accrued secrets that ended merchant families and that made others rich. People sought after me from miles on end. My secrets shaped the coast." Gulamira let the silence punctuate her point.

Isra rolled her eyes at the obvious lie and turned on her side, facing Gulamira. "That's a pleasant story to put kids to sleep."

"Indeed. A cautionary tale come to life."

Voices interrupted their quiet, and within a few minutes, another pair of guards entered the room. The two remained motionless and silent, but as the lantern light passed by, Isra caught a shadowy image of Gulamira. She was still smiling.

Isra stared at that smile until it disappeared behind shadows again. She ran her finger along her sword circle for a moment and then withdrew it. She laid in the quiet, gazing into the black nothing, until the guards were long gone. And she decided.

"I'm looking for an idol of a tatzon warrior."

"Didn't take you for the religious type," Gulamira said.

"Idol's not for me. Been... hired to retrieve it."

Gulamira was quiet for a moment, but then slid onto her back again, though staying close to Isra. "Hope you're paid well for all this trouble."

Isra nodded. Not to Gulamira, but more to herself.

Because the payment was well worth all of this. It was worth every lashing, every sleepless night, every hungry day, every moment of constant danger. It was worth her very soul.

Because this idol meant life and survival for her people.

Her father was dead and gone. There was now only her to act on their behalf.

9

DEATH STALKED BETWEEN THE RIVERS

Ten Years Ago

S pirits danced throughout the river, all under the child's command.

She sent them under the rushing water and high into the drooping boughs of Common willows, dancing and singing to her heart's delight. They were Small spirits, all much taller than her, but her songs were far more beautiful than theirs. Stronger. Better. And her songs directed their paths, shaped their thoughts and songs and even the colors they glowed.

She stood at the edge of the river, water lapping against her bar ankles just underneath her teal robes. This was what she'd needed that she did not get back in Zashai: the chance to really use her power. She counted a dozen spirits and they all listened to her voice. They could not disobey her or do anything other than her will. This was what it meant to wield a higher song. She smirked and closed her eyes, tasting the song on her tongue. It had the hint of strawberries.

A soundless wave of power ran through her, the trees, the spirits, and the river. The trees danced in the wind, but the spirits stopped. Froze mid movement, their glows dimmed. And the girl's voice also froze, stuck, as if air could neither enter nor leave her throat.

Oh, no.

A new song rose through the air from a voice that had soaked in the tongue of spirits, had drank deeper from that Heritage than anyone else. This song broke the girl's song, overwhelmed it as a trumpet overwhelms a whisper, and the spirits descended from their dances, descended into the river, and disappeared.

Gulamira watched them go. Not just because her fun was over, but because she didn't want to see who was behind her.

"Florella Gulamira." The voice spoke in Vei'n and not in spirit song, yet it somehow still held so much power. "Turn around."

She turned and faced her parents.

The High Priest and Priestess of Exkel wore flowing robes of bright yellow and marigold orange, with animal motifs in cobalt blue. Long black hair fell past silvery-gray skin covered in walnut brown markings. On either side of them were the Dasparets, Fadila and her Partner Salma, but Gulamira knew better than to look anywhere besides her father's eyes. In those eyes was all the reprimand she needed, but her father spoke, regardless,

"Gulamira." His voice was even and void of fury or rage. Which only made it worse. "Explain to us what you have done."

Gulamira looked between her father and mother's eyes, but couldn't decide who was more angry with her. She looked at her mother. "I was just playing with them, I wasn't doing anything harmful."

"These songs," Mother said, "are not toys to be played with."

"It wasn't like that."

"Gulamira."

She huffed and fought against looking away. "I'm sorry, Mother, Father. I won't use my birthright again."

She knew it was a mistake as soon as the words left her mouth. Father and Mother straightened.

"Hashai," Mother said, and another girl stepped out from behind a willow's branches. Hashai had protested coming out here, but she had to stay with Gulamira to keep Solitude away from the future High Priestess. Mother smiled at the girl. "Thank you for your service to the priestess. You may return with the Dasparets to the camp. Salma, Fadila, we will return shortly."

"As you wish," Dasparet Fadila said with a bowed head.

The three left, following the river south, and Gulamira faced her parents alone.

Silence hung between them, but Gulamira kept her mouth shut. She already said too much. Better she not get herself in more trouble.

"Child, do you despise us?" Father asked.

Gulamira gaped at them both. "What? No, of course not."

"Then you must think us fools."

"Never."

"Then explain why you disdain our teachings and warnings so much."

She looked away. She wasn't supposed to, but she couldn't handle their gazes anymore.

"I just don't get it, is all. The Heritage holds so many songs, songs that could do so much good and yet we hide from them and don't sing them. The Heritage could give us control of an army of spirits, we could end all the fighting and everyone could be happy."

"We end the war today with our diplomacy, child."

"But we have to give up so much to do that! Those Rajals aren't going to just leave us alone, they want our land and people. But our songs could change that. Our songs could change them, just like they change spirits." She turned away, holding tight to her still-growing left arm. "The Heritage gives us power, I don't get why we're afraid to help people with it."

Father narrowed his eyes. "And where have you been getting such ideas? Because those have not come from us."

Gulamira shrugged. "I don't know. Everyone's talking about it."

She waited for their reprimand, for their raised voices. Neither came. Only a warm wind blowing through the grass and leaves around her.

"Daughter, walk with us," Mother said, and Gulamira obeyed. They took a path beside the river, though they walked slower than a newborn heifer.

Mother looked over the river and Gulamira saw a sad smile. "In some ways, you are right. We have the higher songs, those that can control and change spirits and people and world. Yes, we could use the songs to raise an army unbeatable by any. We could use songs within the Heritage to take over the minds of the Rajal Oligarchs. We could force people to sit side by side, to eat together, drink together, live together. And then what? We rule by fear? By dominated control? That is not the world we are trying to create."

"The higher songs do not belong to us," Father said. "They are Exkel's, gifts from the Mountain itself. And he decides how we ought to use them. There were those in the past who sought to use the power of the Heritage to do the things that you suggest. It did not end well for anyone."

"Abusing these songs only brings more pain and misery into this world. This is why the Heritage's location is kept secret, why its songs are taught only to our family. It only takes a single fool to unleash the Heritage and destroy everything." Mother gave her a stern look that held both reprimand and question, *Are you that fool?*

"But aren't you telling those Rajals about the Heritage?" Gulamira asked.

Both her parents stopped and stared at her. "Whatever gave you that idea?" Father asked.

"I overheard other priests whispering about it."

Mother sighed. "More rumors? Gulamira, why are you putting so much weight behind the whispers of the ignorant instead of the wisdom of your teachers?"

She caught their eyes, for a moment, but looked away. "Is it true?"

They were quiet a moment. Then Father crouched and took Gulamira's prihand in his. "Look at me and understand this: we create peace today, we end a very long war. But never will we hand over the Heritage to any. Not to the Rajals, not even to the Zaruf. It would be better that we died than for it to fall into hands of any other. That is our duty, understand? We shall neither abuse it, nor shall we abandon it." He squeezed her prihand. "That includes you, young priestess."

Gulamira kept her mouth shut. She didn't understand. What was the point of protecting and defending something if they weren't ever going to use it? But they wouldn't listen to her today. Maybe when she was older, they would take her more seriously.

They journeyed to where the river split in two, one veering toward the interior of Veirzen and the other to the enemy nation of Rajalend. When the Oligarchs and Zaruf agreed to peace talks, her parents thought it apt to have these talks on the banks of the Between Rivers. A large meeting tent sat on the bank where the split began, and behind it was a village of smaller tents. Half flew the banner of Veirzen, yellow with the Wolf and the Stallion emblazoned in its center, while the other half flew the Rajal flag, green with the symbol of the Ethereal Tree. The Rajals had not yet arrived, so there were only Veirs here. There were priests and servants with the only contingent of soldiers stationed near the Zaruf's tent, the largest second only to the meeting tent.

Gulamira had heard priests and some soldiers murmuring about it being unwise to have left the war beasts behind, but her parents had been clear about bringing as few elements of battle as possible.

As they entered the camp, a distant, but deep trumpet bellowed over the waters. The camp stilled, and all watched as the tall willows on the other side of the river animated to life, bending out over the river, branches weaving together until the trees created bridges from one side to the other. Rajal Builders appeared outside the tree as the contingent of Rajals marched over the bridges and into the camp.

"Gulamira," Father said. "Find Erasyl in his tent and remain there."

"What? I wanted to go to the summit. I'm the future High Priestess!"

"You lost your right as priestess to attend when you lost all wisdom today. Go. We shall finish speaking with you about this later."

She huffed and left, heading straight for the Zaruf's tent, though she, like the other Veirs, cast glances to the advancing Rajals and the Oligarchs they carried. A moment before she reached the tent, the Zaruf, king of Veirzen, left the tent with his wife. Erasyl was at their side.

The Zaruf smiled at her approach. "Ah, young priestess. Come to join us?"

Gulamira saw the opportunity for the lie. Technically, the Zaruf could out command her parents, but she rarely saw that happen. She looked up into the older tatzon's face. "No. My parents said I couldn't join the meeting. I have to stay with Erasyl."

"Is that so? Hm. Not what I would have wished, but today is their victory. However, I wish Erasyl to come at my side. I will have a maidservant stay with you."

Erasyl, a boy only a year her senior, stepped next to her. "I'd rather stay with Gulamira, if I may."

The Zaruf sighed and shook his head. "They are diplomacy talks, peace accords, boy. There won't be anything to fear here. It is a perfect opportunity to learn what it means to lead."

The boy nodded, but moved closer to Gulamira. "Isn't it also an excellent opportunity for me to learn what it means to stand by my Partner?"

"She is not your Partner, yet."

Arwa, the Zaruf's wife, placed a hand on her Partner's shoulder. "Honor the boy's request. They will need to practice togetherness soon, why not on such a day as this? If we must have the boy there, let's speak with the High Priest and Priestess, perhaps we can request their presence."

Two messengers rushed forward and bowed to the Zaruf. "Zaruf, the High Priest and Priestess request your immediacy to the meet the Rajal Oligarchs."

"We're on our way." The Zaruf looked to Gulamira and Erasyl. "Stay inside the tent, servants will retrieve you shortly. Unless the Zaruf truly has no say anymore."

His wife took his arm and pulled him forward. "Pout after the talks. Today, show strength."

The two children watched them go and Erasyl glanced at her. "What'd you do this time?"

"I did nothing."

"Then why are you in trouble?"

"Who said I was in trouble?"

"Come on, what'd you do?"

She shoved him away. "I punched a future Zaruf in the face, that's what I did."

He smiled and gestured toward the tent. "Up for a game? Doubt your parents will let you back in, which means I don't need to go either."

"Yeah, I noticed you weren't helping."

He shrugged. "Who wants to listen to old people talk about trade deals and borders and stuff."

"You don't even want to see them?"

"See who?"

"The Oligarchs. I hear they don't even have a second arm."

Erasyl pulled the tent flap back and let her go in. "I'd rather not have to meet them. Papa told me they keep Sefaran within their land, so you can't be sure you won't get sick being near them."

Gulamira slumped onto a feathery pillow and stared at the lightstone braziers around the sides. She wasn't worried about a human disease. But she was worried about the talks going well. They could end years of war, or maybe erupt a whole new one. No one knew. Her parents had worked so hard to establish any kind of diplomatic talks between the nations, but what if something went wrong in there today?

If something did go wrong, it wasn't like her parents were willing to do what it took to keep everyone safe. If the Rajals were devious, the Veirs needed someone who wasn't afraid to sing a higher song.

"I need to get in there," she said, half to herself.

"What?"

She turned over onto her stomach, careful not to hit her growing arm, and looked at Erasyl. Unlike her, he hadn't started growing any new arms yet, though within the next year he would. His hair was like the Zaruf's, short on one side and shaved on the other, and he wore golden brown clothes. His markings resembled blossoming roses that followed each other in a spiral down his body.

He didn't like loud areas, preferred history over the present, and couldn't resist a freshly baked fruit pie. And he was going to be her Partner. Her future husband and the man who would help her guide Veirzen for the rest of their lives.

With that being the case, he needed to get used to adventures with her.

"We're going to that meeting," she said.

"You think your parents will change their minds? I don't even know what you did, but I know they won't do that."

"No, they won't. That's why we're going to sneak in."

He frowned. "Don't be stupid."

"I'm not stupid!"

"Yes, you are. Sneak in? The meeting tent is inside two more tents. You have to go through so many sentries, so many guards, and how in Exkel's name do you think you'd do that without getting caught?"

"Obviously you don't understand the word 'sneak'. They won't know we're there."

He shook his head. "No. No way. Let's just stay here and maybe a servant will come get us."

She sat up and furrowed her brow. "Thought you were going to stand by your Partner."

"You may enjoy getting in trouble, but I don't."

"Fine." She rose to her feet, dusting off her robes. "I'll go alone."

He blinked. "What?"

"I'm going. If you want to come, you can."

"Gulamira, that's not funny."

She grabbed his prihand. "Oh, come on, Erasyl. Just for a little."

A grumbling whine stirred in his throat, but he sighed. "Fine. But this was your idea! If someone asks, you threatened me with Solitude and I had no choice."

She beamed and pulled him out through the tent flap.

The camp pulsed with a tense, angry air. Veirs and Rajals stood in their contingents facing each other, none speaking, but all hating. There were songs that could calm them, there were songs that could aggravate them to fighting, but Gulamira held her tongue.

The two children skulked through tall grass, past tents and trees, keeping the meeting tent in their sights. This was not like the times they snuck through the temple or even the palace, avoiding their handlers and parents alike. There were enemies here. Years of war crackled just beneath the surface.

Gulamira led Erasyl toward the back of the meeting tent. This tent stood like a Large beast, overshadowing the other structures with its multi-pointed top and vibrant sheets of color. Veirs stood guard at the entrance, six soldiers armed with ivory spears and sickles. Rajals and Veirs patrolled the perimeter, though as Gulamira watched, she noticed everyone watched each other. No one looked for threats outside the camp.

After one patrol passed in front of them, Gulamira and Erasyl left the tall grass and ran to the tent. Gulamira crouched and grabbed the bottom of the flap.

"No good. It's staked too tight into the ground."

Erasyl glanced over his shoulder. "Don't talk so loud. It's cloth and hide, not stone."

She frowned and pressed an ear to the tent. There were some voices but low and muffled by the many interior layers. "I can't hear anything here."

"Well, we tried. Can we head back before someone catches us?"

"We've barely tried anything yet. We're getting inside."

"How? Are you cutting into the tent? Because it's that or walking through the front opening, and there's no way I can sneak past eight guards staring right at me."

Although muffled, she heard the deep tone of a gong sound. The meeting had begun.

"Come on, Erasyl. It's starting." She rushed along the edge of the tent, toward the entrance.

"What're you doing? We're going to get caught."

The tent rounded, and she slowed as she caught sight of the guards. Eight loyal Veirs, with eight Rajals opposite them, stood at attention. Stood between her and that meeting. And she needed to get in there. If her parents were too scared to use their songs to protect the people, then it was up to Gulamira to ensure that everything went well.

She stepped forward but Erasyl caught her arm. "What're you doing?" he asked.

She smiled. "Just trust me."

He glanced between her and the guards. "I don't know, Gulamira. I don't feel good about this."

There were songs of encouragement. Those that filled a tatzon with vigor and courage and determination to drive ever forward.

A day could come where, as High Priestess, she'd be called to sing such songs for the Veir armies, but it occurred to her she had never once thought to sing them to Erasyl. In fact, using a song on him, changing him, felt odd... or maybe just wrong.

She took his prihand in hers. "If we're going to lead these people, we can't miss such moments like this."

He looked her in the eyes for a moment before he nodded.

Gulamira already had the song in her throat when the first guard noticed them. The song was in the air by the time he nudged his Partner. And before any of them called out to her, before any asked why they wandered around the tent, the song took root in their minds.

It was a higher song, a Song of Blissful Fields. Often used by priests for meditation, this song calmed the mind and caused the individual to imagine their self in the most beautiful of flowered meadows. A harmless, even helpful, higher song. However, it had the added benefit of leaving the person in a dazed stupor. The guards stood as they were, no one collapsed or fell, but their eyes glazed over and they were no longer here.

Gulamira smiled at the dazed adults. Strong, powerful, loyal soldiers. All rendered useless by the power of a child. Why her parents didn't want to use the gifts of the Heritage, she still could not figure out.

The two slunk through the opening, pushing curtains aside. Inside the main tent, was a second tent, of a darker, but still not dull, blue and yellow. Inside the second tent, was a third, itself a somber gray, and within the third was where the leaders of the two nations sat. This set up was the mimic and mirror the sanctity of the temple to Exkel. The first tent represented the life and joy available to all people, thus everyone could see its vibrant colors. The second tent represented joy but seriousness of leadership, and could be seen by those of high rank. The third and final tent was represented the burden of holding together rulers and the ruled. Inside that tent, only High Priests and the Zaruf typically went.

There was a gap of seven feet between the canvas of one tent and the next, so that no tent actually touched another. There were typically benches set up on the ground inside the gaps so that those allowed could take in the wisdom of the next tent. The benches were not put up today, so there weren't nobles or military officers within these tents. Everyone was stationed outside.

Gulamira and Erasyl pushed past the second tent's curtains, but did not enter the third. Instead, they crept along the wall of the tents until they were on the opposite side. Just in case someone did come in or out of the third, Gulamira didn't want them to immediately spot her.

They crouched behind the shadowy outline of someone and she grinned. Erasyl only shook his head. But she could see the gleam of adventure in his eyes too.

"... this is an ostentatious day for both our nations," the Zaruf said inside. "The Florellas shall lead this meeting, so I bow my head to their words."

"Thank you, Zaruf," Father said. "However, I only count four Oligarchs. Where are Oligarchs Argul and Ortu?"

A voice Gulamira did not recognize, a raspy voice with a thick Rajal accent. "They excused themselves for the moment. A long journey we have had, and they needed relief. They shall come soon. We proceed until then."

"I would prefer we not continue until all the Oligarchs are present. We can send a few... who is this?"

A shuffling and then silence.

"Who are you?" Father asked. "Who let you inside this meeting?"

Gulamira and Erasyl looked at each other. Something was wrong.

"Guards! Remove this—"

A scream burst from the meeting as something red sprayed against the tent wall in front of Gulamira. And then chaos.

People shouted, yelled, screamed as bodies ran and dropped and, if her little ears heard right, cracked. Gulamira's heart pounded in her chest as the screams filled the air and then stopped, but there was more shouting to be had.

She jumped to her feet and rushed to the third tent's entrance.

"Gulamira!" Erasyl reached for her but she pushed his prihand aside. She darted to the opening and screamed herself. A body laid in the opening, eyes wide with fear, a pool of dark crimson pouring from their back. A few people ran from the meeting room, ignoring the body at their feet.

People screamed for guards outside, screamed in the faces of sixteen dazed soldiers, but Gulamira, her prihand over her mouth, stepped into the meeting room and all feeling left her body.

The gray interior had a fresh coat of color. The paint came from many, but primarily from the Zaruf, his wife, and Gulamira's parents. In the center of the room stood the artist, an unmoving figure dressed all in black. They met Gulamira's eyes.

They stalked toward her, ivory sickle in hand, ready to paint another wall.

10

A MOST FAMILIAR FACE

I 've gathered a team together to look into this more. These can't be mere coincidences. There's something here. Even in my dreams I've been working on this! I'll keep up my Remnant and spirit research as normal, but alongside that, we will look deeper into these connections. I doubt the Oligarchs are secret Veirs or anything like that. But there is something off about all of this. I feel it in my gut. There's this prickling thought in the back of my mind, ushering me to keep pressing. I have to sort this out.

-Raza, the one compelled to uncover the secret.

Sunlight drifted in through the open window. Actual sunlight. Such a simple thing, such a common thing, yet when deprived from it for even a short time, it became a source of pure delight. For it brought not only light, but warmth, color, life. Even the hues of brown and tan in the room became richer in the sunlight.

But Gulamira had little time to enjoy the sun, to take in all it offered her, to examine the depths of the reddish browns of the wood. Instead, her gaze set on the colors of black before her.

Servants of the *Cleansing* stood before her, lining the walls and waiting for their daily assignments, all dressed in the same black attire she now wore. All tatzon, everyone had two arms and that suffocating iron collar around their necks. She counted near a dozen of them—only two of which were men—none who gave

Gulamira much notice or attention. No one approached her or bothered her, though a few gave furtive glances toward her. Isra had assured her that newcomers were common because of the high death rate of servants, so no one would question her presence there. Isra was also sure that people would avoid her a while until they were certain about whether or not she was a bootlicker.

By Rajal standards, they had cramped quarters. Two long sleeping bars hung from the narrow room's ceiling, giving enough space to fit all of them inside but still tight enough that they pressed against their neighbors while sleeping. Aside from that, there was a single long bench in the center of the room that stretched from end to end so they could sit if desired and a circular window letting in light. However, to Gulamira, this small room was freedom compared to the depths of the *Cleansing*.

Two guards came in and the quiet conversations in the room stopped as everyone bowed their heads. Gulamira followed the example, keeping her smile to a minimum. Isra had been adamant about appearing as subservient as possible. Not that Gulamira needed to try hard. Today wasn't the first day of her being a slave.

Gulamira hadn't known how to even imagine the organization of service on this ship. Everyone here was a slave and, Gulamira had to assume, a dangerous criminal of some sort. She doubted anyone had trained in service and the guards didn't look like they cared. The two guards read aloud some specific requests from some officers and passengers and proceeded down the line assigning tasks, or rather sections of the ship, to each set of two. Isra had mentioned that they didn't assign servants to any one passenger, as things changed almost daily. Gulamira wasn't sure what the logic was in that, though she was on a ship simultaneously carrying hundreds of humans for sale and a contingent of merchants, living a life of luxury. Perhaps logic had little place here.

She listened to each section as the guards assigned them off. As they were all tatzons, they assigned them to the higher paying passengers and the officers of the ship. Gulamira watched everyone's expressions as they accepted their section, noting which places caused elation and which despair. It would be important to learn the dynamics of the place if she were to succeed in not dying.

Most of the assignments were for the second deck. Only one wasn't.

"Right," one guard said, approaching the two male servants. "As before, you two are working topside and the aftcastle."

The two men drooped their heads. Gulamira noted how their expressions had dimmed with every section not given to them. The guards turned to leave, but noticed Gulamira.

"Not seen you before," one said and turned to her Partner. "You heard of any newcomers?"

Her Partner shrugged, and both stared at Gulamira.

"They sent me up this morning," Gulamira said. "Replacement, they said."

"We needed a human, not a tatzon." She sighed and looked at each of the servants. "Whatever. You'll go with those two to the aftcastle."

Gulamira nodded and darted her eyes away, doing her best to hold back the building excitement. The aftcastle was where she needed to go. Although, the almost pitying looks from the other servants gave her some pause to what was awaiting her there. Isra hadn't been able to give her much information since human servants weren't allowed on the second deck and above.

The other servants drifted out of the room and toward their designated areas, some with relief, others with hesitancy, none with fervor. The two men walked the slowest, as if the air itself was thick mud, and gave little attention to Gulamira, which she didn't mind as she followed them to this deck's galley. Cooks, all tatzon, worked over large pots and short tables. Unlike the gruel of lower decks, the residents here were to dine on bright fruits and a hearty broth with a hunk of fish simmering inside, all to be wiped up with warm bread. Gulamira's stomach gurgled and her mouth salivated more than she cared for at the aroma filling the tight kitchen. They'd already received a servant meal today, leftover broth and stale bread from the days before, but her body craved for more.

But she shoved these pesky hungers behind her smile and mimicked the other servants, who she determined were not Partners. Their movements were too asynchronous. They stood near each other as those who must, not those who had the innate need to. Gulamira wondered if any of the servants were Partners, or if, like prisons across Rajal, they separated Partners and denied them access to each other. This brought to mind her lack of a Partner, but, without hesitation, she shoved all the thoughts and associated longings down deep behind her plastered smile.

The men weren't talkative, none of the servants seemed to be, but they gestured and grunted well enough that Gulamira figured out what to carry and what to leave. For all their disgruntled attitudes toward their assignment, she could tell they enjoyed having someone to push around and unload their burdens onto, if even just a little. Gulamira recognized that look in their eyes. She'd seen it in many patrons who'd come to her to have control they otherwise couldn't have, so she knew how to placate these men. She kept her smile small, but still present, head bowed, and voice nonexistent. Gulamira needed to make herself the most subservient of all.

With the three of them carrying trays of foods that tormented and teased her appetite, they made their way through the second deck and up to the... outside. She couldn't believe how delightful that word would be.

The second deck had large rooms, like much of the *Cleansing*, most of which were filled with lavish decorations and comfortable furniture, all filled with plump and overly satisfied merchants, traders, and other opportunists heading to the Maw. They openly displayed their wealth through their ostentatious clothing, with one individual in the far back of the room wearing bright yellow robes. A garish color amongst Rajals, but not so around here, apparently.

No one worried about sea or rainwater flooding into these rooms and ruining everything here, which Gulamira thought would be a much greater concern considering the top deck was just a stair flight away. But the passengers enjoyed their breakfasts without giving a second glance to the black-shirts around them.

The top deck was as different from the bowels of the *Cleansing* as a mjai fruit was from stinkweed. The sun shone over the blue waters and bluer sky, the former sloshing against the massive ship and the latter filled with big, puffy clouds that promised soft rains later. A warm, salty wind kissed Gulamira as it passed by, tickling her ears and filling her nose with smells of sea and vigor. Every deck with windows had hinted at all of this, yet here with the world open about her, she felt some of the *Cleansing*'s darkness melt out of her. But the moment was brief before the two servants ushered her onward.

This was the first time she'd been on the top deck since her exam, since Kamaria vanished from sight, so she took it all in as best she could. Somehow, this deck felt larger and wider than all the rest, perhaps because it had no ceiling and no walls. Six masts stood like Large beasts, their sails filled with wind and their rigging populated with green-clothed sailors at work. Sailors shouted and strove together on several large cranes and an equally large mounted ballista. Based on the shouting and orders given, she surmised these sailors were fishing.

The sailors, of course, were all human. The work of a sailor was a lesser work, not befit beings who could reshape the physical world. She doubted they paid the crew. More likely, they were prisoners from the war or captured anglers and pirates. Human slaves worked the rest of the ship, so it made sense for the main crew to be as well. The only tatzons around were not sailors but guards, keeping watch and issuing orders to the human crew.

The two she followed kept out of the crew's way and moved further and further to the stern, toward the structure looming behind the masts. A few steps elevated the aftcastle above the rest of the deck, and Gulamira noted no human touched those steps. Of all the aspects of the *Cleansing*, this was the most intentionally designed. They'd Built the aftcastle to resemble the Ethereal Tree, with several trunks wrapping around each other until they separated into branches that circled out and back down into the roots, which themselves were part of the deck floor, as if the tree was alive and had grown from the ship's deck. No one could understate the impracticality of such a design, yet Gulamira couldn't decide if that spoke more of the Rajals' confidence or stupidity. As she stared at the tree design, she determined it was indeed more their stupidity. The Ethereal Tree had ten trunks and branches, yet this aftcastle only had eight, so whoever had Built this had not paid close enough attention to their religion.

In front of this structure stood two steering wheels, manned by two tatzons each. Gulamira had heard that on much larger ships, they needed two wheels otherwise steering was too difficult. The four pilots would be two pairs of Partners, though they swapped Partners to work on the wheels. Partners had this uncanny way of synchronizing with each other, so by having a Partner on each wheel there was greater unison between the steering.

Behind the pilots, overlooking the work of the crew and guard, stood the captains whose names she'd heard from guards, Yirig and Juhk. They had two arms each, a sword at their hip, built bodies, and commanding eyes. Yirig had rectangular markings and Juhk's resembled tight rows of spears. They wore simple dark green coats that dropped to their knees and covered most of their body. None of the crew or guard wore coats like these since they flowed too much and restricted movement. The captains having these made a firm statement about their standing. Neither smiled as they watched the sailors hoist their catch of the day, and they, unlike everyone else, noticed the black shirts as they approached. These two paid attention, it seemed. Gulamira had assumed that the captains for a ship like this would have been just as lazy and pampered as the merchants below. She adjusted her assumption.

The captains' eyes centered on Gulamira, so she kept herself small and followed the other servants' leads. One hurried to the railing next to the aftcastle and opened a large chest, producing two short tables and two stools. Gulamira helped him place the table and stools behind as the second servant placed the meals atop the table. The men both bowed and backed away, Gulamira mimicking their every movement. They stayed bowed until the captains dismissed them with a gesture and Gulamira half-expected them to make their way below deck. However, the servants turned to the aftcastle and headed to one of the two openings. As they did, Gulamira remembered what she was even doing up here.

She wasn't just another servant. She was supposed to be looking for the key to the hold. The outside air, as delicious as it was, had distracted her from her true purpose here. She would pay better attention in the future.

Thick beast hide covered the openings, granting better protection than simple curtains while avoiding the indignity of using doors. The servants stood outside the port side opening and hesitated before calling out.

"Yeah, we hear you," a woman said from beyond the hide. This appeared to be akin to an invitation as the two servants headed inside.

The interior was well furnished, though not as lavishly as the deck below, and lit by a sconce with lightstone and the double wide windows at the rear. Small tusks decorated the walls, designed to look like a massive wave. Underneath the sleeping bar, lounging in some over-sized cushions, she found the two she dreaded meeting the most. Isra had informed her they were called Hij Con-Kami and Kami Con-Hij. The two Soulborn.

The *Cleansing* had two Lightless, shadow possessors, on board, but these two were the most dangerous individuals on the ship.

Hij wore flowing green silks with horizontal patterns that paired with his striped markings. Kami wore similar robes, though they contrasted with her speckled square markings. She had her hair done up with wooden carvings, making it look as though branches grew from her temples and held her hair together. Both had four arms, and both had the same spindly and lean stature many Soulborn developed. These were true possessors, able to body-possess and empower. Gulamira's eyes glanced at the iron lock boxes on the table beside them. Inside those would be spirit vessels—crystals with spirits trapped inside, ready to be summoned and possessed by these two.

"Ah, breakfast," Hij said with a broad smile. "Set it on the table, as usual. Then get to the clothes. Had a nasty spill yesterday that I want out by tomorrow."

Gulamira set the food down, trying to glance around with no one noticing as best she could. She doubted the key would be out in the open—Isra had even been sure that the captains would have it—but maybe she'd luck out. Instead, she caught Kami staring at her.

"You're new," the Soulborn said as she grabbed some fruit. "Didn't know they sent odd numbers to serve."

Gulamira smiled, but caught herself before she tried answering. They had not asked her a question, so she bowed and waited for the possessor's eyes to meander away. As she bowed, something drifted into the air and sent tingles down her spine. It started low, soft, but grew in form and force as it tried to grab onto her skin and crawl underneath.

A song. A spirit song.

She glanced over. The two servants did not notice it but they moved slower, and she saw pain creep further into their eyes. Gulamira eyed the two Soulborn, the two humming this quiet song, and saw the gleam of pleasure in both.

Gulamira recognized this song, and it made her stomach sick as she realized why the servants dreaded serving the aftcastle. This song, imperceptible to others, stirred up feelings of grief and loss in its victim. It stole strength, it stole life. It did to the soul what putting a clay jar over a lamp did to a room, or what stripping away all colors but gray did to a painting. This was a song that drew grief into the one who heard it, and it made Gulamira angry to see it used like this. Because this was a song known to her.

It was a lower song she'd heard spirits sing before and one her parents had sung when her grandmother died. The song was supposed to be sung for those lost, those dead. It was a song to help mourning, yet here she saw it distorted and shifted to bring despair, all for the sick pleasure of these Soulborn. These two represented the reason some songs were forbidden. It was easy to imagine the evils they'd commit had they known the song that killed spirits.

However, these two toyed and played with a language foreign to their tongues and far from their understanding. The speech of spirits was hers long before it was theirs. Their attempt to affect her with their song held no sway. She resisted it with ease. But she moved as the other servants moved, slow and shuddering, to not bring attention to herself.

She wasn't sure how long they were in that room, but Hij and Kami ordered them around plenty. The other two servants did their best to shuck the harder, or more demeaning, tasks to Gulamira, but there was plenty to go all around. They had to clean vomit stained clothes, wipe down every piece of ivory, and at one point Hij had one servant finish a plate of days' old food, which had gained a putrid smell. Gulamira numbed herself to the pointless tasks—they were meant only to entertain these two—and kept a vigilant eye for the key. By the time the Soulborn dismissed them, she was convinced the two were not in charge of the key. She didn't see it on their bodies and there weren't many places that seemed an obvious place to hold something of that importance.

When they left, she expected to go to the other opening—the captains' room—but the two servants went to put away the breakfast table and stools of the captains before heading to the forward hatch back to the lower deck. Gulamira wasn't sure if they'd come back up later, but she also doubted she could snoop around unnoticed by those watchful captains' eyes. She followed, noting the Common black-fin tuna mid-deck, with sailors cleaning it and dumping the entrails overboard.

She stopped dead in her tracks as she looked at the human crew, and at one man in particular. He stood out among everyone there, his back unbent, his eyes filled with untempered wildness, with an air about him that when you looked you knew he was unbroken, untamed. The other sailors regarded him with something like respect and Gulamira realized that wherever he stood, it was his voice that issued orders and commanded the people. The guards stood back, obvious in their disdain for him but also in their unease about interfering with him. This man stood among slaves as if the only one free, as if he didn't notice or didn't care about his captors. And around his neck, just as always, he wore a brown scarf that covered his entire neck, with only a short tail blowing in the wind.

Even the *Cleansing* could not change this man, and Gulamira could not help but beam as he met her gaze. His eyes widened. He stopped in the middle of what he was doing, and mouthed a single question, "Amira?"

She resisted waving to him, resisted bringing more attention to herself and him. She only winked at him and gestured with her head toward the hatch. He glanced over his shoulder at the guards and held up two fingers. She nodded and headed down the stairs, slower than the other servants. At the bottom, she slowed letting the two get ahead of her before she doubled-back and ducked into the nearest empty room, but kept her head out to see the servants down the hall, keeping Solitude at bay.

After a few minutes, he slunk down the steps, looking down either way of the hall. She poked her head out of the opening and beckoned him over, and as soon as the curtain closed, he took her into a big embrace.

"Lady above," he said, and his voice, more than the sunlight and wind, brought such joy to her heart. "It is you."

"It's good to see to you, too, Medhi."

He pulled away, smirking as he looked her up and down. "I looked for you when they came through Archoz, but they must've brought you on board while I was down below. I didn't see you and hoped they'd ignored you."

"If only. But how are you here? You headed to the Ashen islands last."

Medhi nodded, stroking his scarf in the all-too-familiar way. "We did. And... well, didn't go too well. Got hit by a dreadful storm, ship hit a reef and we abandoned it there. We got picked up by the Rajals not too long after and they sent me here." He sighed with a big smile and shook his head. "Of all the times I imagined seeing you again, I hadn't thought it'd be here."

"Same."

The two smirked at each other, but voices trailed in from outside their little space. Gulamira pulled him close and whispered in his ear. "Listen, I'm working with someone to get off this ship. Can I find you later?"

"They keep us all in cages on the fifth deck, all crammed next to each other. Others would notice you coming and going." He looked toward the opening in thought. "If we're wanting private talks, we'll have to do with what we're doing now. And if we're escaping, then we keep it private."

"That seems pretty risky."

"Oh, it is, so if you or your friend come up with a better idea, I'm all ears. Otherwise, there's a room forward, a bit of a storage space.

Let's meet there tomorrow after midday. I can disappear for a bit during that lull. You can give me all the details, then."

She nodded with a sigh. "Our big reunion after all these months and we can't even catch up."

"Life's never the fair judge," he said and pulled her into another hug. "But Dragon's Breath, it is so good to see you."

"Let's not ruin this with getting caught. I'll see you tomorrow, so stay out of trouble."

"Never gonna promise that."

He grinned as she left the room and rushed to find the other servants.

Maybe things were looking up. She'd never have wished the *Cleansing* on Medhi, but she could not ignore how her confidence grew knowing he was here. In him she had a staunch ally, an almost friend. And if there was anyone she wanted on her side in escaping this ship, it would be Medhi the Twice Dead.

11

A KEY OPPORTUNITY

B e careful, brother. I know better than to doubt your instincts, but you are treading in dangerous waters. No one would kill a Benefi-cary's brother lightly, but don't think someone won't try. I wish you would do your research here in the West sector and not at home. There is more I can do to protect you, but only here. I can't do much right now anywhere else. Our recent trading expeditions to the Maw have not come back as rich as we hoped. Had some pirate attacks, but our biggest hit came from a quintal ship. Came in faster than wind with the power of thunder in their hands. And then with what happened at the Iron Mountain prison... Be safe and don't add to my headache.

-Beneficiary Syeda Softbark, the one who needs a nap.

Medhi closed the curtains behind them. "We won't have a lot of time. I get maybe ten minutes before someone wonders where I am."

Gulamira gave quick introductions between Medhi and Isra and summarized their plans. Medhi stroked his scarf as he listened, a familiar gesture Gulamira had missed.

"Anyone else helping with this or just us three?" Medhi asked.

"Just us," Gulamira said. "It was just the two of us, but I'm glad to have you with us. Are any of your crew here?"

"Nah, they got sent elsewhere. Still, with just three, this'll be quite the trick to pull off." He leaned his head out of the opening to check for anyone coming and then turned to Isra. "Got means of escape?"

Isra crossed her arms and leaned against the crate behind her. "Working on it."

"So, no outside help, then?"

Isra shook her head.

Medhi frowned, but nodded. "Right. Well, that leaves us with stealing a lifeboat. Not ideal, but we can sneak food and water onto one of them and leave by night. You'll have to figure a way to get me out of my cage without alerting a whole mess of people."

"Can't we get him servant clothes like you did me?" Gulamira asked, looking at Isra.

"Wouldn't work, Amira," Medhi said. "People already know my face too well."

Gulamira didn't doubt this. He had a distinct wildness about him, but she guessed his scarf would be the greater reason for recognition. Regardless, if they couldn't pass him off as a servant, they would need a plan to get him out.

"There's got to be keys we can get somewhere," Gulamira said. Tatzon servants didn't go to the third or fourth decks, where they kept the human crew for the night, so Isra would have to be the one to get Medhi out.

"Keep in mind that when you break me out, I'll probably have a few of the crew in the same cage as me," Medhi said. "Occasionally I'm put in my own. If I'm on my own, great, otherwise we're escaping with a few others."

Isra dropped a hand to the crate and made circular motions along the wood. She didn't look pleased with adding more people to the escape. Gulamira didn't want them to waste their few minutes together to argue about the escape portion, so she blurted, "We'll deal with that if it happens. What about Kamaria, the girl? Have you learned anything about where she is?"

Isra didn't blink. "Key first."

"We'll figure out the key. I just wanted to know—"

"Key first."

Gulamira's mouth pinched tight, and she so wished she could glare and smile at the same time. But she doubted the woman would budge, so she nodded. "Key's not with the Soulborn, so it has to be with the captains. But I didn't look around their room yet."

"Doubt you could," Medhi said. "If you're looking to scrounge inside there, you'll have to sneak in. Never seen a servant go in before. They always take their meals outside."

"When would be a good time to go in? At night?"

"They'll be sleeping, so maybe but you'd have to be real quiet. No, a good time would be during the day when they're on deck, gives you time to look around inside."

Gulamira cocked a brow. "And that'd be easy to do?"

Medhi smirked and glanced out the opening again. "Nothing easy about it. Crew is all over the place, so there are always a few guards. Though everyone gets distracted when someone's thrown over the side or when the captains are punishing someone." Medhi shrugged. "One quick distraction could get you in."

"Alright, let's say I get past the guard and into the cabin. That still doesn't help us. I can't be alone looking."

"There's a window?" Isra asked.

"The Soulborn have one in the back," Gulamira said. "I can only guess the captains do, too. Why?"

Isra moved to the back of the room and pulled some rope from an open crate.

"Rope? How'll that help?"

"Toss it out. I'll climb from below."

"From below?"

A nod.

Gulamira looked at Medhi, but he only shrugged. "Could work. There's windows all over."

Yes, windows were all over. Windows that could let just about anyone see a dangling rope behind the ship. By the Mountain, this was a terrible plan. But it was better than dying to Solitude. Maybe by the time they tried this, they would have a better idea.

"It's worth trying, but we need to be ready to escape before we attempt this, just in case." Gulamira turned to Isra, setting her gaze and smile onto her. "Which brings me back to Kamaria. Have you found her?"

Isra crossed her arms and stared back a moment. A good, long moment. "I'm close." She paused again before sighing and continuing, "Heard others talk of a Wailing Room. Likely she's there."

Medhi leaned toward them, his voice hushed. "Heard about that place. People go by and hear a lot of screaming and wailing and crying from beyond an iron door. Figured it was a story for the crew to tell each other."

"It's real," Isra said. "Hard getting access, but I'm close."

"Hate to end this," Medhi said, "but they'll be looking soon. We should go."

Isra nodded, and Gulamira didn't argue. They would have more time to plan if they weren't caught, so the three parted ways and went off to their individual duties.

Some days passed as the three's preparations went underway. Days of Gulamira eating leftover food, of her bowing her head before fat and crude men, of making deliberate steps to go unnoticed. She kept wanting to work the aftcastle, but after that initial time the guards only sent her with the majority of servants, since they didn't see the point of having three of us topside. After a week of serving the second deck, with only the occasional visitation with Medhi and Isra, she, along with some of the other women, found one male servant in their quarters, his body hanging a foot above the ground, a tight rope around his neck. No one batted an eye as they untied him and handed the body to the guards to throw overboard. While everyone had their thoughts of why he killed himself, Gulamira knew the truth: he'd experienced Hij and Kami's tortuous songs for too long.

Gulamira surprised, and relieved, the other servants when she volunteered to take up the empty position to serve the aftcastle. The guards seemed as confused, but shrugged and let it be.

Over the coming days, Medhi and Isra snuck plenty of supplies onto the lifeboat and, on one night, Isra informed Gulamira she was certain she found where they kept Kamaria.

"Really, where?" Gulamira had asked.

Isra only said, "Sixth deck, stern," and then left. Gulamira wasn't able to get more from that infuriating and quiet human. And so the days continued until their preparations were complete and it was time to act.

In some ways, as Gulamira ascended the stairs to the top deck, it felt like any other day. Humans worked hard keeping the ship sailing, tatzons lazed about with an eye on the humans, the captains oversaw everything, and Hij and Kami enjoyed their amusements. But Gulamira sensed a tension in the air and in her body. The sun shone, but she felt little warmth. Wind blew, but she heard little laughter in it. The sailors toiled and toiled, without a song in their mouths or defiance in their eyes. It was as if the world knew the danger she stepped towards, and it held its breath. Gulamira shook her head at herself, at how ridiculous she was being. She scanned the horizon and noted thick, black clouds collecting and moving toward them.

A storm.

Yes, that was all that she felt in the air. A storm brewing. That was all.

She stared. No telling when that storm would hit the *Cleansing*, but she guessed it would be sometime today, based on how the rest of the sailors rushed around the deck, securing everything. At the least, it wasn't the Dragon's Breath, for which she was grateful. She doubted even this ship could surive that storm.

Gulamira caught Mehdi's eye on her way to serve the Soulborn. He nodded to her, which gave her a strength she needed now. It would happen soon. She headed into Hij and Kami's room with her fellow black-shirt and endured the songs of these self-indulgent little bastards.

A sharp cry from outside was all she needed to know it was time.

"I'll see what's wrong," she said and before the Soulborn said anything, or even noticed, she hurried from the room to see the distraction Medhi caused. It was hard to tell how he'd done it, but she saw a guard dangling in the air with a rope around a leg. He screamed and shouted to be let down and sailors scrambled around the rigging to help the man, while the fellow guards laughed at the misfortune. Gulamira's smile sharpened at Medhi's ingenuity, but her eyes darted to the captains. Just as hoped, they left their post and rushed to put order back amidst the chaos, and likely punish whoever caused this mishap. Gulamira acted fast.

Beside the chest with the captains' table and chairs, Medhi had stowed the length of rope for her. She glanced over her shoulder, but no one looked her way just yet, though if either Soulborn came out, they would see her. Gulamira grabbed the rope and hurried to the captains' opening, though she paused just before it. Being caught was not the worst outcome of today. Being alone was. If she hurried inside and Isra didn't appear fast enough, if there was too much furniture separating Gulamira and the window, if the window was bolted shut… a dark memory surfaced, taking hold of her bones and locking them still. A memory of the whisper of Solitude.

The loud shouts behind drove her from the remembrance. Sailors had grabbed the guard and prepared to lower him. The distraction was done.

Gulamira took a breath, gripped the rope tight, and shoved herself into the room. She took no account of the room, no sweeping glance to assess what was inside. There was only the window in sight and she darted to it with all she had, feeling Solitude already crouching near her. Without a care for noise, she pushed her way past a large desk and grabbed at the window's latch, throwing open the wooden shutters. Light poured in, but she ignored it, tied off one end to the desk, and tossed the other end—the end laden with a heavy weight—out into the open air. Her eyes did not leave the end as it dropped below, ready for any open window to notice. But her mind could not comprehend the dangers of doing this, of her being in this room, of being caught or even of being killed. Not a single one of those thoughts could penetrate past the unbearable need for Solitude to stay away from her.

As the rope dangled below her, time slowed to a saunter, each breath a lifetime of torment.

A hand appeared out of a window far below, grabbing the rope. A head and a short body followed, and an intense release of tension left Gulamira in that moment. She let herself sit back on the sill while Isra climbed, though she dared not let her eyes leave Isra until the woman pulled herself up into the room alongside her.

Isra nodded to Gulamira without a word, massaged her arms, and glanced about. With breath coming back in large amounts, Gulamira, too, looked around. The room was larger than Hij and Kami's—though not as large as Gulamira expected—and where they had comfort and decor, this room had utility and practicality. Maps of Rajalend and the charted oceans covered the walls in between bookcases and a row of spears. Two desks sat in the room, one crowded with books and writing utensils, the other flushed with what looked like a series of reports alongside a small crate of black vials. The center of the room held a simple, yet elegantly carved dining table with plush cushions surrounding it. The table held another large map, this one only of the Dragon's Maw, and had various red lines and markings throughout, though not in a language Gulamira recognized. Perhaps the most ostentatious things in here were two large wardrobe closets.

Isra turned to Gulamira. "Search."

They moved as fast as they could without making much noise, but that was not a simple task. Contrary to what the room would suggest, and what their demeanors declared, these captains were not the most organized. Papers, trinkets, random shells, they were all shoved into the desk drawers without care or order—at least, if there was an order, a madman devised it. Some drawers even had random articles of clothing. The various foot chests were no better, each a disorganized, overstuffed mess that took away some of the captains' fearsome personas.

While Isra searched more diligently through each desk, Gulamira moved to the wardrobes. The first was as she expected now: a clothing disaster more thick and tangled than the deepest forests of Rajalend. Though, she found a rather hefty sum of ivories hidden beneath one pile. She paused at the sight of them, but sighed and passed on. Out here on the ocean, there were greater things than coin. Finding nothing else obvious in here, she went to the second wardrobe, opening it with a growing irritation at the blatant disorder of...

Gulamira pulled back, eyes not leaving the wardrobe's interior. "Isra. Over here."

The human joined her side and stared without offering a word. The wardrobe was empty and had no back. Instead, it opened into a small chamber lit by red-crystal, which cast a baleful glow over a shrine. Burnt out candles sat in a diamond shape around a metal construction, which comprised of six large discs surrounding another disc in a circle. It stood upright in the center of the room and Gulamira circled around it. Each plate-like disc connected to an adjacent one and all to the one in the center via metal wires. Though as Gulamira peered closer, she noted one corner of the circle had a gap, as if there had been a seventh disc once. Each disc had a unique symbol, though none of them resembled anything having to do with the Ethereal Tree. These weren't Rajal symbols, at the very least.

"Do you know what this is?" Gulamira asked, looking at Isra.

The woman frowned and shook her head.

Gulamira looked back at the shrine. *Why do the captains have this?* she thought.

"Key," Isra said and Gulamira nodded, backing out of the wardrobe. Whatever this was, it wasn't why they were here. Though, their thorough search hadn't found even a hint of the key yet.

Gulamira searched through a bookcase near the opening and heard people talking outside. She waved to Isra and paused. The voices grew louder. They grew nearer.

Gulamira spun to Isra. "Hide."

The woman was already untying the rope and latching the window shut. They ran into the shrine-wardrobe and closed the doors as the voices pulled the hide opening back and entered.

Gulamira's heart pounded in her throat and she wished it would be quieter. The wardrobe doors were solid, with the only slit being where they met, providing minimal sight into the room. But they could hear plenty.

"... I'm telling you, this is it," a female's voice said. "This is what they've been looking for."

"Would you stop your prattling?" This was Captain Juhk and Gulamira glimpsed him and Captain Yirig as they passed her view in the slit to sit at their desks. "Abioda, close that hide before someone hears us."

"Watch your tongue, Juhk," a man's voice said, presumably this Abioda. "Don't let this Rajal office make you forget your place." The hide shuffled and stopped flapping, but Juhk spoke quieter as he answered.

"You are right, forgive me."

"Oh, never mind all that!" the woman said, and this time she came into view and Gulamira realized who spoke down to the captains. Besides being bald, the long black robes and markings resembling interlocking rings created no doubt these were the ship surgeons who had examined Kamaria. Yet, didn't a captain outrank a surgeon?

"Look at this." The woman handed something Gulamira couldn't see to the captains.

"It looks just like the other vials you've shown us," Yirig said.

"Exactly! It is exactly like the other vials we gave you."

"Haz, talk slower. We don't do the research as you do."

Haz groaned, and Gulamira saw the second surgeon, Abioda, join her. He too was bald, with the same black robes, though his markings resembled jagged rocks. And there was another oddity about these two surgeons. They had two arms, yes, but both lacked priarms.

"Those original vials," Haz said, "were harvested from the subjects after they died. That's the only time you can find it in such a pure form. Except this girl. She's alive still. We pulled all of that just from her blood."

Gulamira straightened. Had she said *girl*? Were they talking about Kamaria?

There was a pause. "Abioda, what do you think?" Yirig asked.

"I think we shouldn't be hasty about this. Haz is not typically wrong about things, but—"

"I'm never wrong! Ugh, you men. Listen, Solitude hasn't even affected the girl yet. We've tested her since Archoz and she doesn't even have an eye twitch. This is the key! This is what we've been looking for. I'm telling you, she's a shard. This girl could bring back the Isolated."

Gulamira tried to get a look at the captains, but they were beyond what the slit could show. Isra grabbed her arm and in the red light gave her a warning look to be still. Gulamira took her arm back but nodded. Her curiosity was not worth being discovered.

"If you're wrong about this," Juhk said.

"I'm not."

"Fine. What do you need?"

Abioda piped in. "Guards and a fast wind, above all else. We need to move her to a faster ship as soon as possible."

"If she is, as you suspect," Yirig said. "We can post Hij and Kami to protect her."

Haz groaned again. "I'd rather those Rajal pets not come anywhere near our deck."

"I, too, am against it," Abioda said. "It's bad enough they know about the priest. They've not been initiated. Their loyalties lie with Rajalend, not with us."

"Give us regular guards. She is worth more than whatever cargo they look after."

"The Soulborn are loyal as long as they believe we serve the Oligarchs," Juhk said. "They'll do just fine. Besides, if you are right, we want as few people to know about her as possible. There's no doubt the Nightmare would search for her if he knew of her existence."

The room became eerily quiet and still at the mention of "Nightmare". The surgeons in view were still, and Gulamira couldn't determine their expressions. But she *felt* something shift in the air, as though everything became heavier in her chest. As if the Abyssal had manifested before them to claim their souls. Only, Gulamira somehow knew that if they had the choice, these captains and these surgeons would rather face the Abyssal than this Nightmare.

"Just be sure to find us a ship soon," Abioda said as he and Haz went toward the opening. "This is the breakthrough we needed."

The surgeons left, and the captains were silent for a moment or two. Then one appeared in front of the wardrobe doors. Gulamira fought back a yelp and slid deeper into the chamber with Isra, whose hand hovered over one of her tattoos.

The captain did not open the door. However, he stood facing it as he murmured. "It's hard to believe, Yirig. To think... to think that we could bring back the Isolated..."

"A day at a time. Day at a time. There are plenty of duties to attend to. We can let ourselves dream later."

Juhk nodded, though Gulamira could only see the dark outline of his form. After another silent moment, Juhk left the wardrobe and the two captains returned to oversee the crew.

Half a moment passed before Gulamira grabbed Isra. "It's Kamaria. They were talking about Kamaria, I know it."

Isra pulled herself from the grip and gingerly pushed the doors open. Gulamira leaned against the wall, trying to process what she'd overheard. She wasn't clear on what most of it meant, but what she did grasp was this: they were taking Kamaria's blood, which meant they were cutting her.

"We can't wait any longer," Gulamira said. "We have to get her out today. Key or no key, if they are killing her, then we must save her. The deal is off if she's dead and—"

"Agreed."

"—I won't hesitate to... wait, what?"

Isra took the rope and tied it off to the desk once again. "We save her today."

Gulamira stared, sound coming out of her mouth but no words. Isra pointed at the wardrobe, at the still open doors, and tossed the rope out the window. Gulamira closed the wardrobe and approached the woman.

"Wait, you serious?"

A nod. "Deal was saving her alive. We move now." Isra turned fast to Gulamira. "Grab Medhi. Cause a loud commotion and head to the hold. Draw guards if you can. I'll grab the girl and meet you there."

Gulamira could hardly believe it. In fact, something was off about this. "You're going to ignore the key to save her?"

"Key is around the captain's neck." Isra grabbed hold of the rope and looked out toward the water. "I learned what I needed. We'll grab it at night and then escape."

Gulamira wasn't sure how Isra had seen that, though given they hadn't found it anywhere else, it made sense. There was still something about Isra's quickness to agree that seemed strange, but the image of Kamaria in Solitude drove all other thoughts from her mind. She was so close to saving this girl and she would not lose this chance. "Fine, then let's do this." She sidled up next to Isra and readied beside the window. "I'll come after you."

Isra raised a brow and nodded toward the opening.

"No, I'm not going out there," Gulamira said. "Everyone is there and will see me. I'll go to the fourth deck and figure out a way to cause some kind of distraction for you."

Isra narrowed her eyes, but nodded and climbed out of the window and down the rope. Gulamira did not wait long. She wished they could have hidden the rope or something, but after they rescued Kamaria, guards would search for them, regardless. And with Soulborn on board... well, Isra wouldn't get her idol before they left. But Gulamira kept this to herself and climbed after. No point in turning Isra away from them now. Kamaria was all that mattered right now.

Isra passed the window she'd used earlier and descended to the very bottom of the rope, forcing open a window into the fifth deck. Gulamira waved to her and headed in through her window and, without pausing, she hurried into the hall and toward any room with people. The fourth deck held most of the guards' sleeping quarters and she found groups sleeping away down here.

She took comfort that even asleep, they kept Solitude away as she moved through their hanging, balled up bodies. There wasn't as much activity on this deck as the upper decks, but she ran into human black-shirts working various jobs and all gave her curious looks. Tatzon servants rarely made it down here. Ignoring them, she decided she'd make her way back to the top deck and grab Medhi. She didn't have any ideas of what kind of commotion to cause, but when the idea came, she wanted him by her side.

Gulamira was wondering how long it would take Isra to find Kamaria when she heard the shouting. Before she reached the stairs to the upper deck, a few guards clambered down, pushing servants aside and rousing the sleeping guards.

"Abyss take you," a sleeper said.

One guard who roused others, his face quite serious, ignored the curses and shouted, "Everyone up and at it! Captains' orders."

"What time's it?"

"Time for you to shut it and listen. Just found a pinnace alongside the *Cleansing*."

"A pinnace?" another asked. "What're you meaning?"

"We've intruders, you idiots. Someone's snuck on here and the Soulborn are doing a search."

The words struck the waking guards as it did Gulamira. Intruders. But how? Why?

"Captains gave us orders," the loud one continued. "We're locking up all the crew and black-shirts. Fewer bodies for the Soulborn to check. All hands to it!" He turned with his Partner and saw Gulamira, who'd failed to move since the announcements began. "What're you doing down here? Hey, grab her and put her back in their rooms."

A pair of guards grabbed her, and she did not resist. The ship was going on lock down, it seemed, so there would be no moving about now. Medhi would already be with guards, heading to his cages, so all she had to do was wait with other servants until this passed by. Stay put and stay out of this.

Except she couldn't. This was the perfect distraction. These intruders, whoever they were, gave her what she needed. Isra was saving Kamaria today, which meant they needed to escape today. She could not afford to stay locked up. She could not afford a single wasted moment.

Her eyes went down the hall, past the waking guards, to stairs heading deeper into the ship. She would need to run. She would need to hide. These guards needed to lose total sight of her.

She needed to risk Solitude.

This thought, this single thought, grabbed onto her with a greater paralysis than she'd expected. The thought gave the guards a simple time pulling her to the stairs heading up. This thought reminded her of what it did to her, a dark black stain on her soul.

Somehow, by some miracle, a song rose into her throat, one that pushed back the memory, solidified her smile, and instilled courage into her. A song to motivate her legs and give them the will to move. And they did.

She tore herself from the guards' grips and rushed away and down the hall.

"What? She's bolted."

"Don't stand and stare, catch her!"

Gulamira didn't look back to see who chased her. She didn't look for any stair heading up. She only ran and ran. Down stairs, past guards and random servants, back through empty halls and rooms, with those guards fast on her heels. She didn't know where she went or where she was going, but only knew to run as fast as her legs could take her. The shouts of the guards grew further from her, but the awaiting darkness cut this joy short once they were gone.

Solitude seemed to laugh at her panic as it stabbed into one of her legs. This malevolent force, this curse of the Abyss, whatever in damnation Solitude was, it seemed to feed off of the growing fear in her.

She ran as fast as she could with her growing limp. Down the hall, around the corner, though in the briefest of thoughts, in the recesses of her mind, she wished the guards would catch her and never let her go. In this moment, she forgot what she was doing and why she was running. Why was she doing this to herself? Solitude built, and yet she could have stopped it. Why did she run and keep this torment—

Gulamira ran head first into someone. Solitude stopped building, but she stumbled back, panting and wishing for anything that she'd found Isra. She looked up. And she saw a tall tatzon man staring at her.

He did not dress like the other guards. And he had four arms.

He was the intruder.

They looked at each other for a brief second. Then he grabbed her with two arms and covered her mouth with a third. Weakened by Solitude, she didn't even fight as he pulled her back into the room he'd just come out of.

"Got a problem, Nas," he said.

"Who's that?" a feminine voice asked behind him.

"Paralyze first, please!"

Something struck Gulamira's side and a sharp tingle shot through her body. And she couldn't move. The man let her down to the ground, but her body was frozen. She couldn't even move her eyes.

What in the Abyss just happened?

"Who's she?" the woman asked, though she was out of Gulamira's sight. Only the man stood over her.

"Long-lost cousin," he said. "Owe her a bit of money, and all that. Hey, don't give me that look. You ask a stupid question, it's my obligation to give you a stupid answer." He looked back at Gulamira. "She just ran right into me as I was leaving."

Gulamira tried to move again, tried to twist, turn, scream. But nothing. Her body refused her commands, ignored her pleas. The man loomed over her and she wondered if maybe she should have taken her chances with the guards.

"So," he said. "What are we gonna do with you?"

12

THE IRON HOLD

*M*y team just found that Argul and Ortu buy thousands of ivories
worth of crystal and ivory every year, yet we've no record of what
they do with it. It doesn't go to the army or the Temple. It just disappears.
And we're close to proving they are funneling funds away from Al'Rajak
to their own coffers. If it seems like there are fewer ordîns guarding the
streets these days, it's because we don't have the money to pay them! Now,
we just have to figure out where the money is going.

Also, could you tell me more about these fugitives from the Iron
Mountain? I'm confused why a clipped ordîn is considered a far greater
threat than the Red Sword.

-Raza, a giddy scholar with a mystery to solve.

As a girl, Gulamira had once dreamed that a monstrous beast
found her in an open field. She saw the monster, felt its presence,
and tried to run. But she didn't move. She exerted her full strength,
but her dream-self could not budge. She couldn't even scream as
the monster opened its black maw to eat her. At that point, she'd
woken up.

Right now, Gulamira felt the same as the dream. Now was like
then. Except, now had no waking.

The intruders, two from what she could tell, stood beyond her
sight. She only made them out with her peripheral vision, because
her eyes wouldn't move. Nothing would.

"Anyone else?" the woman asked. "Her Partner coming?"

"Didn't see anyone," the man said. "Heard shouts and that's it."

"She was running alone? What about Solitude?"

"Look, Nas, I didn't get the chance to ask for her life story just yet."

The woman huffed, and shadows flickered across the ceiling, the only sign of movement Gulamira could see from her angle. The shadows moved about the ceiling, in and out of her vision, taunting her with their freedom to move. And she just laid there on the floor, every muscle in her body ignoring her commands, though she still breathed. She wouldn't suffocate, at least, but as she tried to test her breath, tried to quicken and slow it, it too ignored her.

"I don't like this, Tsuran," Nas said. "The entire ship is on alert now."

"Well, it wasn't like we could just hide the boat. We lucked out getting even this far."

"Seems like we've run out of luck, then. What are we supposed to do now?"

The man stepped over to Gulamira, passing his hand through his hair. He sighed and glanced up. "I—wait, are you really doing figures? Now?"

"It helps me think. Shut up."

He smirked and whether it was because her panic and surprise had lessened or because the lighting was just right, Gulamira noticed his markings. Black crescents. Covering only his right side, from his face to his arms. Four arms, with a missing priarm.

And it all clicked together. The markings. The name. The lack of a priarm.

This was the man Kamaria had told her about. The man she'd been traveling with. These intruders... they were here for Kamaria.

Tsuran sighed and left Gulamira's unmovable vision. "We don't have time anymore. We just have to find her, fighting whoever gets in our way."

"In a ship this size? Maybe when they weren't hunting us, but now?"

"We can't do anything else. We have to find her before they find us."

Gulamira tried to move . Tried to call out. Tried with all her might to tell them she knew where Kamaria was. But her damn body wouldn't do anything helpful.

"Do you even know where to look?" Nas asked.

Gulamira did. She could take them to her. *Please, Exkel, let me move even a little*!

"If we get close to her, you can sense her," he said.

"Still can't sense energy without touch."

"Yeah, but didn't you do it once?"

"Sure, that once."

Gulamira's eyes stung from not blinking. The shadows widened as if to mock her. And there was this growing realization that this was how she'd die. They would leave her, Solitude would take her, and she wouldn't even scream about it. Some final breath for the High Priestess. She wondered if she'd shed a single tear.

"What about her?" Nas asked.

"What do you mean?"

"Maybe she knows."

"Well, I mean, maybe."

Gulamira thrashed in her mind while her body stayed useless. *Yes, I know! Please, oh fiery Breath, please!*

"I'm out of other ideas, Tsuran, and we're out of time, like you said."

Tsuran sighed and knelt by Gulamira. "Hey, here's the deal. We're going to let you move again. Just remember this: we're dangerous criminals, so don't do anything stupid."

Gulamira stared at the ceiling. As if she could do anything else.

The image of Nas, covered in some shadows, crouched next to her. "Was that necessary?"

He shrugged and grinned. "Have to lean into the persona."

Nas touched Gulamira, and her face relaxed. Her mouth closed and opened and she, finally, blinked. But when she tried to sit up, she still couldn't. "I can't... I can't move."

"I've kept the paralysis in your body," Nas said. "Just in case you had ideas of running away."

Tsuran gave a small clap. "Well, I didn't think of that. Sometimes I love what you can do."

"Anyway," Nas said, "listen, we're—"

"You're here for Kamaria," Gulamira said, moving her eyes to look at Tsuran. "I know where she is."

A stunned silence. She looked at Nas. "I've been trying to... to..."

The light of the lantern shone over half of Nas's face, but it was enough to reveal something unexpected. Gulamira had thought Nas was Tsuran's Partner, a shorter, thinner tatzon. But Nas was not that. She wasn't a tatzon. She wasn't even human.

Head full of bright white hair and skin of crimson red. Gulamira saw no wings, but there was no doubting this truth. Nas was an ordîn.

Tsuran grabbed Gulamira with three hands, and now Gulamira noticed his fourth arm was in a sling, not yet grown to the elbow. "You know Kamaria? How? Where is she?"

As best and as quickly as she could, Gulamira explained meeting Kamaria and them arriving on the *Cleansing* together, as well as her current attempt to rescue the girl. With every word, Gulamira rose a subtle song to her lips. She needed them to believe her, to trust her. A lower song would help that. A song that encouraged trust and dissuaded doubt.

"Isra, an ally here," Gulamira continued, "located Kamaria near the stern of the ship."

"Where?" Tsuran asked. "Which deck?"

"I—"

"Shh," Nas said, rising to the opening.

"Hear something?" Tsuran asked.

"No, it's more that I hear nothing. No one's hurried down here yet."

"It is a big ship."

"Yes, but I wonder..." Nas returned to Gulamira's side. "Are there possessors on this ship? Active ones?"

"There's at least two Lightless and two Soulborn who—"

"We've got to go." Nas touched Gulamira again and this time her entire body relaxed and she could move about again. She got to her feet and saw Tsuran running a hand through his hair, again.

"Soulborn?" he asked. "Icy Abyss..."

Nas turned to Gulamira. "What's your name?"

"Gulamira Con-None."

"I'm Nasna, the man there is Tsuran, though I guess you knew that. Listen, we're all Kamaria's got and you're our way to her." She gripped Gulamira's arm. "Please, lead well."

She did her best. She wasn't sure what deck they were on, but she headed for the stern, though it took her a moment to determine its direction. Her blind running earlier hadn't done her many favors. But they passed a room with an open window and, after a quick check, they dashed down the halls to the stern.

They heard guards ahead, so they ducked through side halls and hid in rooms while the guards passed on. Luckily, the Soulborn hadn't begun their search, or were just on the far end of the ship. Gulamira didn't like the idea of bumping into them.

She followed the winding halls, but they all ended at a solid wall. No rooms for storage or anything. Just a solid wall that did not follow the curvature of the ship. An intentional dead-end.

She led to the deck below and weaved their way toward stern, again. Yet, the halls ended once more with a solid wall. Irritated, they rushed down another flight of stairs, dodging past a single patrol of guards, and ran with all haste, but their run made an abrupt end. Gulamira puffed as she stared at the walled-off hall. Another dead-end.

"Have they walled off the whole stern?" Nasna asked.

"There's got to be a way in," Tsuran said. "Can we come in from underneath?"

Gulamira placed a hand on the wall. Isra had made it seem like she'd head straight to the holds after she grabbed Kamaria. "Maybe, I don't know."

"Well, we need to..." He trailed off. All their eyes saw it at the same time. From the stairs above, blue-white light streamed in, and Gulamira felt the barest touch of a song. The Soulborn were here.

Tsuran took charge, taking both her and Nasna by the arm and pulling them back into the hall, away from the dead-end. He leaned in. "Run as quiet as possible. I don't think they've finished searching the deck above." He then undid a pouch of leather at his hip and faint red-light glowed forth. Gulamira caught her breath. This man... he had red-crystal. Enough to be worth a small fortune.

She pushed it from her mind and followed his lead. Even once the spirit light was no longer in view, he had them creep toward the bow, taking the third stairwell they found. They did not speak, Gulamira hardly breathed. That had been too close. They couldn't afford Soulborn catching them... except, those Soulborn had been close to stern, close to where Isra was. Sure, they had snuck away, but Isra and Kamaria might not be as lucky.

Gulamira slowed. The ship was massive. Massive even for Soulborn. If she somehow drew them to the bow to search, she could give Isra the clear path she needed. All they needed was time.

She removed a lantern and took in a breath. Nasna glanced back and cocked a brow. "What are you doing?"

"Giving us time." Gulamira hefted the lantern into the far wall, and it shattered with thick, oily fire. She unhooked the next lantern as well, but Tsuran grabbed her arm.

"What in the Abyss are you doing? You trying to get us caught?"

"I'm trying to keep Isra and Kamaria from being found." He did not let go of her, so she provided him with her calmest smile and an even softer song. "Listen, people are looking for us, not her. With a little extra fire, we can keep it that way."

Black smoke rose from where the broken lantern burned. Not enough flame to do a lot of damage, but maybe enough to draw guards and Soulborn. She wasn't sure if her lower songs would affect the spirits while Hij and Kami possessed them, since her training had ended before she learned to affect possessions. However, it was a worthwhile gamble.

Tsuran did not let go, but looked between her and the fire, as if he had half a mind to throw her into it. Another lantern flew and smashed into the other. Gulamira and Tsuran turned to Nasna, who walked up and flicked Tsuran's ear.

"Just do it, Tsu," she said. "We can't fight them all together."

"Right, and where are we supposed to go?" he asked, releasing Gulamira. "Huh? We can't hide from Soulborn! Why run if we can't hide?"

"There's a hold below," Gulamira said. "Completely made of metal. We could hide there."

Nasna nodded. "That would work. At least for a few minutes while we wait for everyone to attend to the fires."

"There is a problem, though."

Tsuran laughed. "Of course there is."

"That hold has Remnants inside to protect the cargo."

"Ha, that's it?" Tsuran shook his head, still facing the fire, but then sighed and nodded. "Fine. I'm not stupid, I get it. Let's head there. I hate this, though."

His nonchalance about the Remnants struck Gulamira. Maybe he hadn't heard her. "There are Remnants in the hold. We'll have to be careful."

Nasna took the lantern from Gulamira and threw it. "We heard. Don't worry, we can handle a few Remnants. Just take us there."

Gulamira wasn't sure what to think about their confidence, but the hold had been her idea. Isra had said she'd go there, though Gulamira wasn't sure that would be the safest option right now.

She shook herself. Too many thoughts and the smoke was growing. They descended several flights of stairs and passed through various halls on their way to the hold. The middle decks were quiet as they normally were, but the lower they went, the stronger the oppressive memories became. It was hard to tell if the sounds of crying and constant swib brushing were real or just in her head. The smell, at least, was real. The deeper they descended, the stronger the musk of oil, the stench of filth, the festering of still water and stiller bodies.

But she did not let the darkness take her. Not this time. She grabbed another lantern and tossed it into a room further to the bow, and then another lantern to a random hall. When Tsuran and Nasna saw what she was doing, they joined in, creating a line of open fires for the guards and possessors to deal with.

They heard shouting with every deck they descended. The guards down here lagged to fulfill their orders to lock up the slaves. As they snuck past one group, Gulamira heard a couple guards rush in, mentioning a fire loose on some decks above. After cursing, they left their post and headed to Gulamira's distraction. This opened the way past the narrowest halls and to the stairs leading to the holds.

Nasna went down first, and Tsuran held back, staring off to stern, a hand firm on the red-crystal on his belt. Gulamira worried he'd bolt away from them, but he turned and marched past her.

Gulamira had not been in the hold before, but their destination stood out even as they descended the stairs. They went straight to the wall of iron, stepping into the large alcove and up to the metal door. Nasna, her breathing more haggard than the rest, grabbed hold of the door and glanced back. "Tsuran, statue ready?"

He nodded. "Always."

She swung the door open, and a loud metallic click rang through the hold. Before anyone could move, and before Gulamira could yell, an iron gate crashed behind them, locking them in the alcove. Grinding metals followed, drawing their attention upward to the ceiling, which slid open, and something hissed from the shadows within.

Tsuran grabbed Gulamira and threw her toward the door. "Inside! Quick!"

Nasna shut the door behind them, though there was nothing to lock it. The door would not halt the Remnant for long.

Darkness did not blanket the hold as Gulamira expected. Instead, it had a white glow from the many lightstones embedded in this massive room's ceiling. The perpetual light poured onto the large cages of cargo stored here, stretching for hundreds of feet, but Gulamira looked past them to the other grinding metals in the room. Panels along the walls slid open and a low gurgling moan picked up in various parts of the hold.

The Remnants were unleashed.

"Nas, stick with her," Tsuran said as he removed the red-crystal from his belt. "I'll try to keep them off you."

The groans headed in their direction. The Remnant pounded against the door behind. Gulamira quickened away from there, and Nasna followed.

"Don't go far, Tsuran," Nasna said, flexing her open hands. "There might be Guardian Remnants around."

"You're going to fight them?" Gulamira asked.

Tsuran looked back and winked. "Don't worry. We do this all the time."

"Fight Remnants?"

"Well, maybe not that exactly." The sound of a shattering crate echoed through the metal chamber. "More the doing stupid stuff part."

The groaning grew louder. Another smashed crate. A form appeared.

Gulamira froze. The thing stumbled out from behind a tall stack of crates and chests. Twisting vines made up its body and had four pulsating branches for arms, all covered in spines and thorns that dripped with some sizzling green substance. Its face, if it could be called that, was nothing more than three black holes in a sheet of bark, with that green slime dripping from them like tree sap. It looked at them and, though it lacked eyes, she felt the destructive hunger in that forsaken face.

A Remnant. Once a tatzon, a person, until their magic had consumed them. And this was all that remained: a soulless husk that sought to destroy all it once loved and lived for.

Another loud moaning came from the other side and two more Remnants just like the first came out. From the center, another came. And another. Though this last one looked different. Its body looked like solid wood, no vines or branches, and its face looked like a person's face, but without emotion, like a sculpture.

Nasna cursed. "We've got four Builders, a Guardian, and whatever's in the alcove."

Tsuran tossed his red-crystal lightly in the air and breathed out. "Hate to do this, but—"

"I'll get the Guardian," Nasna said.

"Thanks."

"What are Partners for?" She turned to Gulamira and pointed to one wall the Remnants came out of. "We'll make a path for you that way. Hide in one of those chambers."

"Right." Gulamira paused, realizing what Nasna had just said. *Partners?*

"Go!" Tsuran threw his red-crystal at one approaching Remnant. Then he disappeared and as soon as he did, his red-crystal grew, becoming as tall and as large as Gulamira and... it was a statue. A red-crystal statue resembling a tatzon with four arms. Right. Kamaria had said that Tsuran was a Guardian.

The statue, Tsuran inside it, dove at the Remnant with arms like scythes. The Remnant collided with the Guardian and Nasna shoved Gulamira forward.

"Go." Nasna propelled herself past Tsuran and sprinted straight for the Guardian Remnant. Nasna carried no weapon of any kind, yet she sped forward without a hint of hesitation. The rest of the Remnants reacted fast, attacking with loud screeches and sharp vines. The door behind burst open and the final Remnant joined. Thick fur covered it, its three hands more like wolf's claws, and it crouched like a Rajal cat. A Wrangler Remnant.

Gulamira wasted no more time gawking. She ran through the path Tsuran had created for her. Remnants screeched behind her, and, without meaning to, a song escaped her mouth. She did not know if spirit songs worked on Remnants, but she did not care because it rose from her like an instinctive reflex.

The Remnants did not slow at her song. Instead, they seemed infuriated. They hissed louder and louder and not a few of their viny heads twisted her way. Tsuran sliced through one Remnant, severing off entire arms, and it retaliated with a thick spit of green mucus. Nasna also battled with the Guardian Remnant, and Gulamira couldn't help but stare. The ordîn struck with her palms, and each hit caused the Remnant to be still, as if stunned. But the emotionless creature broke from it and struck back. Nasna dodged each attack, but it seemed she couldn't paralyze them as she had done with Gulamira. She had better have other tricks at her disposal.

Gulamira aimed for the nearest hole in the wall and clamped her songs shut. They were all she could offer to a fight, and all they did was enrage these monsters.

Another screech echoed around the room, one like a tormented beast. The Wrangler Remnant.

"Tsuran!" Nasna cried out.

"Coming," he said, and a gurgling cry followed. Gulamira looked back. Tsuran, with remarkable speed, hastened away from the

Remnant he'd fought, the one he'd slain, and evaded the grasp of the others that swarmed him.

Exkel's Hearth. He'd killed a—

Crates exploded around her as a Remnant burst through. It screeched at her and ran at her, hollow eyes set on destruction. Gulamira needed no one to tell her what to do.

She raced away.

The Remnant chased.

Gulamira rushed headlong through the maze of cages, trying to lose the Remnant, but it drew ever closer with its loud hisses. She ran as fast as she could, but the creature was never far behind.

She saw the surrounding cages, and a desperate thought occurred to her. If she could get inside one of these, maybe that would prevent the Remnant from getting her. They were large, with enough crates to hide behind. It was a tremendous risk, but the Remnant's scream behind decided for her.

She pulled on a cage door, but it didn't budge. She tried another, then another, and another, all with the same result. Locked. She pressed on, not stopping for more than a moment as the thorned monstrosity prowled after her, never leaving sight of her. Tsuran and Nasna were nowhere to be seen, somewhere on the other side of all these cages and crates, so she had no choice but to keep moving whilst the Remnant jerked its way closer and closer to her, a bubbling hiss pouring from its vacant face. If she didn't know better, she'd have thought the Remnant sang its own song, since its very presence, its very proximity, drew strength from her and distracted her mind. But there was no song. This was just a natural reaction to being so close to the mythical nightmare.

Gulamira slammed into a cage, holding herself up as she panted. The Remnant was not far as it shot a series of barbs at her, all of which missed, though not by as much as Gulamira liked. She pulled herself to the side and caught sight of one cage with a large latch instead of a lock. She threw herself toward the cage, opening the door, and shutting it closed behind. There were a few stacks of crates and chests in here to hide behind, but the Remnant saw her and it sped toward the cage with green fumes steaming. Gulamira ducked behind the crates and opened the chests near her. No telling if the Remnant could open doors or not, but Gulamira was trapped if she didn't do something.

Thorns thudded into the crates and bounced off the metal bars. The creature hissed as it rammed into the cage door, its viny arms reaching through, trying to grab at her. It wasn't long enough and so rammed into the door again, then backed up and moved to the side of the cage where she was. The chest she searched through had nothing useful, so she rolled away from the Remnant's arms and pried open a second chest.

The contents drew her attention. Weapons. Dirks, short hatchets, and on top, with a slight glow coming off it, was Medhi's dagger.

The Remnant screeched to the side of her, slamming its arms through the cage bars. She screamed and pushed away, dodging those sharp wooden fingers. The monster backed up to ram again and Gulamira rushed in, grabbed the dagger, and dove to the side. She spun up as vines sprouted from the Remnant's back and stretched toward her. Dagger gripped tight, she struck at the vines and the Remnant reacted, violently pulling back.

Vines erupted at her, bending the bars, smashing crates, gripping her legs. Gulamira screamed and slashed to free herself, each slice driving an unbearable scream from the monster.

She cut free and hurried to the door. This cage was not as protective as she'd hoped.

The Remnant was there in an instant, vines grabbing the door and bending it off the hinges. That hollow face stared at Gulamira and green vapors fled those empty sockets. The Remnant tossed the door aside and all its vines rose to strike. And Gulamira's hand wavered, then lowered, unable to hold up any longer against this foe. She was not a fighter. She was a slave, a failed priestess. And so she would die.

The Remnant stopped and turned its attention. Gulamira looked too and saw Nasna rushing them, arms stretched out to the side, eyes set on the Remnant. Gulamira did not understand, but the Remnant ignored the easy prey and spun to attack Nasna. Its body unraveled into a dozen thorny vines that launched at Nasna like arrows.

And Nasna evaded every strike. She moved as though in a dance, an elegant and determined dance. In some ways, she reminded Gulamira of a stream of water as she moved through and around the attacks. Liquid, graceful, untouchable. There was no wasted movement, no lost ground. With every strike of the Remnant, Nasna weaved her way ever closer to her foe and, as Gulamira looked into Nasna's eyes, she realized something. She saw why the Remnant had turned to fight. Because, in this one moment, Gulamira saw the dynamics of the fight shift from every story about these nightmares.

In this moment, Nasna was the hunter and the Remnant her prey.

She reached the Remnant and slammed a hand into its chest of vines.

The entire creature froze instantly.

The arms twitched.

"No, don't fight it," Nasna said in a strained voice. "Please. Please don't."

The arms twitched more, and the head twisted to the side.

Nasna, hand still on its chest, hung her head. "I'm sorry."

The creature exploded.

13

THE WAILING ROOM

A BANDON YOUR QUEST OR ABANDON YOUR LIFE.
   -From a note found on the door of Raza Softbark. A red-stained dagger pinned it firm.

A few guards, cudgels at the ready, hurried past Isra up the stairs to rally with the rest of the crew. She pressed herself against the wall to stay out of their way, and they paid her no mind. Like the others she'd run into on her way here, they looked distracted. The same thought buzzed between them all: who in their right mind would try to sneak onto the *Cleansing*?

A curious thought. Even Isra wondered. However, she had more important things to worry about right now. There was a girl she needed to grab. A girl who was quite important to these people.

Perhaps important enough that they'd trade the idol of Mirr to ensure her safety.

It wasn't an ideal plan, but Isra needed to think on her feet right now, otherwise she'd lose any opportunity to get that idol. With Gulamira headed toward the hold, she'd serve a perfect distraction for the guards, and maybe in the meantime they'd kill her and remove that liability from Isra. Couldn't have Gulamira telling what she knew, after all. A shame, though. She was an interesting tatzon. But Isra wasn't about to let the life of one tatzon ruin the lives of her entire people.

She headed down the stairs into a circular room smaller than others she'd found on the ship. There was a second stairwell leading down and a short corridor lit with a couple of lanterns. Behind her was a solid wooden wall, cutting off this part of the deck from the rest. She didn't see anyone else around, but she heard plenty.

Down the corridor, at the farthest end, loud screeches and moans echoed from behind an iron door. Every other room in the corridor had curtained openings. This last was a human-styled door. The girl would be there. Inside that room of tormented noises.

The Wailing Room.

Isra crept to the door, checking the openings as she went. They were well furnished living quarters, better than any the regular crew had access to. No one remained inside any of them, so she went straight for the door and checked it. It had no lock of any kind and opened with ease, which revealed just how much noise it dampened. The cacophony of screams and groans and wails hurt her ears a bit, but she pressed forward.

The Wailing Room was not what she expected. Metal covered the room. The walls, floor, ceiling, iron covered everything, and this made the room colder than the rest of the ship. Three lightstones the size of her fist hung from the ceiling, giving off a constant, unwavering white light. Closest to her were cabinets and shelves, all filled with vials, small boxes, and tools for surgery—or perhaps, dissection. Below one set of shelves, Isra saw a worktable with a strange set of equipment.

The center of the worktable resembled a brazier, and it even had some cold coals inside. On either side of it, there were two iron pots and a half dozen glass vials in various bulbous shapes. Some resembled mushrooms, others tear drops, and a few had long necks that curved to the side. Her father had shown her equipment similar to this once long ago, tools for alchemical processes. But... these were Sefaran devices from the quintal lands. Tatzons did not use them, it was forbidden and deemed from the Abyssal itself. Why did these surgeons have them?

Several tables lined the center of the room, and iron doors filled the walls. Red blood smeared the tables and the collection of knives hanging from their sides. The air had a sharp, sour taste, like fruit fermented wrong. And a sharp tingle sped through her back. Whatever these tatzons were doing here, it was not good in the slightest, she knew that much. Isra did not like being in here. These tatzons were using human doors and Sefaran technology. She didn't know why, but this unnerved Isra more than the wailing, and she rushed to the other doors in the room. The sooner she found the girl, the sooner she could leave.

Each door had a parchment with a brief description of who was inside. She scanned over them as she passed by each. Isra expected several humans of varying ages, but there was not a single human among them.

Male, age 35, two arms, entered on the ninth day of Everpine. Solitude entered after three minutes, eighteen seconds. Speaking with subject through door did not reduce Solitude.

Female, age 94, three arms, Builder, entered on the twelfth day of Everpine. Solitude entered after twelve minutes, thirty-two seconds. Mentioning Partner once reduced rate of Solitude for one minute, three seconds.

Isra shook her head. These were all tatzons. Ranging in age, in arms, and sex. Tatzons of all kinds, even active possessors and—Isra was sure—a couple of Remnants, all subjected to Solitude.

This wasn't good. Lady above, what had Isra's step-mom gotten her into this time? One of these days, Isra needed to kill that woman.

The description Isra looked for hung on the door at the farthest end.

Female, age 8, growing a second arm, claimed to be Guardian, entered on the first day of Everpine. Solitude entered after...

The description ended. Isra cocked a brow. This girl had been here longer than some of these other experiments, yet they didn't have a full description yet? Well, she was special to them for whatever reason. Maybe they hadn't subjected her to Solitude yet.

A large padlock kept the door secure. Isra smirked. Simple enough to take care of. She just needed a circle big enough to encompass the lock.

She tapped one of her circle tattoos and her pouch of wooden discs materialized. Many of the discs had runes of unknown meaning in the center of the circles, though after so much time she'd forgotten what most of these had inside. But she only needed the largest one she had. She tapped the circle, Released and tossed aside the lock that had been inside, rested the new lock on the disc, and Caught it.

She stepped back and opened the door. It revealed an iron-laden room that ran back another ten feet to a second door. Isra didn't see anyone inside, but she didn't enter right away. She turned back and found this crate filled with vials and heavy pitchers. She pushed this against the open door, ensuring it wouldn't slam shut behind her. Sure, she had the lock, but doors weren't to be trusted. Especially ones used by tatzons.

She walked in slowly, one eye on the door behind her. The chamber was dark and the only light came from the lightstones in the main room. The door on the other side of the square chamber had little keeping it shut. Only a bolt lock, which was more for keeping people in than out. Still having an eye on the door behind, she undid the bolt and pulled the door open. Dim light filled a cramped space. There was barely enough room for a full grown tatzon to hang from a sleeping bar in here, or even lie down if desperate. And there were no guards. Only a single tatzon girl, glaring at her.

The girl sat cross-legged, leaning against the back of the room. She'd pulled her hair back into a braid and she wore a single rough tunic, which the surgeons must've given her since everyone else sent down this hatch had been naked.

Otherwise, the girl looked... well, fine was a strong word, but she didn't look dead. Given all the horror stories tatzons had told Isra over the years about Solitude, she had expected the girl to be near death at this point. Either tatzons exaggerated or these surgeons were doing something else than subjecting her to Solitude. Though they left her by herself in a small chamber.

"Who are you?" the girl asked.

The kid didn't seem too scared. "Isra."

"You're not those... men... what do you want?"

Well, she wanted to kidnap the kid and use her as leverage. "Here to save you."

The girl perked up at this, but didn't get up.

"Gulamira sent me," Isra said.

"The woman who smiles a lot?"

A nod.

The girl appeared more comforted, but still wasn't standing. Maybe she couldn't. Perhaps Solitude was doing more than Isra thought.

"Can you stand?" Isra asked.

"Yes."

"Let's go."

Isra headed to the second door and felt better being next to it. Even with the crate beside it, something in her kept thinking it'd shut on its own.

"You're a human, right?"

Isra glanced back. The girl was standing, but not leaving. "Yes."

The girl held her undeveloped arm against her chest, looking between Isra and the far door leading to the corridor. And the brat still wasn't moving.

Isra sighed. "Come or stay. Choose."

That seemed to do it. The girl left the small space and joined her in the room.

Now, where were they supposed to go? The hold was not close and there was no way she'd get far towing a tatzon around with her. Though there was a room full of food two decks below. It wasn't ideal, but it'd be a start at least.

Isra stopped as she walked past the bloody tables and looked down. The girl had grabbed Isra's hand and stared at the tables, making Isra wonder how much of that blood was the girl's.

But that seven-fingered prihand of hers felt so weird, and there was no way Isra would hold that for any length of time. She took her hand back.

"No holding," she said and went to the door, but paused and sighed. "Stop."

She turned back to the furthest table where her disc pouch sat. Isra forgot this pouch far too many times. It was too easy to forget it wasn't in her arm.

She tapped the circle on her palm and Released her ivory stylus. This elicited a gasp from the girl.

"How'd you do that?"

Isra shrugged and drew a circle on the table, but the scratching pierced the air, and her ears, like a coiled viper beast. The other occupants had quieted some, so this piercing sound hurt all the more. And, damn it all, it made her ruin the circle.

"Why'd you do that?" the girl asked, rubbing her ears against her shoulders. "Aren't we leaving?"

Isra glanced around. Most of the room, floor included, was metal. There were the crates, but they were made with slotted planks and there were gaps between them. She wouldn't be able to create a continuous circle. Ah, shrivel this. She'd just take it outside the room and do it. It'd be more visible on wood, but at least wood didn't scream in her ears whenever she carved into it.

"Alright," she said, pushing the kid along. "We're leav—"

The door slid open. Two surgeons entered.

"And that's all I was saying about—" the male surgeon stopped. The two surgeons stared at Isra and then to the girl. The two guards behind them also gaped.

Icy Abyss...

Isra threw the girl behind her and slammed a hand on her forearm, Releasing her cutlass.

All the tatzons grew paler at the sight of her using magic. One surgeon stared at the cutlass and then at Isra. "What in the Lost's name are you?"

The two guards pushed past him with their own swords, which were unexpected. These had to be the first swords she'd seen on guards.

"Behind us!" one guard said, though neither looked confident confronting her. A human with magic was a bed-time story told to scare tatzon children so they wouldn't run away into the Rajalend woods.

Isra grabbed a nearby red-clay pitcher and threw it at the advancing guards. It shattered against one, bringing up his defense as he paused. She dove in.

The other guard, the first's Partner, blocked her strike. He returned with his own. She jumped back and grabbed another pitcher. Something sloshed inside. And it smelled pretty foul.

She threw it, but the guard knocked it aside with his blade. The contents splattered around them.

The two guards advanced on her. That was no good. Tables and cabinets crowded the room, and she needed space to maneuver. She ducked underneath a table and jumped out on the other side.

"Get her!" one surgeon said. "Don't let that human escape!"

The guards rounded the table.

Isra kept moving, keeping them from flanking her. She slashed out, then sidestepped, always keeping one between her and the other. They tried to split further apart. When they did, she dove over a table, forcing them to follow again.

One came around and she engaged with him. They weren't masters, but they could hold a sword. What they lacked in skill, they made up for with coordinated movements. Tatzons couldn't go anywhere without their special Partner, but there were benefits to having someone who could, for all practicalities, read your mind.

She ducked underneath one swipe and swung to retaliate. The guard's Partner pulled him back and her blade whistled past.

She was getting nowhere and had no time. She had to kill these four, and fast. Not only had they caught her, they saw her use magic and she couldn't allow anyone to live who knew that. There had to be something in here that could give her an edge. Even a slight one.

The two guards charged her, keeping the right distance to prevent her maneuvering between them. She kicked a chair at them and rushed around a table. One guard tripped over the chair, but the other kept after her.

She ran into the counter, and glass vials clinked against each other. One vial had some black liquid in it.

The nearest guard ran at her, sword raised. She grabbed the vial and threw it. It smashed against his head and the black contents splattered over his face. He shouted and screamed as the liquid blinded him. A bubbling sizzle hissed from the liquid and Isra smelled burning flesh.

He stumbled back, trying to wipe the substance from his eyes, but whatever this black liquid was, it did far more than burn him. He screamed as bulbous growths expanded from the side of his face. Growths that screamed on their own. Growths that resembled another face.

The guard's Partner shouted, sharing in his agony. Isra paused as she took in this horrific image. She had to put this poor creature out of his—and Isra's—misery. She rushed in and cut through his chest. He grunted and swung with his blade. She parried and cut again, this time hitting his neck. Blood ran from his wound. He took a step, stumbled, tried to keep himself up on the table, and collapsed onto the ground.

The second guard stood still, near frozen, looking between her and his now dead Partner.

"Quick, grab her," one surgeon said.

Isra chanced a quick glance. The two surgeons had cornered the girl, who was waving some metal tongs at them. They pounced on her.

"You Unhallowed bitch!" The second guard screamed and charged Isra, slashing her cutlass aside and ramming a shoulder into her. The man battered her into the wall. Isra dropped her sword.

He threw his shoulder back into her. Isra groaned.

"Foul human! Your evil magic made him a monster," the guard said, tears filling his eyes. He gripped her arm and spun, trying to toss her onto a table. But this man was no Colossal of a tatzon, so she let her legs go limp and she dropped to the floor.

The motion threw him off. She kicked at his knee, hard. He yelled and stumbled back.

She scrambled toward her sword. It was on the other side of the man. She hurried. He recovered and grabbed at her feet, dragging her back. Her fingertips glanced off the hilt. He pulled her back and picked up his sword again.

Nothing near her to grab. She turned onto her back and kicked him. He stumbled a bit, but didn't let go.

Damn it.

Wait. Her circles!

She slammed her hand on one of the last circles with any runes and Released a large bag. The bag of ivories belonging to her step-mom's messengers.

The man raised his sword.

She chucked the bag as hard as she could. It hit him in the shoulder and was enough to make him let go. She spun away from him and dove for her sword. He cursed and came after.

Her hand gripped the hilt.

She twisted her body to the side as his blade clanged against the spot where she had just been.

He swung again. From the floor, she parried. She rolled under the table again, dodging strike after strike, and jumped up on the other side. The guard roared and leapt over the table at her.

Her back foot slid behind, she shifted her stance. Her blade whistled as it cut through air, fabric, and flesh.

The guard dropped to the ground. Isra withdrew her blade and turned toward the surgeons. They still wrestled with the girl and were gaining the upper hand. Isra picked up her sword, panting, and rushed the two.

One looked up. The other didn't.

The one who saw let go of the girl and shoved her Partner down. Isra's blade cleaved into this loyal friend.

Blood splattered. The other surgeon screamed, his dead Partner on top of him. Isra pulled the girl away and raised her sword one more time.

The surgeon looked from his Partner to her. It was like Isra had already killed him. Better she made it into reality, then.

She swung.

The surgeon vanished.

Isra clanged against the metal floor and stumbled back. It took her a moment to realize what had even just happened. The damn surgeon was a possessor.

A grunt came from the corridor, and Isra looked out into it. The surgeon leaned against a wall, shadows covered him. A Lightless. That was not good.

The man stumbled out of the shadows and hurried to the stairs. Isra gave chase. Because, damn it all, the plan had changed. He'd seen her use magic. No one could know about that. This man was dead.

"Wait!"

Isra glanced back as the girl came out after her. Right, she'd forgotten about her, somehow. The girl caught up, but the man was getting away. Isra couldn't keep up with him while having the girl tag along. But if they caught the girl, she'd lose her leverage. Though how much would she have if the surgeon had everyone looking for Isra now?

The girl grabbed Isra's hand again, but Isra took it away and stopped just before the stairs. The man was well on the next deck and hurrying for the next. What in the Abyss was she supposed to do? If she went up, the girl could get caught. But, what did that matter? Damn it all. The kid was cute, but Isra was here for that idol and nothing else. Her people depended on it. Her people depended on her.

She looked at the girl, eyes determined, body unaffected by Solitude. Sturdier than Gulamira was. Maybe... maybe could run fast enough to grab the idol.

It was a terrible thought. An awful thought.

And it could work. Isra wouldn't have a lot of time anymore, but it could just maybe work.

Isra sighed and asked the Lady of a Thousand Arms to forgive her. Or, at least only curse her and not her people.

"Come on." She stuck her pouch of discs into her shirt, she'd Catch it when she had time, and grabbed the girl's hand, pulling her toward the stairs. The stairs going down.

"Where are we going?" the girl asked.

"Need to grab something."

Her father's face peeked into her mind's eye, but she pushed him aside and kept moving down into the depths of the ship. The time for words was over. She needed to act for the sake of her people.

And if she couldn't use the girl to trade for the idol, then the girl would just have to be Remnant bait instead.

14

GUARDIAN OF THE SEA

H *ow can I stop now? Don't you see? Someone is getting scared.* *Someone thinks I'm getting close. Yes, of course I'll take precautions, of course. But we must be close. We must be close to something they don't want us to touch. There's something here and those Oligarchs are behind it. Just think, if we uncover whatever plot they have, we could oust them! We could put more power under Hyder and Zaid. Maybe then humans would have a greater chance here. How can I stop when this could be such a significant benefit?*

-Raza, a determined human.

Tsuran faced the iron cages from within his red-crystal statue. Remnants lay dead around him. Nasna was somewhere with Gulamira.

A Remnant yelled far away from him. Then it stopped. Silenced forever.

He let out a pent-up sigh. Not because he needed to let out a breath, while in his statue he didn't need to breathe. No, it was out of forceful habit.

He empowered his statue, shrinking it back to its compact form, and then unpossessed it, his body leaving the statue and materializing right beside it. He groaned as his fourth arm, the one still growing, smacked against his side. The useless limb hung dead, extra sensitive to every movement. Unpossessing often made it fall from his makeshift sling.

Tsuran tucked his developing arm into the sling, his statue on his belt, and he rushed toward the middle of the room where he found Nasna, Gulamira, and a green mess. Vines and Remnant parts scattered the area, all surrounding green bile that splashed against the floor and crates.

It also covered Nasna.

"Oof, what happened here?" he asked.

Nasna wiped off a thick sleeve of the slime from her arm. "Is anything coming?"

"Didn't see anymore Remnants."

"Good. Good." Nasna huffed and leaned against the nearest cage, which had a missing door. "Alright, we've time to... time to breathe."

Tsuran grabbed her with three arms to hold her up. "Hey, you with me? You hurt?"

"I pushed a bit too much, I think. Everything's aching." She met his gaze and attempted a tired smile. "I'll be fine. We're not out of this yet."

Tsuran didn't let go. His eyes drifted to the white scarring all over her crimson skin, scars that were like her very own set of markings. Except these were mere hints at the deeper brokenness beyond. Her body, her strength, it hadn't been the same since the Iron Mountains.

"Take a seat, Red," he said in a hushed tone so Gulamira wouldn't hear. "Not having you pass out or seize up here."

"I don't pass out."

"Right, remind me that next time I'm carrying you over my shoulders just to reach the top of a tavern."

"That happened once, and I was very conscious."

"Whatever you say." He flicked her ear, which brought a smile to her. Tsuran helped her into the cage and onto some low crates. She nodded to him and he turned to Gulamira, who hadn't moved since he'd arrived.

"You alright?" he asked. "Any Remnant touch you or anything?"

She shook her head, smiling. Though that wasn't saying much. This woman was pretty strange. Tsuran was pretty sure she'd been smiling the entire time, even while being chased. Someone must've hit her on the head too many times as a kid, but she'd been helpful so far.

Plus... she said her name was Con-None. A tatzon without a Partner. And with someone at her age not having one... well, Tsuran knew a thing or two about that.

"Who are you?" she asked.

"You sure they didn't hit you?" he asked. "I'm more than sure we already did introductions."

"You've told me your names, but not who you are." She huffed and Tsuran noted the dagger in her hand and the drips of green blood along it. "A Guardian with a statue the size of a hand—a red-crystal statue, mind you. And a wingless ordîn who can paralyze people or make them explode with a touch. That's not a typical pairing."

"Eh, we're not typical people," he said.

"I've seen that." She looked over the small dagger covered in all that internal mucus of the Remnant. It didn't bother her though, since she shoved it into her shirt and pulled her belt tight around it.

But there was something about her. Something about how she spoke that seemed... familiar? No, not quite that.

"Listen," Nasna said. "We don't have a lot of time. Let's wait a few minutes for the distraction to continue. I think we can deal with who we are some other time."

"Fair enough." Gulamira looked between Nasna and Tsuran. "Before we move on, do you two have a way off the ship?"

"We brought some sails with us," Tsuran said.

"I heard it was a boat."

"Well, right."

"You plan to escape this ship and this ocean on a boat?"

"Did I mention it comes with sails?"

She blinked, but her smile didn't falter. Somehow. Maybe he needed to try harder.

"Tsuran." Nasna just gave him a pointed look and shook her head.

He raised his hands. "Alright, alright. Just needing a bit of levity."

"That's great. Just internal levity, please."

"Sure, sure." He grinned and looked back at Gulamira. "Look, it's not a huge boat, but it's quick and should be enough to get us to shore. I'm a Guardian of the Sea and sailed for a good part of my life."

"And you've sailed these seas a lot?" she asked.

"Well, not these seas in particular. But I know my North Moon from my East, so it won't be too difficult."

Gulamira nodded along with everything he said. "Oh good, good. So, you don't know where we are and you'll try to get us to safety while a massive storm is coming?"

Tsuran groaned and ran a hand through his hair. Right. The storm. He'd noticed the telltale signs of one building earlier when they'd climbed into the *Cleansing*, but he'd tried to not think about it. Of all the days for a storm to hit, this really had to be the worst one. He guessed the gods hated him right now. But what had he done to upset them today? He hadn't prayed to them or offered them any reverence, so they should be thrilled he hadn't bothered them.

"I don't suppose you have a solution to this?" Nasna asked Gulamira. "Since you brought it up and all."

The woman nodded. "I've a solution. I have a friend on this ship, a human captive. He's the captain of a ship that sails these waters a lot. With his knowledge and your expertise, we'll have no issues in getting to safety."

Tsuran snorted. A human captaining a ship in these seas? Great. She was asking them to break out a pirate.

Though, on the list of terrible things they'd done, that ranked pretty low.

"Look," he said, "we're just here for Kamaria and we don't have a lot of room on the boat. We can't save everyone on this ship."

"And you're not needing to," she said. "Just me, my friend, and my... well, my other ally."

"That makes six total," Nasna said.

"Yes, thank you, Nas," Tsuran said. "Where would I be without you?"

"You know I'm surrounded by sharp objects I can throw, right?"

"Just be sure to count them off first."

Nasna rolled her eyes and threw nothing, meaning she was tired. "Where are your friends?"

"They keep my friend Medhi on the third deck near the bow. Isra should have Kamaria by now. She mentioned sixth deck at the stern."

Stern. Sixth Deck. "What deck are we on now?" he asked.

She thought a moment. "I think this being the hold, we're just below the twelfth deck."

That made six decks between him and Kamaria. He turned away and started toward the door.

"Tsuran, where are you going?" Nasna asked.

"I'm getting Kamaria. I'll see you two topside."

"What? Wait, Tsuran." She left the table and went to him. "You're not going alone. Just wait for the distraction to work. She already has someone going for Kamaria"

He lowered his voice. "I'm not trusting a stranger to save her, Red. She needs me. Now."

"Yes, I know. But you can't run off alone. You need help."

"And, as much as I hate to admit it, we need that captain of hers." He gestured toward Gulamira. "If a storm is coming, I'll need help. And we can't stay on this ship. So, help get her friend and meet me up top."

He paused and glanced back at the woman, still with her very persistent smile. She'd changed his mind pretty quick. Yes, her words made sense, he guessed. But there was something about them, something nagging at the back of his mind.

Nasna gripped one of his arms, careful to not touch his undeveloped arm. "And what? You're going to face Solitude and Soulborn on your own?"

"I'm just running, Red. Running, grabbing her, and going."

Her eyes met his. One eye light gray, like all ordîn, the other vertically split between blue and green. And that split eye burrowed into his soul.

She flicked his ear and smiled a small smile. "Save her, Tsuran. Keep her safe."

He nodded. "I will."

"I'll try to meet up as fast as possible, but I can't empower my speed like you."

He left her and walked away. "I'll keep them off of us until you get there."

"Good. Oh, and Tsuran?"

He looked back at her. Back at a woman of a different species. A woman with as many external scars as internal. A woman he called Partner.

Her eyes dropped to his chest and his hand drifted to it, feeling where flesh became cold and solid. "No matter what," she said, "do not push yourself."

He nodded.

Statue in hand, he left the iron hold, possessing the statue to cut through the iron gate, and headed to the stairs. Once past the gate, he unpossessed since he needed to conserve what time he had left of possession. He flew up the stairs, one hand keeping his undeveloped arm pinned against his chest. The useless limb stung with every bounding step. At the top, he peered through the door. guards gathered down the hall, shouting at each other about the fires. Tsuran slid across the deck, moving further and further aftward until the hall ended. This time, there was no wall, only stairs. There was a way up through here. Once he was at the top of these stairs, he breathed out.

"I'm coming Kamaria."

He held up his red-crystal statue and body-possessed it. His body vanished, and he became one with the statue. The statue—he—fell. Warmth flooded the crystal as Tsuran empowered his statue, reshaping it and adding to it, enlarging it multiple times over until he was as large as his actual body. As he grew, he also reshaped his statue's four arms, turning the ends into long, sharp blades. It all happened in an instant. Other shapings took a bit of time. But enlarging this statue was like second nature to him. Often, it felt like first nature.

Tsuran looked at the floor, smooth and well taken care of. It wouldn't be rough enough to run across with crystal feet, so he empowered his statue again, reshaping his feet into something resembling claws. They'd help with traction.

Five decks between him and Kamaria.

Time he closed the distance. And fast.

Warmth boiled inside the crystal as Tsuran empowered his speed. And he took off. Like a bolt from a ballista, he sped through the hall and the rest of the deck. He moved twice as fast, reacted twice as quick.

Guards—or rather slavers—cried out at the sight of a full-sized red-crystal statue. For the brave or unlucky ones who were in his way, this was the last sound they made. He rushed through the deck, heading for the next set of stairs he could find. Sliced bodies followed in his wake.

Others rushed off. Time would tell if he could outrun the alarm.

He found the next stairs and headed up, clawed feet scratching up the wooden floor as he did. Each deck teemed with these slavers. And they saw him.

But he had no time for them. He had no time for any of this. If they delayed him, the actual problems would arrive. He really didn't want to fight a Soulborn or a Lightless today.

But the slavers were in his way. So, arms splayed, he cut through them.

A few idiots attacked with wooden cudgels. His red-crystal cut through the pitiful weapons like dried mushrooms. The tatzons were even easier.

And he ran. Flight after flight, cutting through anyone and everyone in his way. There was no subtlety or caution. That was Nasna's specialty. Not his.

He did not need to cover a lot of each deck. There were stairs all near the stern, all behind those dead-ends, which was probably the only reason he didn't run into any possessors on his way up.

Tsuran hurried forward. People were coming from behind, but his greater problem was Solitude. He felt it coming, prowling around him like a starved beast. For most tatzons, it would already be here, ravaging and destroying him in minutes. But other tatzons didn't have the upbringing he had.

He landed on the sixth deck and unempowered his statue, shrinking it, and unpossessed it. His body materialized outside the statue, which he tied back onto his belt. He'd already possessed his statue a lot today and empowering his speed like this was going to sap up his remaining time. After that, Remnancy would start growing. Best he kept his remaining time for when he needed it.

Behind him, the deck was open for a short distance before a tall wall cut it off. Hard to tell if there was a door. Opposite the wall, besides another set of stairs, was a corridor. However, these corridors were anything but quiet and still. Someone—or something—screamed and wailed from the farther door.

In his experience, it was always best to run away from screaming and wailing, but he didn't have a choice now. Of course, the more unnerving aspect of it was that there was a door. Most of the rooms on the ship, including the others in this corridor, were tatzon openings with, at most, a curtain for more intimate privacy. But this room at the end of the hall had a door.

Never a good sign when tatzons adopted doors.

Especially when the door was ajar and something screamed beyond it.

The room was not what he expected. It was huge, but also covered in metal. Metallic doors lined the walls, with only a few light-stones to provide light. There was a strange coolness to the place that seemed to keep out the warmth of the rest of the ship. This place had a nasty similarity with the Iron Mountain prison he'd escaped from with Nasna.

He looked at the dozen doors deeper in the room, a couple of which were open, and listened to the muffled wails beyond them. The loudest screams were more like groans. Gurgling, hissing, venomous groans of Remnants. Was this where Kamaria was?

And there, lying on the ground, were three dead tatzons.

Tsuran checked them over, but they were definitely dead. Two resembled regular crew, but the other wore these black—

Tsuran froze. His body went colder than the room and nearly as cold as the Iron Mountains.

"No. Oh gods, please no."

This tatzon, she had two arms. But didn't have a priarm. Just like him.

He stumbled away, eyes darting to the blood-covered tables. Heart pounding, he peered closer at the blood. There were specks of black intermingled with the red. His head spun, and he turned around, taking in more of this nightmare. One side of the room had cabinets and tables with random instruments and bottles. The other side had an entire wall with tools hanging from them, tools for torture and experimentation. And on one shelf, locked behind iron bars, were several racks of glass vials. Vials of a liquid blacker than the deepest cavern and thicker than the venom of a Behemoth viper. It swirled inside, like an untamable mist.

Tsuran unconsciously put a hand on his right shoulder, where his cut-off priarm had once been. A sign of the people he'd once been with and of every evil trial they'd put him through.

Take the drink, Tsuran child. His mother's sickly voice rushed into his mind before he could protect himself from the memory. *It will grow you strong. It is your true power, Isolated one.*

He shook himself from the past and threw himself back into the present and at those doors. The Seekers were involved here somehow. And if they'd realized what Kamaria was...

Tsuran's breath quickened, and he spun around to the other doors. Each had parchment attached to it, detailing what and who was inside. Some were Remnants. Some were tatzons. Tatzons being subjected to Solitude.

"No."

He rushed from door to door, reading the papers.

Female, age 54, two arms, entered at—

Male, age 89, three arms, Builder, entered—

Male, age 21—

Male—

Male—

Female, age 8, growing a second arm—

Tsuran stopped at this door. The paper described Kamaria.

And it was open and the room empty.

He tightened his grip on his statue. What had they done to her? Where in all damnation was she? She'd be alive. He knew that. But if they were subjecting her to Solitude...

Gods, he had to find her. Before she changed. Before he lost her forever.

He rushed to the door, but paused as the screams of the tatzons in Solitude cried out to him. They experienced the second greatest torment any tatzon could ever experience. And all to create more of that vile liquid. All to further his parents' plans. He gripped the door frame tight and cursed himself, looking from that dead Seeker to those locked doors.

Kamaria was missing, and the storm was coming. Damn it all, he couldn't save them. He could only do what he could for her.

"I'm sorry."

He rushed to the next set of stairs.

But he did not know where to run to now, no idea where to look. It was possible that Gulamira's friend had already grabbed Kamaria, considering he hadn't seen other bodies inside. Hopefully, that meant she was safe.

The wall glowed with blue light. Tsuran froze.

Two spirits glided through the wooden wall as though through air, their bodies a semi-translucent blue. One resembled a droplet of water with two slim pseudopods, while the other had a more beast-like appearance, with six clawed legs and a narrow head. But both had a blank face and those glowing white eyes. Both stood as tall as Tsuran, so they were Small spirits. As if that made them any less dangerous. Especially since they moved with too much precision. Soulborn possessed these.

And they'd found him.

One Soulborn, the droplet one, glowed with a bright blue and the whole body became engulfed in flame, though the wood didn't catch. The other glowed brighter, as well. Tsuran gritted his teeth. These Soulborn could empower their possession. And he had no backup help.

And it hit him. He'd known there was something odd about Gulamira's words, about how she spoke, and now he realized why. Along with her speech, there had been something else, something quiet and subtle. Something that resembled the songs of spirits.

Damn it. And he'd left Nasna with her!

He cast a sidelong glance to the stairs leading up and then back to the Soulborn. He couldn't run. They could phase through wood. Running was stupid. Idiotic. Reckless and pointless.

So, he smirked and threw his statue toward the stairs. "Catch me if you can."

He possessed his statue. And they gave chase.

15

---◆○◆---

LEAVING THE CLEANSING

O ligarchs Hyder and Zaid want to speak with me about you. I think Doyen ratted us out to them, Abyssal damn her. I still do not know what I'm supposed to tell them. They are reasonable people, but even they have limits to what they'll let a human get away with. Lamia would back me up, but the news about the Red Sword has put her in a strange mood and she hasn't been to our Beneficiary meetings. I think he was once under her command. And to make matters worse, there have been sightings of the Black Swallow.

Things are getting pretty rotten here, so please, please don't do anything rash for a while.

-Beneficiary Syeda Softbark, a fish about to be boiled.

Gulamira crept into the holding pens behind the ordîn, Nasna. In all the rest of the *Cleansing, frantic* guards rushed around, shouting and locking up sailors and slaves. The hunt was on. Everyone felt it, even here among these caged humans. Darkness covered the room, save for a couple of lanterns, but that did not stop these human sailors from shouting, whispering, cursing, and speculating.

She stepped over the only guards in the room, their eyes open and their bodies unmoving. Just like she'd done to Gulamira, Nasna had only touched these two before leaving them still and frozen on the ground.

"How long will they be like this?" Gulamira asked as she picked up one of the oil lanterns. She rolled her neck, grateful Nasna had unlocked the iron collar, though being free of it felt odd now, as if her neck were too light.

"It varies on the person. These will be a few hours, at the very least."

Gulamira paused, checking that the tatzons were near each other, before leaving them in the darkness. After enduring Solitude herself, it was hard to let it consume these men. "And what is it you did to them?" And by extension her.

"I paralyzed their bodies," Nasna said. "It only requires me to touch them, but they can't resist it. Usually."

"I didn't realize ordîn could do that."

"Most can't. I haven't met many others who can..." Nasna turned back, an uncertain finger pointing toward Gulamira. "Uh, forget I said anything." Nasna cleared her throat and gestured forward. "How about you lead with the light? I do better sticking to shadows and you know who we're looking for."

While being a bright target wasn't ideal, this was a fair point, so Gulamira hurried down the corridor of cages. Nasna walked alongside her a few paces, but after a moment, Gulamira lost sight of her as the ordîn disappeared into the shadows. And there was something eerie about how well she hid. Gulamira noted it and continued to search through the cages. At first the cages were empty, but it didn't take long to come across those with the sailors in them.

They grunted and shielded their eyes from the lantern. She waved it from cage to cage, but didn't see Medhi.

"Who're you?" one of the caged men asked. "You're not one of the usual guards."

Medhi wasn't in this cage either, so she went to the next. "I'm a visitor. A special visitor, you could say. Looking for someone." Damn, not this cage either.

Another voice, this time a woman, spoke up from a cage in the darkness, "You're not gonna find any of your kind here. Not 'sides the guards."

Another cage scanned. Too many to go. She glanced around. At the moment, she didn't see any other guards. Hopefully, she wouldn't regret this.

She took in a deep breath. "MEDHI!"

Some prisoners grumbled at her, but a familiar voice piped up.

"Amira? Is that you?"

She hurried toward the voice and found Medhi standing against the cage door, looking as bewildered as she'd ever seen him. Which was to say he looked pretty composed, though he cast a wary look at the lit lantern.

"Told you I was getting you out," she said.

"You work fast, Amira. I'll give you that."

"Oh, come now. We both know I prefer to take my time with things."

Nasna stepped out of the shadows and Medhi started and grabbed at his scarf. "Oh! Rotting teeth, you're quiet."

Nasna pulled out a pair of slim metal picks and began working on the lock.

"That's an ordîn. Friend of yours, Amira?" Medhi asked.

"She is today. Oh, I found this." She pulled out her finding from the hold.

Medhi shook his head. "My dagger. You still have it? Thought you would have sold it by now."

"I'd never get rid of such a gift." She smiled at him and he returned his version of a soft smile, his hand stroking his scarf.

Sailors in nearby cages pushed against their bars, eyes on Nasna.

"Telling you," one whispered, "it's white hair, gotta be."

"There's no way," another said. "Ordîn's got wings, remember?"

"But... it's got red skin."

"Can't be a good omen."

As the humans around murmured and pondered the ordîn in front of them, though not as much as Gulamira did, Nasna worked on the lock. It clicked open, and she removed it from the door, letting Medhi come out, though he made a deliberate arc to stay away from the lantern. He looked from Nasna to the door, nodding. "That was... impressive."

"Anyone else in there?" Gulamira asked, raising the lantern.

"Sometimes. Not today though," he said, gaze set on Nasna. This had to be the closest he'd ever been to an ordîn. Most stayed away from humans.

"Hey, you freeing us, mates?" a voice called from a side cage.

"I've got a good ivory stash that's all yours if you getting me out," another said.

A few others spoke up and Nasna glanced at each. She looked conflicted. Gulamira grabbed her arm.

"We're just here for him. We've got to get that boat ready."

She nodded slowly. "Right, right. You're right..." She glanced at her lock picks, as if debating their worth. "These... they are all criminals, right?"

"I was framed," one voice said. "I didn't never come near where they said I killed the man."

"I'm innocent too, total misunderstanding. I'm just wanting to see my family again. Help an old pal out?"

Gulamira furrowed her brow as she watched Nasna. Exkel's Breath. If this woman tried to free these sailors...

She nudged Nasna so they locked eyes. "Kamaria is waiting for us."

This snapped the ordîn out of whatever reverie she was in. She nodded. "Right. Lead the way."

"Medhi," Gulamira said. "Can you take us topside?"

"Sure thing, just keep the lantern far behind."

Gulamira and Nasna followed Medhi as he headed back the way they came. He gave a curious look at the frozen guards on their way out, but Gulamira had a smile that said, *I'll explain later,* and he kept going. Medhi took them to the nearest stairwell and climbed, but Gulamira grabbed his wrist. He gave a wary look to the lantern.

"In case we encounter guards," she said and handed him his dagger.

"Sure you shouldn't hold on to it?" he asked.

"You've a lot more skill with it than me." She backed away from him and he seemed to ease as the flames went further away. He gripped his dagger and nodded.

As they climbed the stairs, Gulamira glanced at Nasna, whose breathing continued to grow heavier and heavier. And maybe it was her imagination, but the ordîn looked like she was slowing as well.

"You alright?" she asked.

Nasna huffed, but nodded. "Just a little winded, is all."

A little winded. Right. Another secret, it seemed.

The next deck had lanterns. They entered a long corridor with passageways behind and in front of them. People shouted from both directions. It sounded like quite a few people were heading their way.

"Where's the next stair?" Nasna asked.

"Down that corridor," Medhi said, pointing.

"Think we can sneak past?" Gulamira asked.

"Maybe. Best hide first before—"

"Kamaria!" Nasna cried.

Gulamira spun around. Nasna rushed toward the opposite corridor, toward the little girl, looking a little worse for wear, and also toward Isra. Nasna ran straight for Isra, hands splayed and tensed, ready to attack.

"Wait! Nasna! Don't!"

Nasna stopped just as she and Isra were about to make blows.

Isra glared at Nasna and darted a glance at Gulamira. "Allies?"

"She's here for the girl."

Isra shrugged and lowered her sword. "Everyone is."

"What does—oof!"

Kamaria rushed straight into Gulamira. The girl shook and held her tight. Nasna didn't look offended. She seemed... distant.

Kamaria looked up at Gulamira. "Is Tsuran here?"

Gulamira looked at her and then at Nasna. The ordîn said nothing. "Yes," Gulamira said. "And we're taking you to him."

Shouts erupted from both corridors, and Medhi brandished his dagger. "We've company."

Isra nodded, backing away from the corridor she came from. "Lightless."

"There's Lightless down there?" Medhi asked. "We're not outrunning those bastards."

"Run for the stairs," Nasna said and positioned herself in front of them. "I'll hold them off."

Isra backed further away, but Medhi and Gulamira shared a look.

"Thanks for the offer," Gulamira said. "But, I don't see how that's a good id—"

"Get Kamaria off this ship and to safety," Nasna said, her voice strengthening with every word. "If I make it, I make it. But she lives." She glanced back with a fake smile. "Besides, I'm an ordîn. I'm the natural predator of possessors."

The shadows down the corridor shuddered, and a chill ran down Gulamira's spine.

Medhi grabbed her and pushed her back. "Thanks then. We'll do just that." He pointed toward the other corridor. "Go."

Gulamira grabbed Kamaria's hand and ran with Medhi. She glanced back to see shadowy figures emerge from the edges of darkness and Nasna lowering herself into a stance.

"Eyes forward!" Medhi said. "We've our own problems to worry about."

A dozen guards stood at the end of the corridor they ran into. Right. She needed to focus. She looked at Isra.

"You and Medhi will have to clear the way."

"I'm going below," Isra said.

"What?" Medhi said. "Aren't you—"

"Soulborn are all over the hold right now," Gulamira said. "Wait for us to lure them up."

Isra's eyes narrowed, and she nodded. "Topside, then."

She pressed on past Gulamira. Medhi charged forward and started roaring. Isra also picked up her pace, raising her sword high. The guards had rallied and were ready for them, but Gulamira saw traces of realization spread through their ranks.

Medhi had a long dagger. Isra had a sharpened cutlass. These guards had whips and small clubs.

The corridor was narrow enough that only four guards could fight at a time. Which meant those in the front had no way to retreat when Isra and Medhi fell upon them.

Gulamira kept Kamaria close as steel clashed against flesh. Medhi attacked like a madman, with an intense ferocity that pushed the guards back. Isra fought with more precision, but with no less fury. They beat at the guards like whirlwinds, cutting through like a beast with its prey. Red blood ran across the floor and once or twice Gulamira winced as steel cut through flesh and bone. And Gulamira recognized the anger and rage of their fight. It was all too similar to patrons that sought her out to hurt her. These two fought with a human's passion to unleash all their hatred upon tatzonkind.

And today, she allied with that hatred.

As Medhi and Isra created a pathway of bodies and blood, Gulamira glanced back toward Nasna, expecting to find Lightless surging past her.

Nasna stood in the middle of the hall, knees bent, hands moving with blurring speed. Beyond her, the shadows looked alive. The shadows shivered, moved, and beings emerged from them. Lightless. Shadow possessors who could make shadows a physical force.

The Lightless sped toward Nasna. Some even tried to speed through the shadows on the floor past her, but she moved faster. She slammed one hand into the ground and another into a Lightless creating a shadow body. Both shadows stopped and two tatzons materialized in front of her. Gulamira stopped and gaped.

She'd heard stories of ordîns, everyone knew these creatures could exorcise a tatzon from their possession, but it was something else to witness it. Lightless were some of the most hated and feared of the possessors, and yet a single wingless ordîn held them back.

Though Nasna breathed heavier than before. Gulamira prayed the ordîn held out long enough.

Medhi and Isra had killed most of the guards, with a few turning and fleeing. Still with the wild fury in his eyes, Medhi beckoned to Gulamira. "Hurry!"

She ran with Kamaria through the carnage and followed Medhi to another set of stairs. They rushed to it.

"You better know where you're going," Gulamira said.

Medhi smirked. "Of course I do. What kind of captain would I—Agh!"

Shadows burst from the wall like a fist, slamming into Medhi and throwing him into the wall. Isra spun around and the shadowy tendril vanished from the air and another shot up from the shadows on the ground into Isra's stomach.

A Lightless had maneuvered past Nasna.

The shadows swirled around them, stretching from their dark corners, and rose into the form of a person. The shadow body had no face or any distinct features. It was a black emptiness standing in front of them, like the Abyssal itself.

Gulamira waved her lantern in front of her and the shadows flinched and retreated, but only to regroup. This pitiful amount of light would do little to protect them. If this Lightless was making the shadows physical, then they had a third arm in shadow possession. They could empower their shadow to resist the light.

Isra groaned and tried to rise to her feet, but the Lightless slammed a shadowy hammer onto her back and she collapsed. The Lightless turned toward Gulamira.

"Whale oil can't stop me, slave." The Lightlesses' voice came from distinct shadows with every word and though the possessor could not have created any wind, Gulamira thought her lantern dimmed.

She took a step back and searched deep inside for a song to help her. Nothing subtle. Subtlety would kill her right now. She needed something powerful. Something even a Lightless could not resist.

From a locked chest within, the song of the Coming Fire stirred. A higher song that would make every possessor bow before her. A song that even shadows could not undo.

The Lightless approached. "Surrender or I'll kill you."

"The fire is enough," Kamaria said, and Gulamira blinked and stared at her.

"What?"

"Lightless can't body-possess for long. And empowering like he's doing will eat up his possession time. Otherwise, Remnancy will kick in." She squeezed Gulamira's hand. "Trust me, I know Lightless. This fire is enough."

"Time's up!" The Lightless vanished into the floor and Kamaria jerked Gulamira to the side as a black tendril soared past her, just missing her.

The shadow disappeared, and Kamaria pulled Gulamira down, causing her to again dodge an attack. Kamaria reacted faster than Gulamira could follow, pulling and pushing her through the hall, narrowly dodging and maneuvering out of the Lightless' attacks. Gulamira allowed the girl to lead her.

Kamaria had an intense focus, and her movements were precise, practiced, and, to a point, prophetic. She expected every attack, every shadowy tendril. And the Lightless realized it. He growled through the shadows and his attacks quickened. Tendrils of shadow struck from the walls, the floor, the ceiling, from behind and in front, but no matter where they originated, this girl moved as if she knew where they'd come from.

After a few attacks, Gulamira could see it too, almost. The Lightless could only possess the existing shadows, couldn't create his own. And the lantern, as pitiful as it was, kept changing where the shadows were, and it made the shadows slower in the light.

But the Lightless grew reckless and his attacks multiplied, no longer stemming from a single point but several. Kamaria tried to keep up, but one rammed into her leg and another swiped Gulamira across the chin. Both fell. The lantern broke and spilled, alighting the ground and wall in fire.

With a groan, Gulamira turned on her side to see the Lightless leaving the shadows and materializing as a tatzon. He breathed hard, and Gulamira noted a bit of his neck, which was no longer flesh, but a wisp of black smoke.

The Lightless strode to Kamaria and picked her up by the throat. "How in the Abyss did you do that? How did you know?"

Gulamira tried to stand, but the world spun and she fell again. She glanced up, but Kamaria smiled.

"My mother was a greater Lightless than you'll ever be." Kamaria raised her leg and kicked hard.

The Lightless growled and went to grab her neck with his pri-arm, to suffocate her.

Gulamira reached out. "Medhi!"

"Get away from her!"

The voice was not Medhi's, but Nasna's. She flew at the Lightless, and her palm slammed into his back. His back arced, and a gasp left his mouth before his hand released Kamaria and his body froze. Kamaria dropped to the ground, but before Nasna could go to her, several shadowy tendrils slammed into her and sent her soaring into the wall.

Gulamira got to her feet, the heat of the lantern's fire burning behind her. The other Lightless approached, but the burning oil created a buffer of light. It wouldn't stop the Lightless and far down the hall, behind the Lightless, a half dozen guards ran toward them.

The possessor surged forward. Toward Kamaria.

Gulamira leapt to her and reached out.

Medhi beat her to it.

The man landed in front of Kamaria and sliced at the Lightless with his dagger. The Lightless screamed and fell back into the shadows, emerging as a tatzon. Medhi grinned and hoisted Kamaria to her feet.

"Crystal embedded iron," he said to the Lightless. "Guess it works against your kind."

The Lightless growled and the guards fast approached. Gulamira grabbed Mehdi's hand. "Let's go!"

They turned and ran. As they passed Nasna, the woman gave them a firm nod and rose to her feet to cut off the Lightless again. Isra groaned on the ground, still trying to pick herself up. She'd need someone to help carry her for a time to escape.

But the guards were too close.

"Good luck to you," Gulamira said and, with Kamaria and Medhi, jumped through the fires and onto the next stairs.

16

---◈---

THERE IS ONE MORE

*D*on't get mad, but in case you hear about the Oligarchs' home
being broken into... that was us. Well, not me exactly. There's no
way I could have done that and lived. But we found it: a trove of letters
and scrolls and writings. We're about to delve into it, so it's just a little
longer. Soon I'll have all the information we'll need to oust these two.
Don't worry, Syeda. We have them.

-Raza, the one who reads with glee.

Strong winds and a warm rain buffeted the *Cleansing*, and Gulamira heard the choppy waters splashing against the hull as she
emerged from the forward hatch. The dark clouds she'd seen earlier were upon them, and the storm's strength would only build.

Rain pelted her face, making it hard to see, but there wasn't any
other movement on deck. Doubtless, they only had a short time
before the guards came because Nasna would not hold them long.

"Quick," Medhi said above the winds. "That boat there!"

He pointed to the pinnace he and Isra had stashed food and
water in. It sat beneath two cranes, which were ready to hoist it out
over the water. She grabbed onto the crank and followed Medhi's
instructions as they hurried to lift the boat over the side. The cranes
carried the boat far enough from the *Cleansing* that it wouldn't
smash into the side once in the water. Even with the cranks, this
was not an effortless task. Normally, they'd be in the boat and other
crew would hoist it out.

"Almost far out enough!" Medhi's voice cut through the rain, and Gulamira hoped it didn't carry far below deck. "There, that's good enough. We'll have to climb across and lower it from the boat."

Kamaria pulled at Gulamira. "Wait, what about Tsuran? We can't leave without him."

"We won't if he gets here in time." She knelt beside the girl, eye to eye. "But your life is his priority, right? Your safety matters. Do you think he'd have us wait for him if it meant you getting caught?"

The girl stared back at the hatch in a way that spoke of rash decisions. Gulamira wouldn't have been surprised if Kamaria attempted to storm back into the *Cleansing* and find Tsuran. She prepared to wrestle the girl into the boat, but Kamaria took in a breath, nodded to herself, and turned away from the hatch.

Thunder crashed overhead and the ever darkening clouds loomed another step closer. And then a clear, white light shone from the other side of the deck, piercing through the darkening rain. Gulamira's breath solidified and lodged in her throat.

Distant lightning mixed with the lightstone, showing more than a dozen guards facing them, though they looked more like Lightless with how the shadows blanketed their faces. Their weapons, though, stood out amidst the rain. A few had swords, but most had crossbows, all of which were trained at her and Medhi's heads. Yet, these shadows seemed less of a threat than the two tall tatzons leading them. Captains Yirig and Juhk wielded no weapons, only a lightstone between them, yet they dominated the scene. Theirs were the only lit faces, though half-shadows still cloaked them, and it was in those faces, in those eyes, that Gulamira saw the true strength behind the *Cleansing*. They were not Lightless, they were not Soulborn. But, as they stepped forward, without a hint of fear of either her or Medhi, she saw commanders, those who spoke and knew others would obey.

"Drop your weapon," Yirig said, just loud enough to be heard over the rain. "Or be relieved of it."

Gulamira looked between Medhi and the lifeboat, a brief thought of whether they should make a run for it. But Medhi caught her eye. He shook his head and dropped the dagger.

The guards with swords rushed them, kicking aside the dagger and shoving them onto their knees, blades at their throats. The two captains approached Gulamira and Medhi, smug satisfaction plastered across their faces.

"You've caused a bit of a stir today," Juhk said. "The fires were a pretty nasty trick. But here's a piece of information for you: no one, and I mean no one, escapes from the *Cleansing*."

"Captains!" A pair of guards hurried up and saluted. "Alier Con-Troih sent us. They captured an ordîn down below. An intruder."

A bit of hope died in Gulamira. Until now, she hadn't realized it was there, but there had been a part of her that thought Nasna would arrive and help again.

"An ordîn? What they have to do with this?" Yirig asked.

Another commotion came from further aft, and another pair of guards came up with their own news. "Word from Hij and Kami. They've captured a Guardian."

Kamaria's grip tightened, but Gulamira had no words of comfort for her. With Tsuran captured, they were finished. They'd come so close, and it just hadn't been enough.

"A Guardian, too? The Abyss is going on here?" Yirig looked back, staring at Medhi and Gulamira. His eyes narrowed, and he gestured toward her. "Pull her up."

The men obliged and not-too-gently hoisted her to her knees. Yirig shone the lightstone above her. "You. Who's behind this mess? Who sent you?"

Before she could think, before she could plan or choose the right words, instinctive reflexes deep within her soul took over. She breathed out and as she did, a song erupted from her like the fires of the Hearth of Life. She threw the song into the air, into the very fiber of these tatzons, a song spirits used when hunting people. Anger was its tempo, fear its melody. The tone would break into their minds, promise the world to them while slowly sucking away all self-preservation. Although a lower song, it was strong. Already, she saw the guards lower their crossbows, and some looked to the edge of the ship, as though only by falling could they find everything they desired. Medhi looked as well, and Gulamira fought with all she had to resist her own song.

But when Gulamira looked at Kamaria, the girl looked... confused as she stared right at Gulamira, as if unaffected by the song. But Kamaria was not the only one the song did not touch. Captains Yirig and Juhk stood before Gulamira without a glazed look. They appeared unchanged, except their eyes bulged upon hearing the song.

Juhk acted first. Gulamira's song cut short as his fist slammed her head into the floor. The shock of the impact dazed her and made the world spin.

"Wake up, you fools!" Yirig said. "Focus on my voice, ignore everything else. You are Rajals on the *Cleansing*. Remember that you are here!"

Yirig's words, and the silencing of Gulamira's song, brought the guards out of the song's effects. They looked around, both at themselves and each other. The rain quieted anything they said to each other, but Gulamira could guess at their utter confusion of what had just happened.

Juhk grabbed her neck and jerked her toward him. She flinched, expecting another strike, but he growled in her face.

"How did you know that song?" His grip tightened and his voice grew darker. "You're one of his, aren't you? That's why you want the girl. Tell me, does he know? Does that damn Nightmare know already?"

She grasped at his hand, trying to gasp for air, but her mind focused on one thing: the captains had heard her song yet resisted it with ease. How on Exkel's Mountain could they? This wasn't good. Not good at all. Juhk's grip hurt, but she knew she needed to get away. These men were dangerous if they could... could...

Gulamira's eyes locked on Juhk's chest. That which froze her blood and paused her heart dangled from his neck. An amulet. An amulet made of ivory with the carved symbol of a mountain with a crown of flames.

A memory flashed across her mind. Exkeldian priests lined up to greet the altar. Her parents stood behind it and began the daily prayer. All voices chimed in,

"We come from His Mountain,
Little embers that rested in His Hearth,
Until the Breath blew us to the world."

In every priest's hand, held against their breast, was this very amulet.

Her smile faltered, becoming little more than a soft upturn.

"Where did you get that?" she asked, forcing out what little breath she had to form the words.

Juhk raised a brow, then looked at the amulet. He became very, very still, his earlier rage settling. "Do... do you know what this is?"

"Where did you get that?"

He let go of her and rose to his feet, a small smile growing on his twisted face. "Not a Bridgemaker," he said, his eyes alighting with every word. "An Exkeldian. Another Exkeldian."

She pushed herself to her knees, still struggling to breathe from his earlier grip. "What do you mean 'another'?"

"Yirig," Juhk called out, his eyes never leaving Gulamira. "Come here. She's an Exkeldian."

The other captain hurried over at the words, his eyes darting between his Partner and Gulamira. "You sure?"

"She recognized the amulet and had a strong spirit song." He grinned. "She's pretty upset seeing it, too."

Gulamira launched to her feet and grabbed the man by the shirt, but he didn't flinch. "What are you saying? You found a priest of Exkel? Where? When?"

Her mind spun too fast, her thoughts going too far. It couldn't be true. It just couldn't.

Yet, that amulet...

Yirig grabbed Gulamira's wrist and pulled her off his Partner. "Don't worry, lost priestess. We'll unite him with you soon enough." He exchanged a nod with Juhk and turned to the guards. "Secure those intruders and then bring the crew back up here! We're changing course for the Floating Treasure." He threw her into the arms of the closest pair of guards. "See to it she is safe and secured. No one touches her or comes near her without our say so."

"And grab that one, while you're at it," Juhk said, pointing at Kamaria. "Get her back to Abioda and Haz."

Kamaria fought against her captors, screaming and kicking. "Gulamira!"

"Kamaria!" She pulled against the guards, but it was no use. The girl, once again, was pulled away from her and down into the depths.

"What about this one?" a guard asked.

"Hm, yes. I remember you," Juhk said. "The pirate that's enjoyed commanding our crew. The Twice Dead, if I'm not mistaken."

Thunder rolled, and Gulamira blinked water out of her eyes, realizing they were addressing Medhi. The two captains looked him over, still keeping him on his knees. Yet, somehow, Medhi did not look defeated as he knelt there. He held his head high in the wind of the building storm, which only added to the intense wildness of the man. There was something about him, something in those eyes of his, that made him almost like a storm himself. And by just looking at him, by just seeing the unfounded confidence in that man's eyes, Gulamira's mind grounded itself back into the present reality. She was not out of danger. Not yet, at least.

"Kill him and toss him overboard."

The guard raised his sword and Medhi turned his gaze to her, those wild, untamable eyes, and smiled.

She reached out to him. "No!"

Lighting crackled overhead and a heavy wave crashed into the ship, sending everyone stumbling back. Medhi reacted faster than any. He jumped to his feet and struck the guard next to him, grappling the sword from his hands and using it to kill two before anyone else moved.

A few raised their crossbows, but Gulamira would not let him die. She would not wait around and let them kill her. The captains could resist her song, but these guards couldn't!

She brought out her song again, set to a different tune, one of confusion and disorder. The guards, distracted by the wave and Medhi's attack, fell in step with the song.

The captains ignored the song and turned on her, ready to silence her. They rushed forward, but Medhi beat them. He sprung in front of her, brandishing the sword, keeping them back.

"Away from her!"

The captains took out their swords and readied to attack. Gulamira did not know how good with a sword Medhi was, but she doubted he could take on a Partnered pair like these two.

She glanced down and saw his dagger sliding across the deck toward the starboard side. Toward the sailboat.

With her song strong in the air, she spun around and took a crossbow from a guard. She took aim at the captains. They dove for cover as she released the bolt, and she did not wait around to see what she hit.

"Medhi, let's go!" She discarded the crossbow, grabbed him by the shirt, and pulled him to the cranes. She picked up the dagger and, as another massive wave crashed into the side of the ship, grabbed onto one of the crane's ropes. Medhi held onto her and also gripped the rope.

She gritted her teeth. "I hope this is the right one."

Gulamira slashed the rope behind and the two leapt off the side.

17

A WATERY END

I t's not just the Oligarchs. I thought that was all there was to this. Just two Oligarchs continuing a war for their personal agendas. And I was wrong. I've poured over everything we found more than a dozen times, and I still struggle to believe it. Oligarchs Argul and Ortu are not bowers of the Ethereal Tree. Their letters show they are part of some cult that worships "the Realized". They are mere puppets for this cult, nothing more. There is a far deeper danger and conspiracy going on here, because as far as I can tell, it's these Realized who were behind the death of the Bramble, Ma'Jra's destruction, and Florella's assassination. They are behind this war.

-Raza Softbark, the fool who is in the water now.

Gulamira and Medhi swung through the stormy air.

Their rope connected to the boat via a pulley at the end of the crane. With it cut, that side of the boat fell toward the water, pulling the two of them up toward the crane while they soared over the water.

Rain pelted their faces as they swung closer to the boat, though now higher than it.

"We have to jump," Medhi said. "Let go... now!"

Gulamira's heart leaped the same time she let go. Time slowed, lighting flashed in the distance, and the pinnace swung away from them.

She reached out as she fell, only just grabbing onto the boat's side, stopping her from falling all the way into the ocean. Her arm strained, and she groaned as she pulled herself up, hand after hand, into the dangling sailboat.

The storm raged against the *Cleansing*. Guards shouted from above, waves crashed below. And the boat still hung from one crane.

Medhi hung from ropes above her. "I have to lower us closer to the water! If we drop now, the boat will smash apart."

Gulamira wrapped an arm around a nearby rope and pulled herself to the sails. "Hurry then!"

The boat swung in the air, but Medhi clambered toward the prow where the ropes attached. He grabbed the spare end of it and dropped it toward her.

Something whizzed through the rain and embedded into the deck. A crossbow bolt.

Another flew by, another struck the boat.

"Wrap that rope around the mast a few times," he said.

"Why?"

"Just do it!"

She did as he said, all while bolts pelted the deck close to her.

"Done."

"Hold on to that rope, Amira."

Whatever he did up top, the boat jerked, as though falling, but caught on the rope in her hands. It burned her palms but in a flash of lightning, Medhi was beside her grabbing the rope and slowly letting the rope pull through.

The boat jerked and swayed but they descended toward the water.

A strong wind grabbed the boat, and the crane swung back and forth. Medhi cursed and yelled as the rope slipped through his hands.

Gulamira's heart dropped into her stomach and they fell straight into the ocean.

Gulamira hit the turbulent waters hard. She fell straight in, no ropes to help her. She went under the water, then above, then a wave shoved her back down, then spat her back out. Water spewed from her mouth and she fought the torrents, spinning around to find the boat. But the ocean was only getting started with its rampage. She felt the intent to kill pulse through every wave that tried to drown her.

She broke through the water and gasped for air and, by some miracle, caught sight of the boat. They had been just close enough it hadn't shattered, though it listed hard.

"Medhi!" Another wave battered her. She sputtered out a cough and swam toward the boat. "Medhi, where are you?"

She made it to the boat just as the water rose and plummeted. She gripped the side of the boat as it hit the water, wood jolting into her ribs. Her cries battled against the thunder above. Hand over hand, she pulled herself onto the boat, dropping into more water.

She spun back, clutching to the rigging to not lose her footing. Her heart leapt as she saw Medhi swimming toward the boat, but the waves were hitting him hard. Frantic, she searched for something to throw at him. Most contents had fallen out with the boat tipping, but she found a rope that someone had tied off previously. She threw it out to Medhi.

He caught the end of it and pulled himself to the boat. She grinned as he pulled himself up to her.

"All that," she said, "and you kept your scarf?"

"Not even the ocean can take it from me." He cast a glance at the *Cleansing*. "We need to get out of here. Can you sail?"

"Some. Just tell me where you need me."

"Secure the rigging. I'll try to—Hold fast!"

She twisted a nearby rope around her arm and braced herself. A wave crashed into them, tipping them, readying to capsize them. Medhi acted fast. He threw himself over the side of the boat and used himself as a counterweight. Gulamira, once she saw him doing this, joined in and they kept the boat from flipping.

Lightning danced through the air as the storm grew ever stronger. Winds wailed around her, ocean spray covering everything in a wet mist. The skies had darkened now, and she saw nothing through the torrent. She went to the mast and grabbed the loose rigging and secured it as Medhi grabbed onto other lines and trimmed the sails windward. He jumped to the tiller, grabbed tight, and shifted the boat. Toward the storm.

"Medhi! You're heading for the waves!"

"I see them."

"You plan to kill us?"

"Shut up and trust me! I need to focus." He pulled on the tiller, wiping water from his eyes. "Hold on!"

They sailed at the building wave, but not directly. Toward the rising water, but at an angle.

Gulamira's smile remained plastered to her face, but of all the times it had been fake, it had never been as big of a lie as now. She clung to the boat, not because Medhi told her to, but because of a greater, deeper, stronger instinct of preservation she couldn't overpower. The stampeding thrum of her heart harmonized with the the bellowing storm.

The boat sailed through the wave, which rose beside them, though the part they sailed through rose last.

Air finally released from her chest, coming out as an involuntary laugh. She turned to Medhi, but he grinned at her.

"Looking pale, Amira. Thought you were made of sterner stuff!"

She swallowed every desire to both vomit and punch him for putting her through that. "I'm not made of whatever insanity drives you."

"The storm's coming that way." He pointed in the direction he steered the boat.

"And that's where the waves are! If we keep this up, one of them is going to topple us."

"You can't outrun a storm you're in. Can't outrun any storm. It finds you eventually. Best to get through it as fast as possible. That means through the waves. Just have to aim for the flattest parts."

She peered out at the black clouds above and the walls of water building toward them. "Can you do it?"

Medhi laughed with maniacal triumph, as though they were already out. "It takes more than a few tall waves to outdo Medhi the Twice Dead! I'll get us out. You just do as I say. Heads up, we're going again!"

They hit another wave, again striking the lowest portion at an angle. She grabbed the mast as the boat listed. Medhi laughed.

The boat sliced through the wave, and Medhi pointed them toward the next wave. He gripped the tiller and held firm. "Hold on with all you got. We're not out of this in the least. Don't know if gods listen to whores, but now'd be a good time to pray!"

Gulamira tried to get as low as possible, lest a stray wind or wave took her from this death raft. A mumbled prayer tried to pry its way out of her mouth, but even she couldn't hear it. All she could do was close her eyes and hold tight as the world tried to kill her yet again.

18

THE SPIRIT'S SONG

Raza, I want you to flee to our home in Tutchal. You were an idiot for going, but we will not ignore what you found. Lamia and I will look over what you sent us, but we both agree this is too dangerous for you now. We can show this to Doyen since we'll need her ordîns on our side for this. Our spies reported that a representative of the Shadow Strikers met with Oligarchs Argul and Ortu yesterday, so head out right away. I will not let my little brother get assassinated.

-Your big sister, worried and praying for your damn life.

The boat floated across the waters, the wind coaxing Gulamira and Medhi along with only brief threats of another storm. So far, none of the threats came to fruition. The two escaped yesterday's storm by the narrowest of threads and this battered craft would not survive another one.

Gulamira's arms ached from bailing water all day, despite the sporadic breaks when she swapped with Medhi. He'd tied the sail off to get a wind, but they weren't going anywhere fast. She plopped down on the bench at the prow and soaked her hands in the salted waters. Strange how the thing trying to kill them was also warm and relaxing. Her tired eyes followed soft lights deep beneath the ocean, small glowing orbs from this distance. She smiled and didn't mention them to Medhi, instead focusing her gaze on the other array of color. The sun was setting and colors of orange, red, and lilac beset the whole of the world. Clouds cloistered to the west, the sun's colors making them appear like roaring fires, and the wind blew them south.

Gulamira turned back to Medhi, who gripped the tiller with waning strength. He looked as haggard as she felt. What disheveled clothes he still had, most notably his scarf, clung to him like barnacles on a dock. His hair was a tangled mess and anyone else would have seemed like a beggar or other destitute. Not Medhi. His eyes kept such illusions away. Even now, a wild intensity filled them that reminded Gulamira too much of the storm they'd just been in. Yet, there was also a fiery warmth in those searching eyes, like a lighthouse calling her to safety. Medhi had his gaze on the horizon, which continued its transition from purple to blue to black. He hadn't stopped staring since the sunset began. Something grabbed his attention. But she had her own thoughts to preoccupy her.

There was another surviving priest.

At least, there was a chance of another being alive. But this was a real chance, no mere delusion or fantasy or hope. Another Exkeldian waited for her in the same place Kamaria would be.

"Medhi?" she asked. "Do you know what the Floating Treasure is?"

He glanced at her sidelong before looking back at the horizon. "It's a black market out on the ocean."

"The captains said the *Cleansing* was heading there."

He motioned to the bucket beside her. "Should bail a bit more. After I adjust our heading, you can sleep a few hours."

Her arms and back protested, but she grabbed the bucket and began the grueling work again. Gulamira waited for him to mention the Floating Treasure, but he stayed quiet. After a few minutes, she glanced up from the never ending work. "Have you ever been?"

"Ah, wait." He turned the tiller and Gulamira saw what he'd been looking for. The first moon rose. Looked to be Chexel, or, as the Rajals called her, the Eastern Moon. "Good. I think we're on course."

Medhi had his thumb out sideways and kept moving it horizontally. "What are you doing?" she asked.

"Old sailor trick. Measure the number of thumb lengths between the last bit of sun with the first bit of moon. Roughly shows where you could be in the ocean. Really glad the Eastern rose first today."

"Don't see how it'd be accurate without a sextant or anything."

He shrugged. "It's not, but it tells me we are moving away from the Meadowlands, which is good. There are islands south of Rajalend. Hoping we run into one." He leaned back and rubbed his eyes. "Hope we do before we sink."

She looked out at the horizon. Chexel rose, a mighty silvery disc shining its holy light upon the world. Its light was not as bright as the sun, but it bathed the ocean in a silvery twilight, making the once blue waters appear like a white slab.

She massaged her priarm and stared into the dark sky. It was strange seeing it again after so long in the *Cleansing*, yet it was just as she'd left it. A handful of stars dotted the sky here and there, but most hid from the sight of Chexel. Among them, only two skybands rose today, long streaks of vibrant blue that on some nights could dominate the whole of the sky. Tonight, though, they did not reach high above the horizon. Not a great omen. But despite that, Gulamira let herself take in the sky's tranquility. After all, somewhere up there, Exkel watched over her. Today, it seemed he had a straightforward task for her.

"Medhi, have you been to the Floating Treasure?"

His hand drifted up to his scarf, where he squeezed water from it. "Didn't I say? Pretty sure I did."

"No, you got distracted by the moon."

"Ah, suppose I was."

She waited. He squeezed more water from his scarf, but he seemed to avoid her gaze. Gulamira stopped bailing and stared at him. He was avoiding her questions.

"Medhi?"

"Hm?"

"Have you been to the Floating Treasure?"

He hesitated. "I... I've been."

"Good, because I need you to take me there."

"No."

She blinked and looked back at him. He twisted his hand in his scarf and avoided looking at her.

"I haven't even explained—"

"Not going to listen to an explanation. It's not happening."

"Medhi, they're taking the girl there."

"I heard."

"Then you also heard what the captains said. You know... what I once was."

He nodded, but looked away. Gulamira hadn't given him all the details, but on one night together, she had told him she'd been a priestess as a child before her entire order's death. He'd been the first person in years she'd talked to about that. It had felt... well, she had a hard time admitting how it felt.

"There's another of my order. I'm not the last."

"I know, I heard. And I know that this means a lot to you, this other priest and this kid, but I'm not bringing you there."

Gulamira's smile waned, and the fluttering of her heart died down. "And why is that?"

Medhi sighed and gave her the look adults gave children when explaining that mushroom people weren't real, and that ended the fluttering. "We don't even know if this priest is alive. I mean, it could be a trap for all we know. This place is dangerous. People disappear there, many show up floating in the water dead the next morning. You think it'd be a good place to bring a woman like you?"

"A woman like me?" she asked, her smile losing its pleasantness.

"Beautiful." He smiled at her, as if she should blush at his words. As if her knees should melt under his gaze and her eyes weep at the foresight of his kindness. Gulamira stayed rigidly upright.

"Wow, you're so sweet." Her grip tightened around her bucket's edge. "But that girl, she needs me. That priest needs me, too. I survived Archoz. I can survive this."

"The Treasure is worse than Archoz. They're not the kind of people you can just spread your legs for and it'll be fine."

"You did not just say that."

"It's the truth." He shook his head and stared out at Chexel, adjusting the tiller as necessary. "They'll eat you alive there. Then spit your bones out into the sea. I'm not risking that."

She narrowed her eyes and inhaled sharply. But she held the breath a moment and then eased it out, relaxing her body as she did. Bailing bucket in hand, she bent down and scooped up some water. She stood up, went to Medhi, and dumped the water on him.

"Gah!" He flailed at her, but she stepped back. "What in the—Amira! Abyssal take you, that wasn't necessary."

"Really? I thought it was perfectly necessary. It seemed like you were getting sick with stupidity."

He wiped the water from his face and glared at her. "Better stupid and alive. Dumping water on me isn't changing my mind, you damn child."

With a single motion, she scooped the water and splashed it at his face before he moved. He sputtered and looked ready to toss her overboard.

"Oh? You sure?" she said. "Then you won't mind if I—"

"Amira, if you do that again, I'm going to—Agh!" Water went right into his mouth and he gagged and coughed. He left the tiller and grabbed the bucket, but she didn't let go. "Enough! Stop being childish, you little filthy—"

"Filthy what?" she said, her smile as tight as her other fist. Medhi, soaking wet again, paused. "Go on. How do you see me? A child? Oh, wouldn't that be great. Easy to tell kids off, isn't it? Or, wait. No, you were probably thinking of a little bitch, right? Makes sense. My other patrons often called me that. A dumb mutt to command." She huffed, still smiling, though it burned almost as hot as the flaming knot in her stomach. Medhi shut up as she let go of the bucket and stepped back. "Or, maybe you were going to say whore. A filthy whore."

Medhi tightened his jaw and breathed through his flared nostrils. "Any of those sound good to me right now."

"Of course they do. Because all I am is someone to bed and then tell off. I'm sure you're enjoying this, so how else may I serve you?" She took a deep bow.

"You're being ridiculous."

"Of course I am, my lord. Please, disgrace me more while I wipe your feet."

"Oh, just stop, will you!" He grabbed her arm and she flinched under the sharp pain. "We don't have time to deal with your childish pouting. Take the bucket and start bailing." He shoved the bucket back into her arms and pushed her back. "You'll thank me later."

It was all she could do to hold back from cracking the bucket over his skull. "You bastard. You're going to yell at me, hurt me, keep me from saving people dear to me and you have the gall to say I'll thank you for it?"

He sat back down at the tiller in a huff. "Yeah. When we're past this and you're still alive, you'll thank me for being a good friend and stopping you from making a stupid mistake. So, just shut up and trust me."

And this right here, him saying they were friends, made the fury rage hotter than anything else he'd said. Because those words were what she'd often hoped to hear from his mouth. So how dare he take those words, those precious words, and use them against her now. Because as he spoke them, as she heard them, it hurt so much to realize just how wrong he was.

"Friend? Please, we're not friends."

He rolled his eyes.

"We're not."

"If you still need to pout, bail water as you do it."

Her mask cracked.

The bucket dropped from her hand. And her prihand slammed against his jaw.

He wrestled against her as her onslaught continued. "Icy Abyss, what's gotten into you?" He grabbed her wrists and overpowered her, slamming her into the boat's watery floor. "Amira, stop."

"Get off me, you bastard. Get off!" She flailed, kneeing his side.

He grunted and shoved off her. "Fine! I'm off. You done now?" Medhi wiped the blood from his mouth and massaged his jaw. "Lady above, what's wrong with you?"

Gulamira picked herself up, though she ached from his rough handling of her. "We're not friends."

He groaned, closing his eyes to take in a deep breath. "I don't know what's gotten into you, but I'm done talking about this."

She stepped forward, water sloshing around her. "We weren't and aren't—"

"How are we not?" He threw his hands in the air, looking just as willing to strangle her neck as she was his. "Tell me that. How, after all we've been through, can you dare say we aren't friends?"

"What we've been through, Medhi, is you buying a service, nothing more. And you can't buy friendship." The words bubbled up out of her. Words she hadn't known her mask hid, but felt the stinging truth of them as they poured out. "You exchanged coin for companionship. That's not how friendships work."

A bit of his intensity died down. "Come on, that's not fair. I didn't always sleep with you."

She rolled her eyes. "Well, doesn't that just make you the greatest gentleman?"

"Abyssal's tail. I've bared my soul to you and told you things I've told no one else. And you've done the same. We've laughed and cried and played together. How's that not friendship?"

Another crack in her mask. This time, anger and fury did not leak out. Instead, it was something colder and robbed her of strength and determination. Her knees buckled, her smile quivered, and she leaned back against the mast, no longer able to look him in the face. "And what if I didn't laugh with you, cry with you, 'play' with you? I'd starve. And every time, you left me there." She looked back at him, and it was these words that finally shut his mouth, that stilled him. "You saw me so many times, Medhi. You saw the life I had. The people that came to me. And then you left. Without me."

"I... I was going to...."

"But you didn't. So, please, don't pretend like you actually care about me. Because you're just another Prikur."

The words left her mouth before she could stop herself, but he only looked at her quizzically.

"What's a Prikur?"

A part of her wanted to cut herself off, but she wouldn't. She stared out over the waters, hoping she looked to the north-east, to where Vierzen lay. "I was twelve years old when Prikur found me, stole and made me into someone's personal slave. He hurt me, took away my possessing ability, and then, then he went and..."

Her throat constricted and the words would not come. How could they? How could she truly explain the deprivations of the man that abused her while simultaneously feeding her, clothing her, and whispering in her ear how much he loved her? No one had praised her more than Prikur had. No one had hurt her more than he. "There've been others like him. People trying to take something else from me. To use me until there's nothing left. They've all been Prikurs." The strength in her legs finally gave way and she slumped into a seat near the starboard side. "I always hoped you'd be different."

The wind picked up around them, with soft musical notes gathering with the waves. But Gulamira didn't look at the water. She glanced up at Medhi, who was motionless, with almost empty eyes. The intensity was gone, and he looked more dead than alive.

"You stopped smiling." The fire fled from his voice and he seemed smaller than she'd ever seen him.

Gulamira froze and then felt her face. No smile. Instead, a trembling lip. She tried to force her smile back, but she couldn't. She'd always been able to smile despite what Prikur and all the others did to her. Why not now?

Tears, angry and hurt and confused, filled her eyes, though she wasn't sure when those pesky traitors had clawed their way out of her. She looked away from him and tried to recompose herself, but to no avail.

"Do you really see me like that?" Medhi sat opposite her on the boat, one hand wrapped in his scarf, and in his eyes she didn't see his usual wildness. Which made it hard to say what she needed to say.

"When you saw my bruises, you ignored them. When you heard I was a slave, you moved to a different topic. You were kind, but you still used me. In that way, you are like him."

The wind picked up around them, and the music of the waters became a clear melody. Near to them, the silvery light of Chexel danced and integrated with another color, another glow. A soft blue light permeated the waters, growing brighter and brighter until six spirits surfaced surrounding the small boat.

Medhi gripped the mast hard and swallowed even harder. The spirits were all Commons, none taller than twenty feet. Each looked as different from the others as could be. One slithered through the water like a snake, one walked bipedal on top, another was all limb and fin. The only shared characteristics were their semi-translucent bodies and those solid white eyes.

Gulamira sat back and listened.

"Lady's skirts," Medhi whispered. "Is this how we go?"

Only two of the spirits even seemed to notice the boat. The others glided together and around each other, in and out of the water. The two had their simmering eyes set on Gulamira, their songs turning dark and hostile and hungry. Gulamira and Medhi were trespassing, as far as they were concerned. Trespassers died.

The spirits approached, their song coursing through the air, so Gulamira closed her eyes, opening her innermost ear, the ear of heart, soul, and life. And she heard. Beyond the wind and the waves and the flapping sails. Beyond Medhi's cries and the creaking boat beneath her feet. Far beyond even the ocean and the land and the skies and the heavens. She heard into the very voice of life and existence. She heard into the world of spirit, the home of Exkel. And the spirits' voices became as clear as white-crystal and as vibrant as a sparrow's call. What was hidden to most ears and disguised to most minds became more real to her than the very breath she breathed.

Their voices echoed through wind and wave and wood and bone, reverberating through the world, tapping into the very substance of life. They spoke, and yet it was nothing like speech. They sang, but it was nothing like a song. It was more like a deep knowing, a feeling beyond feeling. They sang as one and as many. They sang an angry song. Beautiful, quick, and unflinchingly forceful. She could feel, and almost see, their song permeate through the air and into Medhi and herself. The song would ripple through them, causing fear, dread, and anguish to the point of indecision and paralysis. A song that would incapacitate them as foes and make them easier to kill. It was beautiful. It had been so long since she'd heard spirits as she did now.

But she wasn't dying today, no matter how wonderful their song was.

She took in a small breath and left the languages of flesh and blood. She did not need to hold it back, didn't need to hide it amidst Rajal words. Her voice rang out in a clear and powerful note, cutting through the angry song of the spirits and replacing it with peace. The spirits stopped in their tracks, a few even shifted backward, all eyes centered on Gulamira. Medhi stared as well, his breath returning as the spirits' song stopped affecting him. But she sang on, past Medhi's confusion and through the surprise of the spirits. Her song lifted away the anger of the spirits, banished it from the ocean, and as it did, the spirits joined in on the song, letting peace be all there was on the waters. In that peace, she felt her smile slowly reform. She tried to hold on to some of her own rage, but the song affected her as much as it did them.

And she sang her song unto completion, letting her body savor every single melodic note, letting the song take her far, far away to the feet of Exkel. As the song ended, the spirits stared at her a moment longer, and then turned from the boat and left them, whispering farewells only she would hear.

A quiet settled on the boat as both watched the spirits leave.

"Right," Medhi said as the waters grew more silvery than blue. "Explain what just happened."

"Did you know the spirits have a language?"

"Let's assume I didn't."

"Well, they do." She sat back down on the bench, but her eyes did not leave the fading image of the spirits. "They speak in songs. And these songs have the power to influence the mind and change the heart. I sing them too."

The spirits vanished, and she turned to look at Medhi. He gazed at her with an expression she couldn't decipher. She was sure it wasn't excitement, at the very least. "These songs are why I wasn't typically afraid in Archoz," she said. "With them, I could change how people thought about me or how they acted around me. If someone was getting too violent, my songs made them gentler. If someone refused to share a secret, my songs eased open their mouths." She glanced across the waves. "If someone wanted to take me into a dark alley, my songs dissuaded them."

Gulamira leaned back and stared at the moon-filled sky. It was strange sharing this with someone. It had been a secret of her order, and she remembered too many lessons about keeping it hidden from others. Yet, she told Medhi. Just like she'd shared so many other things with him that no one else knew. And perhaps strangest of all, it still felt as easy and as natural to tell him this as anything else.

"Amira?"

"Yeah?"

"Have you ever done that spirit song on me?"

They locked eyes, his expression still indiscernible. But her smile did not waver.

"I never wanted to."

He kept her gaze for a moment until a glint of his wildness returned to his eyes. Medhi gripped the tiller and adjusted their heading.

"What are you doing?" she asked.

"Turning us toward the Floating Treasure." His hand gripped his scarf and for a moment she thought he would remove it, but he let his hand fall to his lap. In his eyes, she saw he had much to say, much he wanted to say. But the proud man couldn't.

A wind blew across the boat, ruffling Medhi's scarf and tingling Gulamira's ears. Throughout these years, Medhi had been the only one who'd come close to being called a friend. But they never had a genuine friendship. In short time, she'd learn if such a thing was even possible.

19

NOT SO DIFFERENT

I'm not leaving my friends behind to cower in some hole in the ground. We've uncovered proof that our Oligarchs are serving an outside force! Why haven't we arrested or removed these traitors? They're working against us! True, we are still working on what this "Heritage" is and who "Regiik" is, but we've figured out where to look next. Argul and Ortu oversee the Temple of the Ethereal Tree right here in Al'Rajak. My companions and I are convinced there is more information kept deep inside there. We'll have all the evidence we need to uproot this cult.

-Raza Softbark, the one who digs to the bottom.

Isra groaned and picked herself from the floor. She winced and sat back, the side of her face throbbing from the beating she'd just taken. *Abyssal be damned,* she thought. *That hurt.*

And now... now she was some place dark. Darker than any night. Isra couldn't see walls or floors or decks or anything. She was in a void of endless black.

She was in the Abyss.

Isra took in a breath and exhaled. She couldn't panic and be a fool right now. She wasn't in the Abyss, and she wasn't dead. They'd been in the middle of the ocean, so she had to still be on the ship. And though pointless, she checked her circles and... she sighed and shook her head. Her sword was missing and in their earlier rush, she had stuffed her stylus in her shirt. It was missing too. Now, the only thing she had, her only possession, was the servant medallion still in one of her circles.

She felt around and found a wall. It was cold, like the floor. She rattled her knuckles against it and there came a metallic ring. So, metal walls and floors.

Great. She was alive. And she was their prisoner.

But not alone. Isra paused, listening. Someone cried nearby in some adjoining room.

"Hey," she said, her voice reverberating against her cell.

The crying stifled, and the person sniffed. "Hello?"

The voice wasn't clear. It sounded distant, like an echo.

"Is this the *Cleansing*?" Isra asked.

"The huge ship? Yeah. Who are you?"

"Where are we?"

"I... I don't know. They just keep us locked up in here. They have other people too, but they are always yelling and screaming."

Isra glanced about at the absolute darkness. So, they'd put her in the Wailing Room. At least she knew where she was. And if that was the case...

"You're the girl," Isra said. "Kamaria."

"You know me?" she asked.

Isra nodded. Then stopped, because she was an idiot. The girl couldn't see her. "Yes."

"You're the human. The one who tried to save me earlier."

Save and then sell, but details weren't important now. "Yes."

"Can you... would you mind... I want to see you."

"It's dark."

"There's a crystal on the wall, behind some metal." It sounded like the girl was shuffling around the floor. "Over here." Her voice came clearer this time. Isra groped her way over and found a spot that felt dented in. A lot, too. Seemed the last occupant had been quite aggressive with the wall. Then light poured out from the hole and Isra started.

"Are you there?" The girl's voice no longer had that distant ring to it. It came clear and straight through the hole.

"I hear you."

"Someone here before made a hole in this wall. I don't think they've been able to fix it yet."

Made sense. Must have been why this room didn't have any tatzons to begin with. Now for the crystal. She felt around the back wall and, like the girl said, found a panel that slid open. The lightstone was small, no bigger than a finger, and kept behind a metal grate, but it shed dim light into the room. Strange they'd give prisoners light, though as far as she knew, light had nothing to do with Solitude. Perhaps they thought to go this one decency.

Or, it was part of some other experiment of theirs.

Isra sat next to the dent and, with the light behind and in front, she noted the hole was larger than she expected. Not enough to be useful for escape or anything. But enough she could see most of the girl's face. And she smiled at seeing Isra.

"There you are," the girl said. "That's good. I didn't have anyone to talk to last time..." Her smile faded and a haunted look flashed across her eyes. She shuddered. "You're Isra, right?"

A nod.

"I guess I should say thanks for trying to save me earlier."

Isra shrugged. "Didn't work."

"But I know Tsuran is here now. We just have to wait and he'll come for me. He always does."

Given the *Cleansing*'s response to the intruders, if this Tsuran fellow could have come for her, he would have already. But Isra just shrugged. No harm in letting the kid dream.

Isra eyed the girl's smile. A small, but genuine smile here in the middle of a metal prison. Just like before, this kid had a strange calmness about her, aside from the few tears. A calmness that prickled at Isra's skin.

"Why..." Isra paused, unsure if she was going to ask another tatzon the same question on this ship. "Why're you smiling?"

The girl averted her gaze, and her gray cheeks reddened. "Something Tsuran taught me." She lifted her chin and straightened her back, as though strength entered her, and she spoke with a power in her voice, "I will fight for those who can't. I will live for those who don't. I will smile for those who won't."

Kamaria closed her eyes and let out a wistful sigh, as if those words wrapped warm arms around her. The same could not be said of Isra. The words did not touch her, nor did it answer her question. Lady save her, tatzons, for whatever reason, sure loved their pithy sayings that, when one looked at them, were vague enough to mean both everything and nothing at all. They had the luxury of nonsense proverbs.

Though, tatzon proverbs was something her father had taken particular pleasure in. As a girl, she'd once seen him studying tatzon literature in preparation to write his own series of proverbs. He had the strange notion that if tatzons understood a human could create wonderful compositions, then maybe they would take another step toward accepting humanity. It was just one of his many attempts. None joined him in it. Not even Isra.

"Do you know the song my mom used to sing?" Kamaria asked.

Isra blinked out of her thoughts and focused back on the tatzon in front of her. "Song?"

"Yeah, she sang it every night to put me to bed."

"Name?"

"Well, I don't know that, but it goes like this."

Kamaria hummed part of the song, and it sounded like a lullaby. But Isra focused on the girl's expression. There was a softness not there before, a kind of stillness and peace that just humming the song brought her. Made sense. Sometimes just thinking of her father's voice had a way of calming Isra, focusing her, grounding her into the earth and making her solid again.

"Nice melody," Isra said. "Don't know it."

The humming stopped, and the hardness returned to the girl. It was like her skin was a carapace and it needed to defend against attacks of predators. Isra recognized this hardness, this defense. It was something all humans learned: everyone else was against them. The world was a dangerous and predatory place ready to devour them. Beasts and spirits the size of trees hunted them and tatzons subjected them to poverty and servitude and annihilation. In every land, humanity learned time and time again that nowhere was safe for them, nowhere was welcome for them. The world hardened them all while it tried to fatten them for slaughter. Only her father had never seemed to learn this lesson.

Yet, Kamaria, this girl right here, wasn't human. She was tatzon.

"Where is your mother?" Isra asked.

Kamaria was hollow faced when she spoke. "She's dead."

The girl started to say more, but her lips trembled and she rolled her head back and forth, as if trying to keep it all in. As if speaking made it more than true.

"Sorry to hear." Isra thought very much about strangling herself. *Sorry to hear*? What an asinine thing to say. But what else was she supposed to say to that? "Do you have a father?"

Kamaria's expression darkened even more. "I don't know him. He never came to the prison, so I didn't meet him. But, Tsuran acts like a father—"

"Stop." Isra raised her hand. "You were in a prison?"

Kamaria nodded, as if this made the most sense in the world. "In the mountains. I was born there. I never even saw the outside world until a year ago when they took me out."

"They?"

"Tsuran. He saved me and has been taking care of me and training me to be a Guardian." She smiled talking about him, but it vanished and her eyes hardened fast. "Tsuran and *she* took me from the prison."

"She?"

"The one who killed my mom. The ordîn who's with Tsuran."

An ordîn? Did she mean the one who'd fought those Lightless? Isra was not sure what to do with that. This was not the conversation she'd expected. Least of all from a child.

"You travel with the one who killed your mom?"

"I don't want to be," Kamaria said, huffing. "I've run away many times, but they always find me."

Isra narrowed her eyes. So, these companions murdered her mother, took her from prison, and found her when she ran away. This didn't sound like concerned rescuers. It sounded more like someone paid these two to capture her. Good thing the child distrusted at least one of them.

"Where were they taking you?"

Kamaria shrugged. "Tsuran said they were trying to find someplace safe for me. But everywhere we've gone, people have chased us away. I think everyone else knows, too."

"Knows what?"

"What I'm not supposed to know." Isra looked over her shoulder and leaned in to whisper, as if to make sure the other tatzons in Solitude couldn't hear. "Sometimes I've pretended to be asleep, but I'm awake. And I've heard Tsuran and her talk. They don't think I understand, but I do."

Isra leaned close too, pressing her forehead against the wall. "What do you know?"

"Someone wants me dead."

She spoke so matter-of-factually, to a degree that Isra wasn't sure she heard right. Because she couldn't have.

"Someone wants you dead?"

Kamaria nodded. "I heard Tsuran talk with her about it once. Someone paid her to come and kill me, but she got it wrong and killed my mom." Her brows furrowed, and she huffed. "Shows how stupid she is."

"Why would someone want you dead?"

The question came out before Isra had time to process it. Because the kid was wrong. Whatever she heard, whatever they told her, she was mistaken. This was a child trying to understand the death of her mother and she blamed herself. Isra could relate to that.

Kamaria, though, had an answer to the unprocessed question. "I think it's because they know I'm going to be an amazing Guardian someday and they're scared."

This kid. Isra wanted to smile, but couldn't manage. Kamaria had a surprising resilience. Kidnapped, on the run, dead mother, born in a prison in the... wait.

"The two with you, a tatzon and an ordîn?" Isra asked.

"Yes, Tsuran and... Nasna." She said the woman's name as if it were a spoiled mushroom.

But Isra leaned back, something clicking together. "Fugitives from the Iron Mountains."

Kamaria lit up. "Yes, that's where I was born. How'd you know?"

"Wanted posters. An ordîn and ex-Guardian." But in none of the bounties was there any mention of Kamaria. So either the authorities didn't know about her or they didn't want general folk to know. Though there was something else that bothered her. When Isra and Kamaria had run into Gulamira and that ordîn, this Nasna did not take Kamaria and run with her. She stayed back and risked her life. As long as Kamaria was safe, she didn't care. And that... that just made little sense. If someone paid them to kidnap this girl, then why would they risk their life like that?

Isra sighed and rubbed her head. She was thinking too much about this. The actions and motivations of this ordîn and ex-Guardian had nothing to do with her. Besides, for all their effort, Kamaria was still here. Trapped.

"Are you a criminal too?" Kamaria asked. "Is that why you're here?"

Isra smirked. "Criminal? Maybe. Not why I'm here."

"Why are you here?"

"I'm here..." She sighed. Lady above, why was she here? Risking her life for a piece of metal, stuck in the middle of the ocean with no escape and no aid, now talking with some child tatzon about how cruel life was. Her finger drifted over the circle with the medallion, with the symbol of her servitude to her step-mom, and the tattoo on her shoulder itched. Sometimes the simplest questions were the hardest to answer. But, at least this time, the answer was one she'd told herself every single time her step-mom had ordered Isra to do her bidding.

And she felt like saying it. "I'm here to save my people."

"Really? How are you doing that?" Kamaria asked. "Do you have family on the ship?"

"Nothing like that." She took in a breath. And maybe because it was a child or maybe because she had nothing to lose, but she continued, "Do you know who the Sefaran are?"

Kamaria shook her head and looked away, as if ashamed about her lack of knowledge.

"They're a group of humans," Isra said. "They're a people. Joined by ancestry, faith, and value. And by so much more."

"They're a family?"

"Yes. A family. Everyone hates them."

Kamaria looked up. "Why?"

"The Sefaran don't come from the Meadowlands. They come from the other side of the Maw. At one point, they left their homelands and came to Veirzen and Rajalend. At first, everyone was glad to see them. They brought innovation and technology people never knew before. They brought scholars and architects and teachers and artists and... and it was good."

Isra paused. She never spoke about this to anyone. Doing so was asking to be killed in most places and total ostracization in all others. Yet it was easy to talk about the Sefaran with this kid. With a slight smile, Isra continued,

"Problem was that the Sefaran brought a sickness with them. It wasn't a problem where they came from, just caused a small fever and runny noses. But the nations in the Meadowlands weren't used to it."

"People got sick?"

Isra nodded. "And they died. But not the Sefaran. Their bodies were powerful enough to live. That's not what anyone else thought. They believed the Sefaran were servants of the Abyss and cursed those they touched."

She leaned her head back against the wall and stared at the ceiling. "Soon, everyone hated the Sefaran and sought to kill them. Many Sefaran died, and the rest fled for their lives. To this day, people still believe the Sefaran to be cursed and to be the Abyssal's personal servants."

And in the three hundred years since those days, nothing had changed. Nothing until her father.

"You're a Sefaran?" Kamaria asked.

Isra's throat constricted, but she swallowed the growing knot. "Yes. I am."

To admit it to anyone was a death sentence. But this was a child. One who didn't seem to know the hatred that other people had. It was strange to consider it: a tatzon who didn't hate her people.

"My people live on a land in Rajalend," Isra said. "Land my family owns. It's become a haven for the Sefaran, a place to live their lives and make fine wages. But there are powerful tatzons who want to see the Sefaran suffer. There's a growing movement among some Rajal elites to take away my family's land."

Kamaria gasped. "Where would your people go?"

"They're going nowhere. I'm making sure they don't. That's why I'm here. On this ship, there's this idol of Mirr, an old religious artifact. If you give one to the Oligarchs, they'll grant one favor to you, no matter the ask." Isra moved over and looked at Kamaria, who hadn't stopped looking through the hole. "I'm getting that idol. And with it, I'm going to make sure the land is secure. The Oligarchs can't change how people feel about Sefaran, but they can make sure we have land. And my people will be safe."

"What happens if you can't get the idol?"

Isra had done her best to not think about it, because there was only one result. "My people are going to lose everything and the Rajals will hunt us down. People hate us, don't want us, reject us. They see us and turn away, hear of us and want to vomit. They speak of us with every foul word they can imagine. We're not welcomed anywhere in the world. If I don't bring back that idol..."

Isra's breath ran hot, but she grabbed her right shoulder and focused on the tattoo there, the one of her family's crest. Losing control in front of a child wasn't something an adult should do. But they were in jail right now. Maybe the typical rules of conduct didn't matter and anything could happen. She was talking to a tatzon about her lineage, after all.

But no. Losing control gained her nothing. She breathed in deep, trying to set aside and ignore the burning desire to scream and wail and pound at the doors and dig her nails into the ground.

"Are there any tatzon Sefaran?"

Isra paused and glanced over, staring at the girl. It took a moment for the question to sink past all the other thoughts. "Sefaran are human."

"Oh." Kamaria looked disappointed. She also looked like she wanted to say more, but she turned away.

"Why?"

"It's nothing."

Isra opened her mouth, but closed it. If the girl didn't want to talk, she didn't need to. Of all people, Isra knew that.

No. Isra would be an idiot to think like that. Everything about Kamaria right now, her posture, her scrunched brow, her distant eyes, everything spoke of a deeper question beyond the one asked.

Because no one ever asked the real question. People hid them inside other questions. Isra hated this. But that was how people were. And Kamaria was no different.

And before Isra started down a path of wondering why she should even care and rationalizing why she was better off ignoring the girl, before she turned away and retreated into herself, before she moved toward being like her step-mom, she made a slight step toward being like her dad.

"Kamaria," she said, and the girl looked up. "What did you want to ask?"

"No, I didn't want to—"

"Tell me."

Kamaria bit her lip, which trembled. "I... I just wanted to know if tatzons could be Sefaran."

"Why?"

"Because... because I wanted to know if I could be one."

Isra blinked and though her mouth hung open, her mind was empty of any response.

"People don't like you or want you," Kamaria said. "But you like each other and want each other. I want that. Back in the prison, no one but my mom wanted me. Everyone wanted to hurt me. Since then, it's the same. No one wants me or likes me." The girl looked up, a twinkle in her eye and a softness to her features. "But if I was a Sefaran, then I'd have family. And I'd work hard, too! I would make sure everyone liked me and I didn't bother anyone. Maybe I'd live with you, but I could also live outside if that's what I needed to do. And I could protect everyone. I'm going to be a strong Guardian one day and so I can protect everyone from beasts and spirits and tatzons."

Kamaria spoke so fast, as though if she didn't say it all at once, none of it would ever happen. But it couldn't happen. It was impossible. It was... was she really asking? She wanted to be a Sefaran. She wanted to be Isra's people.

Isra stared through the hole at the girl, not altogether sure what to say. After all, no tatzon, not even other humans, wanted to be a Sefaran. Want their land and money and labor? Yes. Want to be one of them? Never.

"Kid, I—"

The loud thunk of a door closing interrupted Isra and there were faint voices from beyond the cells. Someone had come into the Wailing Room.

Isra glanced at Kamaria and both stayed still for a moment, waiting for their doors to fling open. A moment passed. And then another. Didn't seem like the newcomers were coming for them just yet.

"I'm going to listen," Isra said.

The door was pretty thick, but this wasn't the most secure of Solitude cells. Doubtful it could be on a ship. Isra pressed her ear to the door, and though muffled, she could make out the conversation.

"The officers can't come by."

"What? Why not? I need their help to move these people. Spirits are perfect for this."

"A Rajal merchant just passed us by. I guess no one thought to tell you."

"So the Captains did a bit of pre-trade, did they?"

"Seems like it. Traded over a good number of slaves to buy the boat onboard the ship."

"A boat? They bought a boat?"

"It had sails. The captains have sent Hij and Kami out into the ocean to look for the escaped priestess."

Priestess? Did they mean Gulamira? No one else was escaping. Well, seemed she'd gotten away, then. And became a holy person. Ambitious woman.

"Fine, if we don't have spirits, then I want six guards for the rest. For now, you two help move the human."

Well, that meant Isra's time here was up. She slunk back to the hole. "Kamaria, they're taking me."

"What? No. Where?"

"Nowhere good."

The girl slumped to her knees and peered through to Isra. "I don't want to be alone again. I don't."

"I know."

Kamaria looked up, a new, determined look in her inexperienced eyes. "We should escape. You saved me before. We'll do it again. Better this time!"

Isra smiled and reached through the hole. Kamaria reached out and grabbed a finger.

"Yes," Isra said. "Let's escape. Do whatever you can to get out. Don't wait for me. If you see an opportunity, take it. Make a plan. Think beyond them."

She shook the girl's hand. The prihand of a little tatzon.

"When I get out," Kamaria said, "I'll come get you."

The talking from outside got louder and Isra took her hand back. "Just get out if you can. I'll manage." She shot the girl a smile. Kamaria smiled back.

The door opened, light blinded Isra, and brawny arms locked iron around her and took her out and away.

20

---◆○◆---

THE SUMMIT OF BLOOD

Ten Years Ago

The young priestess Gulamira watched her parents' killer approach her.

Gulamira did not move. She could not. Her body was unresponsive.

The killer stopped in front of her, a black void amid a patch of red. They stared at her and she, shaking, stared back. Gulamira could not see their face behind the mask they wore, a faceless black clay mask so polished she thought she saw her face reflected in it.

She stared into that mask. She stared into death.

Something grabbed from behind and pulled her hard. The killer's sickle swiped down, but missed.

"Gulamira!" Erasyl held her prihand, his face drained of color. "Run!"

She obeyed. Somehow she obeyed, and the two ran like a gazelle from the hungriest leopard.

The camp was in turmoil when they rushed out. Rajals crowded around, Veirs had their weapons drawn, but the two children ran past everyone, the killer on their heels.

The two pushed out of the encircled guards, leaving them to deal with the killer themselves. Gulamira glanced back, the hint of safety trying to enter her heart. But this hint was squashed when the masked assassin left the meeting tent and engaged with the soldiers there.

The assassin struck four guards down before any reacted. More blood filled the land.

"This way." Erasyl pulled her along, aiming for the road back to Veirzen. But she slowed, unable to look away from the continuous killing.

This was her fault. She did this. If she hadn't dazed the guards, they would have stopped the killer. This was her fault. She killed her parents. She did. And Erasyl's parents. And priests of Exkel. Even now, because of her, more and more people died.

Her fault.

Her fault.

It was all her fault.

"Gulamira, we have to run." Erasyl held her, trying so hard to keep himself from crying. But why would he? She already was. She couldn't stop it or help it. "We can't stay here."

She shook her head, tears falling and falling and falling.

All her fault.

"They're going to come for us too. We have to get to safety."

"What about them?"

Soldiers shouted, yelled, fought, died. Not one of them had even touched the killer.

Erasyl sniffed, his breath shaky. "We can't worry about them. We... we have to go."

"No, I can't... I let this happen." She pushed away from him.

"Gulamira, stop!"

The tears wouldn't stop. The killing wouldn't stop. How could she stop? She wrenched her prihand from him and shoved off toward the killer. Erasyl leapt after her, grabbing her by the waist.

"You can't do anything! Gulamira please!"

"Let. Me. Go!" Her voice filled with songs of highest power. She pushed through his will and mind and dominated his hand, releasing her from his grip. He screamed, fear and pain filling his eyes. Her voice, her songs, filled the surrounding air, like an impenetrable shield. Erasyl fell back onto the ground, eyes wide, but she turned back toward the killer.

Gulamira wouldn't let anyone else die. No one else. Never again. Never again.

Songs swirled inside, all rising in her. Songs carried from Florella to Florella, passed down from Exkel's Mountain by his Breath. These songs stirred in the Hearth of Life, guiding her ancestors, and now they would guide her. One was louder than the rest, needing her to sing it, wanting her to unleash it. But she ignored this Song of the Coming Fire and chose a different higher song.

And she sang.

There would be no more of her people dead. No more would be killed. She was High Priestess. She held the songs of the Heritage. She would protect everyone. And she would kill.

Before the day was done, she would avenge her parents. The killer was not getting away.

The song left her mouth, left her soul, and broke through air and earth and stone. It shook the ground, the trees, and even the sky itself.

Everyone stilled at the quake, even the killer. Everyone looked around, feeling, yet not understanding, what had happened.

A haunting screech pierced through the stillness, followed by another, and another. And from the ground came dozens of glowing blue entities. The people around screamed and shouted as Gulamira's summoned spirits arose.

She smiled. No one else would die. Only the killer.

The spirits filled the land and the rivers. Smalls and Commons and Larges. All beckoned by her power. All bowing to her.

A figure slumped onto a tent pole near Gulamira. Salma bled, but lived. Yet, the elderly priest had a look of horror as he stared at Gulamira.

"What have you done?"

The spirits screeched as one. And as one, they attacked.

They attacked everyone.

21

AN ENDLESS SEA

How stupid are you? Sending a letter through a public carrier? Do you know what could have happened had my men not intercepted it quick enough? Shadow Strikers are involved, you damn fool! You think you can write whatever you want about two Oligarchs? You think it's that easy to rid them of power? Do you forget they are the damn Oligarchs? And what are we? Lowly humans. My office of Beneficiary gives us some leeway, but it has in no way erased all the distrust and hatred and bigotry tatzons have towards us. There are even whispers going around that our family is Sefaran! Do not forget in your excitement how precarious a position we hold. One wrong step and they will feed us to beasts.

-Syeda. Why in the Abyss are you not in Tutchal yet?

A swift wind followed the sunrise, filling the ever-sinking boat's sails. Gulamira scanned the gray horizon for any signs of pursuit. She hadn't seen anything during the half-night and she needed that to mean no one searched for them.

Especially since her boat sludged forward with all the water it took on. She swallowed her panic, prayed to the skies, and roused Medhi. He groaned and waved her off, but he woke and got back to steering. She wouldn't sleep. Instead, she picked up their bucket and mindlessly bailed water over the side, hoping it was just enough to get them to... anywhere.

They did not speak that morning, both too tired to find the energy or motivation to leave their daze.

She bailed water. He checked the horizon, adjusted the tiller, and stared at the sails. And she bailed another bucket. And then another. Her arms were getting stronger, or she was too exhausted to realize how exhausted she was.

There were fewer clouds today, so the sun started roasting their uncovered skin with no remorse. The heat tempted Gulamira to dump a bucket of water over her head, but had the wherewithal to resist, knowing it'd only make her more miserable in the long run. She tried to ignore the heat, the discomfort, the water level that rose in the little boat inch by inch. Her stomach grumbled, which she ignored, and her head ached, which she tried to ignore. It seemed both the outside and inside world wanted to make her miserable today.

Besides the clouds above, nothing changed as they sailed. It was an endless ocean and an endless horizon, which seemed to mock her insignificance and welcome her to the endlessness of her days. It would bury her without announcement. The ocean would bury her deep beneath its waters as easily and absentmindedly as someone kicking a street urchin or slapping a harlot who didn't smile.

"Amira, hey, Amira!"

She shook herself from her sinking thoughts and looked at Medhi, whose eyes were quite serious.

"No day dreaming, girl," he said. "We're taking on too much water."

She glanced down and her stomach twisted. The water was up to her calves now, and was rising faster. She cursed and started bailing.

"How did so much get in?" she asked.

"You must've dozed off for a while."

"I was only thinking. I couldn't have been that distracted."

"Yeah, well, tell that to the boat."

A part of her wanted to growl at him, but she kept bailing. "Why didn't you mention anything sooner?"

"I'm trying to find our bearing and course. I can't be keeping watch on you, too."

"Can't keep... Medhi, we're on a tiny sailboat. What is there to watch? You just say something when you notice I'm not doing anything."

"And I did, if you didn't realize."

"Right, after the boat started taking on too much water. What, were you also in your own little reverie?"

He scoffed. "Please. I've sailed these oceans longer than any, I don't get—"

"You bastard." She threw the bucket at him, and he threw up his arms in defense. "Your mind was wandering just as much as mine. And now you're trying to blame me for all of this?"

"Don't throw things at me," he said, and his grip tightened on the tiller. "And damn you and your accusations. I've done my part keeping us sailing. You just have to do your part. It's not my fault if you're slacking off."

"Ah, great, and now you're accusing me of slacking off?" One fist curled, but her lips were too dry and stiff to do anything but stay in her neutral smile.

He glared at her and rolled his eyes. "Just get back to work, will you?"

She gave a nod and mock curtsy. "Of course, my great and powerful lord. Anything for you."

She bent down for the bucket. Which wasn't at her feet. And it wasn't behind her either. Wait, where was it? She looked on either side of Medhi and then again turned back to her side of the boat.

"Where's the bucket?" she asked.

"What?"

"Where'd you put the bucket?"

"I didn't put it anywhere. You're the one who threw it at me."

"And then you tossed it aside."

He looked at her as if she were stupid and she looked at him with an increasing desire to punch his face. "I didn't catch it," he said. "It hit my arms and bounced over..." He looked in the boat. Both looked at each other, and then behind the boat. Now a good distance away, bobbing a bit in the water, was their only bucket.

Medhi jumped to his feet, water sloshing around them. "You lost our bucket!"

"I lost it?" she said, not backing away from him. "You're the one who knocked it into the ocean."

"You're the idiot who threw it at me. So go."

"What in the Abyss are you talking about?"

He pointed at the bucket. "Go get the damn bucket."

She put her hands on her hips and glared at him. "Why should I? You're the better swimmer, I'd imagine."

"This is your fault. You make it right."

"My fault? You're the one who started all this!"

"You were to keep us from sinking, so no, this is all you."

Oh, her prihand flinched. It was ready to wring that scarf covered neck of his. Of all the nerve of this damn... wait...

"Medhi, where's the bucket?"

He looked confused, but glanced back. "It's... it's..." He turned and stood on his seat, scanning the area. "It was just there. Right there and now... ah, damn it! It sunk."

Gulamira's hand lost its tension, and she leaned back against the mast. Medhi slunk into his seat and buried his head into his hands. Gulamira looked up at the sky again, but there were no answers from the heavens. Only, it seemed, the Abyss' summons.

They continued on, slower than ever, trudging through the never-ending waters. The boat took on more and more water, only mitigated by the wood's natural buoyancy. Though, that'd only last them so long.

She ducked underneath the boom and splashed to her spot at the bow, but stopped as she looked ahead. Something emerged from the horizon, dark against the bright white and blue.

"Medhi, something's ahead."

The man came up beside her, his earlier fury giving way to exhaustion. He squinted for a moment and then lit up and jumped back to the tiller. "Lady, bless us. Thank you. Quick, Amira, duck low. Need to get as much speed as possible."

She did as he said this time, and he adjusted the sails. Even though waterlogged, the boat picked up a bit more speed. "Is it land?"

"Can't be anything else."

"Can we make it?" She looked at the water sloshing around in the boat.

"We will. We will."

Gulamira knelt in her seat and prayed as they sailed forward.

The dark image grew in size and detail as they approached. And it wasn't the type of island she expected. It was a sea-tree, trees with trunks that reached the ocean floor and branches that twisted and curved above the water to create a massive dome. In her addled state, the sea-tree reminded her of a tatzon with long, braided strands of hair that moved around with a life of their own. And it was this tangled mess a braided canopy that made the island.

However, their little sailboat slowed more and more as the hour turned into another. More and more water filled. The sea-tree grew closer and closer, but not fast enough.

The lip of the boat's side sat just above the waterline when Medhi came up to Gulamira. "We'll have to swim the rest of the way."

She looked at the distance. They had to be a good mile or two away. Her arms hadn't recovered from all the water bailing she'd done.

"Can't we break off some of the boat to float on?"

"What're you breaking it with? I've a dagger and that's it. Stop being an idiot and swim!"

They dove into the water and left the ocean to claim the boat. The going was even tougher than she'd expected. She knew how to swim. She'd been on the ocean long enough that it'd been necessary, but she wasn't the best. Medhi looked like he was more of a natural and he swam ahead. She kept her head up and pushed herself as much as she could, because if she didn't, she'd die. There was nothing else for her to do but destroy her arms and lungs in order to save her life.

The water was pleasant, which made it all the worse. If it'd been boiling hot or even chilled cold, it'd have been better. At least then the ocean wouldn't have been lulling her to rest, to sleep forever more. It was deceptively welcoming. So welcoming. It lapped around her and seemed to whisper promises of easing the strain in her arms and taking away her unrest. All it wanted was to embrace her, hold her, suffocate her.

She coughed up a bit of water and shook herself from those damning thoughts. No. The ocean was not her ally right now. So she pressed on. Arm after arm. Kick after kick.

And the tree didn't seem to get any closer.

She swam, and she swam and she swam, but there was only water, water, and more water.

Her arms didn't ache. In fact, she didn't feel them anymore. She barely could move them. Her arms gave up as if they'd abandoned her.

She sank.

"Medhi!"

She kicked, trying to keep herself up, but her legs tired too. Staying afloat had already been so hard. Water splashed her face and washed up past her eyes. She kicked hard.

"Medhi! Help—"

Water flooded her mouth as she submerged. The world dulled and darkened. She shook and thrashed herself above water. She took in a gasp of air. A wave crashed over and she spat out salt-water, losing most of the air she'd gotten.

And it hit her.

She was going to drown.

No. No. Not here.

She kicked hard. Water gripped her and pulled her down. Her arms stayed as useless traitors.

The ocean fought back against her pathetic attempts at life. It grabbed her and pulled her under. She tried to fight back, to get back to the world of light and air. It refused her.

Gulamira wanted to scream, shout, yell, anything but only frantic bubbles sputtered forth.

She was going to drown. She was going to drown. She was drowning.

A hand burst through the waters, grabbed her by the arm, and yanked her up above the waves. Air ripped into her lungs as waters retched out of them.

"Amira!" Medhi said, holding her tight. "Breathe, just breathe. I got you."

She wanted to grab him and hold him, but it was as if she were armless. "Medhi... I can't... I can't..."

"I've got you." He wrapped an arm underneath hers and around her waist. "I've got you."

And he swam, keeping her above the water. She kicked with what strength she had, not wanting him to do everything, but he did not complain or curse at her. He swam. For a time that felt like days, he swam.

He did not let her go.

They reached the edge of the sea-tree, of which the canopy rose above them like a Common sized tree itself. One branch twisted downward and into the water, creating a ramp from the ocean to the trunk. The branch was bigger than the two of them, so Medhi pulled Gulamira and himself up onto it and promptly collapsed on his back.

They were both still close to the water, and she knew it'd be safer to go up further. But neither moved. They coughed and panted.

Somehow, they had made it.

Gulamira's eyes flickered, trying to stay open. But they were so heavy. So, so heavy. She could afford to close them now, just for a moment. They had solid wood beneath them with gentle waves around them. No sign of a storm. They were safe. They were safe.

A breeze blew through the boughs past them, cooling her down but also carrying with it the sounds of the tree. Rustling leaves, creaking branches, lapping water, and... and something else. Something that eerily resembled the low growl of a predator.

She'd need... she'd need to get up and... there could be danger... could be...

Another growl drifted along the wind past her, and Gulamira fell asleep.

22

THE SEA TREE

R az, I don't know how I'm supposed to say this... your companions are dead. My messenger went to collect some new findings from them and... Raza, they were burned alive, in your house. There's nothing left. All of your books, your notes, your years of research. It's all gone. We questioned people around, but no one knows how it happened. Everyone awoke with the screams and... I'm sorry. I'm sending everything we salvaged to you, though it's not much. I am also going to ask Lamia to take you somewhere in Tutchal for a time. You're not safe here and I won't let you die. It's time to stop. This is not a request.

-From a letter to Raza Softbark, found crumpled in the cold hearth.

Piercing yelps and barks shot through the air. Gulamira awoke with a start, jumping to her feet. She slipped on the smooth wood and fell face first onto the massive branch. Her hand found a knot, which was the only reason she didn't fall off the branch and into the ocean.

The barks kept up as she pulled herself back to her feet. She took in a few deep breaths and looked for Medhi. The three moons were low on the horizon, though it was hard to tell if it was the start of a half-night or the end of a full-night. Yesterday had been a full-night, right? Or had that been the day of the storm? Yesterday had *felt* like a full-night at the very least. Either way, the moons flooded the sea tree with silver light.

Medhi crouched further up the branch. Seemed those barks had also awoken him. Careful where she stepped, Gulamira made her way up the branch to him.

"Sounds like a pack," he said as she knelt beside him. "Otters, most likely. As if this couldn't be worse."

"Are they on the tree?" she asked.

"Not sure. Could be. Sea otters are frightful predators. They're comfortable on land as much as the sea. Not the greatest climbers, though. Hoping that means they wouldn't go deep into a sea tree." He glanced over at her. "You feeling up to a brief climb?"

Gulamira looked out at the tree before them, its long branches twisting and curving out from the enormous trunk like Colossal snakes. There were no walkways or bridges here. "I feel more tired than before. Are we not safe here?"

"Third rule of the sea: there's nowhere that's safe."

"Since when does the sea have rules?"

"Sailor expression." He started up the branch. "Besides, I'm hoping this tree's in bloom up top."

Just looking at how far they were from the trunk made her arms quiver and bring up polite complaints about what she'd put them through the last couple of days. But Medhi was moving on. So, she tried to keep her huffing to a minimum and followed behind.

The climb was as hard as she'd imagined, and her imagination had run wild. Most of the wood was smooth but firm. There wasn't much to hold on to or grab since most of the foliage was higher up the tree. Seemed waves rose high enough to hit this part of the tree, a terrifying thought when considering the frequency of storms.

Half of her mind focused on not falling from the high elevation, while the other half listened to the barking of sea otters. These were not playful barks or calls. No, this was something brutish and ravenous, aggressive and primal. It had been a long time since she'd been in Veirzen, but it was a nation of Wranglers and she still remembered the differences in beast calls.

Up here, she noticed that most of the branches, including the one they were currently on, didn't grow from the trunk of the sea-tree, but from other branches. They followed the offshoots like a map to the top of the tree, where the branches connected with the trunk. However, the top of the trunk had a dozen thick branches that shot upward, creating a bulbous cocoon in the center of the webbed dome. There was little spacing between the cocoon branches, but Medhi found a spot wide enough for them.

He sighed as he squeezed through the tight branches and into the area. "Good. Good." He glanced back as she squeezed through to join him. "We're in luck. We've got some blooms here."

She saw what he meant as she entered this open area. All along the branches grew these luminescent green flowers. Not a lot of moonlight made it through the dense canopy and bulb of branches, yet the flowers glowed as if made of crystal. Medhi walked to the nearest and plucked it.

"Some sea trees are like this." He gestured to the open area and dome-like room made by the branches. "They grow these little pockets at the top of the trunk. It's only there you find these."

"Is... is this a honey tree?" she asked, gazing at her surroundings.

"No, though lots of sailors think they are because they make glowing flowers. Far as I know, they're just trees."

She stepped up to the flower. It had a subtle but pleasant smell. It had seven large petals and the whole thing was the size of her prihand. Inside looked like some kind of glowing sap. "What did you want the flowers for?"

"We're eating them."

She turned to him. "What."

He tilted his head back and slurped the green sap from the flower, and then bit off a petal and chewed away.

Gulamira looked at the lunatic with one confused smile. "Medhi, were you drinking sea water the whole time we sailed?"

He wiped a drip of green luminescence from his lips and grinned. "You know what sailors call these flowers?"

"If I had to guess, I would say they call it the drunkard's wife."

He laughed and took a bite out of another petal. "That's a good one. Don't think anyone calls anything that, but that's a good one." He swallowed and gestured to the wall of flowers. "These are called Desperate Saviors. They don't look appetizing, but they're fine substitutes for food and water. Many a shipwrecked sailor has sung praises of these little beauties for saving their lives."

Gulamira looked from Medhi to the flower and back. She thought of objecting, but her stomach hurt from hunger and her throat was drier than the wood they stood on. Even if he was lying, it was worth a shot.

She tore a flower off a flower and poured the green sap down her mouth.

She gagged and spat it out.

"Oh, I should warn you," Medhi said. "This flower's honey is on the bitter side of things."

"You think? Oh, Icy Abyss, that was foul!"

"Get a new flower."

She spat again, but by Exkel, this stuff wasn't leaving her tongue. "There's no way I'm drinking that."

"You got to. We don't know when we'll have water again."

She looked at the flower, wanting to gag again. But the damn man was right. So, she plucked another flower, brought it to her lips, hesitated, watched Medhi eat another petal, and tried to down the honey as fast as possible. The stuff couldn't be called honey. It was closer to a poison. A poison she felt trying to kill her as it went down.

"Good job," Medhi said. "That was the hard part. Now the petals. I recommend rolling them first. Easier to chew. And don't worry, the petals aren't as bad."

"I'm not sure anything could be." She rolled a petal in her fingers and shoved it into her mouth, readying to get rid of the honey's—

Her whole body convulsed with revulsion, and she felt the honey trying to come back up. She held it down, though kept the petal in her mouth only through determine will.

By some miracle, she swallowed. Her smile, still present, shook. "I'm going to kill you."

He rolled up another petal, though he didn't seem eager to eat it. "They're the Desperate Saviors. Because only the most desperate want to be saved by them."

"You're a bastard, you know that? How are you eating them so easily? What's the trick?"

"No trick," he said and stared at the petal. "It tastes horrible. I'm just good at keeping a straight face. But,"—he looked at Gulamira—"I'll tell you now that this is the absolute worst thing I've ever eaten in my life and it never gets easier. It only gets worse and worse." He popped the rolled petal into his mouth, and for the first time, grimaced. "I'm not dying here. Are you?"

She looked at the Desperate Savior in her hand, its green glow warning of what was waiting for her consumption.

But she wasn't dying here. She couldn't.

The next hour was one of the hardest her willpower had ever experienced. After the first flower, Medhi had her eat four more. And he'd been right. Each was exponentially worse than the last, because the taste built on itself and never vanished, or because the anticipation and dread of every bite fed into the torture. Or both, along with some curse placed on these damn flowers. And if they weren't cursed already, she was ready to see if Exkel would do it on her behalf.

Strangely, the hardest part of it all was they worked. Her thirst lessened until quenched and her hunger eased into satiation. She felt renewed, though still pretty tired.

A foul wind blew through the dome, and Gulamira wrinkled her nose. "Oh, Icy Abyss. What is that?"

Medhi peered through an opening in the wall of branches, covering his nose with his scarf. "Smells like something's dead. Probably what's got the otters all excited."

"It'd have to be pretty big for its smell to reach us up here, wouldn't it?"

"Could be. Could be a lot of dead things."

Gulamira walked around the perimeter of the dome, stepping over knobs and random protrusions. "How safe you think we are in the dome?"

"Third rule of the—"

"Just answer the question."

"I did." He turned toward her. She was now on the other side of the dome, so he raised his voice. "There's no such thing as safe, permanent or temporary. If the otters down there decide to climb up here, they could rip through the tree to get to us. Even if they didn't, a random spirit could appear and take us. Or maybe a massive wave hits the tree and breaks off this section and plummets us into the water's grave."

She rolled her eyes and gazed at the ground. Sometimes, he was entirely unhelpful. But, she at least found a nice flat spot where they could lie down and sleep for the rest of the night, and based on how the moons moved through the sky, she knew it was a half-night.

She beckoned to him, but he took a few more minutes peering through the branches before he joined her. "I think I've an idea of where to go next," he said, sitting on the flat surface. "The moonlight showed what I think is another sea tree not too far from here and another after that. I think we could swim from tree to tree until we find an island."

"That will take forever. We don't have that kind of time."

"Time's not even the worst part."

"Oh, it's not?"

He shook his head. "The other tree is upwind."

She stared at him a moment, trying to remember some obscure sailor superstition of swimming upwind, but couldn't come up with anything. Then it hit her. "The dead thing is that way."

"As is all those otters." He stretched out and stared at the sky. "If the Lady smiles on us, the dead beast will distract them enough they ignore us."

"And if they don't, they kill us."

He nodded.

She groaned through a tight smile and leaned her head against the branch wall. As if anything could be worse than trying to out swim a pack of sea otters. But they couldn't stay here, that much was clear and fact. She looked out through the gap in the branches and at the ocean view. Three blaring moons illuminated the sea in swathes of silver. Winds hurried along the waters, creating cascading ripples and small vortexes that hinted at the life the water contained. A hint of its wonder and power. There were old Exkeldian poems and sayings about the ocean. Few dedicated much time to it since—

Gulamira paused and squinted her eyes. Out in the waters, had she seen... yes, yes, something swam out there, its backside visible above the water. This creature moved fast and away from the tree, headed for...

Headed for a set of sails.

She tapped Mehdi's shoulder. "Medhi, there's a boat in the waters."

He stirred and looked out. "Hm, doubt it's a boat. Too big. Looks like a zebec."

"Remind me when I care. But look, a beast is heading out there. Should we do something?"

He sighed. "No."

"But we could use a boat—"

"Ship."

"—to get out of here."

Medhi pointed at the beast. "It's moving faster than we can. There's nothing we can do, Amira."

Gulamira stared, wishing she could shout or yell or stop the beast. But he was right. There was nothing she could do. She couldn't even sing a song. Spirit songs had no effect on beasts.

The beast ripped through the waves, faster and faster until its head breached the water and a loud roar burst from its maw. And it kept getting closer. The beast dove under the water again. It wasn't far from the ship. Gulamira gripped the side of the tree as she waited to watch their chance of escape get dashed to pieces.

And Gulamira heard something faint, like a child's whisper or a butterfly's laugh. The wind did not carry it to her, nor did it drift through the air, but she heard it as it reverberated through life to her. A song. Soft, distant, yet she understood it. A song to beckon, a song to summon.

Blue-white light erupted from the ship and two figures appeared atop it, two glowing bodies.

Medhi leaned forward. "Are those..."

"Spirits."

Before the beast reached the ship, the spirits jumped into the water and sped to the beast. The sea became nothing but chaos. Roars, muffled and clear, ripped through the air, coupled with the hissing of water and churning of thunder. It looked like a pot of boiling water, though the food inside screamed and bled. Blue light coupled with flashes of white and orange. All the while, Gulamira and Medhi did nothing but watch. She had at first wanted the ship to get away, but now she wasn't sure who she wanted to win this fight.

And then everything stopped.

The ocean was a shade darker than before and the beast floated to the top, unmoving, and in two fresh pieces. The spirits left the water and returned to the ship. A moment later, they vanished.

Gulamira's heart raced, and she turned to get Medhi, who'd at some point grabbed her hand—or had she grabbed his? He didn't let go when she noticed, which eased her heart. His hand had a strange, but comforting effect.

"Soulborn," she said and tried to take a deep breath. She felt a little self-conscious still holding his hand, so she let go.

Medhi stared back out at the water. "Soulborn on a zebec is odd and not good news for us."

"You don't think..."

"We'll have to wait and see."

It took a bit of time for the ship to reach the sea tree. For a moment, it appeared as though the ship would sail on, but it stopped and moored just by a branch.

Medhi decided they needed a closer look, so together they made their way along a parallel branch that leisurely angled down to the water. Whoever was on the ship didn't leave it. They might have been sleeping for the rest of the night, though why they were still traveling this late was beyond her.

Their branch dipped just above the other, and Gulamira and Medhi both crawled to a position over the ship. A few sailors sat about. However, two stood near the stern of the ship looking out toward the dead beast, so the moons lit them up with perfect clarity.

Hij Con-Kami and Kami Con-Hij.

23

SOULBORN

L *amia, by the time you find this, I'll either be dead or uncovering the root of this cultish conspiracy. With this letter, I have compiled all of our findings in chronological and topical order. This should provide you Beneficiaries enough to start whatever investigations you can get away with. I need to know what is inside that Temple. The answers are there. I know it. Whether I succeed or die, I have to know. Please tell Syeda I love her.*

-Raza Softbark, the scholar who walks to his death.

"We can't stay here. Not with Soulborn around!"

"Keep your voice down." Gulamira looked over her shoulder, through the branches, and down toward where Hij and Kami were. Medhi paced back and forth, grabbing his scarf tightly. They'd got back to the tree dome without notice, but sound traveled far here.

"We need to get out of here," Medhi said. "I know we're tired, but we can probably make it to the next tree."

"And the otters?"

"They've been quiet. Probably asleep right now. Even they need to do that."

Gulamira walked to the other side and gazed toward the next tree. "There is no way we can make that. I can't make that."

"We'll have to, Amira."

"Why tonight? They aren't searching the tree. We could still sleep and escape their notice."

He twisted his hand around a loose part of his scarf, but it never revealed his neck. "We don't know what they're planning. They might do a quick search of the tree, just in case. Soulborn can do it fast, too."

"Then how would we be any safer on the other tree?"

"They'd search there after this one. Gives us time."

Gulamira looked back at the other sea tree. Just looking was tiring. If they ate some more flowers, she might swim the distance, but she was not eager to eat another Savior today and they'd likely die, regardless.

She straightened at the thought. And she smirked. "We're going to die."

Medhi came over and grabbed her shoulder. "No talking like that. We'll make it."

She shook her head. "No. I mean, if we try to swim, we could drown or the otters will eat us. Even if we made it, these Soulborn would eventually catch up when we're exhausted. Yet, if we stay here, they'll find us sooner. No matter how you look at it, stay or go, we die."

"You know, sometimes I hate how you can say stuff like that with a perfect smile."

"We'll also die if we stay," she said, touching his hand on her shoulder. "They'll search the tree, find us, and kill us."

"Well, if it's all the same to you, I'd rather not mark myself off for the noose yet."

"Me neither. So, let's take a third option." She squeezed his hand. "Let's fight."

He blinked. "Fight? With two Soulborn?"

She nodded.

"You and me?"

Another nod.

"A human and a tatzon who doesn't possess?"

Her smile flickered, but she nodded.

"How? You going to sing at them?"

"Spirit songs don't work on beasts for whatever reason. And Soulborn know about them and so train themselves to resist the effects."

"So, how in the Abyss do you plan on doing it?"

"So, you're willing to help?"

"I..." He looked between her and the ship. He then paused and sighed as he took her hand. "I already said I wouldn't make a mistake twice. What's your idea?"

She kissed his hand and shared the idea she had. It wasn't much of a plan, but it was something. It had the slimmest chances of success. Yet, it gave them the best possible outcome if it worked.

Medhi agreed. They took one last flower to eat and went to their probable deaths.

Gulamira stood at the edge of a spiral branch and stared down at the sea-tree beach. Not a beach made of sand or pebble or rock, but of densely interwoven branches. These branches weaved together like a basket mesh, and instead of rising into the sky or descending into the water, they grew parallel to the water, hovering just above it like a shelf. Every sea-tree had these wooden shelves, these "beaches", and were often used as natural docks.

Washed onto this beach was a massive seal, which from this distance looked as though it were a Colossal. The ship was on the other side of the tree, but that wouldn't delay the Soulborn long.

Gulamira steadied herself on the branch, careful to not slip on the many flowers at her feet.

She looked at Medhi, who was covered in the same greenish glow as she was. "Ready?"

He finished squeezing the last flower's sap over his body. "I would like to state again how terrible an idea this is."

"Noted."

They looked each other in the eyes for a moment.

Then they both took in deep breaths and screamed.

As soon as they did, they grabbed onto the spiral branch, thinner than others, and slid around and around and around, down to the beach.

Grunts and growls picked up into the air as the otters awoke to the noise. They didn't sound happy about it. Gulamira gripped the branch as she slid down, faster and faster, with the spiral closing tighter and tighter. The sap from the flowers acted as a lubricant, making their descent easy but gripping difficult. She held as long as she could, but the momentum built and it was like the air itself was trying to push her off the branch. She held fast as the world became a blur of dizzying vines. The grunts and whines grew closer.

She. Was. Almost. There!

Gulamira let go and flew off the branch and out toward the water. The ocean broke around her and crashed into her lungs. Grateful her aim was true, but understanding the insanity of this idea, she thrashed her way to the top, just in time to hear loud growls and sudden splashes as the otters dove into the water. She had moments to make this work and she would not fail. She swam fast toward the beach.

The latticework of the beach meant people—and beasts—could stand atop of it, but there were also branches underneath that would allow her to crawl between the water and the beach, thus providing protection from the otters above and below her.

She wasn't far, but right as she reached the beach, an otter burst up behind her and two others broke from the water and leapt to the beach. All three turned toward her as she pushed herself to the nearest branch.

They were all Common sized, fifteen or sixteen feet tall at their shoulders. Sharp claws dug into the wood, and long ivory tusks rose from their jaws. They growled, upset that the screams had disturbed their sleep. Gulamira instinctively rose a song to her throat, even though she knew it'd do no good.

"Hey! Over here!"

The otters and Gulamira glanced up to find Medhi standing on the upper side of the beach where the branches were thickest. Seemed he'd stayed on the spiral branch.

With the otters distracted, Gulamira dove under the beach and into the thick network below. A loud splash behind showed one otter followed. But her rapid descent earlier had put her in just the right place, and she pushed herself through the tight holes and into the undergrowth right before the otter slammed into the wood. The otter growled, clawed, and growled again.

Above, she heard Medhi shouting and the otters scratching up the beach, but she couldn't worry about him with her own otter trying to break through. Medhi would be fine. Oh, Exkel, she prayed he would be fine.

Gulamira pushed her worries for him aside and focused on the task at hand. She had to get to that dead seal. She had to get to its tusks. Spirits, and thus Soulborn, were hard to kill, but the ivory tusk of a Colossal would do it.

The water rose and fell around her, making her sometimes swim and other times crawl through the not-passages. The air thickened with the stench of the dead beast as she crawled closer, but the water rose past her nose, rescuing her from that torture. As the water rose past her ears, she thought she heard something like a muffled whine.

Sharp claws breached the branches beneath her and she yelped, sea water filling her mouth. Another claw scratched below her, reaching up through holes and gaps to grab her. She pushed to the side as the otter below her attacked. It was more difficult to maneuver because of the water. The otter clawed its way through the sea-worn tree, the wood below splintering before it. Gulamira, with fierce snarls following behind, scrambled forward as the water level dropped. The otter followed, breaking into the tight space she was in, pushing itself after her.

And Gulamira now understood her position. This was a true predator with the single intention of hunting its prey. And she was that prey. She stared back as death stalked her, clawed for her, hunted her.

Gulamira clambered away from the beast as it snapped its jaw at her. She pushed herself toward a place where there was a gap in the branches above, just wide enough to climb out of. The otter couldn't fit any further and pulled back, diving under the water again. Gulamira hurried to the gap and—

An otter's paw swiped down through the hole and Gulamira cried out and shoved herself back.

One otter from above clawed and clawed at the hole, lowering its maw into the gap and snapping at her. She saw its eyes, its black, endless eyes that looked to consume her whole. She frantically looked around but didn't see another point nearby she could crawl out of, and the otter from behind splashed and snarled in the water, close to her.

Medhi, help!

The beast stopped and sniffed the air. A tense stillness blew through the beach. The otter in front of her lifted its head out of the hole and the one behind stopped clawing at the branches. All the otters growled the deepest, most intense growl Gulamira had heard. She craned her neck and through the slits of the branch work, blue-white light danced about.

The Soulborn had arrived and Gulamira smiled. It seemed her and Medhi's screams had lured them just as hoped.

"Well," one Soulborn said. The possessor spoke from the spirit, which made their voice sound as if it had an echo, but Gulamira was certain it was Hij who spoke. "The pirate captain who left with the priestess. Seems we found them, Kami."

"Where's the woman?" Kami asked, "Don't tell us these otters got her."

The otters snarled, and the one in the water joined the rest on the beach.

"Go to the Abyss," Medhi said.

"Fine," Kami said. "We'll do this the hard way."

The beach above Gulamira erupted into loud roars and wild chirps. Flames and crackling power accompanied it.

She shook it off and crawled to the opening and pulled herself out onto the beach. As she did, two more otters appeared in front of her, rising out of the water. Their grunts joined the cacophony, which only grew louder and louder.

She spun around, water dripping from her, and saw Hij and Kami in full power. Lightning and fire crackled and encircled them as the beasts centered all of their rage toward these forces.

Other beasts joined the initial three, some from the water and others from nooks in the tree branches. More than a dozen Common beasts, each bigger than the two spirits.

But Hij and Kami could empower their possessions and had killed a beast last night that had been ten times the size of these otters.

The beasts didn't care, for there was a law of nature that could never be undone: beasts and spirits were mortal enemies and neither could let the other live.

The otters launched at the Soulborn, and the massacre began.

Gulamira ran from the utter decimation of the beasts and hurried to the dead Colossal. With any luck, these two forces would kill each other. Otherwise, she and Medhi needed a tusk free. They needed that weapon.

Fire erupted behind her, and she glanced back. Hij and Kami sped through the beach at an intense speed. They sliced through otters as through dry leaves. The otters screamed and wailed as their flesh burned and ruptured. But the otters fought back with an increasing frenzy, their ivory tusks ready to rend spirits apart.

She reached the Colossal, Medhi was already there. "We have to hurry," she said as she sidled next to one of the beast's tusks, growing from the lower jaw. It was thin, long, and had a deep blue coloration to it.

"No use," Medhi said. "It's stuck fast."

She grabbed the tusk and tried to wiggle it, but it was as Medhi said. It didn't even budge. "Can you cut through?"

"This is Colossal ivory. Only red-crystal or stronger can even pierce this."

The water splashed and Gulamira glanced back. Otters were flying this way and that as the Soulborn held them off. But the beasts returned just as fast.

"We've no other options," she said and threw her shoulder into the tusk. "So, help me!"

He joined her. They shoved, pulled, kicked and threw themselves into the tusk. No matter their efforts, it wouldn't make a single move—

"Amira, watch out!" Medhi shoved her aside, throwing her into the decaying puddle of cheek flesh. As they both fell into the filth, one otter slammed into the Colossal's mouth, as if the Soulborn had thrown it. The otter screeched and rolled over, a tooth stuck into it. The Common beast staggered a moment and then dropped dead.

"This is not a good place to be," Medhi said.

"Third rule of the sea." Gulamira pushed herself from the muck and examined the tusk. "I think they did us a favor. The tusk is looser now."

Medhi looked out of the mouth and gripped his scarf. "This is insane, Amira."

She grabbed onto the tusk and shoved back and forth. This time it gave way a bit. Not enough to dislodge, but enough she knew it would eventually come out.

The two grabbed it and threw all they had into getting this one piece of ivory.

The otters growled and circled the Soulborn, both of whom were alight with their spirit magic. Glowing white eyes tracked the otters. A battle of hunters, of predators.

Hij and Kami flowed around each other with breathtaking speed and grace, their spirits not creating a single sound or rustled leaf. They attacked as if they were different sides of a single entity. Hij flared his lightning to ward Kami's back as her flames erupted from her. Kami returned with keeping the beasts off Hij as he dove into the fray with crackling power. The pack worked together as well. But Hij and Kami were Partners. Not even a thousand beasts could match that perfect unison.

Kami's glowing white eyes found Gulamira.

Fire flew at the Colossal beast.

Gulamira pulled Medhi with her as they dove backward, and the flames seared the teeth, wood, and bits of Medhi's trousers.

Medhi jumped to his feet, ready to sprint out of here. "The game's up. We need to run."

"No, not yet." No more fire came. She hurried toward the tusk.

"Amira!" He grabbed her arm, but she turned and grabbed his.

"They can't keep this up," she said. "Possessors can only empower for so long before Remnancy grows and those two have not had long to rest from their earlier fight. They're going to run out of time soon."

He looked out at the Soulborn and gripped his dagger. She turned back to the ivory tusk. It was almost there, just about ready to fall out. Maybe one good kick or something would release it.

"They're slowing down," he said. "Damn it, you're right."

"Then help me get this!"

Another burst of flames coursed across the beast's maw. Both ducked, flames licking the tops of their heads. Red flames scorched the wood and blackened the decaying beast. Blue light intermingled with the orange flame and Kami stalked forward, fire dancing along her translucent blue body.

Gulamira froze. Medhi cursed and pulled out his dagger. Kami raised four fiery rings toward them.

Damn it. No. This couldn't be the end. They'd been so close!

An ear-piercing scream erupted through the air. Kami spun around in time to see the otters rip into Hij. And with one more scream, Hij unpossessed and left his spirit.

Everything froze for a moment. The otters stepped back, Kami gaped at her Partner, Hij laid on the ground. And Hij's spirit stared blankly at the beasts. It was as if no one understood what had just happened.

The spirit quickly remembered.

Crackling lightning erupted from the spirit toward the beasts, and the battle erupted anew. But the spirit was significantly weaker without Hij's direction and empowerment. Nothing would stop the otters from slicing through it.

Kami screamed at the otters, flames burning brighter and brighter, and drove herself to them.

They were the last otters. If she killed them, Hij could regain control of his spirit. If she stopped the other spirit from dying...

Gulamira clenched her prihand and punched the tusk. Pain shot through her arm like a fiery splinter.

She punched again. And again. And again.

Her prihand bled. The spirits screeched. Another otter died.

Gulamira screamed, raised her bloody prihand once again. Because she would not die here. She would not let them win. There was still an Exkeldian alive, and she was going to save them!

So, blood thumping, heart pounding, she spun away from the tusk and took in a deep breath. By Exkel and His Mountain, she hoped this worked.

She closed her eyes, and, with a single hope in her heart, she sang.

At first, her mind went to a song she knew but had never sung. A higher song, but one never taught. A song that killed spirits. The memory of it brought a sharp sting to the side of her face, the sting of a bitter lesson. She pushed the song aside, refusing to sing it. Some abominations were even too much for her.

She sang a different higher song, one instilled in her since childhood. A song that reverberated past what could be heard and seen, to the depths and inner places of soul and mind. It was a song that prickled her tongue and made her inner cheek numb, but it would do more to the spirits. The song had a slow, steady rhythm that settled onto the spirits like a heavy blanket used in the mountains. Through it, she coaxed and encouraged the spirits to be still, to cease moving, to become inert. It was a song all priests learned in her order, as it would calm a raging spirit and stun them long enough to escape to safety.

Hij's spirit answered the higher song and became as still as stone. Its glowing white eyes spun around its blue head to face her, and there was an intensity there that was beyond its rage against beasts.

"Amira, what're you doing?" Medhi asked. "The spirit's looking at us."

She nodded and kept singing, giving more and more of her strength to the song. It grew neither louder nor softer. It simply was.

Kami stopped, but only for a heartbeat. She possessed her spirit still and so the song had a weaker effect. But it was enough to slow her movements and give the otters the chance they needed to bite into both spirits.

So, song in her mouth, fire in her belly, she turned back to the tusk and slammed her prihand into it again and again. Harder and harder.

The song numbed her mouth, and she also felt it slow her, change her. She sang the song, but that did not make her immune. Feeling disappeared in her other arm and crept up her neck, trying to hold her still, trying to affect her mind.

As the song's effect crept to the back of her mind, it spoke to her and forced her to remember. Every slight, every insult, every slap, every hit, every abuse thrown at her from the Rajals. Oh, she remembered them all. Right now, she felt them as though the wounds were fresh and alive. The Rajals hurt her, hunted her, robbed her. They took everything from her. Home, family, power, life.

And she'd make them pay. She would make them regret not finishing her. The world would hate Rajalend and see it burned because—

The tusk broke free.

She dropped the song, and the numbness faded from her body, and that rage and hatred faded from her mind—though not entirely. She held onto just enough of that rage. Her hand bled, but she hefted the spear-like tusk into her arms and wielded it like the weapon it was.

While the rage gave her body strength, she ran straight at the Soulborn, to commit an evil that tore at her heart.

Kami's flames burned bright as the Soulborn sliced through the last otter and turned to face the wild spirit.

Gulamira's vision blurred and her senses dulled.

She only heard Medhi shouting at her. Screaming at her. Begging her to stop.

It was funny. He did care.

A piercing cry erupted through the air. It burned the dullness away, along with everything else inside her.

Vision flooded her eyes for a moment. A single moment of clarity.

Kami glowed before her, white-eyes as large as fists. The Soulborn stood still, motionless.

Gulamira looked down.

She'd rammed the tusk through Kami and into the second spirit. Blue blood poured from both.

Kami unpossessed her spirit and materialized near Gulamira, but the two spirits began descending through the wood and toward the water below. And thus, she committed one of the greatest sins to her order and watched the spirits disappear to die alone.

The Soulborn laid on the branches, blood pouring from her chest, as if Gulamira had speared her. The red of the blood glowed, and then other parts of Kami glowed. Blue light crept along and throughout the Soulborn's body—no, that wasn't quite it. Kami was becoming blue light, similar to a spirit. Gulamira stared as half of Kami's body evaporated away and the other half transformed into a Soulborn Remnant.

Gulamira stumbled forward with the ivory spear. She... she could not face a nasnas. She could not let the Remnancy complete.

Kami's eye was the last part to transform. Gulamira looked into that green tatzon eye as it transformed into a single glowing white orb. Gulamira raised the spear and slammed it into the Remnant.

The creature gurgled, and she struck again. And again until the nasnas did not move.

Gulamira stepped away, dropping the ivory tusk and holding her head. She turned back toward Medhi, because right now, she needed to see his stupid face.

Gulamira's clarity ended.

She collapsed to the ground, unconscious.

24

PREPARATION

I'm telling you, it's those demons that did this. Those Sefaran. They poison our waters and now they burn our Temple! Are we going to let them get away with this? Well, if they want fire, I say we give them fire!

-Overheard from a group of Rajal tatzons as they headed toward the human district of Al'Rajak.

Preparation. That's what Isra's power relied on. The more she could prepare, the more she could accomplish with her magic. It wasn't immediate and powerful like possession or even a decent countermeasure like ordîn magic. In a fight, it was only as good as what she'd Caught.

But that's how the fools thought. Because most of life wasn't war.

Remember, little Briar, her father had once said to her. *Remember, the ones who prepare are the ones who prosper. The ones planning for that unknown future, the ones ready to face their days with life firm in their grasp. They are the ones, my girl. That's what life is! A battle of preparation!*

He'd said that to her on the day he introduced her to his new wife, her new step-mom. Strange that she'd think of that day at a time like this. It wasn't a pleasant memory of her father, but not a bad one either. It was just the day her life changed forever. A strange memory for her mind to run to, to escape to, in order to separate herself from the reality of what Abioda was doing to her body.

But, try as she might, she could not detach herself. Her body screamed too loudly.

The surgeon, Abioda, stepped back, an icy grin on his blood-speckled face. Splatters of red covered his robes and drips of blood fell from the short whip in his hand. He stared at her, both satisfied and unsatisfied with his work, and she could see the desire in his eyes, the hunger to continue, to beat her more and more. This was the second day of him doing this, and he still wanted more.

Isra breathed hard and tried not to look at herself. He'd strapped her to a table, tied at the wrist and ankle, and had the table lifted and hung vertically. Gave him a better target for his whip, it seemed.

"I like your screams," he said, setting the whip down on a table beside him and reaching for a red stained towel. "I could listen to them for days on end. And don't worry, I won't kill you. You're too much of an enigma to kill. But you will hurt and suffer as the Unhallowed you are."

Isra only whimpered, tears dropping from her bruised cheeks. Her throat was hoarse from screaming and she now hung limp, waiting for everything to end. The tatzon considered killing only one Partner and not both, to be Unhallowed, to be the greatest crime a person could commit. She was almost lucky that this was all he did to her.

Abioda breathed out a heavy sigh, eyes drifting to sharper objects laid out on his table. "You don't know how much I want to drive these into your belly. To rip out every intestine before your eyes." His hand hovered over a wicked knife. "So easy. It'd be so easy. But that won't be my pleasure."

He motioned to the two guards with him and they unstrapped her ankles and then wrist. She fell onto the floor, moaning, and rolled onto her back, beneath the hanging table. They bent to pick her up, and she whimpered and spun onto her stomach.

"No, please!" she said, her bloody hands reaching out before her, smearing the ground in streaks of her blood. "No more! Please, no more."

"Take her back to her cell," Abioda said. "I'll see her again tomorrow." The two guards grabbed at her, but she kicked and reached out in front of her, more blood marking up the floor. They wrestled her legs, but she thrashed more and more.

"Stop moving," one said, and they dragged her away from the table.

She screamed, kicked, and dug her fingers into the wood. Pain pierced through her fingertips as her nails bit and clawed into the floor. She screamed and Abioda smiled with the deepest pleasure.

The two threw her back into her wooden cell in the room and slammed the door shut. She whimpered and folded herself into a ball, not daring to look at them through the wooden bars. She laid still, a pitiful and abject sight. Everything hurt, especially her throat, but she made sure she cried. Made sure she whimpered. If she couldn't escape this pain, then she'd embrace it as best she could.

She listened to the three return the table to the floor, gather up Abioda's tools of torture, and leave through the opening. Their voices drifted back in for a quick moment, and then there was only the ship and the room she was in.

Sure they weren't coming back, Isra's tears and whimpering stopped. She sat up and cracked her neck. By the Lady, that session had been far worse than yesterday's.

"Hey, you alright over there?"

Isra glanced through the wooden bars to the room. The room wasn't as large as many others on the ship and was empty save for the metal table they'd strapped her to and the five wooden cells. It wasn't hard to guess that this room was for what Abioda was doing to her. Only one of the other cells had people in it, the two intruders, the tatzon and the ordîn. The two who'd come here for Kamaria. The two who'd killed Kamaria's mother and kidnapped her.

Tsuran and Nasna. Guardian and paid killer.

Tsuran leaned against his cell bars, three of his four arms hanging out. "They don't seem to like you that much."

Isra turned away and glanced at her nails. They were bloody and splintered. She took in a quick breath and pulled out the pieces of wood from them, one by one.

"You sure put on quite the show for them," he said. "Screaming, crying, begging. Then the moment they're gone, you're all fine. Smart. Giving them what they want. Saves your strength."

Isra rose to her feet, though she needed to grab the cell bars to steady herself. Faking her screams didn't mean Abioda hadn't hurt her. But the surgeon hadn't done as much as he might have. Isra still had strength, and she needed to act while she still had it. The longer she waited, the worse she'd get.

Of course, she'd already started her plan from the moment they'd brought her into this room yesterday. She glanced at the table and the red blood drying on the floor surrounding it. . The plan was risky and wouldn't put her in the best position, but she had little choice. As long as she didn't bleed out before she was ready, she'd escape.

"The man called you Unhallowed." Tsuran folded his hands together and Isra paused. His markings were black crescents, but they only covered his right side. Weird. "Guessing you killed his Partner?"

"Tsuran, leave the woman alone," Nasna said from her corner. "Anyone can see she doesn't want to talk to you."

"What? Nonsense. Who wouldn't want to talk with me?"

"I'm not always keen on it, and I'm your Partner."

Isra turned away from her torture scene. She was nearly done. She would finish tomorrow. So, she better get going in...

She paused and glanced back at the other two. Partners? Strange. Isra didn't know tatzons could choose an ordîn as a Partner. That was not a Rajal custom. She shrugged. Must've been a fugitive thing.

Something in back of her mind buzzed a small, tiny, near insignificant warning. These fugitives were stranger and likely more dangerous than she'd first assumed. She'd need to be careful with them around.

"If I'm bothering you, I am sorry," Tsuran said. "And I'll stop and let you be, but can I ask you a question?"

She looked up and shrugged.

"Good," he said. "You're the human who was working with that Gulamira person, right? Tatzon woman who smiles a lot?"

Isra nodded.

Tsuran stood a bit more upright. "I thought so. That means you were helping her rescue a girl, right? About this height, growing a second arm, markings looking like circles with broad lines cutting through them?"

Isra didn't move nor show any reaction. She stared back. "What about her?"

"I just want to know if Gulamira got her off the ship. Is the girl safe?"

Nasna stopped whatever she was doing and looked up, too. Both stared intently at Isra, and she stared back. She focused on their expressions.

"They escaped. The girl's gone."

Air released from Tsuran, and he sighed with a small smile. Nasna too closed her eyes and nodded. Both looked... relieved. Not what Isra expected.

"Then they don't have her," Nasna said.

Tsuran nodded. "The ocean's still a dangerous place, though, and the storm yesterday was rough."

"Tsuran, do you need to say that after some good news?"

He smiled a sad smile. "You're right, sorry."

Isra watched for a moment and then turned away, back to her cell room. Her bleeding was slowing, so she needed to act faster.

The cell was large enough to fit several people, so she had lots of room to work with. Though, for what she needed to do, it was only just big enough. It'd be a tight fit.

She dropped to her knees, took in a deep breath, and wiped blood onto her finger with a wince. With no more hesitation, she drew on the cell floor with her blood.

"What do we do now, Tsu?" Nasna asked in a hushed tone, though not hushed enough. "If she's out on the ocean somewhere, I don't know how we'll find her."

"We'll find her. First, we need to get out. You sure you can't pick this iron collar off?"

"All I have are wood shavings. Those will not work."

Isra made her way around her cell, dabbing blood onto the floor and shaking her head to keep herself conscious.

"I can try getting them to come in here," Tsuran said. "Maybe I use my overwhelming charm and when they come to slap me, you do your thing."

Nasna sighed. "After the trouble we gave them, I doubt that will work. Besides, we agreed you'd stay in the shadows while he was in here."

Tsuran quieted, and Isra finished the floor. She didn't get up, though. She needed to be honest with herself, because that beating had hurt a lot and pushing herself more wasn't doing her any favors.

"We don't know for sure he's a Seeker." Tsuran's voice had hardened, taking on a fierce tone. "There could be dozens of reasons he doesn't have a priarm. Could have been an accident or something."

"Maybe. But you were the one who mentioned the aftcastle to me. It's best we don't tempt it. Having a Seeker find you while we're this vulnerable is not good. So far he has paid little attention to us, so let's come up with another idea before he does."

Isra shook herself and pulled herself to her feet. The floor had been easy. Now she had the harder part to do.

"Are you sure you can't do anything, Red?" Tsuran asked. "You broke a mountain. You sure you can't break a door?"

"It's wood, Tsuran. It doesn't have energy."

Isra grabbed onto the crisscrossed bars, readied herself, and climbed. The cell was decently tall since it had some sleeping bars at top. For all their torture, they still gave tatzons a way to sleep with dignity. And it gave her room to work with. She climbed to the top and turned herself around, facing away from the cell door and looking right at one of those sleeping bars.

She covered a finger in blood and made a streak from the cell bars out toward the bar, her other hand keeping her from falling. When satisfied, she turned toward the sleeping bar, breathed in once, twice, and jumped.

Her hands slammed into the bar, and she gripped tight. One hand slipped with all the blood on it, but the other stayed firm. However, she had little strength right now and couldn't hold on for long.

"Abyssal's tail. Is she climbing her cell?" Tsuran asked, his voice no longer hushed.

Isra dipped a finger in her blood once more and drew on the ceiling. Her hand was quick, but steady. She couldn't afford a single mistake.

Her arm shook, her grip slackened, and she fell, collapsing on the ground.

"Whoa, hey! You alright?"

Isra groaned, but sat up, not looking towards Tsuran. She only sat still and held her side.

"You were just beaten for an hour or something," he said. "What in the Abyss are you doing?"

Isra leaned back on her forearms and looked at the perfect circle she drew on the ceiling and at the bloody line that connected that circle with the much larger one on the floor. She looked at her handiwork and smiled. "Preparing."

25

THE LOST PRIEST OF EXKEL

Syeda, I'm sorry. I went. They nearly caught me, but I went. And I found it. Hidden deep inside the Temple, I found a secret room with various shrines, and they were not to the Ethereal Tree. There were eight symbols, seven surrounding the walls, one in the center of the room. I'll send a sketch of the symbols once I have time, but it's hard to form my thoughts right now. Because, sister, I found scrolls. So many scrolls... I don't know who these people are, but I know what they plan. And it's worse. It's far, far worse than I had thought. And I'm sorry about the fire. All those human lives are on my head, I know.

-From a fool. The greatest fool.

Something foul fell onto Gulamira's shoulder like a rotting, moldy, puss-filled mushroom. She clenched her teeth and shook the decaying flesh off her. They'd gone deeper into the beast than she'd like, to where some of the flesh gave way to holes which let in sea water that became contaminated with the death stench of the seal. Much of the throat had already split open, so they stood tall. However, every breath tried her endurance, especially since she'd only awoken a short while ago.

Medhi crouched, tying Hij up with long strands of kelp. He wrapped the Soulborn more times than was likely necessary, but he was a large tatzon and this wasn't rope, even if he was unconscious.

"Alright," Medhi said, standing. "That should hold him."

"It won't if he sees a spirit," she said, crossing her arms. "Only ivory and metal keep spirits out, so one can easily float on in here."

Medhi took out his dagger. "A problem only if he sees them. Turn around."

She looked from his dagger to him, but did not move. It hurt knowing what Medhi needed to do, but she would not stop him and she would not look away.

He nodded and crouched next to Hij and raised his dagger.

Gulamira forced herself to watch. And, to her surprise, she barely flinched as Medhi sliced through the man's eyes. She didn't even blink as Hij screamed with a hoarse voice that reverberated into her spine. Hij thrashed and wailed and blood poured from his now ruined eyes. Medhi stepped away from the man and wiped off his dagger. He was less fazed than she. In fact, he tore off one of Hij's sleeves and stuffed it into the Soulborn's mouth to muffle the screams and whimpering.

Medhi looked up at Gulamira, eyes hollow and expressionless. "He can't do anything now."

The two stood in silence, watching Hij thrash in pain. Medhi pulled him up by the throat twice when Hij rolled into the water. Otherwise, they waited for him to regain control of himself. And all the while, Gulamira watched feeling... well, she wasn't sure what she was feeling. Pity? Disgust? Guilt, maybe? They were all possibilities, all options. None fit right. Those all had thick build-ups in her stomach and often constricted her throat. This felt like none of those.

She felt... light. Not quite cheery or happy, but it had a similar tingle.

Hij calmed his screams and thrashes to a minimum, so Gulamira stepped forward. However, Medhi grabbed her.

"Hey, maybe I should take care of this."

She smiled at him and patted his hand. "No. You should not."

He stared at her a moment and then let go. She crouched in front of Hij, fragments of dawn creaking in through the open maw and places where the flesh had rotted away.

"Hello, Hij Soulborn," she said, bringing her smile into full bloom. He wouldn't see it, but it had a way of affecting how she spoke. "My name is Gulamira Con-None, and I have a few questions for you."

Hij breathed through his flared nose, jaw clenching on the gag.

"Now, I'm going to take this sleeve out of your mouth, and I hope we may have a civilized conversation." Careful to not stick her finger inside his mouth, she pulled the gag from him. He spat and ground his teeth.

"I'm not telling an Unhallowed like you nothing," he said.

Gulamira winced at the name, something in her abdomen stinging as if someone squeezed it. Along with it came this empty feeling of shame that made it hard to breathe, made her smile waver. Being Unhallowed was more than criminal and painful. It was... wrongness. But she'd deal with these feelings later. For now, she wiped the spit from her cheek and stood.

"I have a few questions."

"Go freeze in the Abyss."

Medhi held up his dagger. "Do you want me to stab him?"

"I'd rather not kill him, Medhi," she said.

"A few stabs to the leg won't kill him."

Hij tensed and held his chin high. "Do your worst. I'll still sleep in the branches of the Ethereal Tree while you lot are drowned and frozen."

Medhi raised a brow and nodded at his dagger, but Gulamira raised a hand. "Thanks, but no."

He shrugged and put the dagger away. Though a part of her wondered if that was the best course of action. Because with Hij just losing his Partner, and them being the cause, there wasn't anything she could offer to get him to talk. That was problematic.

Bribery wasn't an option, threats wouldn't do much, and, despite what Medhi wanted, torture would get them nowhere because what more pain could they cause this man who'd lost the one he'd Formed his soul with? Loss of a Partner meant he'd even let some of his country burn if he could see Gulamira and Medhi dead and hanging.

And maybe it was the lack of food and sleep over the last few days, or maybe because the only "food" she'd had were flowers, but Gulamira was all out of patience. She needed answers, and she needed them now.

Which left her with only one option. Only one choice.

A crueler tactic.

A much, much crueler tactic.

It turned her stomach to think about it... but she had to.

"You invite me to do my worst. Well, I hate turning down a man's invitation." She forced her gaze into Hij's bleeding eyes. "So, I hope you enjoy your time in Solitude."

Hij froze. She wasn't even sure if he breathed. It seemed even his bleeding hesitated and wasn't sure what to do. "You wouldn't." His voice did not have the same confidence as his words did.

Gulamira started walking away. "No, I suppose I wouldn't. After all, you know me so well."

She nodded to Medhi, who walked with her.

"You're bluffing," Hij said. "You wouldn't... you couldn't. I... I'm a tatzon. I'm your kind! Where are you? I know you're there! Go on, speak. Speak, damn you!"

Hij's voice became more and more muffled by the beast around them as they walked away. With every step, it was more shrill, more panicked, more desperate than before. It continued up to the point they stood by the mouth where Gulamira stopped them and waited.

Had the waves crashed hard against the tree, had a torrent of a storm swept through, had a mythical ship of quintal with their powers of thunder appeared, still, she would have heard—felt—those screams deep inside her very marrow. Because they were the screams of Solitude.

There were two evils that far exceeded all else. Two evils acknowledged and hated by all tatzons across the world. It was written in the very blood of being a tatzon, so that only by denying their own soul could anyone enact these crimes.

The greatest evil of all was to murder someone's Partner but let them live. To be Unhallowed was worse than damnation. And the second evil was just as unspeakable: subjecting another tatzon to Solitude.

In a single morning, she'd committed both.

Gulamira turned to Medhi. "Let's head back."

"It's barely been ten minutes."

"That'll be enough."

They returned into the putrid depths, but this time it wasn't the decay that made her stomach curl. Hij's body spasmed, jolting this way and that. It eased as Gulamira made her presence known, but the effects of Solitude were fast. It hadn't been in long enough that his outer body showed any effects of Solitude, but she knew his insides would've started to waste away.

Hij whimpered and said something, but it was low and hard to hear.

Gulamira bent down to him. "Are you ready to tell me what I want to know?"

A tear of red-black streamed down his cheek. "... yes..."

Medhi grabbed Hij and pulled him up into a sitting position. Gulamira crossed her arms and breathed out. "The priest. Tell me everything. Is he alive?"

Hij gulped at air, but all his composure, all his projected strength, had vanished. "The priest's alive, far as I know."

Gulamira's heart thumped into her throat, but she held her excitement back and listened.

"He's kept at the Floating Treasure in this secure tower."

"How?" Gulamira asked. "How did you find him?"

"I didn't. Someone found him in Ma'Jra and brought him to the Floating Treasure. Man like that would go for a lot of coin. Lots of people were interested in Veirzen's old priesthood."

Her gaze dropped to her chest, toward the scar under her breast. She knew all too well the extent to which people wanted her order.

"How long ago did your captain purchase him?" she asked.

"He's been at the place for over a year, but the captains didn't buy him. No one did."

"If he's still at the Floating Treasure," Medhi said, "means those in charge of the place kept him."

Hij nodded, though at an awkward angle, as if he didn't have full control over his neck. "That's right. The big ones wanted him, wanted what he knew. That's what they're after. Just want what he knows."

"What could he know that they'd want?" Gulamira asked.

A scratchy, breathy, squeaking came out of Hij's mouth. The only laughing he could manage now. "You kidding? What they've gotten out of him has changed the war with Veirzen. Tactics, weaknesses, developments, spies, whatever you could ask for, he's given them. Veir secrets they've been trying to get for years has just fallen in their laps."

Medhi crossed his arms and stroked his scarf. "Hm. That would give the Rajals a needed advantage. And I'm guessing he didn't willingly hand up these secrets."

"What do you think?" Hij said and coughed hard. Gulamira clenched her fist at the thought of one of her priests being tortured by Rajals for an entire year. And, for a moment, some part of her wondered if they did to her priest what she'd done to Hij.

The moment passed, and that part of her quieted.

"So, you torture him and then sell his secrets to the Rajals?" Gulamira asked. "You are just scum in disguise."

"I'm a proud Rajal!" Hij said, spitting in her direction. "Sell to the Rajals? We are the Rajals! We're the Rajals that do what the people can't stomach in order for them to sleep at night. Or do you forget who owns the *Cleansing*?"

The *Cleansing*? What did that have to do with...

Her protective smile faltered as everything hit her. "The Oligarchs. That's who you work for. That's who bought the priest."

"Oligarchs Argul Con-Ortu and Ortu Con-Argul," Hij said. "They've owned and operated the Floating Treasure for seventy years. It's the backbone of their money and power."

"That doesn't make any sense," Medhi said. "The Floating Treasure is illegal. It's a black market, a port of piracy and dissidents who are no allies to Rajalend."

"And it's run by two Oligarchs." Hij smiled, as if he could feel the confusion emanating from them. "And it's because of them we're turning this war around. It's been their ideas that's made us strong.

The *Cleansing*, the plantations in the Maw, the Floating Treasure, the priest and his secret treasure, all of it! Rajalend is rising because of them. The other Oligarchs are nothing but figureheads and—"

"Stop right there," Gulamira said.

"I won't stop! I know you're a filthy Veir and you're getting what's—"

She grabbed him by the throat, her voice hard. "I don't care one damn about that. What is this about the priest's 'secret treasure'?"

He gurgled in his throat, his cut eyes glaring at her. "The Veirs have a treasure hidden, one that would end this war if we got our hands on it. They call it the Heritage, or something or another. The Oligarchs want it, and this priest knows where it is."

Her heart sunk like a ship with a breeched hull, pulled under by a Behemoth beast with no chance of return.

The Heritage.

The Oligarchs knew about it, somehow. And now, they were trying to pull its location from another priest.

"Amira," Medhi said, taking her aside. "This all have to do with you?"

"More than anything in the world." Her smile thinned into a determined line. "We need to get there. Now."

He nodded. "I'm all for impeding Rajalend. But it will not be easy. Sounds like your fellow is stuck in there real deep."

"We'll figure it out." She turned back to Hij. "Your ship, are there other possessors there?"

Hij shook his head. "A few sailors. That's it."

Gulamira leaned into Medhi. "I think it's time to steal a ship."

He smiled and nodded. "Then let's go. I have one thing to do, though."

He walked over to Hij and grabbed him by the hair.

"Ah! You bitch," Hij said. "Mark me, you've not won here. You've not won anywhere. Go on! Head to the Floating Treasure and see if you find anything! The Oligarchs are taking that priest away soon, if they haven't already. And when you arrive, they'll carve you like a boar and eat you like the whore—"

Medhi's dagger plunged into his neck, and this time, Gulamira looked away. When Medhi joined her, he held Hij's belt which, among a couple of other things, held the metal box with a blue-crystal inside. And with it, they left the carcass of the beast, neither looking back. The future was too uncertain for her to look back now. The blood of the future demanded her attention far more than the blood behind.

26

---◆◇◆---

THE FLOATING
TREASURE

T *his war fuels him, gives him strength and power. With every bro-
*ken family, he forces his influence deeper and deeper into the hearts
of the weak. Humanity bows to his every whim, unworthy tatzon flock to
his lies. All of Rajalend is weak before him now, just as Oushwala was
before. We fear even the ordîn are soon to be our enemies. Prepare your-
selves, every one of you. We shall cull the Nightmare's power. We will
burn every source of strength he has. If humanity and lesser tatzonkind
flock to him, then we shall butcher these beasts of burden. If he would
stoke the flames of this war, then we shall douse it with blood. The war
ends when one side stands victorious. Let us make Rajalend's fall entire
and complete. The Bridgemakers shall not win.*

*-From a scroll found under the Temple of the Ethereal Tree. Author,
unknown. Date, unknown. Our future, uncertain.*

On the ocean, it's said, you can see unto the ends of the world.
There are no mountains, no mighty hills or massive forests to block
your view for miles and miles, even without a spyglass. Even now,
with the sun overhead and the skybands faint amidst the blue sky,
Gulamira thought she could make out the edges of the Meadowlands from here. If she squinted, she thought she saw the vague
outline of the Iron Mountains rising beyond the trees, trees that
were so small from this distance. In this same manner, she saw the
Floating Treasure days before they reached it.

At first, it was just one of many distant dark shapes on the horizon, one of many sea-trees. But with every passing day, it grew in stature and detail. The dark vagueness gave way to a bulbous tree with branches that stretched high and stretched far, covered in bright orange leaves and green flowers. The size of the tree stole Gulamira's breath as they approached. Although its trunk and roots reached down to the ocean floor, the part that rose out of the water was as tall as a Large cypress, rising several hundred feet, its trunk many times larger. The overhanging branches cast a mighty shadow for the ships to sail into, as though it protected the illicit dealings from the very light of the sun.

A massive maze of root and branch stayed just above the water, creating a natural barrier to the trunk, protecting the tree from mighty waves and ships of law enforcement. Gulamira stayed next to Medhi as he directed their new sailors. These humans had at first been relieved they didn't need to sail with Soulborn, though they hadn't been excited about a stranger commanding them. But with a firm voice and a promise of giving them the spirit vessels, Medhi kept their new sailors in order, sailing the ship through the correct channels, staying a safe distance from the roots that, whether natural or by a Builder, had spear-like thorns surrounding them. He navigated the maze as one accustomed to it and brought them before the opening in the bloated trunk. It must have taken many Builders many weeks to shape this opening. It gaped open like the mouth of a Behemoth, as tall as any tree and nearly as wide. They passed by ships leaving and sailed alongside a few entering, and already it surprised Gulamira to see so many ships in the area. They passed through the opening, into the tree itself, and she joined the sailors in their stunned silence.

The Floating Treasure was a proper port, one even larger than Archoz. The interior of the trunk was hollow, with two large entrances to allow ships to come and go, and along one side was what could only be called a town. Buildings and constructions filled the entire side, most coming from a wooden "ground" and some even protruding from the wall. Docks lined the entire place, with several on the opposite side of the tree for the ships too large to properly moor otherwise. Lanterns lit the town, those small lights standing out amidst the dimness of this hollowed place, though several non-flickering lights showed that someone had lightstone here too.

Gulamira counted dozens of ships of various kinds and sizes, some resembling pirate ships and some that looked too much like a merchant's to be a coincidence. However, one ship, in particular, drew her attention. She came up next to Medhi and pointed.

He nodded. "Saw it as we came in."

"Think they're waiting for us?"

"Let's hope not."

He turned them toward the docks, being sure to keep a wide berth between them and the *Cleansing* that sat motionless at one end of the port. Gulamira had a hard time taking her eyes from it as Medhi chatted with the dock masters and the sailors tied the ship off.

The *Cleansing* was right there. Which meant that Kamaria and Isra were there. Well, Kamaria was, at least. They would have killed Isra by now. But they wouldn't have killed Kamaria. There was no way.

"Amira?" Medhi came up beside her, away from the others. "What's the plan?"

"Hij said they kept my priest in a tower and I only see that one." She pointed to a tall Building in the center of the town, standing higher than all the others with white light drifting from the top. "So that's where I need to go."

"Not much of a plan."

She shrugged. "I'll be fine. Can you look at the *Cleansing*, though? I don't know what's the best way to get the girl."

He glanced at her sidelong, his shoulders stiffening. "You're going alone, then. Didn't think tatzons were supposed to do that."

They weren't. Going alone was one of the most dangerous things a tatzon could do. It was foolish.

"I'll be careful, but we can't waste time. We have two people to grab and... and if that means I have be more human-like, then that's what I have to do."

She tried to instill courage in her words, because she believed them. But the memory of Solitude hung in the back of her mind.

But Medhi took her hand and gave it a gentle squeeze, and that was enough. "I'll do what I can to keep this crew with us. Likely sell the crystals to do it. Not sure how many will stick around, though, so try to be fast."

"Thank you."

"Don't thank me yet." He stroked his scarf and pulled out his dagger. "You should take this."

She grinned and shook her head. "I appreciate the gesture, but I'll be better off without it. I'll cut myself before anyone else."

He sighed. "You're testing my trust here. I'm still not convinced I'm doing the right thing here. So, I beg you, prove me wrong."

"When don't I?" She winked at him and headed into the Floating Treasure.

Gulamira had never been to a nectar tree, trees so massive they held entire cities within them, but she imagined they couldn't be too different from this place around her. Every structure here grew from the wooden floor and resembled constructions, except there were no seams or cracks or individual pieces. Every Building around here was a single whole and a part of the entire tree.

The Buildings showcased the fact that the Floating Treasure was more than a single market. It was a town of markets and homes and businesses. She passed through lantern-lit streets with vendors selling their wares from stalls, shops, and random street corners. Her thoughts of a black market made her imagine the most vile of things for people to sell. Gross and detestable. Instead, in many places she saw fruits and dried meats from Veirzen, spices and dyes sold at a premium, and one shop, with guards and people clambering to get inside, selling small pouches of the Maw's greatest export: sugar. In these things, she didn't see nefarious or even dangerous items, just anything and everything that was illegal to sell in Rajalend, was heavily taxed, or which was reserved for the elite.

However, the deeper into the town she went, she saw signs that these were not all that were sold here. Several stalls had human children chained together, ready for purchase, and Gulamira could not help but think back to when Prikur sold her. Her gaze fell to each of the girls there and the empty look in their eyes told her more than any tome. She pushed herself away from there but found herself in front of one store with a sign that said it sold the skulls of slain Veirs. A few passersby stared at her, at her lighter gray skin, and she hurried to a different place.

The time was blessed just as much as it was cursed.

In too short a time, Abioda discovered a shard of Solitude while also losing his Partner, his Haz. In many days he had laughed in worship, and he had cried in worship.

Soon, he would kill in worship.

Abioda stood on the deck connecting to the *Cleansing* with the shard, this girl, clasped in iron and held by two loyal guards. He grimaced at the sight of the Floating Treasure. A disgraceful pit of despair. Such places as these were why the Lost had disappeared so long ago.

Soon, they would return. And the world would be bright with a cleansing flame.

"They're here," one guard said.

Abioda beheld the entourage approach, stared past the Tifran ordîn and the Soulborn to his fellow Seekers.

The two Seekers stopped before him, and he forced himself to not glare.

"Abioda," Argul said, adjusting his garish silk robe.

"Argul. Ortu."

The two Oligarchs glanced from him to the shard, so dismissive of his presence. He refrained from clenching his fists. These two encouraged much of the evils in this place, and in Rajalend. Unworthy to Seek the Lost, they had not even surrendered their priarm to please the Lost.

Abidoa was loyal. Abidoa was true. Why did he share the same rank as these frauds?

"Is this her?" Ortu said, looking the shard over. "So young. Why is she gagged?"

"She has a foul and violent mouth. But, yes. This is the shard Haz and I discovered."

Argul nodded, not once looking to Abioda. "And where is Haz? I miss her company."

He hesitated to share more. These were not his superiors. But they were his equals, and he had to honor that. "She is dead."

With as few words as he could, he informed the two Rajal leaders what had transpired on the *Cleansing*. Ortu sneered at the tale, but said nothing. One of these days, Abioda would rank higher than them. One of these days, he would put their pomposity in its place.

Argul frowned and looked across the harbor to the *Quick Passing*. "I am glad to hear you did not lose her, for your sake. Though, if you nearly lost her already, I think it best you hand her over to Hais and let him deliver her. Perhaps this magical human, too."

Abioda stepped forward, not raising his voice, but ensuring it did not quieten either. They would not cow him. "I discovered the shard. Haz discovered her. It is our honor, our right to deliver her. What happened on the *Cleansing* was a fluke."

"Flukes are not a minor thing with a shard of Solitude. Not when the Nightmare searches so fervently for one. Put your pride aside. This is of greater importance than you or us."

Abioda turned away, huffing. The *Quick Passing* was just across the water, the ship that was meant to take him and Haz to the Realized with all their findings.

But they would not smile on his near failure.

"I admit you are right, so I'll hand the girl over. But the human is mine. She took my Partner, so I will rip out her secrets and deliver her myself."

Argul exchanged a glance with Ortu and they both nodded. "I do not doubt they would grant you that leniency. We, too, would be quite interested in what you discover."

"Yes, I'm sure I will send a full report throughout the chapters."

Ortu smiled wide, her eyes rolling up to the ceiling in a way that sent a chill down Abioda's spine. "The Lost bless us these days. So much aligns itself with us. It shall not surprise me that today we finally uncover that priest's secret."

Abioda hesitated and glanced back at the shard. "If that is the case, is there any point in sending her along? Our orders are explicit. I would rather continue experiments as long as possible before."

Argul stepped up to the shard, who had not stopped glaring at her with an intensity that gave even Abioda pause. Argul smiled. "We should send her along, just in case. Her life is forfeit only after we have the Heritage in our hands." The old man crouched and looked the shard in the eyes. "It is a wonder to be so near one. Do you suppose she even knows what she is? What she means?"

"Only the Realized truly do," Abioda said.

The two Oligarchs departed and Abioda brought the shard to the *Quick Passing*, handing her over to Hais. He stayed a moment, watched the ship prepare to set sail.

Yes, much sorrow had come to him. But today was the greatest of blessings. He turned back to the *Cleansing*, a smile creeping back to his lips.

Now. He had a particular human to dissect.

Gulamira's goal was the tower, but the town was more of a maze than she expected, with no direct path to it. Before long, she found herself back near the docks and unsure of which street she was supposed to take. She glanced over the harbor, watched one ship depart, watched a few more dock.

That's where she saw them.

The ordîns stood out the most. Among the brown and tan tones of the town, these creatures were an intrusion of bright colors. Three had vibrant green toned skin while a fourth had blue, and all four had bright white hair and large wings, which they kept pressed against their backs. Four tatzons stood with them, two that, by the looks of the metal boxes on their hips, had to be Soulborn. The other two, though, were something else entirely.

She saw past their retinue, past their fine silk clothes, and straight to their markings. Markings that told who they were. One had markings of brown and black dots that made tight spirals, while the other one's resembled brown forked tongues. She knew these markings. She'd seen them long, long ago, and her parents had prepared her to meet these two. Back when she'd been a true priestess. Back on the day her parents died, she was supposed to meet these two.

Argul Ustre Imil Con-Ortu and Ortu Hajr Ghimpa Con-Argul. Two of the six Oligarchs of Rajalend.

Unwelcome memories barged into Gulamira's mind.

A parade through the streets of Zashai, celebrating the soon-end of a too-long war.

A contingent of tents standing tall at the Between Rivers, tatzons of Rajalend and Veirzen facing each other in tense silence.

Rajal soldiers surrounding the six Oligarchs of Rajalend. Gulamira's parents and the Zaruf greeted them.

Fake smiles, faker promises, hidden lies, disguised daggers.

A figure dressed in shadows, striking without mercy and without fail.

Bodies. Memories of bodies were all that remained. Zaruf, father, mother.

The figure standing before her, bloody sickle raised to strike.

No!

She shoved and pushed those memories down, using the rising anger to lend her strength to lock those hauntings tight behind her smile, behind her walls. But she could not rid herself of the emotions that came with that flood of memory. She could not help but seethe at the sight of those two. It took all of her willpower to fight the urge to rush them and kill them where they stood. Those Oligarchs. Those liars and betrayers. Two of the six responsible for her parents' deaths.

They headed into the Floating Treasure, on their way to the tower and her priest and she remembered what Hij had said.

The Oligarchs are taking the priest away, soon.

It seemed she didn't have much time anymore. She started to followed but paused and glanced once more toward the *Cleansing.*

Don't worry, Kamaria, she thought. *Medhi and I will grab you right after I get my priest. Just hold on a bit longer.*

She turned her gaze up the street to the Oligarchs, to the path to her priest, and followed.

27

THE TRAP IS SET

L *amia and I have shown all the evidence to our Oligarchs and the other Beneficiaries. They seem as convinced as we are, but there's still nothing we can do. Hyder and Zaid don't have the resources right now since they've used a lot of their fortunes to keep the soldiers at the Wall paid. We'll need the other two Oligarchs on our side before we can remove Argul and Ortu, but it doesn't look like we have that kind of time. Especially with the people being so enraged towards humans right now because of the Temple burning. If it gets out that this evidence is from a human, people will dismiss it. Oligarchs Hyder and Zaid are under a lot of pressure because of me. We'll try to come up with a plan, but the people want blood, Raz. And our enemies know it.*

-Syeda Softbark, human.

Isra's screams pleased the surgeon. He stepped back, putting away his iron mallet, and gestured to the guards.

Another day of torture done.

Isra couldn't find the energy to even thank the Lady.

They dropped her to the ground, picked her up, threw her into the cell, and slammed the door shut.

When they left, she grinned, but didn't stop groaning. Today, she hadn't faked as much as before. By the Lady, she was getting much too tired.

But she was ready. When they dragged her out today, she had finished. She was ready for the last step in her preparation.

Tsuran and Nasna didn't speak to her today. All the better. The more focus she had, the easier this would be.

She sat in a corner of the cell, just outside her blood circle, though it was a tight fit. She placed a hand on the circle and her eyes traced the dried blood to the cell door where the wood was dug up by her dragged nails. To where her nails had dug a line from this circle to the metal table in the center of the room. To the table where, with her own blood, she had drawn a circle around.

The plan had come into her mind as soon as she'd entered the room for the first time. To fake exhaustion and flail on the ground in order to mask the fact she was drawing a perfect circle. It'd taken a few days to finish, but she was now ready.

Not waiting for anyone's permission, she touched the circle and Caught the metal table. It vanished from sight, and a large rune appeared in red letters in the center of the circle on her cell floor.

Now came the tricky part.

She Released the table, but channeled it away from the circle she touched and up the blood line to the circle on the ceiling. The table materialized on the ceiling. And then it fell.

Right before it struck, she Caught it using the large circle on the ground. And then she Released it through the ceiling circle. It dropped. She Caught it again. She Released it. It dropped. And it crashed into the floor.

"Icy Abyss!" Tsuran cried out. "What was that?"

Isra ignored him and breathed in a slow breath. She could do this. Focus.

Isra Caught and Released the table again, Catching it this time before it hit the floor. She Released and Caught it successfully again. And then again. And then again. Each time the table fell, it fell faster and faster. As long as it didn't hit the floor, the table would continue to build speed. From its perspective, it never stopped falling.

She groaned as a shot of pain erupted in her side. She didn't Release the table until she found time to breathe again.

But she kept at it. She couldn't tell for how long. But it was long enough that the table fell so fast she barely had time to Catch it again. So, one more time, but this time she connected the line on her finger to the blood line. She hovered a finger over a circle on her arm and stared at the blood circle containing the table.

Sweat dripped into one of her eyes and she wiped it away and returned the hand. She took in one, two, three breaths.

She Released the table, and it soared down toward the floor with rapid speed. Without thought, she slammed her finger into the circle on her arm and Caught the table, putting it and all its momentum into her arm.

Isra stared at the rune formed in the circle. And she laughed.

She eyed the cell door and rested her hand on her lap. Now she couldn't wait for them to come back. Oh, yes. That was going to be fun.

28

ASCENDING THE TOWER

I played into their hands. I thought I was helping, but all I did was ready Rajalend to destroy us all. The more I read what I stole from the Temple, the more I see how powerful these Realized are. They weren't just the minds behind Ma'Jra's destruction, they enacted it. Not all of them. Just one. One of these Realized leveled the town. And there's six of them! Six insanely powerful possessors. Even one is stronger than half of our armies. And I'm a human. What did I think I could do against forces like these? What can any human do?

-Raza, the one who doomed his people.

"I don't want to try again!" the child priestess said, pushing the glowing crystal away from her. Priest Salma scowled at the blatant disrespect, but he would not strike her. Even if he could strike a future High Priestess, Gulamira doubted he would.

"Priestess," the man said, his voice calm and collected. "You must continue your practice. It is an imperative that the High Priestess can stand shoulder to shoulder with the Zaruf on the battlefield."

"But it feels weird, and it hurts."

"And what of your undeveloped arm? Does that hurt any less?"

It was an odd memory to sprout up right now. As Gulamira trailed the Oligarchs, she'd kept most of those painful remembrances deep below the surface so she could focus. Yet, somehow, this event leaked through. It wasn't a bad or good memory. Just another day of her training, perhaps a year before her parents' death. She focused on her steps ahead of her, but the memory played on.

"Why do I need to do this now?" little Gulamira asked. She frowned at the arm growing from her shoulder, ending past her elbow. "Alir and Hashai don't need to yet. I don't see other kids doing it."

"Ah, but you are not some 'other kid'," Salma said. "You are a Priestess of Exkel. A Florella. You are many things, but not some 'kid'."

Gulamira followed the Oligarchs to the tower. The Builders had designed it much like someone had the aftcastle of the *Cleansing*: several tree trunks wrapped around each other until they sprouted into the canopy above. Given how much the Ethereal Tree frowned on the depravities filling this port, it was strange to find such a religious symbol in this place.

Even with the tower in view, she stayed to the shadows, which were plentiful around here. The street had traffic in both directions, but most people seemed intent on heading to the tower as well, so she was sure the Oligarchs hadn't noticed her. However, her pursuit took a rather unexpected turn.

The Oligarchs ascended. The ordîns grabbed hold of them and flew up, up, up to the heights of the tower and beyond her reach. Gulamira stared longer than she should have, but then she realized they were likely heading straight for her priest. Since she couldn't fly, she'd have to walk fast if she were to get there in time. Along with many others, she entered the tower.

"Well, I want to be just a kid, you know." She conveyed this with more depth than words could provide. As always, during her lessons, they spoke only in the tongue of spirits. It allowed more understanding to transpire, more knowledge to be passed on. But it also allowed every emotion to come across in its most heightened form. Nothing could hide in such a language.

And Salma felt more than heard the emotion her words carried to him. His song returned, and she understood how much he wished the same desires for her.

"Priest Dasparet, please do not encourage her."

Salma bowed his head and Gulamira looked over to her parents who, as always, sat cross-legged in front of the central fire, with Salma's Partner sitting with them. Mother focused on some kind of writing, though they never told her what it was about. Father was looking right at Gu-lamira in that way only he knew how. Somehow, his gaze pierced deeper than any song did.

The first floor of the tower was a tavern. A large one at that. Dozens and dozens of sailors filled the place, taking over every chair, every table, every inch of the bar. Candle-lit chandeliers hung from the tall ceiling, yet it was still hard to see for all the tobacco smoke filling the air. Now that she thought about it, this was the first tavern Gulamira had seen in this port, so the number of patrons made sense. It didn't seem unlikely the Oligarchs had a monopoly here. She pushed through the crowds, searching for the stairs. All around her, people laughed, sang, and, after many drinks, they danced.

She broke through the densest cluster and saw a group of people heading up a winding staircase to the next level. Gulamira left the drinking behind and hurried up.

Father fixed his stare on her. She tried to look back, tried to look him in the eyes as she was trained, but she focused on his markings instead. His weaved around his body like hers, but they resembled leafy vines instead of branches.

"My daughter," he said, and he poured so much love and care and expectation into that single melody. "Your emotions are to serve you, not you to them. You disrespect yourself when you burst out like this. You also disrespect Priest Salma. That is not the way of a High Priestess."

Gulamira nodded. What more could she do? Argue with Father? No. You couldn't argue with the very voice of Exkel, no less her Father. But neither could she forget how the other children laughed and played.

On the second floor of the tower, there was a drug den. The place was dimly lit, showcasing the wide selection of iridescent mushrooms for sale. Nightsingers. Many ways to use them, many ways to experience them. By far the most common method, and what she saw here, was grinding it into a fine dust and pouring it over a fire. The fumes grabbed ahold of those nearest the flame, drifting into their lungs and taking them to worlds beyond. The sailors here huddled around their small lamps, which prevented the Building from alighting and also allowed each to hoard their nightsinger for themselves.

Seeing the drug left a sour taste in her mouth and a bitterness in her stomach. Many of her masters had used it to make her docile and compliant, to steal her thoughts and lock away her mind.

The stairs were on the farthest end of the floor, so she weaved through dazed humans and oily dealers. One pair of tatzons tried to stop her from going upstairs until she bought nightsingers from them, but she ducked around them and up the stairs.

"I apologize for my disrespect," she said. "But I don't understand why I need to be different. No one else has to worry about these things." She tried to cut her words off there, but nothing could hide in the song. Her song carried the secret thoughts of her heart through those words. "Sometimes I don't want to be the High Priestess."

The third floor was too familiar. It took a single glance to recognize the elements that had been her home for many years.

A brothel.

Rich fabrics flowed from the ceiling, handsome men played soft music, half-dressed women flirted with the patrons. There were some drinks sold here too, but they would brew these to enhance the growing desire in the indulging sailors. A few of the men and women started up conversations with her, some offered drinks, others flirted with thoughts of more. Gulamira knew her priest would not be here, but found it difficult to move on. It was too surreal to stand inside a brothel, yet not need to throw herself at the nearest human wanting a lay.

However, despite what made sense to her, being here, being surrounded by the only life she'd known for so long, she felt something akin to a yearning to stay. For a moment, she even wondered what kind of life she would have made for herself had she been here instead of Archoz.

It would have still been a lesser life than what awaited her, so she smiled to her fellow workers and headed up the next flight.

Gulamira expected her parents to raise their voices and shout at her. Instead, Mother set her papers down and both she and Father came over to her. Mother hummed a comforting melody, which helped ease some of Gulamira's shame of them knowing that terrible secret. Mother, with her markings resembling a tree's root system, beckoned to Gulamira. They left the two Dasparets and led her to the balcony overseeing the city of

Zashai, and Gulamira pulled her furs tighter around her as a snowy wind blew past.

"It is a hard duty to be High Priestess," Mother said. "We do not deny the hardships ahead of you. You will be unlike the other children, for you must be unlike every Veir, every tatzon." She turned her priestly smile toward her, and Gulamira felt the warmth it offered. "But this need not be a bad thing. You are a chosen of Exkel, which brings both duty and freedom unlike anything else. You must endure many hardships, and you must now, for the days will come when those children who laugh and play will need someone to look to. They will need someone to comfort their pain, to give leadership to their confusion."

"Their hardships shall come," Father said. "As they do for all people. But when they do, they will look to you for their strength. You must bear a thousand sorrows, and a thousand more, for then when they come with their few sorrows, you may give them what they need."

The fourth floor of the tower was much like the third, except the services were more expensive, more exotic. Here, they offered more than simple carnal pleasures. Here they offered any and every pleasurable fancy. Unlike the floor below, Gulamira found no sense of safety here. It brought back too many memories of the more violent encounters she had, and the more humiliating ones. Sounds of ecstasy and pain flooded through the closed openings.

The floor below she had wondered what kind of life she would have had. This floor was her answer.

She rushed onward to the next set of stairs.

"And it is hard now," Mother continued. "But it won't be forever. When we began our training, it was so very hard. But it became easier as we found our purpose and as we found each other."

Father stood behind Mother and wrapped his arms around her, giving the back of her head a small kiss. They were rarely affectionate in public, so Gulamira craved these moments that let her see the love of their Partnership and marriage.

Mother smiled, and it was not her priestly smile, but something that was just her. "You are jealous of your friends today. But you must overcome such feelings, because a day will come where they shall envy you, and you must not lord it over them. A day will come when people look at you and will wish they could be you."

The fifth floor reminded Gulamira of an inn. It held many rooms, and each looked rich, wonderful. It seemed this was where the well-to-do merchants and ship captains stayed, and where they enjoyed the private services of the tower. But no priest.

She tried to move on, but stopped. Where she expected the stairs to be instead was a solid wall. In front of it, two guards, each with four arms, sat playing a game of some sort. Builders, and the wall would be a proper opening. Either they had to open it up for her, or she had to find a different way up.

"You will have what no one else has. You will have a Partner like no other."

In one empty room, she found open windows and a way to climb up. But no one was with her and Solitude waited that way. So she headed back into the hall.

"You will master weaponry that can upend the world and cease all war."

If she were Medhi, she could have fought her way through, but she hadn't brought a dagger or a sword. Even if she had, she didn't know how to use them, because she was not him.

"You will have the songs of our people, songs that can bend minds and soften hearts."

She looked at the Builders. They would be more susceptible to a lower song than a Soulborn, but she didn't have any songs that would force them to open the wall. Even if that somehow did work, as soon as she passed them, they would come for her.

"You will stand alongside the Zaruf with many arms, your possessions shall be sights to behold."

Her hand drifted to the scar under her breast. She had no power of possession. She didn't even have whatever magic Isra used.

Her parents knelt beside her and took her prihand. "And you will have us."

Gulamira stood at the end of the hall by herself, looking toward the Builders. She had no one. She had nothing.

No allies. No weapons. No magic.

Alone. She was all alone. She only had herself.

Only herself. Just as she had in Archoz. Just as she had for ten years.

And she was enough.

She squared her shoulders, held her head high, and looked the Builders in the eyes as she approached. They glanced up, ignoring her at first, but when they saw she walked for them, they waved her away.

"We're not servants," one said. "Find someone else to order around."

She walked on, a song rising in her throat. It would not control them, it would not have them open the wall for her, but it would lower their defenses and help her words take root.

One turned in his seat toward her. "We told you, we're not servants. Who're you? What do you want?"

Gulamira smiled as the question hung in the air. A thousand sorrows had indeed shaped her, and she had become unlike anyone else. She had not grown up like other children and she did not live like other people. Yet, she was not who the priests trained her to be. She was not who her parents envisioned. Gulamira was not who she was supposed to be. And she was not less for it. She was herself. She was who she needed to be.

"I am Florella Gulamira, High Priestess of Exkel, Sign of the Merciful, Sworn of the Zaruf, and the Holder of Heritage. Your bosses have my priest. I want him back."

29

HER PEOPLE

*I*t's late here. I just woke from a nightmare that I don't want to return to. Everyone was dying. Our family, our friends, our people. Everyone was dying... I can't go there, Syeda. I can't let it happen. We can't let them win... I have an idea. It's a terrible idea. An awful idea. But it will save a vast majority of humanity and a lot of tatzons. Many will also die. But I think my idea will give us time and an opportunity to survive the fall of Rajalend. And if we do it right, these cultists will think we're playing into their hands. I know your Oligarchs can be sympathetic, so this is up to you to convince them to do this. I'm sorry, sister, but for our people to live, we're going to become demons.

-Your brother, the one who needs your forgiveness.

Isra breathed through her nose. Doing anything more flared the burn on her neck and the slices along her ribs. Yet she waited with a grin. A delirious, beyond caring grin.

She'd spill blood soon.

Voices came through the opening. Abioda returned. He entered, cheerful and eager as ever. He came in with the two usual guards and they stopped dead in their tracks.

"Where's the table?" Abioda asked.

And Isra leaned her head back with a mighty smile.

"Who moved my table?"

"I don't know of anyone moving it," one guard said.

"Then why's it gone?"

"I, well, maybe it—"

"Idiots." Abioda stomped to Isra's cell. "This your doing? Where's my table?"

Isra made a nonsense gesture and dropped her hands in front of her. She faced the door, sitting with her back against the wall.

"Get this door open," Abioda said. "Beat out some answers."

The two guards moved past Abioda and unlocked the door. The door opened, and she sprang forward. One guard jumped back, the other reached for his—her—sword. But they were too slow.

Isra opened her hand, fingers splayed wide, showing an empty circle on her palm. And with a quick tap of the finger, she Released the table, channeling it from the Capture circle through her tattoo lines and out of the palm circle. She Released it with all of its force and speed.

The table materialized out of her hand, and it met each of the three tatzons.

The table did not shove them back. It did not knock them to the ground. It didn't even knock them unconscious, as she'd planned.

The table pulverized them.

It bisected the one directly in front of her and obliterated the second's head and much of his chest. Red blood erupted and covered everything in sight as the table stopped for none and collided with the wall, creating a loud metallic crash that echoed in both the room and her ears.

It happened so quickly. The first didn't have time to make a noise, the second sounded like a god struck an over-ripened peach with a hammer. Abioda, though...

Isra stumbled forward amidst the gore and red coating to a screaming man on the ground. The table seemed to have only clipped Abioda's side, shattering leg and arm and caving in one side of his rib cage.

"Abyssal's tail," Tsuran said from his cell. His mouth hung open as if to say more, but he seemed to forget to speak.

Isra walked to one of the side tables where Abioda had dropped his torture tools. She unwrapped a cloth and found her ivory stylus, her red blood covering it. And she smiled. She'd likely not find her sword or her pouch of circles, but at least she had her stylus back. With it in hand, she walked to Abioda, blood pouring from his broken body. The man gasped and tried to flail with his good arm, but he screamed in pain. He wasn't going anywhere.

"How did she do that?" Nasna asked. "She's... she's human."

Isra kicked Abioda. "Hey. Few questions."

Abioda's face crumpled into a twisted growl and he spat blood. Which helped. It meant Isra could skip the gentle portion she was too tired to deal with.

She slammed her foot into his broken leg. The man screamed.

"Please!" he said. "Stop! I'll talk."

Huh. That worked better than she hoped. She bent down, staring at him in his bloody face. "You know about the idol of Mirr?"

The man glared at her, but nodded.

"We just docked. Is it still here or did you sell it in the port?"

"Why do you—augh!"

Isra pulled her foot off his leg again. "Is it here?"

"Yes! Yes, it's still here! We're delivering it to the Maw, damn it."

Isra smiled. Good. She could still get it. She could get the idol and her people would be...

She sighed. They'd be in the same position until she got back to Rajalend with the idol. And that was many decks away, and she was tired. But she could get it now. It was hers.

"Second question." She gestured to the ceiling, to the deck above. "Where's the girl?"

Tsuran and Nasna shuffled behind her, but she kept her gaze on Abioda, who didn't seem as keen to share about this. His lips tightened, and he closed his eyes.

"What girl?" he said.

Isra drove her stylus into his prihand. The ivory cracked through bone, and Isra grimaced at the wailing.

"Where is she?"

He tightened his lips and shook his head. That was far from a suitable response, and Isra let him know with her stylus. Abioda screamed again and bit his lip, shaking his head again and again. Her nostrils flared, and she punched his broken knee and then stabbed him again. She stabbed wherever she could, pressing, shoving, piercing. He screamed and wailed, but he did not beg for her to stop again. This time, he readied himself for the worst. Why? Why did he become so determined to anger her?

She pulled the stylus out and wiped it off on the man's robes.

"Is she meaning Kamaria?" Nasna asked. "She's here? You said she got away."

Isra didn't look away from Abioda. She did not appreciate his silence. "What did you do to her?"

He grabbed his sides and kept shaking his head. She raised her stylus.

"Stop it! He's not talking, just stop," Nasna said and her red hand reached through the wooden bars toward Isra. "I can get him to speak. You don't need to torture him. Just let me out and I can get him to talk."

Isra glared at the ordîn and then at Abioda. He squirmed in agony, red leaking onto the floor, which gave her pause. If she kept this up, he'd die, and she'd be nowhere.

Nasna met Isra's eyes. "You said Kamaria escaped. But you torture him for her whereabouts."

Isra used the nearby table to pull herself to her feet. "Yes."

"So, you lied earlier. She never escaped."

"Correct."

"What?" Tsuran asked. "You mean she's here? On this ship? Why in the Abyss did you tell us she left?"

Isra looked away from them, and through the room's opening. No one rushed down the adjacent hall. Somehow, no one heard these screams. Or perhaps people just thought they were hers.

"Could you get him to talk?" Tsuran asked, turning to Nasna.

"I... I don't know for sure," Nasna said. "But I could do something in his energy."

"You don't sound confident."

"I've never done something like that before. Not sure if it can be done."

Isra looked down the hall. The ship seemed pretty quiet right now. Maybe she could make it to the iron hold with no one noticing.

Her people's hope waited for her down in that hold.

Damn it. She was too lightheaded for all of this. She needed a moment to sit and think. To plan.

"Hey, human," Nasna said. "I'm sorry, I never got your name, but can you please let us out? If Kamaria isn't safe, we can't wait in here any longer."

Isra was on the sixth deck? Maybe the seventh. Somewhere near the middle. If she were careful, she might go down and back up in an hour. Though she'd be looking at over two hours given her level of strength and all the potential problems that could arise.

"Hey! You hearing us?" Tsuran said. "Let us out! Now's no time for gawking and reminiscing."

Isra glanced back. "We're not friends."

Tsuran slammed three hands against the wood. "Damn you and friendship. We just want out. It doesn't risk you anything! We just need to get the girl. Two minutes is all we need from you to let us out. Come on."

Isra limped back toward Abioda, stylus gripped in her hand. She had to try one more time to—

"My gods," Abioda said in a raspy voice. "Those markings... it's you. The hidden one, the eighth one. The Isolated."

Isra paused and followed Abioda's gaze straight to Tsuran. Silence ripped through the room like a collapsing tree, so only the *Cleansing* spoke or moved.

"You're... you're mistaken." Tsuran's voice was hushed, only a strained whisper. It was hard to tell with his gray skin, but it seemed he lost some color as he spoke. "I don't know what you're talking about."

"I've been a fool," Abioda said, and he twisted himself, throwing his shattered limbs over to get onto his one good knee. He groaned and cried out in pain with each thrashing movement. "I was so focused on this magical human I failed to see my salvation right before me. Forgive me, forgive me!" He planted his forehead on the ground and Tsuran stared back with an indiscernible expression. Fear? Frustration? Confusion? Maybe joy? Compared to his ordîn friend, he did better keeping his face from betraying what was going on inside. She looked baffled and anxious.

Nasna placed a hand on his shoulder. "Tsuran?"

He kept staring at Abioda, though there was a hollowness to his eyes now. "You know where Kamaria is?"

Abioda held up his head. "The girl? Yes, yes, I do."

"Just tell us where she is."

"Yes, yes, of course. She's your key. I see it now. I knew it. I knew it."

"Tell us."

Abioda smiled, as if Tsuran's frustration fed his enthusiasm. "We sent her to the rest of the Realized, down in the Maw's heart."

"When?" Isra asked, grabbing the man's shirt. "When did they sail?"

His smile turned into a frown looking at her. "The secluded one sails now. I just handed her over to the ship, *Quick Passing*." He returned a wide smile to Tsuran. "I do not know what act I've done to deserve such a blessing. To be here, to witness the dawning of the Eventual Return. We await you, my lord."

Isra shook the man again. "Where in the Maw?" She breathed hard, the pain of the last few days of torment becoming more and more real to her. But she held onto the man. But... why was she caring so much about where they took Kamaria? She hadn't taken the time to wonder.

Because the answer was strange to admit.

"They did not bless me with the knowledge of the Realized home." Abioda's intense gaze was almost yearning, with Tsuran being his target. "Those who are blessed, they know."

Isra threw the man to the side and held up her stylus. "Who knows? Tell me a name."

Abioda smiled, his gaze still set on Tsuran.

"Tell me!"

"I know."

Isra lowered her stylus and turned toward the cell. Tsuran stepped back, his dark eyes drifting this way and that, as unfocused as a dying rat. "I know where they're taking her," he said.

Nasna reached out and helped steady him. "Are you sure?"

He nodded. "There's only one place he could mean. I... I'll explain later."

Isra glanced between Tsuran and Abioda. She sighed and got to her feet and looked around. Next to one guard was her cutlass, and it looked like the Released table hadn't damaged it. Isra picked it up and walked back to Abioda.

Abioda coughed and one hand spasmed, and he cried out from the pain. He was about to greet the Abyssal with or without her.

"What are you doing with that?" Tsuran asked. "Hey, I know he tortured you, but we need him alive."

She hovered the sword over his throat.

"Stop!" Tsuran rammed into his cell door and Isra rolled her head to the side to see him. There was an intense fury in his eyes. "Please. He knows things. I'm not done asking him questions."

Isra held his gaze, not looking away, and shrugged. "I am."

She plunged the sword into Abioda.

"Damn you!" Tsuran said. But Isra was as far from caring as she could be right now. She limped to the cell and met Tsuran's pointed rage. He was a lot taller up close, but there was thick wood separating them. However, that didn't prevent his fury from washing through. "You didn't have to kill him. He had answers."

"You know where they're taking her?" Isra asked.

Tsuran tightened his jaw and looked away. His hand drifted up to his right shoulder, where the priarm should have been. But this space was empty and no other arm took it. Isra glanced back at Abioda. He was missing a priarm too.

"I know where they're taking her," Tsuran said.

She glanced at the iron lock on their cell. The guards would have the key. If all else failed, she had her stylus. Even the weakest of ivory was at least as strong as iron.

"Why do you want Kamaria?" Isra asked and this question she directed more toward the ordîn, who stilled and looked away.

Silence followed. A breath passed. Two breaths. The woman took in a deep third and looked up. "I stole from her the one person in the world who cared for her and there are people who want to hurt her. We're the only ones who'll try to keep her safe."

"You murdered her mother."

Tsuran stopped at the door and the ordîn's face blanched, making it more pinkish. Neither spoke for a moment.

Isra nodded. So, it was true. Those trying to save Kamaria were the reason she needed saving to begin with.

"Yes," Nasna said, taking a breath and recomposing herself. "I did. Tsuran tried telling me otherwise, but it was me who ended the life of Kamaria's mother."

"People want Kamaria dead," Isra said.

Nasna nodded. "Yes. Someone paid a lot of money for me to kill her. I doubt they've given up on that."

"And you," she said, turning to Tsuran, "you're connected with these people that've taken her?"

"That... that was another life," he said.

"You murdered her mother while getting paid to kill her. And you're with the people who took her." Isra looked between the two of them, sword still gripped in her hand. "Why let you out?"

Tsuran leaned forward, jaw set, eyes determined. "I am not with them. And I have done everything I could this past year to keep her away from them. Yes, we're the reason she needs protecting and all that. But, damn it all, no one else will protect her now! We're all she's got, whether she likes it or not."

"We made a promise," Nasna said. "To give her a better life. Well see that promise through."

It wasn't easy to believe them. They could have been lying, of course. She knew that. Half of her life was lying. And Kamaria hadn't been keen on the ordîn being around, though she seemed to like Tsuran. Lady above, this was not why she'd come here.

She searched through one guard until she found the cell key. She paused in front of the door and looked at the two of them. Isra had a sword, but the last few days had exhausted her. If it came to a fight, these two would overpower her.

She unlocked the door and stood back.

The two pushed it open and walked out.

Tsuran nodded and spun to Nasna. "Nas, help with the collar?"

"On it." Nasna rushed to the wall sconce with the lightstone and placed a hand on it. "Tsuran come here. I don't want to hold it for long."

She placed her other hand on the lock of his iron collar. Isra cocked a brow. Did they want her to get them a key or—

The lightstone flickered and there was a loud thud followed by the cracking of metal. Tsuran stumbled back and the iron collar fell to the floor. The place Nasna touched had shattered.

"Are you alright?" Nasna asked, coming beside Tsuran.

"Abyssal and her icy—Gah!" he said. "Damn, that hurt."

"Can you sense your statue now? We can't waste anymore time."

Tsuran closed his eyes and rubbed his neck. "Yeah, feels like it's above us. Captains' quarters, I'd imagine."

Nasna nodded and turned to Isra. "Tsuran is a Guardian. He'll possess his statue and start paving a way for us. Hopefully, the ship Kamaria's on hasn't sailed yet and we can get to it. Can you walk?"

Isra nodded and walked to the nearest wooden table and carved a circle into it.

"I'll head over now," Tsuran said.

"Wait, maybe don't until we're closer. Better you not endure Solitude if no one is around."

Isra placed her stylus down and Caught it into her palm. Sword in hand, she headed to the door.

"Fine by me," Tsuran said. "Let's go."

Isra made for the hall, which opened into the wider space with two sets of stairs. One led up. The other stairs led down. Down into the depths of the ship, down to the iron hold. Down to the idol.

Tsuran and Nasna would be plenty of a distraction for her. Icy Abyss, they could even get Kamaria if the Lady was with them. Isra had always been here for one reason. She was here for her people and her people alone.

"Are you coming with us?" Nasna asked, heading toward the stairs going up.

Isra did not look away from the other stairwell, from the path to the hold. After all this time, she would finish this damn mission. All she needed was one hour now. One hour to go down and get out. Within this next hour, she'd have the idol in her hand. Within this next hour, she...

Within the next hour, she could lose Kamaria forever.

Isra paused and the girl's face became vivid in her mind.

Do you think I could be a Sefaran?

"We're going," Tsuran said. "Catch up if you can."

"I am not coming with you," Isra said. It was what needed to be said, because she decided. Lady forgive her. She turned toward them. "You're coming with me." She pushed past them and headed toward the stairs leading up and out of the *Cleansing*. Not toward the idol, but toward Kamaria.

Tsuran walked up next to her, brow raised. "Leading with a limp? You want me to carry you?"

"I'm carrying a sword."

"Point taken." He paused. Isra glanced at him sidelong and he had a stupid grin on his face. Nasna groaned to the side.

"Focus, Tsuran," Nasna said.

"Right, right. Sorry. Actually, I have a question." His grin faded, and a serious expression replaced it. "Why do you care what happens to Kamaria? You couldn't have known her before and, no offense, you're a human."

Isra smirked at this. The line between tatzon and human was often far thinner in her life than Tsuran's kind would think. Especially with Kamaria. Because there was a simple fact they wouldn't understand, but Isra would acknowledge.

"Kamaria's my people."

30

ONLY THE BEGINNING

Ten Years Ago

The Temple and its gardens burned with flame and the screams of priests.

The city of Zashai quaked with the chaos. Spirits rampaged through the ivory gates, attacking all in the Cubling districts, while Veir warriors possessed their beasts to push the invaders backs, and the citizenry fled from spirits eating and Buildings toppling. Trees and constructions burned, streets piled with bodies and ran with streams of Veir blood.

Gulamira watched from the balcony of the Temple. She watched what her songs had brought to pass.

She watched as below, Veir citizens joined with priests of the Three Sisters as they threw flame and torch onto the Temple of Exkel, as they dragged Exkeldian priests out into the streets to slaughter.

The people knew the songs of the Exkeldians brought the death of the Zaruf. They knew it brought the spirits to their city.

And the Temple burned.

"Priestess, away from the balcony!" Salma grabbed Gulamira by the elbow and pulled her away from the sight of her failure. "It is not safe here. Grab what belongings you can. Clothing and essentials only."

She stared at her wardrobe, covered in ivory tusks, yet everything the room blurred, both vision and sound and smell. She and

Salma had run from the Between Rivers. The spirits had ignored them, failed to follow. At first. Then more came. And then more. All like an army descending onto the capital.

Gulamira looked out of the window. "I need to help them."

"Priestess, please. There is nothing to do. We must leave before the flames catch us here."

"But... the people... I did this."

"And they know it, child. Grab your clothes."

"Salma, I have to stop this." She walked toward the balcony. "I can protect the people. I can save them."

She knew she walked out onto the balcony, she knew flames climbed the Temple and that people screamed and shouted. She knew, yet it was as if everything was still, silent, empty. The flames offered her no warmth, and the screams were hollow in her ears. She did not even realize a song rose in her, for even songs were silenced in her heart. All she saw was the blood-covered faces of her parents.

"Priestess!" Salma pulled her back and grabbed her shoulders. "What do you think you're doing? How could you dare have that song in your mouth?"

Gulamira blinked, eyes focusing on Salma. That song. Without thinking, she had begun to sing a higher song she was not supposed to know. One she had learned from going to the Heritage itself.

A song that killed spirits.

She looked back to the burning city. "It's the only way... I can save them, Salma. I can save everyone. I just need to—"

Salma slapped her.

"Shut your mouth child about things you cannot, should not understand!"

Gulamira stared up at Salma, unable to grasp what had just happened. That he had hit her. He never struck her. Never. But in his eyes now, she saw.

Pain.

Hurt.

Anger.

So much fear. Fear of her.

He gripped her shoulders tight and breathed even, but shallow breaths. "Have you not done enough evil already that you would desecrate the land with that song? Do you know and understand nothing? Look. Look, Florella child, at what you have brought us. This, this is what happens when you abuse the higher songs. The higher songs do not bow to you, you bow to them! But because you thought yourself greater, Veirzen sits without a leader, without spiritual guidance, and it burns itself alive."

Salma let go of her and stumbled back, shaking. He stared at her and then his hands. His expression fell, and he buried his face into his hands, sobbing.

Gulamira cried too. The Temple, this room, this man before her, they were supposed to protect her. To keep her safe. But she lost that. And it was her fault. She killed her parents, her Zaruf, her order. All with those higher songs.

Never again. Never again would any of those vile songs exit her lips.

"What do I do, Salma? How do I make it right?"

The aged priest knelt before her, wiping away his tears and then hers. His hand rested on her cheek where he'd slapped her. "There is nothing to do, but flee. When the people find you, they will kill you."

A priest burst through the opening, panting. "The people charge the stairs. They come for the High Priestess."

Salma rose and ushered Gulamira towards the second opening. "Then there is no time to grab anything. We head for the river, are the guards there?"

The priest nodded. "They are ready to take her to sea. We are trying to save the texts but will come after."

Salma took Gulamira, and they fled. She watched her world burn as they fled through secret stairs, down under forgotten tunnels, and into the turmoil of Zashai. A boat waited for her at the river, six soldiers loyal to the Exkeldians standing by. They ushered her into the boat but Salma did not enter.

"What are you doing?" she asked.

"I must help the rest of the priests. In three days time we shall meet with you by the sea."

"Please don't leave me!"

He turned to her and smiled a priestly smile. "Come now, why the tears? Why the frown? You are now High Priestess."

"Salma, no."

The guards shoved the boat off, grabbing their oars and taking their seats.

"Why do we smile, High Priestess? Why do we live? Come, you know your lessons. You know why we priests must smile. So never forget."

"Salma!"

The guards rowed down the river, distancing her from her priests, from her dying Temple. They left Zashai in ruins and made their way to the sea where a ship waited. Some guards tried to speak to her, to comfort her, but her eyes did not leave Zashai's direction and her ears heard nothing but Salma and the screams of her priests.

She did not speak to the guards. She did not speak to the ship master or any of the sailors. When they brought her food, she nibbled. When they brought her water, she sipped.

Three days passed. And the three days became a week, the week became three. Not another priest arrived to the harbor.

When a month had gone by, word came by the river: the Exkeldians were no more and priests of the Three Sisters now hunted for the High Priestess.

The ship sailed. No one knew where to go, only that Gulamira would live.

And in that time, she tried to smile. She tried to force her priestly smile onto her lips. To smile for those who couldn't, for those who wouldn't.

But that smile never came. Because the worst of life had only begun.

31

---◆◯◆---

HIGH PRIESTESS OF EXKEL

T　*his is an impossible request. This would doom our people. There's too many things that could go wrong and... do you understand what you ask? I understand your logic, but to do this to our own people? It is uncertain that it would work. We can't be sure that you can gather them all. We can't be sure that we aren't just killing everyone! Raz, if we do this, we are selling our souls to the Abyssal, and we won't find redemption for this.*

-Syeda, the one who pleads for your soul.

Gulamira stood outside the opening to the Oligarch's suite, a large archway of twisting branches with long drapes hanging to the floor. One Builder vanished from sight, possessing the still-living wood, and traveled ahead to announce her. There were no chairs or cushions for her to sit on, so she and the other Builder stood in silence as they both waited for several long minutes.

When the first Builder returned, he nodded to both. "They'll see you."

Gulamira readied her smile and followed.

They passed through the drapes, only to meet a second row of silks, just as tall, just as vibrant in their green. She slipped through three more sets of these, a gaudy design, but one with a not-so-subtle message: those within had money to spare. The messaging strengthened as she passed through the final curtain and entered the suite, which was like an entire Building. The room was spacious enough to fit two Large beasts inside, and they'd replaced an entire wall with an open balcony. Beast furs covered the ground, and the head of a Large panther hung on the wall above the hearth, streaks of red marbling its curved tusks. In the center of the room, another depiction of the Ethereal Tree grew like a column, wrapping around itself to the ceiling, where it branched out and along the ceiling. Perhaps the most impressive display, though, was the chandelier hanging from one of those branches, a chandelier predominately made of green and red-crystal, with, unobscured for all to see, a yellow-crystal the size of two fists hanging in the center. That rare crystal would fetch enough ivories for most families to have the most lavish of lives.

It had been a long time since she'd seen any.

She tore her eyes from the wealth and centered her attention on those who sat amid the grand room. Oligarchs Argul and Ortu.

The Oligarchs sat in over-sized cushions underneath the chandelier, their ordîn guard standing behind them and the Soulborn leaning against the hearth. Argul was a small man with deep wrinkles, but that did not disguise the calculating mind behind those sharp eyes. Ortu was a long, yet terribly thin woman with a single arm compared to Argul's two. Where he resembled a squat boulder, she reminded Gulamira of a dried out branch.

A still tension thickened with every moment until the very air seemed to choke Gulamira as she stood before probable death. But she took one breath. And then another. She had come with a purpose, and they would not defeat her before she began.

At last, Argul leaned back in his cushion, eyes still firm on her. "Why does the mountain cry in the summer?"

Gulamira struggled to not let her mouth drop as those words flittered through the air. He had not spoken in Rajal. That was Vei'n, the tongue of Veirzen, and that was a pass phrase belonging to her order. Something no outsider would know.

She swallowed and, in Vei'n, said, "Because we have shed it of its furs and left it without a friend."

Both Argul and Ortu smiled. Beamed even. Ortu grabbed Argul's hand and squeezed it, whispering something to the air. They approached her, cautious at first and then eager. They circled her as if she were a domesticated beast for sale.

"Amazing," Argul said, in Rajal again. "To think, all these years, you lived. A Florella lives."

They stopped in front of her, their gazes transfixed by her markings. She smiled, but did not miss how the ordîns and Soulborn had also drawn closer and encircled them.

"How are you alive?" Ortu asked, but before Gulamira answered, Argul placed an arm around his Partner.

"Come now, Ortu," he said. "That should not be our first question when greeting the High Priestess who is back from the dead."

Ortu shot him a quick glare but recomposed herself just as fast. "Of course, my surprise stole my manners. It is an honor, High Priestess. You seem well for one supposed to be dead."

Gulamira made a polite bow. "Likewise."

"Yes, yes." Ortu's spindly fingers twisted around a section of her robe, which had patterns of forked tongues to match her markings.

Argul snapped a finger at the guards. "Bring us food and drink, and be quick about it."

The ordîns, these glorious beings of legends, rushed about like simple servants. The Soulborn brought over two pitchers of wine, while the ordîns brought short tables and filled them with platters of dried fruits and meats. Argul took a goblet of wine and drank deep. Ortu stabbed a fruit with her fingers, yet her eyes fixated on Gulamira, who did her best not to stare at the food. Given that her last few meals were stale crackers and flowers, her stomach gurgled with longing.

"I do not wish to be rude," Argul said, wiping his aged mouth. "Especially as this is so unexpected, but I don't want you to waste energy or breath. We are more than aware of your affinity for the spirit song. We had many lessons to prepare us to meet you and your parents all those years ago, and we remember them well."

"I wouldn't presume to do such a thing." Even as Gulamira spoke the words, she quieted the songs she'd coaxed. She hadn't thought they would work, but she'd wanted to try at the least.

"I will be honest with you," Argul said. "When our Builder first told us you were here, I denied it. Everyone knew that the High

Priestess had died in that unfortunate raid." He was all smiles, but there was no life in his eyes. They had the same feel as the eyes of a dead fish on the dock, which made it hard to focus. Gulamira stared at his spiral markings instead.

"The pass phrase was a clever way to determine my identity," Gulamira said. "How did you know of that, if I may ask? I did not know my parents had ever shared that knowledge with the Oligarchs."

"Oh, they didn't." Argul took a drink from his goblet and became distracted by some of the dried fruits. Gulamira sat and waited, but neither Argul nor Ortu offered any more explanation. But she could guess which priest they'd pulled it out of.

Argul looked back and laughed. "Really. This is almost too much to believe. Tell us, where have you been all these years?"

Gulamira hesitated. This conversation was going better than she'd expected. She had thought they would lock her up the first chance they had. Though, that was still an option, so she needed to be careful. "It's been a long ten years, let's put it that way. I have stayed as inconspicuous as I could."

"Very inconspicuous." Argul swirled his goblet around in his prihand, letting the wine draw to the edge before he put it down. "Seems strange you would reveal yourself in this manner instead of in Veirzen. Strange indeed you would announce yourself to us this day."

"There was a time," Ortu said, "when we suspected your Partner had hidden you away, but we dismissed it as the years went on. It seems we had been correct, after all."

Gulamira took great effort to keep her breathing even as she spoke. "He does not know I'm alive."

Argul raised his brows at this, but Ortu leaned in with a most predatory smile. "Is that so?" she asked. "How most unfortunate."

"As much as this is a thrilling conversation," Gulamira said. "We all know these pleasantries are a veil. Perhaps we should cut out this side talk and get straight to the point."

Argul smiled and spread out his hands. "You returned from the dead before your people's enemies, so perhaps that is a fair point. The High Priestess has the floor."

"You have one of my priests."

Argul nodded. "You want him back."

"And I would then like to leave with him, alive."

"A very rational desire. Unfortunately, he acts as an ambassador to us and he has been a great help in sorting out our business with Veirzen. If someone would like to acquire him, we would, of course, need to see a formal request from someone with the... proper influence."

"Which is why I, the High Priestess of Exkel, am here to collect him."

Ortu danced her finger up toward her neck like a spider and her eyes narrowed. "High Priestess, the years must not have been kind to you, for you misjudge the position you've put yourself in. Don't misunderstand how generous we are, humoring you with a long-dead title." Her spider-prihand crept down and found her Partner's and tapped each finger rhythmically. "In fact, it's quite generous of us to even allow this talk, isn't it? We have a wealth of iron chains around, I assure you, and it would not be difficult to find you a new sleeping bar. We have plenty of room here."

Those words stung and snapped at some of Gulamira's confidence. But her smile did not falter.

"If you wish us to get to the point, then I shall," Argul said. "It seems obvious to us that, along with gathering your priest, you likely have desires to avenge your parents' death. If neither your Partner nor any in Veirzen are aware of you being alive, then it also appears you do not hold any actual power. Thus, we have no reason to listen to your requests."

This was true. So she needed to make them listen. "I am not here to kill either of you. My priest is the only thing that I want. I did not know that anyone else survived and that's all I want."

"And we are to believe that?" Ortu asked. "That you've walked into a beast's den without plans to put the monster down?"

"You can see I'm unarmed and alone. If I came to kill you, wouldn't I have come with a much better plan?"

The two Builders materialized beside the Oligarchs, both of which gave little reaction, though Gulamira started at their sudden appearance. "Ah, what wonderful timing," Argul said with a smile.

The two Builders leaned in and whispered to the Oligarchs. Both Argul and Ortu lost their smiles and appeared more confused than before. Argul nodded and waved the Builders away. "Thank you. Keep searching, just in case."

The Builders vanished, and the two Oligarchs stared at Gulamira. "What was that about, if I might ask?" Gulamira said.

"We gave them orders to search the tower," Ortu said. "To look for anyone suspicious or attempting to take the priest or find a way to our balcony."

Gulamira scrunched her brow and leaned back. "Are there many people trying to get my priest?"

"You mistake us," Argul said. "We sent them to find associates of yours."

"Because," Ortu said, "we truly did not think you to be so foolish as to come here alone and without help." Ortu sat forward, her confusion giving way to a sneer. "It seems we were wrong about that."

Gulamira froze, realizing that the Oligarchs had only been talking with her because they thought they stalled her. Stalled in order to locate her nonexistent team. But she had no one with her. And they had no reason to humor her any longer.

"I have to say, I am amazed at your brazenness," Argul said. "You, my dear, are a rare, near extinct species that we cannot find again. And now you have walked freely and openly into our arms, without help or a plan. Do you even understand that situation you've placed yourself in?"

Gulamira eyed the Soulborn and the ordîn guard. They did not move. Yet. But they understood the Oligarchs as much as she did. So she needed to speak fast, to bring to light the idea that had been percolating in her mind since she first saw the Oligarchs.

"I may not understand everything," she said. "But there are a few things I do. I understand you two are not as in control as you'd have me believe."

Argul and Ortu both smirked. "And what would make you think that?" Ortu asked.

"You came here to get my priest."

"Ah, yes," Argul said. "How could I forget that collecting one's property showed a lack of control."

"I understand that the information he's given you has been invaluable, but you came here personally to see him moved. You didn't send for him. You came for him. Oligarchs who own a third of Rajalend and who could have easily hired a fleet to transfer my priest, yet you didn't. And when you came, you didn't come bearing on the port with an army or even a large guard. You brought six with you. This, to me, speaks of people who don't trust anyone else to do this. I don't see two Oligarchs wielding grand power. I see two individuals nervous about something going wrong. Which brings me to a frightening question." She leaned forward, smile firm, eyes piercing. "What has you so scared?"

The Oligarchs stared at her for a long time, and no one moved during the silence. And Gulamira beamed. She had touched something, just as she'd thought. Even in the riches of the Oligarchs, no one was immune to fear.

Ortu broke the silence by raising her goblet. "One of you, pour more wine." The two Soulborn obeyed, though Ortu did not take her eyes off of Gulamira as she drank. "You're observant, you know that?"

Gulamira only smiled.

The two Oligarchs leaned in to each and exchanged quiet whispers. After a minute or two, Ortu sighed and nodded, turning back to Gulamira. "What do you know of the land of Oushwala?"

Gulamira took her own pause, though not as long as they had. "I've only heard stories. It's a land far north of Tutchal, I think."

"It was. Once, long ago. That land has been destroyed for many decades now. But before, it was a rising power, a land with holds on fertile lands and rich mines. It had a standing army of possessors strong enough to buffet both Rajalend and Veirzen. And today, the land is an empty wasteland, with not a single living thing for miles."

"Have you heard of Regiik?" Argul asked, and Gulamira shook her head. "Yes, I doubted you would. It was a land even further than Oushwala, yet it received the same fate. And there was another land even further than Regiik, one whose holy name we are not to utter, who received the worst fate of them all."

"Each of these were mighty nations," Ortu said. "And now the only inhabitants are spirits."

"I don't understand the point of this geographical history," Gulamira said.

"As do so many." Argul took his goblet, but only looked at his wine and did not drink. "But I think you understand more than you say you do. You were young when tragedy struck your order, yet you must have learned the history of the priesthood."

Gulamira shifted in her cushion. "What does that have to do with anything?"

"You do not recognize these Rajal names, yet perhaps you would know the names in their own tongue." He turned his gaze toward her, and something went cold in her as both he and Ortu lifted their voices to speak three words. Words that were not Rajal and not Vei'n, for they were not words at all. Three names spoken in the spirit song.

In Rajal, Oushwala. In truth, His Fiery Breath.

In Rajal, Regiik. In truth, the Hearth of Life.

In Rajal, they would not say. In truth, she could scarcely believe, for it was the Mountain of Exkel.

Breath. Hearth. Mountain.

Gulamira jumped to her feet, though she neither spoke nor moved. She thought she would call them liars and manipulators. But she didn't. In the spirit tongue, nothing could hide. Deception was impossible. The words they spoke, the names they declared, had to be true.

Ortu grinned and leaned into her Partner. "It seems you recognize those words, at least."

"How do you know..." Gulamira's words faltered. She didn't even know what to ask. But she shook herself from whatever spell had hold of her and she sat down, regaining composure. "Those names are Exkeldian. They are not of lands of this world, but of the world beyond."

"Perhaps that is as much as they taught you at your young age," Argul said. "But you must realize how foolish that is."

She glanced up, finding it difficult to form the right words. "You say that the Breath, the Hearth, and the Mountain... they are..."

"Actual locations in this world, yes. Ones from which your order originated from."

"We come from His Mountain," Gulamira said. "Little embers that rested in His Hearth, until His Breath blew us to the world."

"A simplification of history to teach a theology and to teach a child." Argul smiled as the realization continued to sink into her. "Your order was relatively new to Veirzen, but its history is far, far older. As is the destruction they had to continuously flee."

"Are you saying my order destroyed them? How do you even know any of this?"

Ortu smirked. "There is much we know that you do not, High Priestess. But no, we are not saying your people destroyed those lands. However, someone did. We're not told if your people followed the destroyers or if the destroyers followed you, but the results are the same."

Argul looked at the hanging beast's head, though his eyes seemed to go far beyond. "I would like to tell you something you will not believe, yet is still true. We are not behind your parents' assassination."

The words hit her stomach like an iron fist and she found no response to give.

"True, both Veirs and Rajals commonly believe that the six Oligarchs were behind it. Even within the six, Hyder and Zaid have had their suspicions about the two of us. But, at the day's close, we did not do it. Your parents' death was a supreme failure, one we wished had not happened. And yet, the crux of the matter is that someone *was* behind their deaths. Someone wanted them dead, for the war to erupt again, for the order of Exkel to fall." He turned his gaze back to her. "We are not your enemies, High Priestess. It is a fact that we share a common foe with you."

"Those who destroyed your Exkeldian lands were called the Bridgemakers," Ortu said. "We destroyed most of them almost a century ago, except we failed to kill the most dangerous of them all. And he is the one behind your life's destruction. He is called 'the Nightmare'."

Gulamira's mouth tasted dry and was empty of every sound. She stared at them, not blinking, not knowing how to look away. The things they told her... they couldn't be true...

"Who is he?" she asked.

"A powerful possessor. He's evaded us for many years, but we've seen his hand rising in our recent past." Ortu fixed her gaze on Gulamira. "He had a particular desire to see your entire order erased from the world."

Gulamira looked at her hands and followed her branch-like markings, her eyes tracing those familiar shapes. She needed familiarity right now, because these things they told her were too much to believe. Yet, they had spoken true about her order's original homes. Could they be right about this Nightmare?

For years, she had assumed—no, she'd *known* that the Oligarchs had killed her parents. This... she didn't know what to do with this. And it brought another question.

"Did... did my parents know about this Nightmare?"

Ortu frowned, her prihand skittering around the fruit plate beside her. "They knew of the Bridgemakers and their history, but not him exactly. Information about him was partially what they planned to bargain for during that Summit."

Argul nodded solemnly. "It was to be a fortuitous day. We would share our knowledge of Nightmare, and they would assist our masters in their aims." He tapped the side of his goblet for a moment before leaning forward. "High priestess, I understand we have not begun a relationship under the best of circumstances. I also understand that you may not believe all we say. Regardless, there was a time when we were going to make a deal with your parents, when we were going to unite in a common goal. Perhaps we can still achieve that. Yes, I realize the two of us had been hasty when you first came in, and we indeed saw you as easy prey to add to our collection." Argul gestured to the guards and had them move his table away, allowing him and Ortu to rise from their cushions. "I see we were wrong in judging such. Your words, your mind, your... demeanor reminds me much of your parents. We would rather have an Exkeldian as our ally than our enemy. I think it is appropriate to extend an offer of cooperation between you and us."

Gulamira eyed them as well as the Soulborn. "Earlier you called me brazen for walking into a beast's den. Now you think I should walk into its open throat?"

Ortu smirked. "You may stagger at what we've said today. But there's more we haven't told you. More you don't know. But you could."

"And that should entice me? Unverifiable stories that I must take at your word?"

Ortu did not lose her smirk and Argul even seemed pleased with her response. "Perhaps not," he said. "Though what we know is far from unverifiable. However, given what your alliance to us would mean, we would also, of course, compensate you generously. You will have all our resources in searching for your parents' murderer and we shall grant protection to you and your priest. We will care for you and elevate you in status and power beyond what you are currently capable of."

Gulamira wanted to scoff, to dismiss their offer with a flick of the wrist. Yet, she didn't. Years of slavery washed over Gulamira at that moment. Years of hunger, of beatings, of tears and curses and abuse after abuse. If anyone could end all of that, it would be the Oligarchs. If anyone could grant her relief and safe refuge, it was these two. However, nothing in this world came free.

"And what would you want?" she asked. "It's too generous an offer to stem from the kindness of your heart."

Argul smiled. "Cooperation is all we ask. We will give you access to all of our resources and in return, we ask you to give us access to all of yours."

"You want the Heritage."

A yearning, a deep hunger flashed across their eyes. "Astute observation, yes. We believe it to be something the Nightmare needs, but also what we need to defeat him."

"You don't even know what it is."

"True." Ortu extended her bony prihand, an enormous grin forming on her lips. "So, enlighten us."

Gulamira looked past the Oligarchs to the open balcony, toward the harbor, where Medhi waited for her. She could almost hear him whisper in her ear, *Third rule of the sea.*

She took a deep breath and looked back at the two. "I appreciate the offer, but I will not be joining you. The only deal we'll have today is the one where both me and my priest leave here alive and free."

"If that is all you desire, then so be it, though what we want remains the same."

"The Heritage is not for sale."

Argul's smile twitched. "High Priestess, I understand it is of great importance to your people, but—"

"There is nothing you may say that will change my mind about this. You need to ask for something else."

Ortu's prihand tightened, but then relaxed. "Do not be so quick to assume what is and is not on the table to trade. Do not be so quick to forget your presence."

The Soulborn turned toward Gulamira, hands resting on their lock boxes, and the ordîns, by some unspoken order, moved along the walls to stand behind her. Gulamira did not flinch.

"I do not appreciate threats, Oligarchs."

"Neither do we," Argul said. "But if you refuse to work with us, then we must assume you work against us. We do not wish to be your enemies, High Priestess, but that relies on you."

"It relies on us all." Gulamira kept her gaze on those two, a song rising in the back of her throat, though she did not usher it. "There has to be something else you want."

"All you have that we want is the Heritage."

"And yet, that is not an option, so I shall offer something different."

"What could you possibly offer that is worth the Heritage?"

A sickly knot formed in the center of her stomach. She knew what she had to do, but prayed her parents would forgive her, anyway. "Are you aware of the song that would kill a spirit?"

The two Oligarchs paused, though the Soulborn appeared more stunned.

"Ah, so you do. Good." Gulamira crossed her legs and looked up toward the Oligarchs "Here is my offer: I will take my priest and leave here free and alive. You will not pursue us or bother us again.

In return, I will teach your Soulborn here a song that will give you an advantage unlike any other."

It was a bitter thing to say, with the ghost of a slap on her cheek. But they were right, she only had the Heritage to bargain with. Better that she give them only a small piece of it without them realizing the magnitude of what they held.

The Soulborn looked between each other, but all other eyes were on Argul and Ortu. The two pulled back and whispered to each other. As they spoke, a glint came to their eyes and their lips upturned into wicked smiles. Gulamira knew their answer before they turned back to her.

"We accept these terms," Argul said, placing his prihand over his chest to signify the agreement. "And we even have a spirit in another room you can demonstrate on."

Ortu gestured with her prihand toward the opening in the back. "Shall we begin?"

Gulamira placed her prihand on her chest and nodded. She ignored the cold pit in her stomach and followed the Oligarchs and Soulborn beyond the opening.

And in order to protect the Heritage, to save her priest, Gulamira taught the Soulborn this abominable song.

32

---◆◇◆---

A THOUSAND
SORROWS

D *o it.*
   - Anonymous

The Oligarchs led Gulamira to a spiral staircase hidden inside the Ethereal Tree in their suite. It wound up and up, bathed in the soft glow of small lightstones, the stairs widening with every turn until it opened to a large platform, which Gulamira recognized as the top of the tower. From this vantage point, she could see all the Floating Treasure, every ship coming and going, and she could even make out people as they went about their illegal business. The tree trunks of the tower branched out from here, rising into the ceiling as if holding it up. Strangely, she counted only eight branches instead of ten, just like the *Cleansing's* aftcastle.

Crystals of various colors rested in seven braziers surrounding the circular floor, creating shadows of blues and greens. A tatzon stood at each brazier, wielding spears tipped with lightstone and wearing iron masks that held no expression. There was no wind inside the sea-tree, yet Gulamira felt colder here.

But her attention left the crystals, the soldiers, the view of the Treasure, and centered on the man chained to the center of the floor.

The man before her was an elderly tatzon, being at least a hundred-thirty. The markings covering his body reminded her of the hooves of the rams native to the Esotork hills. She knew these markings. She knew this man.

"Dasparet Salma."

The priest opened weak eyes, one gone milky white. This man, one who'd been present at her ordination, one who'd seen the stars at her birth, one who'd held her as an infant and played with her as a child, this man looked up at her from the ground.

Tears pooled in the man's eyes. "High Priestess. You live."

She knelt in front of him, unable to take her eyes off of what they'd done to him. She remembered him as a tall, spindly man, with hair growing in odd places. He was old when she was born, yet he'd always been full of laughter and a knowing smile. Exuberance was his gift that he shared with all. It seemed the Oligarchs had been rather exuberant themselves in how they mutilated his body. There was not a part of his naked body untouched. They marred one side of his face black from some fiery torture and the rest of his body showed intense scarring. And if that hadn't been enough, these... these bastards had taken his limbs. They had taken her tutor, her guide, and sheared off both legs and severed all five of his arms just above the elbow, stealing his ability to possess. She dared not even imagine all the things they did to him. To Salma. To her brother and teacher.

"Yes, I'm alive," she said, though her throat constricted. What was she even supposed to say now? "I'm here to take you with me."

"Alive," he whispered. "All this time, you lived. Oh, mighty god, oh Exkel. I've failed." He hung his head and started to weep.

She grabbed him, cupping his scarred cheek. "No, don't say that. You've failed no one."

He wept, and his long life had taught him how to cry well, for these tears were full and thick and made her eyes water.

"Salma, it's going to be alright. I'm going to take care of you. You're going to finish my lessons, if you'd like."

He wept even harder. Her eyes pooled, but she smiled still. After everything, he needed to see a friendly smile.

"I've learned a lot, but I could still use a teacher. And I'll make sure you have everything you—"

He wept harder still. And it was the only thing she heard. The only thing she saw. An old, mutilated man weeping. And it was not a joyful weeping. She knew this kind. She'd heard it every night in the slums of Archoz, whether it'd been from another prostitute or from a street urchin or some random human who'd found the end of their rope.

The tears of total defeat.

"I'm sorry, High Priestess, I'm sorry." His voice cracked through the tears. "I'm sorry. I'm sorry. I'm sorry..."

He sounded both here and not. Gulamira's mouth twitched, and she took deliberate and slow breaths, refraining from looking at the Oligarchs. Because if she did, the temptation to throw them off the tower might have been too great.

"It is amazing, you should know," Ortu said. "We have learned so much from your priest friend here. The secrets he held, it was like a treasure trove waiting to be unearthed."

Argul sighed with a wistful smile. "He single-handedly advanced our plans by years. What he's given us, what we've found, shall bring victory to a lost world."

"I want him unchained," she said. "I'll leave with him and be done with this."

The Oligarchs nodded. "Yes, of course," Argul said. "Would you care for one of our guards to carry the priest out of the tower? It is a long way down."

"I think your guards have done enough with him. I'll carry him."

"Oh?" Ortu said. "Well, that shall be a sight."

Argul motioned to one of the masked soldiers who approached with a key. Gulamira kept one eye on the guard and another on the Oligarchs, who leaned to their Soulborn, whispering something.

The soldier made no movements except to unlock the chains before backing away. Gulamira crouched and removed the iron from her priest, who continued his mournful refrain. He was so small now, not only without his limbs, but they'd starved him to the point he would have been right at home on the *Cleansing*. He was light enough she could carry him.

"You know, there was one last question we wanted to ask," Argul said, and Gulamira's stomach churned. "The very question we came all these miles to ask."

"Is that so?" she asked, her smile straining to remain. "Well, unfortunately, he's no longer under your supervision."

Ortu sneered and leaned onto Argul. "We are Oligarchs. Everything is under our oversight."

"Indeed," Argul said. "And all we want is one last question. I know you refuse to speak about the Heritage, but I'd like to ask, regardless."

Salma shivered next to her and muttered, "No, no. Please. No. Don't ask. Not that. No questions. Don't hurt. No more hurt. The Heritage... the Heritage..."

Gulamira rubbed his back, but kept her focus on the Oligarchs. "I already told you, the Heritage is not on the table. Information on it was not in our deal."

Salma wavered and burrowed his face into her shoulder. "... Heritage... the Heritage..."

Ortu smiled as the Soulborn let their hands settle on their spirit vessels. "Yes, it was not part of the deal. Yet, it is still something we want to know. And you two are the last to know anything about it. Please, look at this from our perspective. It would be unwise for us to lose the opportunity."

Gulamira rose to her feet, noting the ordîns who stationed themselves in front of the stairs closing off that escape. "We had a deal, your Excellencies."

"Indeed, we did," Argul said. "And we'll hold to it. You shall have your priest and you both shall leave alive and free, that you bought with your earlier lesson. But naturally, before you leave, we would like to receive simple answers to simple questions."

She smiled with utmost grace, though her eyes scanned the area. "Here is the simplest answer: we won't speak about the Heritage." Where could they go? The stairs were the only obvious choice, but there was no way she could outrun them all. Especially not Soulborn.

"Once again, you don't seem to understand your position," Ortu said, looking out over the Floating Treasure. "The view up here is beautiful. It's an endless drop."

The soldiers moved toward Gulamira, spears pointed toward her, and formed two loose walls on either side of her. The other paths were to the Oligarchs or to the edge of the tower. Argul and Ortu stepped forward, grinning. "Let's make this easy, shall we?" Argul said. "You tell us what the Heritage is and its location, and you two shall leave unharmed and unbothered."

Salma muttered beside her, but Gulamira focused on the Oligarchs. "How do you even know about the Heritage? Salma wouldn't have mentioned it, even with what you've done to him."

"No, he didn't, but why not an answer for an answer?" Ortu said. "Tell us where it is, and we tell you how we know about it. We could even share a secret about your order that even you don't know. See? Another deal to be made."

Argul raised a finger. "We wish to be civil, and I'd hate for you to make us desperate enough to resort to violence. As you can see, our men are quite proficient in dealing pain."

Salma jerked upright and cried out, "No! Please, no! No more. The Heritage! It is two, and it is one. It is both a knowledge and an artifact. It is—"

Gulamira spun, slapping a hand over his mouth. "Salma!"

He stilled. The Oligarchs stilled. Her heart raced.

Argul gripped Ortu's hand but his gaze went out beyond the tower. "A knowledge..."

"And an artifact," Ortu said.

Both looked as stunned as she felt, but their reactions turned into jubilation. "Tell us more, Salma," Argul said, walking toward them. "Tell us about the Heritage."

The old priest's body shook and quivered. He fell back and away from Gulamira, sobbing loudly again, a sight that made those damn Oligarchs smile with gleeful satisfaction. An arrogant smile that said they won. A smile that declared themselves victorious. But they were far from it. Gulamira still stood and if she had to fight through every one of these soldiers, if she had to put Salma on her back and run, then she would. They would get nothing more from them. They would learn nothing more about the Heritage.

But then... then Salma met her gaze.

And she was wrong.

"Please." His voice echoed in her ear with a hollow resonance of absolute emptiness. It carried more than words, it carried a song. A spirit song which conveyed his pain, conveyed the truth inside him. It sucked at her heart, as if trying to siphon life from her as Salma sang things she did not want to hear.

Salma had no strength. Not in his body, nor in his soul. They had taken everything from him to the very last piece of strength that had kept him together. He was truly defeated.

Now he had nothing.

He was nothing.

A shell.

Empty.

Broken.

Salma. Her last brother. So glad, so happy to see her once again, with so many things he wished he could say. He was done and could hold out no longer. As soon as they asked again, he would tell them everything he knew about the Heritage.

His song ended and Gulamira sunk to her knees, staring at the ground.

"Take them, if you would," Argul said. "I am quite eager to hear more about this artifact, Salma."

Gulamira didn't move. Salma sobbed and whimpered.

"I'm sorry, High Priestess, I'm sorry," he said through thick tears. He shook as he bowed his head to her. "Forgive... forgive me..."

The two Oligarchs chuckled and Argul pulled his Partner close. "You know, your parents taught us a song once, when we met long ago. We have sung it on occasion. Perhaps you'll recognize it."

With a glint in their eyes, and foul breath in their mouths, the two entered another spirit song. A lower song that declared victory and triumph. No doubt her parents had taught it to them as a way to signal peace, and no doubt these two meant to gloat by it, to relish in this moment. But her parents had never taught a song to anyone without good reason.

Neither of these two understood the songs of spirits. They did not understand that nothing could hide within the song, that all was laid bare. There was only truth.

And Gulamira heard in their song what they did not mean for her to know.

It did not come in images or sounds, but the deepest seated feeling and impression.

Kamaria. A tatzon unharmed by Solitude. A shard of Solitude. She was their key. Their to key to drawing the Isolated and to defeating the Nightmare.

She was the Nightmare's key to destroying all.

Already gone. She sailed to the Dragon's Maw, where knives and cages awaited.

Many truths and hidden lies flooded through their song, but one struck her in the heart. One shook her soul.

Kamaria. The Heritage. One or the other.

The Nightmare needed only one or the other to succeed. Only one or the other was needed to defeat him. Once the Oligarchs, once their masters, had one, the other need not exist.

When they had the Heritage, they would kill Kamaria.

The song ended, and the Oligarchs laughed and beamed, not knowing the secrets they shared with her.

Gulamira was quiet. She was still, closing her eyes and letting only a few more tears to fall down her cheek.

One or the other.

She shifted back toward Salma, toward the last remnant of a life stolen from her. She cupped both Salma's cheek, bringing his eyes up to meet hers. And with all the power she could muster, with a song that drove through the pain to Salma's heart, she smiled the brightest smile she could as the soldiers surrounded them. "Priest Dasparet Salma, chosen of Exkel, servant of Veirzen, I do right now say two things. First, you are forgiven beyond all measures."

Tears streamed down the man's face and his lips trembled.

"And the second thing is a promise I make you. A promise I've already made before Exkel and my parents." In her words, in her song, she carried all the determination and fury of her heart to him, using the song to push aside all pain and anguish. Only a blazing fire remained in her and for a flicker of a moment, she saw the same fire in Salma's eyes. "I promise you, they will never touch the Heritage. Before Exkel I promise you they shall never have it as long as they shall live."

"Guards, please take them," Ortu said. "The reunion has ceased its excitement. And, unfortunately, High Priestess, today you have lost."

Gulamira turned her burning fire and blazing smile toward the Oligarchs, causing their smiles to falter. "Yes, I have. And so have you."

She dropped her prihand to Salma's throat.

And she locked it shut.

The guards yelled. The Oligarchs started. Salma choked and tried to reach his throat with his severed arms.

Gulamira stared at the Oligarchs and kept smiling.

"Stop her!" Argul said and two soldiers tackled Gulamira. Two others grabbed at her hand and tried to wrench it off of Salma's neck. Two pulled her away, but this only dragged the dying Salma with them.

"Let go, you bitch!" One guard struck her with the butt of his spear. He struck again and again, pummeling her side and face.

"You can't open my prihand. It opens for no one!"

The Oligarchs shouted. The guards swore and beat her. Two started wailing on her priarm with their spears, but the priarm was stronger. It would break, but not yet. Not before...

Salma squirmed less and less. His thrashing weakened. While the guards struck her again and again, Gulamira turned her head and looked at Salma.

His eyes had bulged and his gray skin was turning ashen-white. And maybe it was her imagination, maybe it was her hope, but she thought she heard the gentle whisper of a song.

Thank... you...

Salma went limp and Gulamira became once again the last of the Exkeldians.

The guards pulled her off and tossed her to the side. They rushed to him and the Oligarchs grabbed one guard.

"Nectar! We need nectar!" Ortu cried. "Send someone—anyone! There must be—"

"Forgive us, your Greatness," the guard said. "He's... there's nothing we can do."

Ortu shook her head, and Argul pushed past them to the priest. He looked over at Gulamira, who had not moved.

"What have you done?" Argul gaped at Salma's dead body. His nostrils flared, and he straightened. "You've doomed yourself now, I fear. You think we'll let you go after that?"

Ortu came beside her Partner and glared at Gulamira. "Guards, lock her in iron. Make sure she can neither possess nor escape." She spun to Argul. "This time, I think we bring her to the Realized. We cannot lose her."

"You are fools." Gulamira lolled her head back and stared at the ceiling, the walls, the great big open balcony. "You do not know what the Heritage is, nor its power."

"Maybe not. But, don't worry. You'll show us in time."

Gulamira shook her head. "No. I'll show you now."

She took in a deep breath, air and life and power filling her lungs. Her mind traveled back through every song she'd learned, every lesson of the spirits' language drilled into her, every time their songs reverberated through her being. She thought back to a single song, a song her parents taught her once and then commanded never to use. A song carried from generation to generation to her. The highest of the higher songs.

And as the final High Priestess, she sang the Song of the Coming Fire.

It poured out of her like a river bursting from a dam, like a stampede of wild beasts, like a single leaf falling to the ground. She was deaf to the words, but not to their power. It first flooded her body, tingling through her arm and every place they'd beaten her. The pain vanished, or rather, it traveled. It left the arm and fueled the song. Her body, her strength, her pain, it all became the fuel for the fiery power of this song. The air steamed around her, as though her very person became made of flames. The Soulborn exclaimed as their spirit vessels glowed brighter and brighter, and the Oligarchs stumbled as the power of this song slammed into them. Some guards tried to reach her, but they moved as if the air itself pushed them back, burning them.

And she felt the song rise and build within her, within the world. The song soared through the very life of the world, cutting through the barrier to the Spirit World, beckoning and summoning the Fires to Come.

The song burned her throat as she sang, though no air escaped her. This song was beyond sound, beyond what even her heart could hear. But even as she sang, even as she spoke change into the world, she felt the song changing her too. As it would unmake the lands and sea, as it would bring ends and destructions, so it would unmake her.

But she did not quiet the song. She poured all of her pain, all her determination, all of her soul into it. She fought. Because if her parents had been wrong about anything it was this: the higher songs did belong to her.

Gulamira raised her eyes to the Oligarchs, eyes that could see the fear building in their hearts. She held her head high and hummed a single, declarative song into her words. "And so, the Fires shall Come for you."

The crystals on the platform, lightstones and spirit vessels, glowed like miniature suns and colored stars. She could not see, but she felt as the song built to its climax.

Ear-piercing screeches ripped through the air, causing the Soul-born to curse as they became the first to realize one effect of this song. It was then they heard the cries of the spirits Gulamira had summoned. Spirits on a rampage.

The song built, burning and yearning for more and more, demanding life as payment. Demanding Gulamira's soul as a sacrifice.

It built, built, built.

The climax of the song came like the Dragon's Breath, sweeping through the seas and oceans and all across the lands.

And as the last note left her being, as the forbidden song was sung, Gulamira's body lost all substance as she phased through the floor beneath her and fell.

33

⬤

THE COMING OF FIRE

O *n this day, we Oligarchs of Rajalend, leaders and guardians and protectors of the land of the Ethereal Tree, declare that, in order to combat the blasphemy and the evils that keep us weak against the Veirs, Rajalend shall be purified. No longer shall we harbor those that poison our wells and corrupt our hearts and burn our Temples. Today, we send out our three mightiest Built ships: the* Blessing, *the* Healing, *and the* Cleansing. *They shall root out the human disease of Rajalend and remove every corrupted Rajal and take them to end their days in the Dragon's Maw. May their souls burn into the ash that feeds the Ethereal Tree.*

-From the Declaration of Purification, Eleventh of Sespen, Year 371 of Our Eighth Age

Gulamira fell.

Wood passed by—no, it passed through her. And she fell. The wood rippled through her body, a buzzing sensation that was neither painful nor comfortable, and she fell. She passed through level after level of the tower, briefly hearing startled curses before she continued. As the tower passed her by, she wondered if she would continue falling forever, if this was how her life ended.

She burst from the ceiling into someone's private room and collided with the floor without phasing through. The sudden change jolted through her and she groaned on the floor.

"Burning branches!" someone said from the massive cushion near her. Four tatzons, none clothed, peered over at her. Seemed she'd interrupted someone's fun.

"Who are you? Where did you come from?" the man asked and Gulamira picked herself up from the ground. Somehow, she could stand, even though she'd fallen through the entire tower. That fall should have killed her, or at least broken a leg or something, and yet, besides some dizziness, she felt fine.

"Get out this instant!" the man said. She was all too ready to comply. This tower was not safe for her. She needed to get out now.

The lightstones in the room dulled, a dim shadow falling over the room. Then blue light bled into the space and Gulamira turned around. A face as large as her body emerged from the wall. Its two glowing white eyes centered on her and it sang into the air, singing a song that told her that the spirits were angry with her and they came for her.

The four on the cushion screamed at the spirit. Gulamira stepped back and summoned a song into her throat, to become invisible to the spirit. As the song left her lips, fire surged in her veins and she cried out and fell back, huffing. She couldn't sing. The song of the Coming Fire was still swirling inside her, changing her. Any spirit song would speed up that process. So, she did the only thing she could.

Gulamira ran.

An ear-bleeding screech ripped through the tower, emanating from the spirit. She covered her ears as she ran, but the screech didn't end. Another joined it. Then another. And then a fourth. All from different directions.

The spirits had come. The Fires were stoked, and she had pronounced doom over the place. Now she just had to escape with her life.

She looked over her shoulder and went cold. The spirit behind shot several limbs from its head into the room and hall, following her. The screaming of tatzons ended with a sickening sound of flesh rendered asunder. And the limbs were coming for her.

She sped up and turned a corner fast, heading for the stairs. Dozens of people, the servants and the served, rushed around in panic. Two glowing blue limbs phased through the wall behind her and the people screamed. Gulamira shoved people out of her way and scrambled for an exit. The spirit would not take her. She would live.

The spirit limbs pierced into those in the back, diving for every fallen or tripped tatzon. Gulamira turned to the stairs and kept shoving her way through the chaos. As best she could, she closed her ears to the massacre behind her.

Wood cracked and shattered around Gulamira as she rushed out through the tower's opening. She gazed up and covered her head from falling debris. Three Large spirits wrapped around the tower, claws and limbs cutting into it and squeezing it.

One turned its gaze, as if drawn to her.

She ran into the streets to the marketplace which surged with chaos. Overhead, Common spirits flew or jumped from building to building, attacking anyone and everyone around them. Panicked people pushed and shoved and swore and cried around her, most grabbing their belongings and fleeing in every direction. Many held up iron shields to protect themselves against the spirits. Some lowlifes, though, turned on the merchants and rob them.

A Common spirit landed amid the panic and issued a song of challenge toward Gulamira. It resembled a beast with spear-like barbs along its back, which shot out, piercing people and even pinning them into surrounding buildings.

Gulamira dove to the side as the spirit lunged at a nearby woman, pinning her like an insect while her Partner tried to bash the creature with a wooden mallet. The tool sunk harmlessly into the spirit.

A few braver men and women with iron swords rushed over and cut into the spirit, which caused it to scream as the iron burned it. They struck again, but before they gained an upper hand, a second Common descended upon them, biting their heads.

Gulamira pushed herself up into a run. She couldn't stay to be killed like the rest of these fools. They defended their gold and ivory and crystal, and so they'd burn with it. She had to get to the docks before people killed Medhi and stole their ship. Hopefully, she wouldn't be too late.

A loud crash and shattering snapped her gaze back. The tower, with the body of her dead priest atop, crashed into the surrounding Buildings. Worse, the three Larges left it and collided with other Buildings, breaking through them like through twig constructions or a burning straw hat. The spirits were pure destruction, and their lust for death would not be sated.

One of them, the same that had gazed toward her before, stopped its rampage and stared at her. She froze for a moment. A foolish move.

The Large screeched and launched itself toward her, body crashing through some Buildings and phasing through others. It loomed over all Buildings—itself being close to seventy feet tall—and no matter where she went, it would see her.

She acted out of instinct. Before she thought, before she could stop herself, the higher song was in her mouth.

Her song left her without an audible sound, yet it rose through the air in an intense chorus. The song rose and rose, growing in power and force and will. As it grew, she felt the fire inside her burn and twist as something *about* her shifted, changed for always. A piece of her soul, lost forever. But she kept up her song and directed it with accuracy at the Large, and the song soared to the spirit, penetrating its very essence, telling it to stop and freeze.

The spirit slowed, its rampage letting up. Its massive eyes stared her down as her song rippled through it. The Large froze, unmoving. Gulamira breathed out, leaning against the side of a Building.

She steeled herself. The song had done its work to the Large, but it was only just beginning with her.

She turned and headed away.

A whisper danced through the windless air, like the falling of a single tear. "You've made our Watcher cry."

She stopped. That whisper... that had been a spirit, a song to her. She turned back and those white eyes didn't leave her.

"You will have your Fire. And you will Hate it."

Gulamira took a step back. Then another. She turned. And she ran.

"What in the Abyss?" Tsuran said.

Spirits seemed to have sprung up from the ocean as though blooming flowers. One moment Tsuran was fighting off sailors, the next dozens of spirits were wreaking havoc everywhere in sight. But Isra tried to not let it distract her. Their primary goal was the same, so they rushed off the *Cleansing* and onto the docks.

"Find a ship," she said.

With Nasna's help, Isra hurried alongside them, Tsuran with his small statue in his hand, though only a moment ago it'd been full size.

Nasna pointed at the ships they passed. "Any of these good?"

Tsuran shook his head and ushered them along. "Too big for us to manage. Without a crew, we have to steal the smallest one we can."

"That's going to be slow."

"I know, but we don't have other options."

Shouts and sharp cries poured down from the docks ahead. And steel clanged against steel. A dozen tatzons were storming a zebec, most with swords, fighting with the humans who held the ship.

"That one," Tsuran said. "That should do it."

"It's occupied," Nasna said.

"Then we help someone take the ship in exchange for getting out of here."

"Help the tatzons?" Isra asked.

Tsuran paused and looked at her. "Well..."

A bellowing voice broke above the chaos. "Come and face death, damn cowards!"

On the ship, one man launched forward with a sword in one hand and a dagger in the other. Some others on the ship had weapons, but it seemed this one man was the primary force keeping the tatzons back.

"I know him," Isra said.

"What?" Tsuran looked at the tatzons fighting. "Who? Which one?"

"The crazy human killing the tatzons."

Nasna gasped. "Yes. I know him too."

"What? You do?" Tsuran asked.

"Medhi," Nasna said. "The friend of that Gulamira woman."

Tsuran clapped and rushed forward. "Wonderful! Then let's get on that ship."

He tossed his statue into the air and vanished from sight. The statue enlarged to the size of a man and Tsuran, possessing the statue, rushed the attacking tatzons who were all too surprised at the newcomer.

Nasna and Isra hurried to the ship, while Tsuran broke through the steel swords and pummeled several of the men into unconsciousness, if not eternal sleep. The crowd backed away, no doubt terrified by a Guardian in red-crystal. Tsuran created an opening for Isra and Nasna, so the two rushed to reach the ship. Medhi stood with his sword out, his eyes watching Tsuran, though he raised a brow at the sight of Isra.

"Need help?" she asked.

Medhi looked at her and shrugged. "This world is getting too small these days. Fine. If you're not here to kill me, you might as well make yourself useful."

Nasna helped Isra up onto the ship and Tsuran unpossessed his statue. The crowd debated whether or not this ship was worth it.

A deep, but loud, hum vibrated through the air and Isra felt it reverberate in her chest. People in the crowd panicked and Nasna's face blanched.

"Icy Abyss," she said, and Isra looked to see what everyone else noticed.

A blue glowing claw phased through the wall of the Floating Treasure and overshadowed all the chaos. This massive claw made the Large spirits seem small, as any two of them could have fit inside that palm. Lady above, how big was that spirit?

"We should head out now," Tsuran said.

"Not yet," Medhi said, one hand on the tiller, the other on his sword. "We're waiting on two more."

"What? Are you insane?" Tsuran pointed toward the gigantic claw as it raked into the tree, tearing out entire sections of the town. "Do you see what's happening?"

"If you want another ship, get one. I'm not leaving without my friend."

"Gulamira?" Isra asked.

"She's coming," Medhi said. "Don't you worry about it. She's coming."

Tsuran sighed and shared a look with Nasna. "Fine. I'll try keeping the people off the ship. But, if she doesn't come in the next five minutes—"

"Then to the vortexes of hell we go!"

The sailors around didn't look as certain as Medhi. Push come to shove, Isra could get them to turn on him. But Kamaria liked Gulamira.

So, she had five minutes.

Gulamira sucked in a gasp of air. That spirit claw... that was a Behemoth spirit. The massive hand shook the ground like an earthquake and the entire sea tree groaned in protest. Had... had she summoned that? Exkel's Breath. The legends of this song had not prepared her for this. But she had to focus on getting away. Once away, she could contemplate all of this. For now, where in Exkel's name were the docks? These streets were as chaotic as ever and her song wouldn't keep the Large frozen forever and she just had to—*there!* She thought. *The docks! Thank Exkel. Please, let Medhi still have the damn boat.*

Throngs of despondent men and women flooded the ships and boats. Even here, the stench of death grew thick. Spirits attacked from further down the docks, but she needed to be around here. That's where they had docked. Please, he had to still be here. She couldn't let the Fire consume her. Not just yet.

She threw herself on top of a cart and scanned the water. Every ship in the harbor was setting sail, with some trying to save as many people as possible and others trying to shove off unwelcome guests.

Wait, one set of sails wasn't heaving off yet. Was that... yes! Her ship. Hard to say if Medhi was there, but—

The screech of the Large spirit ripped through the streets, and the crowd in front of her screamed. Many scattered, many more stampeded the small ship.

Gulamira glanced back. The Large was no longer stunned. And it was enraged.

To the side, five Commons rushed toward the crowd, ready to slaughter. She took in a breath and jumped off the cart. There was nothing else to do but to run and run. She dove into the chaotic fray. She pushed and ducked around the terrified tatzons, but they shoved back as the spirits collided with the people. And much too close to her. The Commons attacked with greater ferocity, and the screams of the dead were the only thing she heard as she weaved her way forward, ever forward, to the ship.

She burst from the dying crowds and had a direct path to the ship, where Medhi stood.

She rushed toward him. "Medhi!"

The blessed man spun. "Damn all Abyss, Amira!"

With a genuine smile, she hurried to him, noting the red-crystal statue and the ordîn. How had Tsuran and Nasna gotten here?

"She's here," Medhi called out. "Hurry, everyone! We're leaving. Guardian, keep any stragglers away from us." Gulamira reached the ship, and he clasped her arm to pull her in. He stopped and looked behind her. "Are we waiting for..."

"It's just me," she said.

He gave her a somber nod. "Right. Get on."

Another deep hum, a song of a Behemoth spirit, pushed itself through the ruckus of noise and two more massive limbs pushed into the tree. Before she could curse, the Large spirit smashed into the area just behind them, blue flames trickling along its many limbs. It still glared at Gulamira.

"Damn it," Medhi said. "Guardian, can you—"

"I've empowered too much already," Tsuran said. "I don't think I can take it on."

The spirit growled in a melodic tremor only she would hear and understand. The Guardian beside her straightened, eyes on the Large.

"Not good," he said.

Gulamira spun to Medhi. "How much time do you need to set sail?"

"I need time we can't get," he said.

Gulamira gripped the edge of the ship and locked eyes with the Large. The air shook with the destruction and chaos permeating the Floating Treasure. Hundreds of tatzons screamed and Buildings shattered, all falling into despair and endless silence. The spirits called out louder and louder with every passing death, their songs stretching into the tree and sea, stirring and cultivating and preparing a power Gulamira had incited.

A Coming Fire.

And she would live to see it manifest.

She stepped toward the bow, another song burning in her soul like a slight ember slowly eating away parchment. A waiting, patient flame, ready to erupt when she opened the airways to her innermost being.

But it would not consume her today. No. Not today.

She took in a deep breath and ushered a different song to her lips, a song to give them all the time they needed.

Before the song left her mouth, the Large spirit's eyes turned black.

All the spirits in the tree screamed. Not in harmony. Not with melody. Only with passionate hatred. Their screams burrowed into her ears, slicing into her mind. The attack flooded her with unimaginable excruciation. She collapsed to her knees as though the very air shoved onto her like the weight of a Colossal beast.

The song vanished alongside all vision and sound. The spirits' screams struck her again and again and again and again.

Her screams joined theirs.

———◆○◆———

Gulamira thrashed on the prow, nearly falling into the water, screaming her head off. Medhi and Nasna reacted the fastest, pulling the tatzon into the ship. Isra turned her gaze back to the Large spirit and its now swirling black eyes.

"Amira!" Medhi called. "Calm down. Amira, stop. Hold yourself!"

"She's not responding," Nasna said, grabbing onto her. As she did, she looked as though something invisible pushed her back. She looked to Tsuran. "Her river of energy is in total chaos. I sense spirit energy. I think the Large is targeting her, somehow."

"Great. Can you help her?" Tsuran asked.

"Yes, but it'll take a lot of concentration. This... this is new."

Nasna closed her eyes, and within a moment, Gulamira stopped screaming and flailing. In fact, she stopped moving, as though frozen.

Isra sighed and rubbed her head. Gods, she needed to sleep before the world threw anything more at her.

And as if the world heard her thoughts and spited her, flames burst from the Large's back. Everyone on their little ship froze. The flames flew above the spirit and grew into an ever-increasing ball of fire. Medhi grabbed his scarf, Tsuran gripped his statue, and Isra... well, she lost feeling in her left hand. So, that wasn't good.

She glanced at Nasna and Tsuran. "What can you do?"

"I can stop the spirit," Nasna said and stood up. As she let go of Gulamira, the tatzon went right back to screaming and wailing.

Tsuran pushed Nasna back to Gulamira, and the woman quieted again. "No, you stay here with her. There is no way you're erupting that thing."

"We die if I don't."

"You die if you do."

"Then I die!" She spun toward him while keeping her hand on Gulamira. "Better one than all. At least you'll save Kamaria."

The spirit's flames were growing too big and too fast for Isra to stomach this couple's griping any longer. She tapped a circle and Released her stylus.

"Guardian, with me." She shoved past him to the prow. They hadn't gotten far from the dock, so she might make the jump. But it wasn't likely.

"You've an idea?" he asked.

She nodded. "Get in your statue."

"What's the—"

She gave him a stern look as she pointed at the ball of flame. He sighed, but got the message. He possessed and enlarged his statue next to her.

"Take me to the spirit," she said.

"You want what?"

"This or death."

He grabbed her with his crystal arms, which were smooth and uncomfortable, and leapt to the docks. And he ran. She expected the speed, but that did not prevent air from lodging in her throat. She had seen possessors empower their speed a few times before, but she'd never been strapped to one.

Tsuran yelled into the wind. "I can't do more than run fast for a short bit. What's the plan?"

"Run around it. Keep a wide berth. Hold me tight." She took in a breath and leaned hard to the side, dropping herself near to the ground.

"Abyssal's tail!" He grabbed at her, nearly letting go. "What are you doing?"

"Hold tight and run." She gripped her stylus and prayed upon every prayer that this would work. She slammed the ivory into the wooden ground, digging a deep line into it. "We're making a circle."

"You're insane, you know that?"

The spirits roared, and the Large now seemed to see them. The Guardian swore again, but ran on as Isra let her arm relax while keeping her grip tight. She directed Tsuran, shouting out directions and jerking him best she could to keep him on track, keep him to a true circular pattern. The man didn't even realize the depths of her insanity. The circle had to be perfect. It had to be to work. A circle large enough to Capture a spirit. An insane task to do in the arms of a speeding Guardian. No one could do this. To think one could would prove their insanity and idiocy.

So she did not think. She let the circle form without thought. Instinct born from her very blood created this circle. As they made their last turn, in her sleep and energy deprived mind, she thought she felt the start of the circle just ahead of them.

A blue claw appeared in her vision, swiping toward her.

Tsuran dove to the side and Isra fell from his grip. She hit the ground with all the speed of the crystal, but with none of its protection. She rolled and skidded, the wood slamming into her. A high-pitched chime rang in her ear as she laid still for a moment, but not long. The circle wasn't done.

She tried picking herself up, but her body didn't respond, days of torment catching up. She had only another ten feet to go, so she gritted her teeth, gripped her stylus, and clawed into the wooden to pull herself forward.

The spirit's movement drew her gaze. The ball of fire had grown to be the size of a Common spirit itself and two new arms sprouted from the spirit's back up toward the fire. By the Lady, the damn creature was ready to throw it.

Isra reached the unfinished circle, body shaking, and plummeted her stylus into the wood. And she carved.

She carved shallow and fast.

She carved inch by inch like her life, like the very life of her people depended on it.

The spirit made this unsettling noise, like some deep-throated, hissing gurgle. She glanced up. The spirit made a single step toward her and lowered its head. A black empty void of a mouth opened. A fear as primal as the very jungle of Tutchal grew deep in her belly, as cold and petrifying as the Abyss. The fear gripped her very bone, freezing even the bloody marrow within. She would die now. This spirit would end her. She died now.

And as the fear took root in her, a fear deeper and stronger and more foundational than the very world, the image of a little tatzon girl came into her mind. An image of Kamaria standing side by side with Isra's father and her people.

Isra finished the circle. And whether it was to the spirit, to the fear, or to only herself, she whispered, "I have a people to save."

She slammed her finger into the massive circle and tapped a tattoo.

And Nu'Isra of the Brier, hope of her people, Caught the damn spirit.

34

━━━◆○◆━━━

EVER ONWARD

I know you think I'm wrong. I don't blame you. Every day I wake here in the Maw, I doubt everything I've done and wonder if I should have kept my mouth shut or found another way. I'm not a leader, not like you. Yet, now I have to figure out how to save these people? Every day I wait for those ships to arrive, I wonder if I've made the right decision. I don't know that I have... yet, after all this time waiting and doubting, I'm still here. Because I must. I started something, something with consequences I can't even guess at and I will see it through.

-From an anonymous letter delivered to Beneficiary Syeda Softbark on the back of a red thistle leaf.

Gulamira sat close to Nasna as their little ship sailed away from the Floating Treasure. She didn't need Nasna's touch anymore, since they were far enough from the spirits' screams. No one spoke as they sailed. Medhi kept his gaze forward with his hand on the tiller. Everyone else watched as seven Behemoth spirits, each several hundred feet tall, rose from the ocean and surrounded the sea tree. The silence on the ship was palpable. A spirit of this size... people spoke of those only in myths and legends. And, unbeknownst to anyone else, Gulamira had summoned them. With a single song, she'd summoned spirits larger than most trees.

Many ships had escaped the destruction, though only one caught her eye. The *Cleansing* escaped, and did not sail the same direction as they.

After a short time, everyone took their positions on the ship, directed by Medhi. Nasna kept watch over Tsuran, who laid exhausted at her feet, while Isra slept at the bow, as though to be as far from everyone as she could. Tsuran had carried her unconscious body back to the boat and, so far, no one yet spoke about what Isra had done. The Floating Treasure's destruction was enough for today.

With the image of the Behemoth spirits snapping a massive sea-tree in half, their little crew sailed on. They sailed on into the full-night, and even then no one spoke. The human crew would tomorrow. Once they regained their courage, they'd demand they head back to Rajalend. But, of course, that was not an option.

As the full-night wore on and sleep failed to find her, Gulamira took a seat near Medhi, who also couldn't sleep.

Neither spoke at first. They only sat together under the silvery light of the moons. But after a time, Medhi placed a hand on hers.

"Sorry you didn't get your friend."

She smiled, although he'd see through it.

"You don't need to talk tonight," he said. "But you've a listening ear with me."

"Thank you, Medhi." She leaned into him, desiring to lay her head on his shoulder, but she stopped and pulled away, shifting in her seat. He glanced over at this, dropped his gaze to where he held her hand, and pulled his away.

"No." She grasped his hand, and he paused. "No, I... I need to feel something genuine right now." His rough sailor hand squeezed hers and those wild eyes met hers. So inviting.

She tore her eyes away from him and focused on the distant horizon. A cool night breeze blew over the deck, causing a slight chill to run over her, except for where she held his hand. That stayed warm.

"He's dead," she said, and though she did not look at him, she felt his wild gaze center on her. "I don't know what I'm supposed to feel right now. I'd spent years mourning everyone's deaths. I don't want to do that again."

He nodded. "Do I ever understand that."

"But I still feel like something was hollowed out of me and I don't know what to do about it."

"Fourth rule of the sea."

She looked over, brow raised.

He smirked. "Can't outrun pikefish if you're anchored."

"And what's that supposed to mean?"

"Means that if you want to live, you keep moving. The sea's rough, it's dangerous, so only those who're moving, who're acting, only they survive."

She nudged him with her shoulder. "You're making these up."

"Come on, you think I got the mind to make these things up?"

"Of course I do."

"There's that coy smile I've missed." He kissed her hand and stared into her eyes for a time, his gaze flitting to her lips. But he cleared his throat and pulled back. "My point is, life's hit you hard. But life's too short on the sea for the hardships to last. Either you move on or it drowns you. So, what're you going to do?"

She still felt the song, deep inside her, stirring but calm for now. Life was indeed short, but Salma's death was not the only thing trying to drown her. A change was taking place inside her. She knew that. A change that would, according to legend, prepare her for the Coming Fire. No one knew how fast the change would occur, but after singing it, she thought she understood a portion of what it did.

Piece by piece, it would make her more like a spirit.

And when that happened, Gulamira would die.

Without taking her gaze off the horizon, she pressed her hand against the wooden bench. And then she pressed harder, but she did not phase through as she had in the tower. She sighed, glad to not phase through the ship into the water. Hopefully, that was only a onetime thing, or, at the least, it wasn't a random thing she could not control. But she supposed that was the point of the Coming Fire. It could not be controlled.

But before the Fire Came, before the change in her finished, she would see Kamaria safe again. The orphaned girl would smile again. And if Gulamira had to fight and conquer Oligarchs, Nightmares, Solitude, or even the Coming Fire to do so, she would.

"I will not drown," she said.

"Thought not. Then what are you going to do? Easier to swim if you've a destination in mind."

"Another rule of the sea?"

"Just practical advice."

She shook her head with a smirk and looked up. The three moons shone in their full brilliance, but Gulamira's eyes traced the black sky for the skybands. Twelve crisscrossed the sky this night, long blue swathes of light winding through the night and around the moons. And perhaps it was a trick of the eye, but they looked far more vibrant than she'd noticed before.

"They're taking the girl someplace in the Maw. That's where I'm going."

Medhi leaned back. "We'll need to pick up my crew then. I don't trust these sailors here, and if we're facing the Dragon's Maw, we'll need some crazy fools to follow us."

She paused and glanced over. "We?"

"I'm also going to teach you how to use a sword. If we're going to war with a pair of Oligarchs, you'll need more than just songs to protect you." He looked over at her and smirked. "And yeah, I mean 'we'. If getting this girl shoves a fistful of thorns up the Oligarchs, then I'm in. Besides,"—he brushed a strand of hair out of her face, letting his finger trace her markings—"a friend of mine is heading that way."

She rolled her eyes and pushed him away. "You think you're that charming, don't you?"

"Made you smile, didn't I?"

"I'm always smiling."

"True, but I can tell when it's real. Always have."

She looked down at his hand holding hers and thought back to the first time she'd held his. "Yeah. You have."

Medhi smiled and stared at her for a long, quiet moment. He cleared his throat. "So, then... to the Maw?"

She placed her hand on her chest, sensing the reverberating song deep, deep inside her. Gulamira looked out across the darkened horizon, in the direction of the Dragon's Maw, and gripped Medhi's hand. "And to whatever awaits us."

A Word from the Author

Thank you so much for reading Song of the Coming Fire! I hope you enjoyed it as much as I did writing it.

Please don't forget to give this book a quick review!. Even just a two-word, "Liked it" or "Hated it" review helps so much and would mean a lot to me. Positive or negative, I am grateful for all feedback from my readers.

And be sure to sign up for my newsletter receive updates on all new releases. Sign up at tylerjamesbooks.com! Thanks again!

- Tyler

A Study of Worlds

Possession

T atzon magic is best understood through the Seven by Sevens, a teaching tool used by most possessor teachers. In it, it explains that tatzons are able to possess seven "types", or categories, and within each type there are seven "layers" of power. While the types all differ from each other, the layers are the same for each.

Layers
Mind-Possession: the first kind of possession a tatzon can learn, it entails the possessor projecting their soul out of their body and into what they are aiming to possess. This leaves their body inanimate where they left it.

Body-Possession: the possessor now brings their body along with them when they possess. They also bring along any clothing they were wearing as well as other very small things. Larger pieces of clothing, such as a cloak, or other items do not go with the possessor and drop to the ground.

Body-Possession with Empowerment: while body-possessing, the tatzon can now use the three Empowerments: Harden/Strengthen, Speed, and Specialized.

Total-Control: the possessor can fully posses while also remaining in their body. This splits their mind, placing half in the possession and the other half in the body, and thus they become and feel like two people.

Total-Control with Empowerment: while in total-control, the tatzon can now use the three Empowerments.

Multiple Possession: the tatzon can now body-possess or use total-control with more than a single possession.

Types

Statue: commonly known as Guardians in the Meadowlands, these can possess any sculpture of a person or animal. Used predominantly upon naval vessels, Guardians are not the most common sight on land, though you will find them fighting on the front lines of the war between Rajalend and Veirzen.

Harden/Strengthen: This Empowerment doubles the hardness and strength of the material of the sculpture, and usually results in the statue being difficult to maneuver in.

Speed: the Guardian's speed is doubled. (Note: if used in conjunction with Harden, the speed normalizes.)

Specialized: Guardians can alter the shape of their statue in two ways. The first, and easiest, is to only change the shape of the statue without losing or gaining material. The second can only be done with a bonded statue, since it involves changing the shape of the statue by adding or removing material. The most basic example of this second form is when a Guardian enlarges their statue.

Beasts: commonly known as Wranglers in the Meadowlands, these can possess any animal. This is the most common possession type in eastern Meadowland, with the majority residing within Veirzen. While they do make up a sizable portion of the military,

Wranglers in all nations are the main sources of transportation through the Meadowlands.

Harden/Strengthen: this increases the beast's toughness and strength, while slowing its movements.

Speed: Wranglers can double their beast's speed and increase their reflexes.

Specialized: this grants the Wranglers access to the beast's inherent reflexes, instincts, senses, and even memories, if applicable. This sharing of senses even occurs with Total-Control.

Plants: commonly known as Builders in the Meadowlands, these can possess any form of plant life. The most common possession type in western Meadowland, especially in Rajalend. Builders make up a large portion of the military and an even larger portion of the working class of possessors.

Harden/Strengthen: this Empowerment doubles the strength and durability of the plant, but slows both movement and growth rate.

Speed: this Empowerment allows the Builder to either increase their movement as the plant or to increase the growth rate of the plant.

Specialized: Builders can alter the shape of the plant in two ways. First, they can change the shape without adding or removing material. This can often be seen with them possessing trees and hollowing out the insides and creating rooms. Second, they can change the shape by adding or removing material. This can be seen as rapid growth, in some cases.

Shadows: commonly known as Lightless in the Meadowlands, these can possess any shadow. Criminals tend toward this possession due to its many applications in theft, blackmail, and even assassination. Because of this tendency, many nations outlaw shadow possession.

Harden/Strengthen: (can only be used in conjunction with Specialized Empowerment) using this Empowerment, a Lightless can triple their natural strength while in an embodied shadow.

Speed: Lightless can use this Empowerment to either double their movement through the shadows or they can triple the speed of their embodied form (this second option can only be used in conjunction with their Specialized Empowerment).

Specialized: this Empowerment gives the shadow they are possessing a physical, embodied form. It may take whatever shape the possessor chooses but the total mass of the form typically cannot exceed that of the possessor's physical body.

Spirits: commonly known as Soulborn in the Meadowlands, these can possess any spirit. Of the accepted types, this is known as the most difficult to master. Due to the need of specialized crystal equipment known as vessels, it is common for only the children of wealth to have access to this type.

Harden/Strengthen: this Empowerment doubles the spirit's natural durability against iron and ivory. The spirit cannot phase while using this Empowerment.

Speed: the Soulborn's speed and reflexes are doubled.

Specialized: every spirit has a unique magical ability that is unlike anything else on Vicoluntas. This Empowerment allows the Soulborn to use this spirit magic.

Dreams: commonly known as Dreamwalkers in the Meadowlands, these can possess dreams of other soul-beings. Though some in Vicoluntas attempt this possession, there are no records of anyone ever discovering how to move beyond mind-possession and into body-possession. Either the Seven by Sevens is flawed in this way, or dream possession has no further layers.

The Dead: commonly known as Disturbers in the Meadowlands, these can possess the deceased bodies of other soul-beings. Disturbers are strictly outlawed in most nations within the Meadowlands, and even where it is partially allowed one must receive approval from the governing body for any possession.

Preventing Possession

It has been long known that tatzons cannot possess through any kind of metal. Neither can the metal be possessed, which is why most statues are made of or lined with metal as to prevent Guardians from stealing the monuments.

The most common way of securing a tatzon prisoner is to latch a iron collar around their neck. This prevents possession and thus instantly neuters the possessor.

Remnants

Remnants are the unfortunate end of any possessor that cannot learn how to temper their magic.

Every tatzon is able to possess for a single hour without any issue. Afterward, if they wish to possess safely, they must refrain from possessing for a certain time. For every two minutes they rest from possessing, they regain one minute of safe possession (up to one hour of safe possession).

However, there are times when these time constraints are impossible to follow, such as during a battle. And there are possessors who wish to push the limit of their time. What results is Remnancy.

Remnancy appears as a "growth" at first. This growth takes on the appearance of whatever the possession was at the time. In the most direct terms, a Remnancy growth is the possessor's body becoming what they possess.

Once the growth has spread over the entire body, the Remnant is created. These creatures have no memory of their past life nor do they hold the same desires or goals or dreams. Every Remnant has the same inherent desire: to consume and destroy living soul-beings.

Statue: Guardian Remnants are the most humanoid in appearance. They are a detail perfect replica of the tatzon they once were, with the caveat that they are now made entirely of the material of the possessor's statue. Most of these type are made of either wood or stone.

Special: the touch of a Guardian Remnant is dangerous to possessing Guardians. Their single touch can sap the strength and vigor from a Guardian, though it has no such effect on other possessors.

Beasts: Wrangler Remnants take on the bestial aspects of whatever beast they possessed. This can take the form of fur, claws, snouts, fangs, hooves, and more. Some cultures refer to these as the "smallest" beasts.

Special: the bite of this Remnant causes a most excruciating disease in less than an hour of infection. Those infected experience the sensation of their internal organs dissolving. There is no known cure.

Plants: Builder Remnants resemble walking trees and creatures made of branches and vines. They typically have a wooden head that no longer has a face but instead three holes, two where eyes were and one where the mouth was.

Special: these Remnants create a toxic ooze that corrodes metal and eats through flesh. In many ways, it's comparable to Iron's Fear.

Shadow: Lightless Remnants become living shadows. Unlike other Remnants, these are particularly difficult to kill and are often considered the second deadliest. The only upside is that these Remnants are not mobile creatures and instead remain as floating voids of darkness in the exact place the Remnancy took over.

Special: any organic substance that enters the Remnant is instantly decimated, leaving not a single trace of its existence.

Spirits: Soulborn Remnants take on the appearance of spirits in a humanoid shape. They resemble the vague shape of the person they once were, with the exception that their face is now only the two glowing white eyes of a spirit.

Special: the touch of this Remnant is deadly to a soul-being. A single touch kills. Couple that with their incredible speed, ability to phase through material, and the difficulty in killing them, these are the most feared of all Remnants.

Dreams: given the rarity of anyone spending much time in this possession, I have only found Dreamwalker Remnants in bits of folklore and various legends. It is said that such a Remnant becomes a living nightmare, slowly killing its victim while they sleep.

Special: unknown.

Dead: Strangely, Disturbers do not create Remnants. Although they do have Remnancy growth, which takes on the appearance of decaying flesh, once the growth takes over the person, they die. The remaining body is harmless to people and there are no records of any coming back to life.

Conjuration

An unknown magic to most in the Meadowlands, Conjuration is also known as the Circular Art, since its power relies on the formation of circles. Although its concept is simple, its application can be quite complex.

There are two basic aspects of conjuration: the Containment and the Conjuring.

Containment

This is the process of containing something which can be conjured later. Colloquially, this is also known as "Trapping" or "Catching".

This process requires two circles connected by a line. These circles are known as the Containment Circle and the Activation Circle.

The Containment Circle is what must surround that which is to be contained. These are the most difficult circles to create since they must be large enough to encompass the whole of whatever is being contained.

The Activation Circle is what the Conjurer must touch in order to engage the containment. This can be of any size.

The connecting line must touch both circles, but otherwise can take any shape or form.

Once the Conjurer has connected both circles with a line, they touch the interior of the Activation Circle and then capture whatever is within the Containment circle, which instantly dematerializes and its essence is imbued within one of the circles, the Conjurer can choose which.

The Conjurer cannot discriminate what is contained. If the Containment Circle surrounds a table and a chair, they cannot choose to capture the chair but not the table. Everything within the circle is contained.

If any part of a thing lies within the Containment Circle, it will be part of the containment process.

If any part of a living soul-being is within the Containment Circle, containment is impossible.

Conjuring

Once something has been contained within a circle, it remains there indefinitely until one of two conditions are met: the circle is destroyed or someone conjures it.

Conjuring is a far simpler process than Containment since all that is required is the conjurer to touch the containing circle. This returns its contents back to the material world in the same state it left.

It is also possible to conjure something from a circle without touching it. To do this, a conjurer must connect it to a second circle with a line and then touch this second circle. The conjurer can choose which circle the contents appear from.

The Standard Categories

Name	Height	Tusk Color
Small	5-10 ft	Full Ivory
Common	15-25 ft	Ivory with Brown marbling
Large	50-80 ft	Ivory with Red marbling
Colossal	100-200 ft	Ivory with Black marbling
Behemoth	500-800 ft	Full Blue

One of my criticisms of the Standard Categories of Vicoluntan Fauna is that the system blatantly displays the issues inherent with it, yet without pausing to wonder if the system could thus be correct.

For instance, a Small size has a max height of 10 feet and a Common size has a minimum of 15 feet. There is a five foot gap here. Does this mean there are no beasts that have a height of 12 feet? Are there no creatures that have height of 30 feet, or 300 feet? Those who adhere to the Standard Categories say, "No".

I hope the absurdity of this thinking is clear.

Crystal

Throughout Vicoluntas, there has been discovered a resource more valuable than gold or silver. It takes on the appearance of crystalline formations which emit a natural light. The Vicoluntans, in general, refer to this simply as crystal.

Crystal has various shades of color which corresponds not only to its rarity, but also to its overall strength and toughness. However, even the weakest crystal, blue-crystal, has the same relative strength of wrought iron, which is why crystal weaponry is most highly sought after.

In order of most fragile to most unbreakable, there is: blue-crystal, white-crystal (also known simply as lightstone), green-crystal, red-crystal, and yellow-crystal.

On Vicoluntas, the finest of metal tools are able to work blue and white crystal, though not without difficulty. However, even the best metalworkers have yet to create something that can even scratch green-crystal and up. Thus far, only two materials have been found that have any hope of even chipping these higher colors: other crystal and the ivory from beast tusks.

In general, crystal is only able to break away weaker crystals or a crystal of one color greater.

The Meadowlands

The continent known as the Meadowlands takes up almost the entire northern section of Vicoluntas and hosts the most varied biomes throughout the world. From what I have gathered, tatzons were first placed in the Meadowlands, as far north as can be, and then slowly migrated south over many generations. However, history has not been kind to the northern-most lands and currently there is no living kingdom or community that still touches the ridged ice mountains.

A majority of the flourishing nations reside in the south of the Meadowlands, where they touch the Ashen Sea and the Chromatic Strait. There are over twenty nations that call the Meadowlands home, but there are truly only two powers: Rajalend and Veirzen. All others act as vassal states or are simply too small to consider.

What interests me most is the name, because there are strangely very few meadows within the so-called Meadowlands. Rajalend and most of the western continent are made up of jungles and dense forests, while Veirzen and the east are filled with plains and mountain ranges. But there are few true meadows. As I have walked the world and spoken with a splattering of scholars, it seems there is this collective memory of an ancient land far to the north. They have no name for it, but it is believed that this ancient land was the first tatzon nation, and was situated in a lush meadow. As tatzonkind moved ever south, the memory of the flourishing meadow stayed with them and eventually became the namesake of the continent.

Acknowledgements

I would like to express my deepest appreciation to my wife, Havah. Your constant encouragement and willing ear were beyond essential for this book to become a reality. Without your sharp eye, and your deeper heart, I would not have been able to create a book half as good as this one. Thank you, my dear.

I also want to express my thanks to the folks over at the Write Practice, since it was under their wing that the first drafts of this book came about. Specifically, I want to thank my mentor, Abigail Perry, and my editor, Rebekah Olson.

Abby, you never had a wasted word and always had time to help answer my very specific questions. I still think about your writing advice whenever I sit down at my computer. Thank you.

Rebekah, you gave me a much needed boost in confidence when I wasn't sure how viable my books could be. I won't ever forget that, nor the absolutely essential guidance in honing my story to a greater finale.

I want to extend my sincere thanks to all the wonderful people who beta read my early drafts. I couldn't have done this without any of you, but I'd like to shout out Morticia, Anne, and Marcy from my Mingle cohort. I am beyond grateful for your support and am so glad we get to walk this writing journey together.

Finally, I want to pass along my genuine thanks to you, dear reader. You and your support are the reason I can do this whole "author" thing. From the bottom of my heart, thank you.

ABOUT THE AUTHOR

Tyler James is a writer, world-creator, and author of Song of the Coming Fire. Born in Tukwilla, Washington, James has been reading and writing fantasy since he was a child. When he's not creating epic, blood-thumping adventures for his Dungeons & Dragons group, James dives into the far-reaches of human possibility, crafting worlds and stories never before seen. He lives with his wife in Santa Barbara, where they work together to create art that stirs the heart.

You can connect with him more at his website:
TylerJamesBooks.com

www.ingramcontent.com/pod-product-compliance
Lightning Source LLC
Chambersburg PA
CBHW070840260626
47170CB00007B/2446